BRINGER of DEATH

WORKS BY SYK KELLY

CRUEL GODS SERIES:
BRINGER OF DEATH

CRUEL KINGDOMS SERIES:
SINISTER DESIRE
FATEFUL CHANCE
MALICIOUS INTENTIONS

CRUEL GODS

BRINGER of DEATH

SYK KELLY

FOR THOSE LITTLE DEVIANTS
WHO CAN'T HOLD THEIR
TONGUE,
LIVE FOR BANTER,
WITH AN UNHEALTHY
OBSESSION FOR DARK
FANTASIES.
IT'S JUST THE BEGINNING.

Content Warning

This book contains sensitive material with depictions and references to bullying, parental abuse, death, graphic violence, manipulation, off-page sexual assault, some BDSM elements, voyeurism, and exhibitionism.

Chapter One

KORE

"Not all of us can swing our tits to sell overpriced, dry tarts, *and* get free coin thrown at us."

Disgust stares back at me, deepening the wrinkles on Alice's withered face with every grumble under her herbal breath, twisting back into that sweet-old-woman grin as she turns back to her waiting customers. The very customers who are now eyeing my chest with equal distaste.

"That's because no one wants to see your tits," I bite back, immediately regretting my quick reaction when those passing by toss their pointed curiosity in our direction.

Today is *not* the day to be noticed.

I tug the gilded necklace around my neck, gripping it like a lifeline— a reminder to tame my emotions and hold my sharp tongue.

I will give Alice one thing; her teas smell heavenly, and it isn't because my stomach has been groaning and aching for food since yesterday morning. The earthy aroma, the floral scents, the spice…

I peek down at my own table, and my chest flutters. I should sell my last tart, but the pooling under my tongue rejects such sensibility. Just thinking of the lemon treat I'm saving for Dora—the perfect balance of sweet and sour—but that's her favorite, and I wouldn't dream of tempting her tantrum.

For once, my undying hunger wins and I reach for the last strawberry tart, grabbing my eye instead when another coin strikes above it, earning me an exasperated grunt from the old tea merchant.

Fucking Styx.

I turn my back on the crowd, hiding that I'm holding anything but a smile.

"Let it out now." A faint tangle of envy and wrath seeps from Alice's pores, a commonality she shares with many of the other nearby merchants. "We don't need another one of your hysterical scenes." Smirking proudly, she ties back her thinning, white hair from sticking to her forehead. It's as brittle as she is, but she isn't wrong. The coins, her glances, the sun, the very air, everything is clawing under my skin more than usual today.

That hunger deep within my core stirs, that need for balance tipping off scale. One that could be so easily centered with a bump of Alice's tables so one of her precious teacups takes a tumble to the ground. Or I could place a tart on her chair so when she sits back down the filling would ruin her patchy dress.

I wield both hungers by taking a bite of my tart. It isn't chocolate, but the sweet flavor bursts on my tongue and softens a tiny bit of the spice I'm overflowing with.

Next week can't come soon enough, Hel, tomorrow can't. This week-long festival will finally be over, and the outsiders can return to their wealthy homes and their tea parties where they can gossip and pass their judgements out of sight. The locals can go back to ignoring my existence.

This time of year always drags out the worst in others, especially the outsiders. We're nothing but entertainment, families and servants selling every last bit of our goods only to continue struggling. Our bartering is the most amusing, and I can't blame them for posing themselves near tables and carts, snickering and taking wagers on how low sellers are willing to take, who will sell out first, and if someone will snap. What bothers me is how close I am to being the reason someone collects on the last one.

With everyone in black for the day of Hades, it's harder to differentiate an outsider from a local, but there are signs: the wealthy walk straighter, their posture perfect with their nose to the sky, their jewelry clinking beneath their cloaks because even though someone will be sacrificed tonight, they *must* flaunt their wealth.

When I lift my tart again, a hand wraps around mine, spilling the sweet red filling out of its toasted cinnamon dough. My throat tightens at the memory of my father, Celius, and the way his neck—

"I came to warn you." The stranger leans against my ear, their grip tightening around my wrist, holding me in place. "You're running out of time here. You must drink this and run before they find you."

Something cold is pushed against my palm.

I jerk back, trying to remove myself from the stranger's embrace, but my head is pulled right back into their shoulder.

"I think you have the wrong person." My struggles weaken as the strong scent of something familiar fills my nostrils, like a minty, herbal balm that clears a sickness and allows you to breathe clearly for a moment.

This has to be another trick. A new form of throwing coins. Another way to single me out.

"Your name is Kore. You used to be *very* wealthy until your father died five years ago. You and your mother lost everything except the estate. You've become a servant working daily—"

"You might know *of* me," I start, trying to place the unfamiliar voice. Everyone knows my past, so I'm not surprised by her knowledge, but our town is small enough that it's odd I don't recognize her from her voice alone. "But I still think you have the wrong person."

"I don't have time." The plea in her voice is unsettling enough that I stop squirming against her hold. "This isn't how I wanted to do this, but I need you to listen *very* carefully. You were made for a much bigger purpose. I don't know how, but they've managed to find you. Anyone you care about will be in danger soon, and if you don't drink this before tonight, we'll lose any chance at—"

"What are you doing?" The woman jumps back, releasing the back of my neck, allowing me to take her and her friend in, both draped in dark cloaks that look too thick to wear in the high heat of the day. The new one is noticeably taller with a voice that is just feminine enough to clock her as a woman, that, and her blood-red braid slithering out of her hood as she takes in my space with disinterest. "There's nothing here."

My jaw tightens, biting into my cheek to keep me from saying something I'll regret. Instead, I take them in with the same unimpressed assessment.

3

Their cloaks hide most of their faces, but it's enough to know that I don't know them. The one with the ominous warnings has a pretty, angular, feminine jawline that tightens the way one does when they've been caught doing something they shouldn't have been doing and they don't know what to say.

When she leans in again, my body instinctively does too, sighing at the touch of her soft fingers brushing the back of my hand. "*Trust me.*" Her whisper is so low, so breathy, that I can hardly hear it over the tingling shiver that rushes through me, settling in the depths of my mind where a dull ache would.

Before I can say or make sense of anything, the two blend into the sea of black, leaving me baffled at the curious encounter. A glance at Alice gives me nothing. The old woman looks half asleep with a book in her hands, oblivious to the world moving around her.

Opening my hand, I find a small, corked vial filled with red liquid and a note attached that reads: *Drink me before the moon falls.*

"Who was that? Did they cause you any trouble?"

I quickly shove the vial into my cleavage before Dora can take it and toss it out—as it probably should be. I'm curious about it, though and I can't look at it with her here.

"And how did you end up in the slumps?" Her mouth is already full of the lemon tart I saved for her as she kicks the sandal I wedged under the table's leg. The plates clank together, threatening to shatter. "This is the third week in a row. Do I need to come earlier to make sure you get a good table in the town center?"

Dora's constant abandoning of questions is a habit I find the most enjoyable, a trait that I admire because I could never be one to let go of anything so easily.

"One, I don't know who they were. They wanted tarts, and as you can see, I'm out." I wiggle my finger between us for emphasis. "Two, I came late because—"

"Adonis?" Dora smirks, already knowing.

"No!" I can feel the blush creeping up my neck, my pulse racing just thinking about the lie.

If there's anything to say about this day, it's that he gives me all the distraction I need to avoid thinking about it.

Dora's brow rises, unconvinced, lifting three fingers for me to continue my explanation—*lies.*

4

"And three," I continue, "You should come earlier anyway. You know it's boring without you here."

Her lips curl, taking in the brick buildings surrounding the tight alley. Most of the windows are boarded up to keep the sun from overheating the homes, leaving the alley to feel even more shallow and narrow.

The set-ups farther in town have more room and far more customers than here in the slumps, where everything is placed closely together and the uneven ground has our tables teetering throughout the day.

I slide my arm behind my back to keep her from seeing the cut I managed to get while climbing under mine earlier. It would only make her more dramatic and hound me to take better care of myself and stop being so *clumsy*.

"Besides," Dora's icy blue eyes light up at seeing the bag of coin I take out of the pocket of my dress. "I'm thinking a dry white wine for me, a sweet red for you, and those chocolates from—"

"The Tempered Caterpillar!" She's practically jumping on her toes, both of us squealing at the rare, expensive delicacy. As defensive as she is about how others treat me, we both see the benefit of a few bruises to my skin and ego in exchange for free coin.

"Dora, always around when the work's over." Adonis wedges his way through the crowd and playfully bumps her shoulder.

I cover my giggle with the palm of my hand. The thought of Dora actually working is something I would pay to watch.

Since we met five years ago, to this very day, the only work I have ever witnessed Dora attempt was when she helped sell my family's treats, wine, and oils. Her gift of gab allows her to sell more and faster than either Adonis or I ever could. She's brilliant at knowing what people need to hear, but the daughter of a priestess isn't allowed to work. She is expected to dress and act in a way others can emulate, making her more of an outsider than a local, but also neither.

The way she openly teases and nudges Adonis, a servant, but also gives him a side hug, further proves that she doesn't care about what others think of her or the roles she's expected to play. To my benefit. She's the only other person besides Adonis who speaks to me after what happened, the embarrassment that led to my family's ruined reputation.

"I was preparing for the final feast," Dora explains. "The priestesses are losing their minds because the oracle predicted this year to be chaos with the full Harvest moon tonight. They've ordered more guards and wooden stocks." When she casts a quick glance back at me, all amusement is gone.

That cautionary look has me taking another bite of my tart, but I can't savor it, not when she continues, "I can't be with you during the play or sacrifice." I immediately regret taking such a large bite when I nearly choke on her words. "I'm needed elsewhere, but I'll come get you right after. We'll take our wine and chocolate to the river and drown ourselves in all of it."

My cuticles suddenly need picking, something that doesn't stop the tremor of panic I'm positive is showing on my face. This will be the first sacrifice since my father's death that Dora won't be by my side. Who is going to hold my hand until it's over? Who will whisper distracting questions into my ear?

"I'll be there." Adonis' hand jerks like he wants to reach for me but remembers where we are. The chivalry alone makes me smile, just a little.

The type of distraction he provides isn't what I had in mind, but I'll take anything to get me through this night.

I want to beg Dora to skip the sacrifice altogether, to go straight to the forest instead, but along with all servants, one member of every household is required to be in attendance tonight, and I am ours.

I can't blame my mother for forcing this role on me, not after everything I caused. That is one internal scale that will never be balanced, a wrong that can never be righted.

"Adonis!" The last voice I want to hear rings through the tight alley. "You forgot your sticky bun."

Blonde has never looked so much like kindling before, and by the warning glares others shoot her as she shoves past, they're thinking the same thing I am.

Meg makes it through, handing Adonis the bread. His accepting smile sends a wave of heat straight to my clenched fists.

"Oh, I didn't see you there, Kore." The curl in her lips isn't kind, but at least it's honest, where the pity that follows in her pinched brows is anything but. "I do hope tonight isn't too hard for you, with your dead father and all."

I've tried to avoid glancing too closely at the crowd all week, especially today, but Meg's reminder makes everyone's stares and whispers all too apparent.

"It's an honor that my father was chosen." The forced smile and rehearsed phrase are ash on my tongue, my heated glare unmoving from hers. "I hope you get that honor this year."

A lightness fills me as the words slip off my tongue, but Adonis' gaping mouth has me biting my lip with mild regret—*mild*.

Dora squeals, her hand clasping over her amusement to keep from laughing any harder. A reaction that has me struggling to bite mine down.

"*Kore*." Adonis releases a strained breath. His floss-thin patience for mine and Meg's bickering is on its last thread.

I tried to be Meg's friend years ago, with his help, but she's always found ways to cut me down and twist anything I say or do into something either embarrassing or offensive, which only leads him to come to her defense.

Seeing them both now with their worn-in matching chitons has my tongue slipping and forgetting my promise to play nice. No matter how much things have changed in the last five years, I will never have that connection or understanding that they do, both raised in the orphanage and trained to serve.

I'll only ever be a former outsider turned servant.

I envy both sides.

All week, I've pined after the white silks the outsiders wore on the day of Zeus, the emeralds for Demeter, the ambers for Hestia, rubies for Hera, citrines for Chiron, and variant blues for Poseidon. I miss my own silks and gems, but now my clothes are either too thick or too thin, the colors too plain, the dresses too short or too long, and the only accessories I wear are the pins to keep my hair out of my face.

Then there are the locals. Their close-knit connections, their bonded struggles, how they accept their place, growing and loving their families and friendships without appearing as if they yearn for more.

That yearning is all I have. A chaos that despises the way things are simply because they are that way. They expect a smile, and I do, because I know this town too well to think I would survive if I did anything but conform. But I detest the forced acceptance, and I can feel my mask fading, my restraint thinning with every passing day.

"Your master was looking for you a moment ago, Meg."

Knocking Dora's hand off her shoulder, Meg visibly pales. "Where?" Dora points, and she rushes in the opposite direction. "I'll see you tonight." She waves back to Adonis.

Would she see him tonight? Why? Do they have plans? Didn't he say he'd be with me tonight? I keep my questions to myself, refusing to sound jealous.

The accomplished smile on Dora's face vanishes. "Can we... Can we talk after? I have something— I just— Will you forgive me?" I hate that I'm the reason her light dims, that I can feel her worry without having to look at the pout on her round face. I know she's talking about the sacrifice, but whatever she wants to talk about sounds heavy if she's stumbling over her words. "You'll be okay, right?"

Being the skilled liar I am, I smile. "Drown me in wine before and I'd forgive you for murder." A terrible joke, one that has all three of us tensing.

My finger loops through the black ring at the end of my necklace, brushing against the vial tightly tucked between my breasts.

Trust me, the stranger's last words send another shiver through me, coiling around my instincts not to.

Chapter Two

KORE

"Why are you seeing Meg tonight?" I give in and ask the question that has been nagging at me since leaving the market, hoping Adonis misses the snarl in my tone.

The black omen birds cawing in the trees above us don't settle my uneasiness one bit. Not when every chirp and click adds to the dreadful lullaby that bears an aura of warning.

I'm overreacting. This time of year always leads me down dark spirals and paranoia, looking over my shoulder and second-guessing every intention, every sentence.

Adonis' tightened grip on my hips, the rough feel of his palms rubbing against my skin, hiking my dress higher, draws me back to him and that hazy look in his eyes when he steps back, leaving me with the strawberry flavor lingering on my lips.

"She's my friend, and servants are required to be in attendance. Of course, I'll see her. We both will."

He's so casual, so matter-of-fact, leaving little room to argue, which forces me to take his answer for what it is and shove away that green ache. His mind shouldn't be wrapped up in blonde waves anyway. And I trust him. We've known each other for far too long and too intimately to keep those kinds of secrets from one another.

I let out a high-pitched squeal as he lifts me by the back of my thighs, shushing me with another kiss before looking around the forest. "*Quiet,* Kore. We can't get caught."

CRUEL GODS

I kiss him harder, refusing to think of the bitter truth. We've found these stolen moments over the years, but a nobleman's daughter isn't meant for a servant, even if I am now our house servant. It isn't the same as being born into it. The punishment if we're caught wouldn't compare to the embarrassment it would bring my family, and my father's memory doesn't need any more tarnishing.

Stupid girl! The whispers of the crowd as I cried out cycle through my mind. I lock my hands at the nape of Adonis' neck and brush my tongue against his, breathless when he pulls away again.

"I know today is hard for you." He sets me down, pushing back a lock of hair that falls over my face. The soft gesture only reminds me how gentle and caring he is.

He was just a boy when he started working for my family. A boy who snuck out with me to roam the forest and swim in the rivers, who taught me how to swim, how to kiss, all while my father was away selling our oils and wines.

He was my first real friend, but not even he understands the weight of guilt today brings, the secrets I can never tell.

"It's the same as every year." I lift my chin with the perfected smile, my fingers slipping down the gilded chain, finding the ring at the end. So much for distractions. "We should get back to the house."

I don't get to turn to leave before he's pulling me flush against his chest. I feel his lips first, taste the sweet strawberries as he bends down and kisses me. It's soft, always soft, leaving me wanting more but too afraid to ask for it.

Part of me wants to push him away before things go too far, before those feelings deep, deep inside of me take over and leave me with an aching regret when I don't get what I need, but Gods, he tastes good.

The fire in my belly roars to life as he pulls me even closer so there's hardly a stitch between us.

My tongue wraps around his. That *need* building, eviscerating every hesitant thought when his grip tightens on my waist as if to keep himself steady, to keep them from roaming any farther.

It doesn't matter how many meals I skip, my hips never shrink, and I couldn't be more thankful that he has something to hold. I'm not embarrassed by my full figure, and it's thanks to him, the way he grips and pulls at every piece of me like I'm dough he has to knead.

His legs brush against mine, and every hard inch of him turns me molten.

My skin tingles waiting for his touch, has me damn-near praying this is the day he finally can't control himself, that he can't resist taking me against the tree or the forest floor.

My soft moan against his lips has whatever internal battle he's fighting lost and waving a white flag.

My back hits a tree, but no puncture of a branch or scraping against my flesh can stop me from seeing where this goes, from touching him without shame—up his back, feeling every bit of hardworking muscle beneath the thin fabric.

Watching him work in our groves, the way every curve and cut of him moves and glistens under the sun, has been its own special kind of torture.

When his fingers slide beneath my straps, I still, my pulse rising, my skin pebbling as he slides them down my arms at a pace too slow.

It's been years of waiting for him to want me this way, and part of me feels guilty that he doesn't know just how badly I need this, that it isn't just a distraction for me.

A scorching shiver runs up my back as his lips brush along my chin and down my neck with the same unhurried tease. We're tucked beneath a canopy of branches, shading us from the harsh sun, and yet it feels like I'm being showered with its rays.

My breath hitches as the fabric falls to my waist, leaving me bare, those rays burning through the pit of my stomach with nerves, spiking with pleasure when his fingers wrap around my nipple.

His mouth finds mine again, fondling my breast with the same kneading motions he was giving my hips.

It's still too soft. It isn't enough to stop the memories I'm desperate to forget. This moment is what I've wanted for years, but *this* isn't what I want, what I *need*.

He hisses, grabbing at his ankle, taking all the built-up heat with him as he stumbles back.

I cover my chest, quickly grabbing the vial that fell to my feet, finding a raven hopping away before setting off to a branch. Its neck twists back toward us, cocking its head to the side, its beady eyes taking us in as if studying us closer.

How curious.

Adonis doesn't take the same interest I do. He leans in to pick up where we left off, but the bird is back before he can so much as touch me, swooping down and flapping its wings between us.

In one quick motion, Adonis bends down and grabs a rock, cocking his arm back.

My stomach drops. "What are you doing?" I grab the rock from his hand and throw it deeper into the forest. "Tell me you weren't about to hit that bird."

"It attacked us."

It attacked you, is what I want to say, but that wouldn't help my argument. I'm stunned by witnessing such a violent act from him, especially toward an animal. He's always so quiet and passive, never one to cause trouble or so much as speak up unless it regards mine and Meg's hatred for one another, or when he teases Dora. Servants are supposed to be silent and unseen, and it's a quality he naturally possesses, but violence? I haven't seen him so much as bat a bee away.

He grumbles with disappointment. I mimic him with an entirely different type of disappointment, that familiar unmet needy ache pissed at me again for hoping today would be any different. "We should run home before Metanira makes herself useful."

He chuckles, adjusting the strap on my shoulder, lingering as if contemplating leaving it there or pulling it back down.

Before he can decide, I right it myself. "Race you?"

I quickly set the pace toward the house, knowing my small legs are no match for his, but I purposely left the baskets by his feet, giving him no choice but to run slower to avoid breaking the plates.

I'm not one for signs, but there's something disquiet in the air, a despair that has me noticing things I would otherwise overlook or brush off: strangers with riddles and odd omen birds with their following songs and inconvenient interruptions, Dora not attending the sacrifice, and Adonis taking it a step further with me.

12

My pulse races with a nervous anticipation I can't decipher from the flicker of fear that excites me or the kind that shouldn't.

The windows in the front room are wide open, carrying a light scented breeze of fresh fish and baked bread throughout the house I've always called home.

"Mother?" I call out, making my way toward the kitchen. "Hello?"

Adonis follows closely behind with the basket of plates lightly clanking together, pointing a look in my direction that leaves no misunderstanding; he wants a rematch. One thing he hates more than being a servant is losing.

I watch his face shift from challenge to confusion once the smell catches up to him. There isn't another person who prepares food in our home aside from us.

My mother, Metanira, hasn't been able to afford another servant since my father's death, and there isn't a chance we'll find her in the kitchen unless she drank too much and stopped in for a snack, but even that doesn't involve cooking anything. The woman favors cheese and bread to soak up the copious amounts of wine she spends her days drowning in.

Adonis takes the lead, stepping in front of me to peek through the swinging kitchen door. His protective stance has me take a step back, only to lean closer into him a second later, too curious to stay behind.

"Hello?" His voice deepens as he pushes the door open.

I cover my mouth to hide my laugh at his attempt to sound intimidating while looking just as nervous. I have no doubt that whoever is behind the door isn't going to harm us. I haven't known a harmful intruder to bother cooking.

What we find behind is much, much worse than a stranger here to rob us of what little we have left.

"*Ooo!*" The old woman clutches her chest. "You scared the living soul out of me. You must be Adonis. Metanira told me you'd be here to help soon, although I'm nearly done now." She looks as disappointed as she sounds about having to do all the work herself.

"Where is my mother?" I ask, not that I need to. There are two places she could be, and it's nowhere near a kitchen if help is around.

"Courtyard, speaking with Theseus. I've already set the table if you'd like to freshen up. They're waiting for you." Her perky tone is marked with warning, her wrinkled judgment dancing between our flushed cheeks and sweaty clothes.

"Do you need help with anything?" Adonis steps into his servant role, placing the dirty market plates on the counter. He immediately begins helping the woman plate the cheese, bread, fish, and fruit—a rather elaborate spread for lunch, which only further confirms my suspicion about this surprise visit.

Before I can decide between offering to help or freshening up as the woman suggested—maybe running away—the front door sings with nonstop eager, little knuckles.

My feet can't carry me fast enough away from the keenly observant woman.

"Kore!" The children scream as I sneak out the front door.

"We're not picking grapes again, right?" a little girl asks.

"Can we pick the olives instead?" one begs; a boy who usually ends the day cradling his stomach and looking greener than the olives.

"No, I want to take care of the roses today!" one of the older girls pleads.

"Enough!" Their housemother shouts. She's a younger woman, not much older than I am, and usually returns smelling of sweat and wine. "You will listen and do whatever Kore tells you. I'll be back soon." She gives me a curt nod and has a speed in her steps as she makes her way down the dirt path that leads back toward town, while all six children wait patiently for me to answer them.

Their mismatching chitons, usually donated or made from found fabric, are cut above their knees that are too often bruised from kneeling all day. For the day of Hades, they all wear a black piece of fabric pinned near their shoulders that are freshly burnt from daily sun.

If we didn't have guests, I'd take them to the courtyard for some shade and a plate of food before they start.

"Grapes today! You know how your housemother loves her wine." I wiggle my brows and stumble jokingly, earning an applause of giggles.

Since one of the kids broke a vase, interrupting my mother from her afternoon nap, they are no longer allowed indoors, so we follow the

14

footpath around back, where the children run off with their baskets toward the rows of endless grapes. Every year, they seem to grow farther back, adding more work for us to maintain.

"Kore?" My favorite orphan, the shaggy, auburn-haired girl, tugs my arm.

"We have a guest today, Atlanta. I won't have time to help or race." It's too bad because I enjoy listening to her talk about her dreams of being a hero like the Gods in the stories, and her relatable complaints about having to learn ladies' work at the other houses. Like me, she detests cleaning. She would rather learn to forge weapons like the God Hephaestus and hunt like the Goddess Artemis. She is at an age when most girls would mature and dream of marrying, having babies, but her childlike wonder has yet to fade. Something I wish I still possessed at times.

"That's fine. I don't feel like running anyway. Will you at least sit with me for a little bit?" Her softness curls around my heart. "Today is always hard, and you're one of the only people that really..." Her head lowers, her pink cheeks brightening, "listens."

I let out a soft sigh, glancing back at the house. My mother and her guest will have to wait a little longer.

"I have time for one story." I hold my finger up for emphasis. We'll get lost in too many if I don't set the rule now.

The top of her head doesn't reach my chest as she jumps on her toes before ushering us to an isolated area away from the rest of the children, who are already in their usual flow. The older girls care for the baby boy while gawking at the older boys from a distance. The older boys run around or throw grapes into baskets, backing up farther and farther, making a game of it.

I pride myself on being a sanctuary for them. Adonis told me they were trained brutally to be subservient, silent, and unseen, that if he had a place to be a kid, maybe he wouldn't have had as many punishments that he refuses to tell me about. Anything to do with the orphanage is off-limits.

We sit, hidden in one of the rows, the grass cool against my once-pale legs, now tanned from the daily sun. A sign of a working woman. A flaw that makes me less desirable to any potential suitors, but it's the price I pay for putting food on our table. A happy price if I'm honest. If tan skin ensured I never had to marry, I would pull my bed outside to sleep all day and night, bathing under as many rays as I could.

"Are you going to marry Adonis?" Atlanta's question brings me back to the present, to her sitting back on her knees, gathering grapes and peering up at me sheepishly.

Thinking perhaps she's starting to grow into the inevitable woman who finds boys cute, I bite my cheek to keep from smiling too wide. "Why would you ask that?"

"Well…" Atlanta pauses, her cheeks reddening as she focuses on plucking grapes to keep from looking at me. "I was excited to see what treats you had for us today, so I ran ahead of everyone. I know the woods are a shortcut to your house, and I saw you two kissing."

My mouth dries. It's my turn to grow hot with embarrassment, to have to explain myself to a thirteen-year-old, and the fact that we were watched without realizing it. Anyone could have seen us. The scandal it would have caused… How could I be so stupid?

Stupid girl, the memory assaults me.

A callused hand grabs mine, too rough for a girl so young. "I won't tell anyone." As if sensing my worries, she adds a gentle promise.

"It's complicated." My voice holds more heartache than I expect. "He's a servant. There are expectations when you're born into a family with money or status." I'm not exactly sure what to say to a girl who already knows too much, let alone an orphaned servant who's likely never to marry.

"I know." She glances up with a look I know too well. A look so distinct, I can feel the emotions behind it: pain, grief, and loss. "My mother tried to marry me off." It's like looking into a mirror when I speak of my father.

"What happened to her?" I ask before I can stop myself. Orphans aren't allowed to speak of their past just as we're not allowed to ask. A strange rule, but one that I've abided by, until now.

She doesn't seem to mind or hear me at all because she doesn't stop picking grapes or look back up.

I open my mouth to apologize when she starts, "I've never told anyone."

"I shouldn't have asked."

"No, it's okay. I never get to talk about her." She glances around, making sure the other children are still too far away to hear, her voice lowering to ensure it. "I didn't see her often. Weeks, sometimes months, went by before I saw her again, and she never stayed long. But when she did come, she would hug me tighter than before, and lie in bed with me, listening to me tell her everything I had learned and done since her last visit." A soft smile creeps up her puffy cheeks at the vision in her head, one that will fade as years pass. "When she found out I was better at hunting and fishing than weaving and whatever else wives do, she was different. It was like she was scared. She would talk about marriage and how important it was to be a lady. Then, one visit, she brought a boy my age along."

"To marry?!" My shriek catches the attention of the others, but not for long after I wave them off and make an excuse about a spider crawling on me.

Atlanta's confirmed nod leaves me baffled and peeking over my shoulder at the house. "We didn't get a lot of visitors in the tower, and I only heard of boys from the myths and stories. They were heroes I wanted to be, not marry. So, when I saw him, I was disappointed. He was hardly bigger than I was. But my mother told me to impress him, that she had gone through a lot to set up the arranged marriage. I didn't want to make her more upset or disappointed in me, but I also didn't want to marry him. I knew I couldn't reject him, but I figured he could reject me, so we arranged a race. If I won, he'd tell my mother that he was not interested in me and leave, but if he won, I'd marry him with a smile on my face."

"Would you have, though?" I raise my brow, knowing how headstrong she is. A fact that Adonis reminds me of when she shows up with bruises and her head lowered.

Atlanta bites her lip like she wants to laugh. "I offered the race because I knew I'd win. I knew the woods better than anyone. I'd lived there my whole life. I knew exactly where to turn to avoid rocks or floating roots. It was supposed to be easy, but he cheated. He threw apples at me from behind. I lost my focus, and he won. He was boasting about it, how he'd sooner lock me in a room to birth his heirs, but he never finished the thought." I swear I see a smile before it drops into a haunted look that has me counting the seconds until she continues,

"A lion attacked him from behind. I ran to my mother and maid for help, but they were dead too. I didn't know what to do, so I ran deeper into the forest than I ever had. I'd hidden weapons for hunting in trees and under rocks. Eventually, the lion found me, but I killed it. I was too scared to go back, so I skinned it to keep warm."

I try to hide the disbelief. Atlanta is small now; there is no way she would've been able to kill a lion by herself. And skin it? She must have been no more than eight at the time.

"If you take out the legs first, it doesn't chase you," she adds, reading me all too well. This girl is always too perceptive.

"Anyways," Atlanta plops a handful of grapes into the basket. "I don't even know how long I was out there before hunters found me. I let them take me to the orphanage. I'm not sure what happened to the lions' fur."

"I'm sorry." It's all I can offer without thinking too much of my own loss. It's easy to offer sympathy for that part of her story, whether it's true or not.

"You could run away, too. If you want to be together."

A giggle escapes me, one that makes her throw a grape in my direction and let out her own fit of laughter. All sense of sadness evaporates at the sound.

Childish dreams.

I've thought about it before, running away to travel outside our small farming town, something few ever do. I ache for the chance to leave and be free of expectations, for a chance to make my own decisions.

I've never seen a boat, but I can imagine jumping on one, letting it drift me away to a new place, to start fresh somewhere else. But they are only dreams.

I would never be able to leave my mother to fend for herself, and the thought of not seeing Dora or Adonis every week is unimaginable. Then there's the children, who would no longer have a safe place.

I shake my head and begin to stand. "I've seen what happens to those who venture outside of expectations." It pains me to continue, but it feels necessary to teach a young girl the heavy lesson I was forced to learn. "Stay hidden, Atlanta. Those who know your name will use it."

18

I turn, ready to face whatever my mother has planned.

"Do you care about me?"

I whipped around so fast, my hair strikes my face, and all I see is dirt-colored waves. "Why would you ask that? Of course, I care about you."

"I told her I wouldn't say anything."

"Told who?"

Atlanta's shoulders curl like she's in trouble. "A woman stopped by the orphanage today. She was asking who knew you. When I told her that I did, she asked a lot of questions. She said I had to watch out for you. To make sure no one unfamiliar came around. She also said I needed to convince you to drink whatever she gave you earlier, or anyone you cared about would be in danger."

My pounding heart falls beneath my feet. "Is that all she said?"

"She was different, like you. And when I told her that, she said it was because I was similar. That we were made for more, that our past is something we need to face before we can fully embrace who we are."

The story about her mother makes sense now. All great myths started with tragedy. This girl wants to believe the strange woman who spun her childish promises. Who wouldn't want to hear they're special?

My fists clench knowing the woman manipulated Atlanta, but I can't figure out her motive. It has to be the same stranger from earlier, the one with the pretty jawline and vial.

I open my mouth to ask more when the bell rings—my mother's call that means I'm requested, immediately.

Atlanta clutches my arm one last time. "You should drink it, but if you don't, just know I can take care of myself." Her smile is too mischievous. "Be careful tonight, Kore."

Fucking Fates and their omens.

Chapter Three

KORE

Splashing cold water over my face isn't enough to calm the rising panic of the unknown waiting for me in that courtyard, or the dread for what comes after. If there was a freezing lake that could rid me of all these worries and unwanted thoughts, I would dive in headfirst without question. And if there was a fiery pit that promised to send me straight into the morning, I wouldn't bother to shed my clothes before leaping into the flames.

With my hands resting on the edge of the washroom counter, I hang my head between my shoulders and repeat the daily mantra for the hundredth time today, "It's almost over."

Removing the mirror from the wall, I place it backward on the ground, and finish getting ready. My annual ritual to keep from seeing myself in the long, black dress. My mother gifted it to me as more of a punishment and reminder that I now represent the family at the sacrifice rather than the lavish, loving gift it appears to be. The soft fabric covers the entirety of my back and reaches my neck but isn't tight enough to choke. If we cross paths again, the old hag, Alice, would have no reason to stare at me with that disdainful look.

I'm determined not to give anyone a reason to look at me tonight. I'll be a shadow in the dark night, or so I hope.

The ring I never take off sits snug in my cleavage. I smile, remembering my father's laugh when he came home from months of traveling to find me and Adonis with swollen lips and red cheeks. He walked us out to the gardens and showed me the black ring. "I would

20

never tell you who to marry, you know that, but when you decide who that is, I want you to tell me so I can give you this ring. That way, you will never forget me when you have your new family." I slapped his arm and wanted the ring right then and there, so he knew I would never forget him. "When you get this ring, it should be the best day, a start of the rest of your life," he told me as he slid it onto his own finger.

That ball in the back of my throat isn't as suffocating as it used to be, but it's still there. And I swallow it down just as that desire for something *more* stirs. I never know what it is, just that I don't feel right, ever—not in my body, not in this home, not when I'm walking to the market, not even when I'm soaking in the bath. I've always felt like I don't belong, like I'm a throw pillow on a dusty couch, floating in an ocean. It doesn't make sense, and neither do I.

Admiring the stranger's vial one last time, I slip it next to the ring, the *Drink Me* label still attached, enticing me to try it.

Any normal person would have tossed it out immediately, but every time I pull it out, something tugs at me, telling me not to drop it into the waste bin or pour it down the sink. Intuition, maybe, but ridding myself of it is impossible, and keeping it close feels strangely right.

With everything in place, I make my way toward the center of the house, feeling rats clawing at my insides. My mother hasn't entertained in years, and while I have my suspicions, I have a feeling that whatever is waiting for me on the other side is another sign or omen to add to the riddle that is today.

Straightening my back to appear more confident, I inhale through my nose and push the doors open.

A waft of freshly baked bread and floral hit me first, wild hyacinths, roses, lilies, and other flowers of opposing shades and varieties flourishing, weaving, and climbing without pattern in every corner. The dreaded wildflowers that most murder from their gardens find a home in mine.

The rare visitors who are unfamiliar with our home often trip over the tangled vines that slither across the patio.

Our old servants would cut them away, severing the poor plant's limbs, making each bed identical to any other garden standards, but I despise gardens like that. What is the point of having the same as

21

everyone else? Flowers are meant to grow freely and intermix within one another, each one unique to itself, growing and dying at its own time.

"Here she is!" My mother's perfected hostess grin spreads in greeting. It's the way she stands from the table and holds her arms out wide that startles me, more so than the unfamiliar man whose back is to me.

Never has my mother been *excited* to see me.

When my father was alive, she chose to spend her days with other wives, gossiping around this very table while servants waited to fill their never-ending cups, all the while, I played in the garden with the other children, the same who now throw their coins at me.

Taking the hint, I round the table and hug her in an awkward embrace. The passing kiss on my cheek makes me flinch, and I step back to assess her better.

My mother never fails to put herself together when guests are over but today is even more impressive. She wears the silver-embroidered green dress that makes her matching emerald eyes sparkle, and her golden hair is freshly washed and curled, shining extra bright in the sun. Her makeup is soft, giving her a more youthful glow.

The man across the table stands and bows in greeting. "It's a pleasure to meet you, Kore. Your mother has been telling me so much about you."

I hold my face expertly still so as not to frown at the pleasantries I despise so much. It makes sense to greet one another, but it's always the same hollow words with the same shallow smiles, even if neither is in fact happy.

It's all fake and disingenuous.

"Don't be rude," my mother hisses and nudges my shoulder, shooting me with a warning glare to behave.

"The pleasure's mine." I, being the hypocrite that I am, offer my hand that he accepts with too much enthusiasm. Nothing about this man is remarkable—his flat dishwater hair, the dullness behind his stare. He is a little older than me and isn't a man I'd stop to look at twice. In fact, I'm a little annoyed he's taking up space in my sanctuary, likely here to tell us we're too poor to keep up with our annual tithe. We've been barely skimming by for years.

His light kiss on the back of my hand is warmer and more welcoming than my mother's, and I can't help but notice his palms are soft against my callused ones.

"Like I was saying, she donates her time to help the orphans. Always looking for ways to help. Too much if you ask me." The spite laced in my mother's calm demeanor doesn't miss me.

She should be thankful. It's because of me, Adonis, and the children that we're able to continue producing our oils and wines, that we're able to keep our home and the large bed she sleeps her drunken days in.

I immediately regret choosing the seat next to her when sharp nails pierce my thigh beneath the table in another warning to behave.

The man doesn't seem to notice my struggle to keep my composure, to keep myself from gasping for air as my skin breaks.

"That's quite impressive." His praise is swift and curt, a glance of acknowledgement in my direction before returning to my mother.

Typical, and just as well. As curious as I am, I'd rather not speak at all, or I'll likely earn myself more bruises and broken skin. While servants are to be unseen and unheard, it's the daughters that need to be *seen* and unheard, the latter being my biggest struggle. Already, my nerves are on edge, and I want nothing more than to take that bottle from the center of the table and run before I finally snap. It's been five years of holding my tongue, and I'm not sure I can make it one more of fighting my instincts to speak without being spoken to, to frown when I'm supposed to smile, or punch back when kicked down.

"Your reputations precede you. I've often heard how close and loving your relationship is. It's quite a sight to see in person. And she is as beautiful as you described, the spitting image of you."

"Theseus, you flatter me." My mother takes a long sip from her cup in self-celebration that her hard work had not been for naught. She's worked tirelessly to ensure our reputations are flattering amongst our peers for as long as I can remember. There was even a time when people flocked to our home to see the painted smiles and public displays of affection and doting.

People see what they want to see.

The perfect mother. The perfect maiden.

That's what I had been before it all went away because I trusted the wrong person. My elegant dresses were replaced with rags, my optimism turned cynical, and everything around me dulled.

"Me as well." I follow the gesture, taking a long sip, to hide my silent snicker behind the cup.

Metanira is tall, thin, and blonde with fair skin. I am anything but— shorter, dark hair, and curvier, with a chest I do my best to hide away in public.

"How is it you two know each other?" My question is simple enough, but my mother shoots me a side-eye that tells me it is the one question she will allow.

It's the only question I have, and now that I've asked it, I don't wait to eat. It has been too long since I've indulged in such an elaborate spread, and my stomach will surely be the fourth guest at this table if I don't feed it soon.

Filling my plate with bread and fruit, I nibble while listening. That's always been my tactic to stay out of trouble: ask a simple question to get everyone else talking so I can sit back and listen. People love to talk about themselves when given a chance, and it gives me less opportunity to say something I shouldn't.

A subtle movement behind Theseus catches my attention. He was so still when I first walked in that I didn't notice Adonis in the statuesque stance, waiting for someone to call on him. It's easy to pretend we're just two people living in a house together, earning a living like everyone else, until days like today when we're forced into our roles.

"Oh, well," Theseus glances between me and my mother, clearing his throat, and shifting uncomfortably in his seat. "I've come for a wife."

I choke on the piece of bread. Nails dig into my leg, urging me to be quick about it.

I was wrong, very, *very* wrong about this impromptu visit. I can't begin grasp it. How could my mother even think of marrying again? She hardly leaves her room. To be a wife to another man? How could she forget about my father? And to marry a man so much younger than she is? It's absurd.

To marry before even I....

24

My spiraling thoughts pause when I realize my mother and Theseus haven't stopped staring at me.

No!

"You're here for me?" I sit up straighter, dropping the bread from my lips, my heart with it.

He can't be there for me. My mother wouldn't sell me off. For what? What could this man offer that I can't, what I haven't been providing these past five years?

"Yes," the man asserts himself as if we hadn't met minutes ago.

Cautiously, I steal a glance at Adonis, who remains still, but his raised brow gives him away.

He knew.

Metanira's grip on my thigh tightens again, but this time, I welcome the pain I learned to embrace as a child, the promise of crescent-moons carved into my skin.

"Why me? How did this even come about?"

"*Kore*," my mother warns.

I hiss, taking in a sharp breath at my breaking skin, the warm liquid soaking into my dress.

Theseus chuckles with a playful shake of his head. "It's fine, Metanira," he assures her, looking back to me with more interest than I care for. "I apologize for being so upfront, but we've been in an arranged marriage for some time now. My younger cousin Pirithous…"

If it wasn't for the lack of food in my belly, I would throw up at the mention of that name instead of swallowing the bile back down, focusing on that lingering pain stinging my thighs to stay present enough to listen.

"I understand your father was a mentor of his. I'm not sure if you crossed paths. He isn't much older than us. Regardless, he came to me after your father died and said that you two would need help one day, and it would be best to align our families to help alleviate the reputation you two have endured. Metanira and I agreed to the arrangement with the request that we wait until you were… *more agreeable*."

I'm at a loss. I'm in an arranged marriage I had no knowledge of, and with Pirithous' cousin of all people. If he set this up, I can't imagine what this means. I thought he was out of my life.

"You agreed to this?" I find my mother sitting back, tapping her nail on her cup, not at all pleased with his admission.

Theseus clears his throat, dismissing my question as he goes on, "I've heard you're very successful at earning a living without much help, but you won't need to any longer. As part of our agreement, I'll see to the continued success of your family's estate. We'll bring servants back to ensure it. As for our home, it's quite large with many servants. You'll want for nothing."

I scoff. "How generous of you."

The words are out before I can stop them. The lack of fingernails biting into my thigh isn't a good sign either. My mother will see to it that I learn my lesson later.

Misunderstanding my corrected smile, Theseus chuckles. "You're a funny one."

To keep myself from saying anything else that would lead this man to believe I'm agreeable to this marriage, I bite the inside of my cheek until I taste blood.

"Metanira wants this wedding sooner, but I think we should enjoy a long and public engagement. My maid has already sent out the notice, and by this time tomorrow, all will know of our upcoming union."

"Theseus, are you sure about a long engagement?" My mother leans forward and reaches for his hand. "Do you really want to wait for heirs? We can do a small ceremony here tomorrow. A celebration after the long festival."

I watch in disbelief as my mother barters for my early departure.

"In time, Metanira." He pulls away, dismissing her with a simple look that says she's being improper. He's the kind of man who would scold a child for not saying thank you or have his servant whipped for unpolished silverware. "You needn't worry about anything now that the announcement is being made. My maid is yours, and I'll have servants sent over to help right away, so you can ensure Kore has all the time she needs to prepare to be my wife."

"Of course." They both stand and embrace each other like old friends. "She'll be nothing short of perfect."

Theseus stalks around the table, and my body stands on instinct rather than thought. It takes all my willpower not to frown or shudder away as his eyes travel up the length of me, eyeing the woman he officially bought.

"I look forward to our wedding night." When he kisses my hand this time, his lips linger a few seconds too long, turning to leave without waiting for my response, which is a vulgar gesture at his back.

As Adonis leads the man away, Metanira's usual glower is replaced with a smile of a job well done. "At least you had the sense to shut up for once. You managed *not* to ruin everything I've worked too hard to put in place."

"I don't understand. Why would you marry me off? Why now?" I fight to swallow the thickening in the back of my throat that threatens to suffocate me this time, not of guilt but of utter betrayal.

My mother floats across the floor back to her seat. "Please, you're twenty. I've let you stay here long enough."

"We don't need the money. Adonis and I have managed, and with the children's help every week, we've been able to sell more—" Reasonings stumble out, hoping for something, anything to change her mind.

"Mom?" I plead, the strange word catching in my throat.

Standing with an icy calmness and an even colder glare, she makes her way to me. I hold my head high, knowing exactly what's coming, but the sting doesn't grace my cheeks as usual.

The hard shove takes me by surprise, and I hit the ground with a yelp. My head lands on a clump of flowers instead of the stone. Thank the Gods for that. The pain-relieving tonic I bought last week is already out, and I don't need another week-long headache.

"I told you not to call me that!" Metanira reclaims her seat, looking even more satisfied with herself, finishing her drink before slamming the cup back on the table, hard enough that I flinch at the impact.

My head clears, and I manage to stumble my way to a nearby chair, my lash line flooding with unshed tears that I wipe away before they fall.

"Be grateful your… Celius isn't here to see you now."

Her words hurt more than they should. We don't speak about my father, or at all, choosing to avoid each other as much as possible. Since she's usually in bed, our paths hardly cross, except when I return home and see bottles of wine on the counter. That's one sign I can never overlook. I know to grab the healing salves and head to my room for whatever awaits me when I see them. Still, hardly a word passes until she's finished and leaves me to tend to my wounds in peace.

Blinking back tears, I grab the cup Metanira was swirling and refill it for her, pouring myself one, too, before I sink into my chair and sip, savoring the numbing tannins on my tongue.

"I tried when you were younger." Metanira chuckles to herself, taking a long drink. In this, we're alike. Maybe not in looks, but we both enjoy the fleeting bliss that comes with a bottle. "But I couldn't love you, not like Celius. He loved you right away. He couldn't understand why I didn't. I tried though. I pretended. As you have tried and pretended to love me."

The way her voice begin to slow into a slur reminds me that this is just the alcohol talking, though, there is something in her gaze that stills me, the words I can see she's contemplating, as if she's been waiting for this conversation and wants to cherish it.

"I've never pretended to love you. You're my mother." We've never truly bonded, but I never once thought she didn't love me. She shows it differently, with rare gifts like a beautiful, jeweled dress, a vase that depicted my favorite story, or an extra blanket in my room when the shutters broke during a windstorm. It's the small things I've held onto over the years.

"I am not your mother!" Metanira snaps. "You took everything from me."

I've heard this too many times to question the remark, but as pure hatred stares back at me, my mind begins to falter.

"I should have gotten rid of you after your stupidity caused his death."

"Then why didn't you?" I bite back. I don't need a reminder of what I did, of what I caused. Guilt eats at me every day, but I'm growing frustrated with the turn of this conversation. "Why didn't you get rid of me then? Why keep me around? You could have married me off and had more money to pay for servants long before tonight."

"I made a deal." Her empty cup falls to the table again. "I promised Celius I'd try, and I did. Do you think anyone in this town would take you? After being labeled a nonbeliever? After the scene you caused at the sacrifice?" she scoffs to herself.

28

Feeling the hatred radiating off her, I embrace it as my own because *I* am pissed.

"Where were *you* that night?" My skin heats with every passing word. "You blame me, but you weren't even there. Maybe if it had been you who died instead, we'd all be better off."

Her laugh sends chills down my spine, all the way to the shaking wrists on my lap.

"Is that what you think? That your life would be better off without me?" Her slurs thicken, filled with a dripping venom. "You have no idea what I've given up for *you*."

She stands, catching herself on the table, swaying before the old woman from the kitchen ushers her away.

If my mother hadn't kicked the door closed that very second, I'm certain the cup I threw would have hit her head.

When they're no longer in sight and their feet no longer pad against the floor, Adonis comes out from behind one of the pillars.

I focus on the untouched plate in front of me at his shuffled approach, barely feeling his gentle pull at my elbow, or aware that I stand and follow him absentmindedly out of the house.

It doesn't matter that his hand is on me or that we're headed to our favorite spot; I can feel myself crawling further back in my mind, watching my body move without feeling connected to it.

We zag our way through the tight trees without talking until we make our final climb over the fallen one that marks our hidden clearing next to the river.

Adonis turns, raising his hands in defense, a plea to hear him out. "I swear I would have told you if I could. That old woman told me right before you showed up, and by then it was too late."

Physically and mentally exhausted, I slump onto the log. The rough bark scratches at my leg, bringing me out of the hiding pocket in my mind.

"I know I shouldn't complain about any of this to you, of all people, but I miss him. If my father were here, we wouldn't be struggling, we wouldn't be overworked, there would be no arranged marriage, and my mother wouldn't be able to—" I catch myself before admitting to the abuse.

It isn't that he doesn't know. He's seen the bruises I hide behind bandages and makeup. He notices the increase in healing salves in the pantry, but like the orphanage, we don't talk about it. He doesn't ask, and I don't offer.

"This was always your fate." He lowers himself to my side. "You're the daughter of one of the wealthiest noblemen, with the largest vineyard and groves. One who helped run our town. A king in his own right. Celius might have been able to reject any man's offer, but Metanira wouldn't have been able to. The deal she made was the best option, given your father's tainted reputation as a nonbeliever. And Theseus is Pirithous' cousin, which means he's just as wealthy."

He lifts my chin to look at him, emphasizing his next words, "*When* you marry him, all the problems you listed won't be there. You'll get to raise babies and order servants like me around to do all the dirty work you don't want to do. You'll have all the free time you want to bake and garden."

His words, the lingering wine within my veins, the life within these trees that has always brought me peace, nothing can make me agreeable to this situation.

"And what about you?" His frown fades into a reassuring grin, and with a quick turn of his head, he reminds me of the tattoo on his neck. "My fate is sealed, too."

My family sigil is bold, branding the small patch of skin below his hairline.

The silence stretches between us, filled with ravens cawing and the river's soft trickle.

I spin the golden chain between my fingers.

There is no running away. Theseus would pull any help he offered, and that would leave my mother alone to fend for herself. But marrying the man is out of the question. I simply don't want to.

That's something I haven't thought much about. What *do* I want?

From the black metal between my fingers, I look at Adonis, his sun-kissed curls, sharp cheekbones, and tan skin. That lingering lust from earlier nudges me. There is one thing I want, one thing I need before everything changes.

Not giving doubt a chance to hold me back, I throw my arms around his neck, picking up where we left off earlier.

My kiss isn't soft.

I don't want the soft gentleness he usually gives, as if he fears breaking me, but it's all he offers.

This could be our last kiss, our last chance. I need this, a memory I can come back to that replaces the others.

He isn't gripping hard enough, but at least he's kissing me, at least he's pulling me onto his lap, the bark no longer digging into my flesh. A discomfort I don't need at all so long as his lips are on mine.

Straddling his waist, I don't wait for him to make the next move. I lower my straps to my elbows, and this time, there are no birds to stop him from fondling me. I don't even care that the vial fell to my feet again. I'm too focused on his lips trailing kisses down my neck. They're too slow, too sensual, and I rock my hips so there's no denying what I want.

Feeling his reaction beneath me, the heat from before returns with a vengeance. The *need* inside me begs for more, but I'll accept anything he is willing to give me.

A raven perched in the tree catches my attention, taking away my focus. Its wings flap at its sides as if ready to cut in if I drop my clothes any farther.

Curling my fingers at the hem of my dress, my eyes remain locked on the bird's cocked head that twitches side to side, challenging the thing to see if my mind is playing tricks on me or if the bird really is stopping us.

As I rock again, Adonis tenses.

His lips leave my collarbone, pulling my focus back to him.

"Kore, we can't." His eyes are searching in a lust-filled plea to understand.

"Why not?" I pout, dazed and confused, and again disappointed.

Maybe it isn't normal to have this craving inside of me, for wanting *more* all the time.

"I can't... I can't ruin you."

"You wouldn't ruin me." I cringe at the neediness in my voice. "Besides, if I am ruined, I won't have to marry him."

He looks at me as if I'm being childish and presses my shoulders. I take the hint and swing my leg over, peeling myself off him and adjusting my clothes, ensuring I grab the vial and tuck it back in place before he notices.

"He will provide everything for you."

"I don't want everything." Childish or not, my mind holds firm on that front. I've had everything and it still wasn't enough to fill that aching void.

I'm not changing my mind on marrying Theseus either. I will die before I let that man or his cousin touch me again.

Chapter Four

KORE

My steps are heavier than they were this morning. Each step back towards town drags along the worn trail, the crows and ravens mocking above, the trees rustling with the swift breeze.

Had my mother not ambushed me with an arranged marriage, I would have circled back and grabbed a bottle to keep me company, but thinking of running into Metanira again sounds as appealing as skinning my fingers one at a time with a dull knife—a form of punishment I would never say out loud in case she finds that appealing enough to use. With enough wine, I wouldn't put it past her.

Spotting the temples peaking in the distance, the names carved into the top still too far away to see clearly, almost makes me wish I had risked it, if only to dull myself enough to make it through the next few hours. But as I take in the dimmed mauves and ambers in the sky, my nerves aren't because of the sacrifice alone, and my feet move a little faster.

I know every step, could point out every boulder and fallen tree, but walking through the woods in the dark alone is foolish, no matter my lack of fear.

While some might hear Atlanta's story and think she was saved by those hunters, I see the truth of it. They sold the girl to the orphanage for quick coin.

Others weren't so lucky. Stories of girls disappearing, never to return. The few who have come back forgot what had happened to them or became the strongest of believers. One had even lost her tongue.

33

CRUEL GODS

I shouldn't have insisted Adonis run ahead to deliver our house offerings for the final feast, but we both needed the space. I couldn't listen to him justify this marriage, and the sting of his rejection made it harder to look at him. All I saw was pity and the comfort of the small life we've made, the path I should want to fight for, but find that both directions give me the same hollow fate.

The ravens cawing above agree, in fact, I'm realizing now that they probably follow me because they recognize the dead and find it amusing to see one walking around.

I give them a vulgar gesture, reminded of how everyone is too willing to give me up, as if I'm a sacred offering and Theseus is their God.

Gods be damned if that's the case.

I cross the bridge that separates the locals and outsiders, stepping onto the streets lined with scaffolding on one side and crumbling homes on the other, shared apartments that could once fit a small family now crammed with too many.

I'll take callused hands, late nights, solitude, and work my bones to dust, so long as I never have to replace my forest, river, and gardens for tight alleys, crows, and construction.

Children bump into me, too giddy to see the play that marks the end of the festival, some holding looks of fear, lingering behind parents who urge them to walk faster. Women clutch their husbands with that same nervous excitement, and a few women stumble, laughing and pushing each other with playful banter.

I held that same ignorance long ago, now silently judging them for having the grim confidence that death won't be coming for them tonight. He will claim one, though; a lover, a friend, a neighbor.

"That damn little..." Dora huffs, coming up beside me as the familiar black stray runs ahead of us, swaying its hips.

I laugh. "Still can't catch her?"

A hint of her cherry-tinted cheeks is my confirmation that she's been chasing the thing for a while. "One day."

It doesn't matter if she leaves food scraps on the porch like I do; the feline waits until Dora leaves to devour it. If Dora calls for her, the thing hisses and runs away. It's become a game where I'm the only winner, laughing at her failed attempts and cuddling the stray for myself.

I stifle my amusement, my mouth hanging open at the golden braids atop Dora's head that leave wisps framing her face perfectly to draw attention to the black dust along her eyelids. Dora's always been pretty—petite, full chest and even fuller cheeks, bright round eyes, and a lightness that makes her fair skin glow—but tonight, she's stunning.

After I adorn her with compliments and beg to know the man's name, who is obviously the reason behind this added effort, she turns it back on me to keep from answering. Unable to keep anything from her, I tell her everything from the moment we departed, trying my best not to leave out one single detail.

"A raven stopped you and Adonis from—"

My hand flies over her mouth, cutting her off while I look around to make sure no one else heard her. When I see it's only us taking the long route, I drop my head, feeling her smile beneath my palm, and let out a bemused sigh that only she can pull from me.

"Yes, a bird stopped us. Is that seriously all you took away? I'm to be married. My... Metanira arranged for me to wed Pirithous' cousin."

"Wasn't that always the plan?" Dora shrugs, knocking my shoulder with hers as we continue down the narrow alley, the fluttering lights bathing our path in chilling shadows that make it harder to ignore my rising pulse. The dark has always hummed to me. The night sky, hidden corners, dense fog, and that pocket in my mind.

"Besides, it's not like you're marrying Pirithous," Dora adds, too sweet and naïve to understand. Priestesses marry their souls to the Gods, never a man, unless an oracle blesses it, but even that's rare. This is one thing she'll never have to consider or worry about, let alone contemplate how to get out of.

"I'd sooner spill my blood and seal my soul with Hades than marry either."

"Always so dramatic." Her eyes roll to the back of her head. "But you've always been different. I'm not surprised you'd want to fight this too."

"Too?"

"Are you serious?" She chokes like I said a joke, rounding in front of me and lifting her arm. "Give me your hand."

"What? No. Why?"

35

Her brow lifts in victory before taking my hand into hers and setting our pace again. Touch has always been Dora's comfort—one I learned she needs as much as I need to stay busy—always grabbing a shoulder, a hand, nudging an arm, or brushing hair from someone's face, all while teasing or saying something sweet in such a way that would lift a smile on the most stubborn of faces.

"Gloat all you want, but I'll find a way out of this situation by the end of the night."

A moment of silence passes that makes her soft whisper clear, "You were meant for more than this."

You were created for a much bigger purpose, the stranger's words come back to me, and Atalanta's, *We were made for more*.

"What do you mean?" I press. The highest any woman could wish for is to marry into wealth, to bring heirs that will thrive and continue a family name and successes. Being born into riches helps ensure that prospect, but it's never guaranteed. It's something I thought I would never have to endure thanks to my father's fallen reputation.

The weight of my reality is growing heavier with every realization. I am achieving the highest dream anyone like me could have, and rejecting it would not only be selfish but a slap in the face to my mother, my father's memory, and any other woman who would kill to be in my position.

Why don't *I* want this? Why isn't it that *more* that I crave?

"Really, what more could I be?" I ask, the question coming out as more of a plea for an answer I've sought for years. "A priestess like you? Marry myself to serve the Gods who let us murder each other in their name? Oh, please, Hades, God of the Underworld, let me serve you for eternity so I can never have a life of my own."

"Being a priestess is an honor. "Dora looks as if I just slapped her. "Not to mention that Hades doesn't have his own priestesses, which you should know, being that his temple is the only one you visit."

The way my insides writhe at her reminder has me flushing and cursing myself for mentioning the dark God twice now. The part of myself I've hidden deep down was already starting to climb out when I was with Adonis, now it's poking and whispering for me to go back home for release. A temptation I've only given in to a few times.

"I'm going to let all of this slide because I know today is hard for you." Dora's brow rises cautiously, which means whatever she has to say, trouble is likely to follow. I'm thankful she steers the conversation from Hades and intrigued by what could make her look so mischievous. "There is a Goddess who might be able to help you. Unfortunately, even the priestesses are too scared to speak about her, let alone know her name."

My eyes strain not to roll at the seriousness in her tone. Like my father, I don't really believe in the Gods or theories like the Fates. They were all stories and figures of speech. Except one. I have always hoped one God was real.

"Alright, since you asked." Dora tosses her hair behind her shoulder, never able to stay silent for long. "Some say she's a Goddess, others say she's a witch, and few have speculated she's something else entirely. I read that she was cast out of our world into another before she came back. Regardless, she does make deals with those who are desperate. There was something about a forked path, and you must call upon her three times for her to appear."

"But we don't know her name? The book you read never said anything?" I'm baffled that I'm even asking these questions, as if Gods are actually real.

"Nope. Not even the restricted books I read when everyone goes to bed say anything further. They all refer to her as *The Triple Goddess* with no name."

How ominous. I'm more than a little intrigued.

On cue, the sun's last rays disappear in the distance, draping the town in a layer of shadows, the alley swallowed by darkness as the last lamp burns out. Ravens and crows caw ahead once more—unkindness and murder—*fitting*.

An icy breath slithers up my spine, and I shiver, the vial shifting between my breasts.

Drink this and run before they find you.

Lines stretch from each temple with those waiting to pray and complete their offerings.

CRUEL GODS

Even though it's the night of Hades, his line is practically nonexistent, mostly giddy children huddled together, waiting for their chance to catch a glimpse of the fearsome, dreaded God.

Dora perches herself next to one of the front pillars as I make my way inside after them.

The first time I chanced a peek inside, I was a child, but just as elated with nerves as I am now. My belief then wavered with uncertainty of anything, but there was always the question of *what if* —a question that led me to this very temple more than I care to admit.

It's for appearances, I remind myself, ignoring that other lingering feeling that distracts me every time I enter this place. The few candles casting dancing shadows along the pale walls have me moving faster before I can act on it again.

The giggly children find their exit in the back with their shoulders drooping in relief and mild disappointment that the God wasn't here to run them off or collect their souls for the Underworld. A feeling I know all too well when I leave still intact.

Along the farthest wall sits the statue that prickles my skin, a silent presence with a heavy gaze, unmoving but always watching. The crown sitting high on his head holds candles that reveal soft glimpses of the distressed stone, warped by the wavering flames. He is so tall, the priestesses use ladders to light it, but by the looks of it, they haven't been here in some time, with only two of the seven candles lit, nearing their end.

That looming darkness calls to mine, enticing that side I struggle to keep buried when I'm here. If I didn't have to follow tradition, have to be seen walking into a temple with an offering, I wouldn't have tempted the restless ache uncoiling inside of me since mentioning the King of Soul's name.

I pass the near-empty slab of offerings, quickly tossing a cinnamon apple tart on top, and continue toward the back. As the treat lands, the candelabra's dimmed light flickers out, drawing out a reaction that has my breath growing heavy.

With every step, I fight to convince myself that I'm normal, that I'm not imagining the King of the Underworld behind me, following me into the shadows. That the subtle tremor of fear doesn't incite deranged, obscene thoughts of him abducting me from this life, giving me no choice.

At the sight of the crumbling fountain, my anger rises on his behalf. The other temples are better lit, the Gods' statues are front and center, and their fountains aren't crumbled to dust with birds nesting where water should be.

If Hades were real, he would damn them all for caring so little for him. It's a thought that makes me smile while imagining my own apology on behalf of all mortals, one that requires more than useless words.

The heat pooling at my core, the pulse thrumming between my legs at the thought is too much to ignore. I fall to my knees before the sculpted man who carries a bident in one hand and the other holding a rope that leashes a three-headed dog, each one snarling angrily at his feet. Hades glares straight ahead like he couldn't be bothered.

My neck strains to look up at the features that aren't as defined as the others, focusing on the intense, veiny details of that grip around that leash.

My cloak covers enough of me that if anyone were to come in, it would look as if I were simply on my knees praying.

My ears grow more alert as my hand travels up my thigh, lifting my dress, and finding that spot I've touched only three times before.

Four years ago was the first time I lost control. The horrid memories I wished to forget and the voices I hoped would mute had suffocated me so deeply that I was desperate enough to run here in the middle of the night, begging the God to be real and take my soul.

At the plea, the vivid images I conjured, I realized then just how sick I am because, on instinct, I found my hand between my legs.

Since then, I haven't been able to stop hoping that one day he'll hear my begging—because I refuse to call them prayers—and finally appear behind me to claim me once and for all.

It doesn't matter that I don't believe in the Gods; his lure is enough. Is it wrong that the only thing in life I look forward to is death?

I bite my lip to keep my moans from escaping as every inch of my body grows more sensitive, a wave of heat coursing through me.

My eyes shift to meet his glare, and my fingers slow to long, drawn-out circles. I want and need so much more, but this is all I can give in to right now. All I will ever allow, because the *more* I want is too profane, too crude, and the soft touches Adonis gives me aren't enough.

Because his statue isn't too detailed, it's easy to imagine Hades' scowl flickering to me, watching what I'm doing because of him, *for* him—my own personal offering. My fingers dip lower, gathering the slickness, and dragging them back to that spot, finding a rhythm that has me coming with a metallic taste on my tongue as my lip bursts between my teeth.

The rush of shame and regret washes over me immediately.

I wipe my fingers on the hem of my dress and look around the temple, making sure no one else had entered. Before the reality of what I've done again can fully hit me, I pull out the vial of liquid to examine it once more.

That what-if, the unknown aura of it, is the same I hold for the statue being before me. The *Drink Me* note attached catches my attention, noticing black marks at the bottom that look like crumbs, only when I try to rub them off, they don't wipe away.

Getting to my feet, I find a lit, tapered candle and hold it to the paper. In small black lettering, reads: *A butterfly without wings is a terrible thing. Drink me and become what you were fated to be.*

The sound of shuffling feet takes away my chance to think more on the riddle, and I quickly stuff the vial back in my dress before heading toward the exit, another step closer to whatever fate awaits.

The merchant tables throughout the town center no longer hold goods for sale but gifts for the final feast for all to enjoy, a required tithe: meats, cheeses, fruits, breads, oils, wines, and meads. My stomach rumbles at the sight.

My family's plum-colored bottles are scattered about, our empty ones we save year-round for this very night to make it appear as if others have already had their fill, while those who have lost loved ones due to the sacrifice are gifted the real wine in a basket with my baked treats. It won't bring them back or dull the pain, but it's all I can offer. A token of understanding.

I take Dora's hand and follow her through the crowd, tightening my hold when we shove past a tight group of women unwilling to move from their spot in line for Hera's temple, no doubt to pray for what I was offered tonight: a husband with promising wealth. If they were smart, they would be sure to ask that he be kind and caring, loving even, but those traits are often overlooked by girls so innocent and naïve.

We slide past children skipping with wooden swords and ducking beneath clinking glasses. I can't hear anything Dora yells back over the laughing, joyous banter, and stringed instruments playing somewhere in the distance. Everyone is in celebration, honoring the end of the bountiful year with high hopes for the next one to be just as prosperous.

I scan the running children for Atalanta and the other children, but they're likely sneaking food or climbing the unfinished buildings. I've warned them to be careful, but I still hear them whispering and snickering about how far they climbed without falling.

As we pass Zeus' temple, I can't help but notice the stark difference from Hades'. The priestess, clad in white robes, stand at the entrance, welcoming all who enter with a tender greeting, overseeing the generous offerings piled high on the slabs.

To the right, a pissed-off man is locked in the wooden stocks, red-faced and heavy-eyed, with a finger missing and dripping blood that's formed a pool at his bare feet. The price for thievery. A balance I can understand, but with a cost too violent and cruel for something so meager.

When we find our seats in front of the center stage, I slide into the one next to Adonis.

Before meeting Dora, my father and I lingered in the back of the crowd, wandering the streets and grazing from tables, not paying any mind to the play or the inevitable tragedy to come. After his death, Dora insisted I sit beside her to prove I'm a believer who supported the tradition, and what better way than next to a priestess's daughter.

At Dora's squeal, I jump, thankful the attention is stolen before I have a chance to find words for Adonis, unable to decide if I should apologize, demand one from him, or ignore our tiff altogether.

"This is Swan," Dora says, practically bouncing on her toes at the introduction.

Heads from all directions swivel toward us. Not us, *her*. Wives, husbands, and even children stop to gawk at the shapely blonde; the golden waves that flow to her hips, the fair skin glowing in the blush dress, slitting up the hem to her upper thigh, exposing the entirety of her pale leg. A golden chain glints between her generous cleavage.

I reach for my own. A motion the woman tracks.

"We bumped into each other at the market, literally," Dora explains, sharing a giggle with the woman. "She's passing through and stopped to see why everyone was gathered, and since I won't be here all night, I figured she could sit with you."

Swan's gaze lingers a second too long on Adonis before doing the same to me, a graceful, unhurried gesture. "If that's fine with you, of course. Pandora here insisted."

Dora tenses at the use of her birth name. "It's Dora," her correction edges with irritation, meaning she's already mentioned her preference.

Swan offers an apology. "It's just a little surprising one wouldn't want to use such a beautiful name with such history."

I felt the same when I first met her, but being named after the first woman ever created has its own type of pressure, according to Dora, especially because her mother is a priestess. No matter how much I've attempted to pry or loosen her up with drinks, she never elaborates.

"Really?" I don't hide my disbelief while also trying—and failing—not to get lost in Swan's striking violet eyes I want so desperately to ignore. As if I need another strange omen today. "Dora, *insisted* you stay?"

"You must be Kore." Rather than offer her hand as expected, she offers a poised grin that is sure to imprint into all our minds for eternity, while taking the seat on the other side of Adonis, who introduces himself swiftly before glancing between us.

"Are we..." I already know what Adonis is going to say before he finishes, "Forgive me, but are we just ignoring that you two have the same eyes?"

"Except the gold," Dora adds, because of course she noticed that small detail flecked in Swan's. "You know, it's said that purple eyes—"

"Are a sign of the Fate's blessing," Swan and I finish in sync, to Dora's giddy delight.

I've heard the term *waiting for the other shoe to drop*, but at this point, I'm waiting for the other boulder. Every hour is putting me on an edge that feels inevitable to leap from.

"Where are you from?" I ask, holding onto my uncertainty rather than pushing it away.

This woman radiates an aura like nothing I've ever been in the presence of. Not even an outsider with all the luxury and riches has whatever it is Swan possesses—confidence or arrogance, a dangerous beauty or deadly lure, a seductive, elegant suavity. All of it is emphasized with intrigue, hope, and subtle fear seeping from her being, latching and manipulating my own feelings.

I loathe this night. My sensitivity to others' emotions is too heightened. The only upside is I feel a little better when they're gone, a little less dull and a little more… alive.

"Not here." Swan offers a soft smile that has me crossing my arms and cocking my brow.

"You're not one to elaborate?"

"You didn't ask for specifics."

"You two are more alike than I first picked up on." Dora drags her chair in front of us, severing the tension swirling through every question and closer glance. I stand down, sinking deeper into my chair but not fully dropping my guard.

Her dress hides it well, but I notice Swan's leg bouncing, her attention shifting to the crowd, scanning as if in search of something or someone.

"We need to find you something black to wear." Adonis visibly strains to keep his attention on Swan's face; a gesture those passing by don't bother attempting. "You don't want to stand out tonight."

I almost laugh because I'm positive there isn't anything that could make this woman blend in. Her presence radiates with something impossible to ignore.

"I don't wear black. It washes out my skin." The way she brushes him off so casually enrages me. This self-assertive, insufferable woman—

A raven caws above, something no one else seems to pay attention to except for me and Swan, our necks craning to spot the black-feathered wings passing by. It only serves as a reminder for what's to come, and as much as this woman unnerves me, I don't want her to be at a disadvantage. I wiggle free from my cloak and hold it out. "You can wear this."

It feels like a truce when she accepts it, but not before giving me one last questioning look with the same hesitant trust I hold for her. As she pulls away, I hiss, feeling her nails rake across my knuckles.

Her apology is quick, and she's even faster at wiping the blood that breaks past my skin.

"No!" I shout when she pulls my cloak over her stunning, shimmering dress, but it's too late. It pains me more than the cut, knowing the soft material will be stained with my blood.

Swan shrugs, brief and uncaring, searching through the crowd again. "I need to blend in, right?"

With how many times I've caught her looking over her shoulder, I have a feeling it's not the sacrifice she's concerned about standing out for.

A grunt has all of us turning toward the stage where five guards struggle to carry the altar to the center. I think back to Hades' temple, wondering if it's he who tells the oracle who to choose, *if* he's real. If so, why hasn't he chosen me yet?

As the hour passes, I try to pay attention to Dora speaking with such adoration about Swan, but I can feel myself slowly disassociating from the conversation, from the rest of my surroundings. Their voices fade, and soon, there will be nothing. Until then, I force my ears to pick up as much as they can.

From what I gather, Swan travels selling wine, or maybe it's candles. Dora is talking much too fast for me to keep up. Adonis might have said Dora should join her on the road, and I can't help but silently agree. It would be the perfect life for Dora, collecting stories from different places, and writing books about the people she meets. She is like a caged crow with the priestesses—an omen bird with clipped wings, unable to mystify people.

Adonis' knee grazes mine, and I let myself enjoy the butterflies flapping their wings in the pit of my belly while fighting the urge to pull him back to the forest to see if he would *ruin* me this time. He looks at me with an unspoken apology, and I brush my knee against his with my own unspoken acceptance. I couldn't stay angry with him if I tried.

Sensing eyes on me, I look up to meet Swan's before they fall to where Adonis and I are pressed together with a lifting grin. An expression that has me jerking my leg back and crossing it over the other. Even if I'm willing to destroy myself to get out of this marriage, I won't take Adonis down with me. If anyone besides Swan sees us touching so intimately, the rumors would lead to him being punished, or worse.

The thought has me swiping the bottle Adonis lifts to his lips, his face contorting between confusion and disgust at what little he tastes, using the back of his hand to wipe what spilled down his chin. I don't care how bad it is as long as it floats me closer to oblivion.

The wine slides down easily, the sweet flavor barely catching on my tongue before I'm finished, warmth already spreading through my empty belly. With only the nibbles of tart and bread, nothing will slow the wine from doing what I need it to do, drowning my senses and smothering away all unwanted thoughts and memories.

No one says a thing as I take another drink and when I pass it back to Adonis, he shakes his head and pushes it back toward me, insisting it's all mine.

The instant bliss keeping the emptiness at bay has my curiosity front and center, and has me leaning over Adonis to ask Swan about the dangers of traveling.

"Everything is dangerous, darling. Your husband can decide he wants another woman, but you're in his way. He could kill you so he can have her. You could be attacked by a deer in the woods on your way home. You could be struck by a stray arrow. Your heart could suddenly stop for no reason at all. You could choke on your own tarts. Life is but a dangerous game we all play. Why not have fun doing it?"

As inspiring as that concept is, she speaks as if there are no rules in this world, no roles to play, as if there are actual choices. A fantasy that will get her killed if she's not careful.

Swan looks around, tightening her hood before continuing, "As long as you have something someone else wants, you can make a living on the road. People are willing to accept as little as hearing stories in exchange for a cot and a hot meal. If you feel like running away from that engagement of yours, I could use the company."

With all the signs and omens, her offer feels like a gift, the perfect opportunity to get me out of this town once and for all, to get me out of this engagement. That need for more stirs, agreeing when something suddenly gnaws at me. How does she know about the engagement?

Before I can answer, Dora clears her throat and straightens with excitement, literally gripping the edge of her seat. "I have a story I recently heard. It's about Psych and Eros. Have you heard it?"

The question is angled toward Swan, but Adonis and I shake our heads, soon followed by Swan, whose concern is evident by the tiniest crease between her brows. I can understand how someone who doesn't know Dora's quirks and excitability would be wary.

Dora's mischievous smile lifts as she starts,

Psych was adored and admired by all men, which caught the attention of the Goddess of love and beauty, Aphrodite. She grew jealous that another woman could rival her beauty and sent her son, Eros, to kill her. He was about to strike her down with his arrow, but fell in love with her instead.

All the while, Psych's parents grew restless since no man wanted to marry her. They sought an oracle for guidance. The oracle told them to send her to the mountain where, in her darkest times, she'd find her true love. Psych couldn't live with the embarrassment she'd caused her family by being a spinster, so she stood at the edge, and jumped off the mountain, only to awake in a castle.

A voice answered her calls, but the man never showed his face. Over time, she fell in love and married this voice, on the promise to never attempt to look at him. But she grew lonely and invited her sisters to visit her. Because they were jealous that she lived in such a beautiful castle and was happy to find love, they convinced her that the voice had to be that of a hideous creature tricking her.

Psych couldn't get her sisters' warnings out of her head, so she lit a candle and peeked at her husband, finding not a beautiful man but the God Eros. The hot wax dripped, waking him up.

Heartbroken by her betrayal, Eros flew away, but not before telling her, "Love cannot live without trust."

Desperate to find her husband, Psych prayed at the temple of Aphrodite for guidance. The Goddess heard and was filled with rage that her son betrayed her by not killing Psych, so she agreed to help her if she completed three impossible tasks.

No one has heard from Psych since.

We're all silent while Dora finishes the story I recognize pieces of. I recall hearing my mother talking to others at brunch about a young woman named Psych. They claimed she slept around with any man who would take her, though her family denied it, of course. Then, one day, she disappeared. Her family didn't bother looking for the daughter who had caused their family such humiliation. Metanira believed she must have gotten pregnant and run away before anyone found out.

Completely captivated by Dora's every word, I can't stop myself from asking no one in particular, "How would you have ended it?"

Although I don't believe the myths and stories are true, they do have elements of truth to them that have me pondering for days after. They're like little riddles with hidden meanings and morals.

"Happily, of course." Dora doesn't elaborate before directing us to the beautiful blonde, a look dancing with prying intent that's accentuated with the added lean. "What about you, Swan?"

"I guess that depends on who you're rooting for." Swan's already-arched brow rises in question. "If it's Aphrodite, she would've locked Psych away from her son. She wouldn't want to kill the *beautiful* girl too quickly. Maybe complete multiple tasks, always hoping to see Eros as she grows older with no one to see her beauty ever again."

I stare, stunned at how dark yet intriguing I find her answer. Not that I would want something like that to happen to anyone, but to end a story in such tragedy is appealing in some way.

An *almost* perfect balance.

"What would happen to Eros?" I ask.

"What about him? He never had to think about that traitorous woman again." A bitterness catches behind her tone.

I'm lost in thought, contemplating my own version, when everything clicks into place. "I'd clip Eros' wings, deafen Psych, and blind Aphrodite."

Swan's jaw slacks, her eyes widening with a horror-laced shrill. "Why would you do such a thing?"

"Balance." It's a simple answer and the only one I have, feeling that contentment flowing through me, the sweet wine taking hold and easing my mind even further.

I swear Swan's lips cock with amusement, but it's gone too quick to be sure. An intrigue Adonis and Dora don't share, their brows pinched at the center with more alarm than Swan had.

"I see where you're going, but why blind Aphrodite?" It's Swan who asks without judgment, more a mere curiosity.

"The story begins with Aphrodite being jealous of another woman's beauty. Clip Eros for running away, deafen Psych for listening to others, and blind Aphrodite for being jealous of another's appearance."

That look returns, the soft turn of her neck like she wants to scan the crowd again, but her focus remains on me as if seeing something she hadn't noticed before. "Interesting."

Priestesses step onto the stage, lighting the torches to mark the start of the play.

"I have to go," Dora's tone dips apologetically. "I'll come find you after." She squeezes my shoulders as she leaves, turning back when Swan grabs her arm, whispering something I can't hear. Whatever it is makes Dora's back stiffen, and her eyes glaze over before she runs off behind the stage.

When I turn back to Swan to ask what happened, she pulls the hood over her head, her jaw poking out.

That angular, *pretty* jaw.

"You," I mutter. The stranger from the market. *She's* the stranger.

Adonis has no choice but to lean back as I lurch over his lap to ask what was in the vial, who is after me, and what purpose I could possibly have, but the questions are drowned out by the loud applause erupting for the monstrous man standing center stage.

I swallow the bile that rises as he begins, "It started twenty years ago today. Some of you might remember. Some of you were too young. But we've all heard this part of our history year after year. Tonight, we honor those we've lost during that tragic winter. And we honor the Gods who have blessed us with this food, this wine, this land, this weather, and this beautiful night. We honor each other, and we will honor the chosen. We ask now, does anyone wish to be honored as a sacrifice, to walk through the gates of the Heavens and be welcomed by the Gods?"

Those words are chosen carefully. To walk through the gates of the Heavens, not the Underworld, even though it is believed all dead must pass through the Underworld. The Heavens are for the Gods.

Heads swivel left and right to those seated and standing, waiting for someone else to offer themselves to Death. Some appear worried, others excited, but most look hopeful. If someone else offers themselves first, then it isn't a random pick from the crowd, but there hasn't been a volunteer in over ten years, and there certainly won't be one tonight.

To hope would be equally monstrous and foolish.

Silence has never echoed so loud.

"No volunteers this year. If Charon grabs your hand, you have been chosen by the oracle, the voice of the Gods, to be the sacrifice. I needn't remind you what an honor it is to be chosen."

Pirithous leaves the stage to be replaced by seven priestesses, each representing one of the seven Gods.

The play is always the same: the Gods were angry at the mortals for starting to lose faith and they withheld their gifts; the ground froze over; mortals died; a man sacrificed himself; everything went back to normal; the Gods began to bless us with their gifts again; mortals continue the sacrifice year after year with a seven-day festival to honor each God.

I avert my eyes, pushing down the building nausea and wishing I had grabbed a plate of food before it started, before drinking the entire bottle of wine.

The skin under my thumbnail grows sore from where I pick at it. It's when I bleed that I know I'm too anxious and need to find another outlet, usually by busying my hands in the kitchen or garden, but without either, I settle for watching others while twisting my hair between my finger.

Swan's the first one I look to, admiring how she watches the play with such interest. Her face lights up in a way when someone finds something comical or absurd. Her head both bobs in agreement and shakes in disbelief as the scenes go on. It is such an unusual mix of reactions that I could have watched her all night if that familiar sense of being followed hadn't torn my gaze away.

Sure enough, from across the stage, Meg's scowl points in my direction.

Maybe it's the wine, but I give her a small wave and lean into Adonis' shoulder. He looks down, startled by my sudden closeness, but relaxes into me. "I'll give you tonight, but I'm not a tool to get your engagement called off. This is the best thing for you."

Meg's lips tightened to a thin line before stalking off. I rarely feel triumphant when it comes to her, but at this moment, I feel like I won a battle in a long war.

"You said that already," I counter bitterly, righting myself.

The story of Psych replays in my head, and I can't help but wonder if I'm like her, waiting for others to decide my fate for me. I want to believe that I wouldn't let my mother leave me on a mountain, but Theseus, in a way, is my mountain.

I set my sights on the night sky, full of blinding stars, searching the constellations and admiring the full harvest moon.

The note said to drink the vial before the moon falls, and I can't deny that urge to listen, to trust the stranger, Swan, for reasons I can't explain.

Taking a deep breath, I reach for it, my fingers fumbling to grasp it as my knuckles graze my ring. A reminder that today could be the start of something new.

I don't believe in coincidences—the omen birds, Atlanta's warning, the marriage arrangement, being rejected by Adonis, this strange woman with the same unique eyes as mine.

Fate or not, *something* is urging me toward a different path, giving me a choice to trust one stranger over another: Theseus or Swan; Marriage or freedom.

Drink and run. Swan's voice coils around my mind and makes the choice for me.

The crowd gasps.

I must have missed something.

Adonis nudges me, bringing me to his strange reaction. Something similar to pity, only... sadder?

Then, to the black hooded figure, and their hand stretched toward me.

Chapter Five

KORE

Slim delicate fingers hang in the air before me. My tongue sticks to the roof of my mouth, drying more with every passing second.

This has to be a mistake.

I blink hard, trying to wake up from this horrid memory, but when I dare look up at the cloaked figure, they remain before me, unmoving, with every detail I don't want to see: the seven-pointed star amulet hanging around their neck, the gold stitching along the hood, and the massive scythe looming above my head.

There is no denying who stands before me; Charon, the taker of souls, has chosen *me* as the sacrifice.

This shouldn't be happening; it *can't* be happening. I played my part as a believer. I attended the offerings and blended in with the town. Against all instincts, I became a shadow in the dark.

No! Please! You can't! The cries and pleas I once screamed are now silent on my tongue, the memory disappearing when the hood shifts, revealing a familiar face hidden beneath, those light blue eyes bearing into mine.

"Dora?"

Her mouth hangs open with the same astonished terror I hold, her eyes vacant, a single tear sliding down her pale cheek as she pulls her hand back within the cloak's long sleeve as if she can take back what she's done. "What…" she staggers back a step.

51

CRUEL GODS

No one moves or speaks, but I feel their stares and confusion all around me, their walls and safety crumbling away with mine. Never has a family been chosen twice.

Two guards in silver armor shove Dora out of the way to grip my shoulders, rough enough that I cry out at the sudden sting that shoots down my arm.

A few gasp, but the wave of silence is so thick that one comment draws everyone's attention, "Dear Gods, I hope she doesn't cry again," earning a few agreed murmurs.

If I were a witch, I'd curse every one of them on my dying breath. A thought I quickly cast away as the guards pull me from my chair, their strapped swords banging against my hip.

This night won't be my last; I won't let them take me. As much as I beg Hades to take me, I'm not ready to die. The choice—the paths laid out before me today—the signs... I can't settle here. I can't die not knowing what that *more* I'm pulled to is.

I won't give them my fruitless cries or pleas either, not again.

With every step closer to the stage, I drop my weight to my heels, dragging like the stone beneath me is thick caramel. As I pull and yank back, fighting to get out of their grasp, their fingers burrow deeper, imprinting on my skin, penetrating my muscles with the weighted resistance.

It's useless.

These men are too strong, and I'm no more than a child compared to them, weaker with the wine flowing through me.

There isn't a face I pass that I'll forget, their silent compliance and gaping mouths confirming that they, too, realize that no one is safe, that anyone can be chosen.

To my utter shock, there's no clapping or bowed heads of gratitude, just a collective acceptance, and the panicked prayers thundering through my chest that I'm certain everyone's bearing witness to.

In one last attempt, I stop moving my feet entirely, the effort futile as I'm hoisted off the ground and hanging between the guards. They exchange quick glances and snickers that say they should have done this from the beginning, their pace quickening up the steps.

My grunts and struggles fall on deaf ears from those I've come to know. From the woman I buy strawberries from every week to the man who supplies our flour; the outsiders I once played with as a child, and their parents, who doted on how I was such an angel.

We pass one of my old servants who remains seated, clutching her heart with soft eyes I don't need—pity—a look that only reflects their favor for selfish judgments over useful actions. Yes, please belittle me with your eyes instead of using your mouth to stop this.

None of them are going to help me, just as I never helped any of the ones before me.

With a rough toss, I'm dropping onto my feet, my hip clashing against something hard. Their hold on me remains firm as I take in what it is; the sleek stone shimmering under the moonlight, the faded maroon hindering its shine, and the seven-pointed star carved into the top, an emblem sealing the fates of those who look upon it.

"Quiet!" Pirithous' voice shakes my core with the command that travels through every crack and abandoned corner.

The answering silence is met with equal stillness of those too afraid to speak or move for fear they, too, will be chosen and dragged to the altar, their minds questioning if that's a possibility.

Unlike everyone else, I refuse to look at him, the man who demands respect without ever having earned it, a man my father had once called a friend, a man who tore away my childhood facade and showed me what the world truly is.

As he speaks again, my eyes seal tight. "Charon has chosen Kore as this year's sacrifice, and we honor that decision. Please, everyone, show your respect."

The crowd gasps again. My eyes fly open, all the dread I felt thickening at the sight of Dora removing her hood, revealing herself to the sea of surprised faces.

Charon has never been revealed, for the safety of the one playing him and to keep the awe and wonder of the myth being portrayed on stage.

The scars on my back tingle with phantom memory of my own punishment for causing such a disturbance at a sacrifice, and what Dora just did is much, much worse than my screams and pleas for my father's life.

"I didn't mean to!" Dora starts, grabbing for Pirithous' arm in plea. "I don't know what happened!"

"Silence!" His command is sharp enough to cut through every held breath. "The Gods have spoken through you, child. Don't be upset."

"But she is unwilling. What if the Gods won't accept her?" Desperation is warped on Dora's face, her shoulder shaking as hushed murmurs begin to rise.

"That is enough, Pandora." Pirithous snaps his fingers, and two more guards step forward to ensure she can't run from the inevitable repercussions.

I shouldn't be worried about her right now, but the thought of Dora enduring any similar torture has me struggling against the guards once more to no avail.

"We will start the final toast." Pirithous clasps his hands together, and two priestesses clothed in white make their way to stand on either side of me. The silver band on their heads marks them as priestesses of all Gods, rather than one in particular.

One woman is carrying the prayer-etched kantharos brimming with ambrosia—the drink of the Gods—while the other bears the white pillow cradling a knife. I can't help but notice how ordinary it looks. I'm not sure what I expected, but not something so simple and small. The blade and hilt together would barely fit within someone's palm. It's something I'd peel a potato with, not murder one with.

The thought stills me. Had this been the one to kill my father? The sight of the blade has me wondering if he became a believer in the end. Did he stare at this weapon and pray to Hades to accept him into his kingdom of the dead, or to Zeus to strike Pirithous down before his so-called friend could slit his throat? Or did he stick to his beliefs that there's nothing after this?

As stupid as I feel doing it, I send a quick prayer to Hades, demanding that he exists so my father's death wasn't in vain, and that anyone who was taken from their families for this ridiculous ritual hadn't died for nothing. And for the Hel of it, I send a prayer to the God Hermes for guidance. They say he's fast and clever, and that's exactly what I'll need to escape this.

With his dimpled chin in the air, Pirithous dips his head toward the priestess. The one with the black braid, holding the kantharos, grips my unwilling jaw and begins pouring the warm ambrosia down my throat. Every attempt to resist is impossible with my arms held out to the side, my scalp stinging as someone fists my hair to keep my head steady.

"Swallow," the priestess silently demands. "You're causing a scene."

Good. Let them see my defiance. I should have been fighting against this tradition a long time ago instead of cowering in the shadows like everyone else. All that resisting my instincts has gotten me is a forced marriage, offered as the sacrifice, and a fucking headache from the bastard at my side.

The irony that I thought Swan would get herself killed by living by her own rules isn't lost on me. I could laugh if I weren't seconds away from dying, by either drowning on this wine or a sliced throat, I'm not sure yet.

I force my throat closed and let the liquid spill out the sides of my mouth, down my cheeks, and neck. I've never tried ambrosia, but I know the taste of wine. I've drank and made enough to know the exact grape used, which only proves my suspicions that this entire festival, the murders, it's all done in vain.

Realizing I'm not going to drink any of it, the priestess stops pouring, shaking her head with a disapproving snarl. Her eyes snap to the guards, and their hold on me tightens, expecting me to continue my sorry struggles. Maybe I should have played obedient because I'm not going to get out of here with them holding me like a rabid dog about to be put down.

"Drink it!" Swan moves to the front of the stage, her head swiveling left to right before facing me once again. "*Before the moon falls.*" Desperation clings to her, those violet eyes separated by the crease between her brows, her wringing hands.

That familiar shiver slithers up my spine, something willing me to trust her, finding myself, again, asking, *What do I have to lose?* My life? That's about to end anyway.

"I'd like to do it myself," I tell the priestess loud enough for the crowd to hear. "I'd rather not drown on wi— ambrosia before I die."

The braided priestess looks to Pirithous, who gestures his approval. The guards release me, their stances wide and ready in case I make a run for it.

Pulling the vial from between my breasts, I flick the cork off with my thumb and dump the contents down my throat before they can stop me.

The moment the warm liquid touches my lips, a lightness falls over me, like taking a dress off after a long day.

The mix of sweet strawberry, honey, and metallic leaves me quivering. It's thicker than I expected, and I desperately need water.

More. My insides stir, that hunger deep within starving for more of whatever was in that vial.

I look over, ready to beg Swan for another vial, but she's gone. The seats we were all in are now empty with Adonis nowhere in sight either. I search every face in the crowd, but nothing. No violet eyes or caramel curls.

But then I see someone who has my heart sink.

My mother watches from the depths of the farthest alley, her lips tight, face etched with disappointment. A glower I'll never forget as she turns back down the alley and leaves me to fend for myself— to *die.*

Everything blurs, but it's not from tears. A darkness unfurls, tunneling my vision until there's only that golden hair in the distance, so far away it looks like a thinning string. One my twisted hurt wants to smother as it settles into a simmering rage.

She left me. No tears, no pleas, no last words. She just… left.

"Take me!" My stomach drops, taking all my anger with it, faster than it came. My attention snaps to Dora just as the priestess on my right nearly drops the pillow bearing the blade, recognizing her daughter's voice. "I am willing. Take me in her place," Dora repeats.

"No!" Vienne and I shout in unison. I may not wish to die, but this world needs Dora, her light and sheer goodness. I'd slit my throat before I let her take my place.

Abandoning her pleads with Pirithous, she runs toward me, pushing past her mother. "I'm so sorry." Her hug knocks the breath from me. "I don't know what happened. I was talking to Swan, and she— There's so much I need to tell you. I should have told you a long time ago."

I can barely make out what she's saying as a rush of euphoria fills my veins. The cool breeze I suck in runs down my throat, and it's like I can taste the air, like my skin is made of it.

I watch in a daze as Dora's lips move again, noticing the freckles speckled across her cheeks and nose for the first time, losing myself in her blue eyes. There's something different about them. A band of silver I've never noticed before.

My nose wiggles, inviting in the strong scent of roses and something spicy, like cinnamon, only angrier. A feeling that strikes deep in my ribs and rips the breath out of me with a tight pulling sensation.

I catch myself on the altar while the entire world seems to light up in color, a rush of emotions beneath my skin, too many to count or put names to, while the shadows in every corner darken once more.

It's too much... I can't—

"Kore?" My body sparks to life at Dora's light touch, prickling with sensitivity. The colors vanish, taking the heightened emotions with them.

"Why?" My breath is heavy, but my mind is clearer than ever. "Why did you pick me?"

"*Dora*," Vienne hisses, pulling her daughter to stand by her side. Somehow, I hear her faint whisper as she leans into Dora's ear, "You did well tonight, but don't make this worse. She'll be safe with the Gods soon."

"You're volunteering is too late, Pandora," Pirithous says. The glee hidden behind that apologetic smirk brings me back to a time I wish I had the strength to say no, to move, to not be so fucking silent and still. "Fortunately, Kore has already accepted the offering by drinking the ambrosia."

When he glances at me, I find no remorse or care behind the eyes that have been the cause of too many nightmares. I shouldn't be surprised, but I am. After everything he's done to me, he has the audacity to look at me with a grin, minutes before ordering my death?

A soft breeze pushes back my hair, a glint catching my eye—the blade.

For once, my impulsivity is a blessing. Vienne's eyes widen with realization, but I'm quicker, snatching the weapon with my sweaty palms.

Having never used a knife outside of the kitchen, I still, stuck without a clue of what to do next, until a voice pushes through my mind, *If you cut them off at the legs, they can't chase you.*

I drop to my knees, swiping the blade across the guard's calves, the left one first, then the right one, repeating the same cutting assaults, deeper this time, the sliced skin vibrating against my palm. The guards fall to the ground, clutching their bloody legs.

I'm a little more inclined to believe that Atlanta killed that lion after all, and I tuck my apology for ever doubting her in the back of my mind.

Jumping to my feet, I start towards the steps, cut off by a smirking Pirithous blocking my path. The whip at his hip mocks me, reawakening the phantom pains across my back. The weapon in my hand trembles.

His fingers inch toward the whip, his grin deepening, sharing the same memory I do.

Never again. I swipe the knife at him, slicing through the air, and he stumbles back, barely missing the tip. If there was any blood I wanted spilled tonight, or ever, it's his, but I don't have the luxury of time to play this cat-and-mouse game. More guards will be here any second to strap me to the altar and slit me open to be done with it, final toast or not.

Bracing myself, I sweep the blade through the air once more. This time, when he steps back, I pivot and sprint to the other end of the stage.

I'm closing in on the steps when a short woman with dark, wild hair and dirty clothes steps up, blocking my freedom once again.

"Found you." The woman's lips curl with a sharp grin that holds an unmistakable determined ferocity. "You're coming with me."

The arrow poking above her shoulder has me stumble back a step.

"It's over, Kore," Pirithous' victorious laugh claws at my ears, but it's the wild woman who holds my focus. Her head cocks to peer past me, that determination shifting from me onto him as she draws the bow, nocks an arrow, and releases it before anyone can blink.

That laugh turns to shrieks, no longer grating at my ears but blessing them with a song I've longed to hear. His eyes widen at the arrow stabbed through his shin, and I can't help but tilt my head with a boasting smirk.

"Pig," the woman spits.

My bliss is short-lived, replaced with a need to get off the stage before this was all for nothing.

"Let's go," the woman orders.

I'm not going anywhere with a stranger who radiates mayhem and fury, and eyes that promise chaos.

A moment of understanding passes between us, and she glares while reaching for another arrow.

Pure adrenaline keeps me on my feet as I turn and jump over Pirithous, who grabs for my heels with bloody hands that are too slick to keep a hold.

I run as fast as I can down the steps, seeing more guards coming through the tight crowd as I round the stage and sprint down the back alley.

An arrow whooshed past my face, landing in front of the path, forcing me to weave around it.

I don't know or care if anyone else follows me; I push harder and faster, the wind whipping past my flushed skin. Every step is in sync with my jumping pulse.

"I'm not going to hurt you!" the woman yells. She's close, enough that I push myself harder, but not close enough to tackle me.

"What's with the arrows then?" I shout back, staying focused on the road before me, cutting between alleys and construction that aren't on the beaten path.

When I can no longer hear steps closing in, I jump into one of the abandoned buildings overgrown with wild hysteria vines, crouching in one of the shoddy corners, and wait.

In through the nose, out through the mouth, I repeat the breathing pattern to calm myself while looking through the cracks of the wood panels. Through a small opening, I see the woman come to a stop, scanning her surroundings. From what I can tell, she's neither outsider nor local, not from this town anyway. She's too wild to be the former and too... well, wild to be a local. No one steps out of pocket here, not during this week.

My heart is relentless, pounding against my breast, while I cover my mouth to hide my unsteady huffs.

A loud whistle pierces my ears.

"The easy way is you come out willingly." My pursuer sets her bow with another arrow. "The hard way is I have to hurt you, which I already told you I don't want to do. But we all have choices we must make here. What is it going to be, *Kore?*"

I don't move a muscle. Don't so much as blink.

"Hard way it is."

An arrow shatters through the panel, inches from my face, shredding my cheek with wooden splinters. I bite down the urge to scream, physically straining to clench my teeth tight and throat closed.

Scrambling on the ground, I quickly right myself and rush out the back of the building, stumbling down the crumbled steps. I don't stop or dare look back. If I see her determined face setting pace for me, I just might topple over and give up.

The few low-burning lanterns are few and far between, and the roads are uneven with loose cobblestone, forcing me to lift my knees a little higher to keep from tripping.

As great as the shadows are for hiding, they're even greater for stalking, to the advantage of the woman. And with my footsteps and breaths bouncing off the brick walls, I fear I have no upper hand.

My advantage will be in the woods on the other side of the bridge a few blocks away.

As more constructed buildings begin to line either side of me, I hear the townspeople grovel in the distance.

"What is going to happen now?"

"She wouldn't be dumb enough to go home."

"I'm not surprised she would abandon our town now. Always an outsider, that one."

"I never trusted her."

Taking a chance, I peer behind me, the knot in my belly unraveling when I don't spot my peruser. I slow to a light jog before stepping behind another building to take a breath. Not that I need it. I'm sure I just spent an hour of constant sprinting, ducking, hiding, crouching, and circling the same streets to confuse the unrelenting woman, but I feel like I just started, like I can do this long after the sun rises.

"Hiding?" I jump at the sound of Swan's voice, turning to cover her mouth before she can say another word. Even shrouded in shadows, her features are striking, like she should be on a tapestry depicting the Gods.

Glancing around the corner, I hold my defeated grunt when I spot the wild woman closing in, her steps strong and growing impatient.

Mother of Muses, this woman does not give up!

Swan's brow lifts, her fingers curling around my wrist to remove my hold on her, passing me with a lifting smirk that looks odd, forced. "Stay quiet and stay put until she's gone."

I try to explain that we need to run, try to open my mouth to call after her, try to reach out to stop her from walking into the alley, to stop her from revealing herself to the dangerous woman, but my body won't move. My arms remain stuck at my sides without so much as a flicker.

A coldness washes over me just as it had in the market when she grazed the back of my hand with her soft, *trust me.*

Before my panic sets in, a slight warmth wraps around my arm and another above my hip. Adonis' touch is as familiar as my own, and I can't help but calm knowing he's here.

Swan waves to where we can't see past the corner of the building we're hidden behind. "Hello Artemis."

If I could move, I would roll my eyes. People who name their children after Gods should be chosen as the sacrifice for damning them to such disappointment.

"Where is she?" Artemis snaps, that little patience I noted before fraying to its last thread.

"Who?" Swan admires her nails with a tilt of her lips. "I have to say I've seen quite a lot of women today."

"Don't even start. You know exactly who we're looking for. I can smell her."

"Oh." Swan wiggles out of my cloak and hangs it out by a finger. "I found this bloody cloak earlier. You're welcome to it."

Artemis, now inches from Swan, snatches the bloody fabric and holds it to her nose. "You think you're clever, don't you?" she sneers. "I will find her, and I will collect that reward."

"I'd hurry before your other half gets the best of you." Swan pats her cheek and whispers something too soft for us to hear.

When Artemis' eyes lock on mine, I swear the shadows darken, but to my utter shock, she doesn't move for me. All I feel is a surge of pure relief when she turns and runs back the way she came.

"She's gone."

The freeze that held my body hostage immediately melts away.

"What was that?" I shake my arms and legs to make sure every piece of me still works when I'm nudged forward by Adonis, a harmless gesture, but one that makes me scramble to find a reason for it.

"Artemis is not a threat." Swan waves me off like I'm being childish.

"Not a threat? She was shooting arrows at me! And what reward is she talking about? What the Hel is going on?"

My questions stifle her amusement, sharpening her features into a pointed stare that focuses my hearing onto whatever she's about to say. "There's a lot you don't know, Kore. All I can tell you right now is to be careful who you trust. The Gods are cruel."

"The Gods?" I scoff. "Do you actually believe that was the Goddess Artemis?" A familiar shiver crawls up my spine and wipes away my skepticism. The birds *were* odd, I did freeze unexplainably, and the wild woman was brilliant with the bow just as the Goddess is said to be.

Swan's gaze drops to where I'm still holding the knife, still wet with blood at my side. Instinctively, I want to wipe it on the back of my dress. Instead, I tighten my hold around the hilt, letting it serve as a reminder that I will do whatever it takes to survive—a warning for anyone who tries to step in my way.

"Yes," her answer is swift and sure. "And if you come with me, I can keep you safe from the rest of them."

The rest of them? "Safe from what, exactly? Or is it that you want to collect whatever this reward is for yourself?"

I take a step back at the same time she motions toward Adonis, who assumes his servant position off to the side. "Your friend is coming with me. Don't you want to join us? I could see you contemplating taking my invitation earlier."

That crack in my chest cleaves more. He was going to leave with *her* while they slit my throat and dumped my body in the dirt?

"I thought you were going to die." When he reaches for me, I lean away before he can so much as graze me, not wanting a tender touch to sway me one way or the other. He frowns, disappointed by my rejection, and drops his arms at his side. "When I saw you up there, I knew I couldn't stay here. Not with Metanira. Not without you." His eyes sweep over me again as if still not believing I'm here. Alive.

"You were fine with it a few hours ago," I snap, the pressure around my heart building from all the betrayal. The arranged marriage, Dora, my mother, and now Adonis.

He glances back at Swan, giving her a look I can't see that has her shift her weight from one foot to the other, subtle but as someone who is constantly restless I see the signs. "Please, Kore." He turns back to me. "Please come with us."

Us. They're already an *us*, as in, I'm an option, an addition to their plan, and only because I survived. Because *I* got myself off that stage.

I glance between them, and it hits me. I should have seen it. I *did* see it, but with more information, things are starting to become clear. Swan planned this. She's been begging me to come with her since this morning, cornered Atlanta to convince me. Whatever this reward is, she's using Adonis to get to me.

"What did she promise you?"

Swan's eyes narrow at my question, but she doesn't bother to interject, letting Adonis answer, "A way out. She said she can get my tattoo removed so I can be free." The desperation in his voice—the hope—physically pains me, the way he looks at me, pleading for me to understand. "Once I get this removed, we can go anywhere without worrying about being bought or sold. I can earn money. I can finally be worthy of someone like you."

"Adonis," the pity I hate so much is all I hear when I speak, and this time, when he reaches for me, I let him grab my elbow and pull me in. I can't blame him for wanting to believe someone who promises to make him normal, but with the town looking for me, with these strangers talking about a reward for me, so many unanswered questions and omens, he's vulnerable.

I let him wrap his arms around me and kiss me one last time, remembering the feel of his lips on mine, and for one final time, I let myself pretend we're a normal couple, kissing without any restrictions. It's short-lived when he pulls back to ask, "So, you'll come?"

It's nearly impossible to refuse him, even tougher to pull away, but with a soft shake of my head, I do before I can change my mind. Hardening myself once more, I face Swan and ask again what is going on.

"I'm trying to keep you out of the hands of extremely dangerous beings. If they get to you…" All the confidence that I saw in town withers with every word, like she needs to say as much as she can before it's too late but can't. "Everything would have been for nothing. You have no idea what I've been through to ensure your safety all these years. To ensure they couldn't find you. If they know what—who you are, they will use you to do terrible things."

"And who am I exactly?" I ask, a plea so similar to the one I asked Dora before the night started.

"I can't say here." Her lips tighten, rolling between her teeth before continuing, "I can and will explain everything, just not here. Not when others could be nearby. What I can tell you is that the vial held ambrosia, which you needed to drink willingly and preferably in a time of absolute desperation for it to work correctly. Now that you drank it, we need to hide you before the others find us. Artemis is the least of our worries, trust me. I would have taken you earlier, but I was being followed too closely." She dares a step forward, offering her hand. I follow by taking the same step back. "There's too much to explain in such a short time."

I can't understand why I suddenly believe in Gods and their myths, but at the mention of ambrosia, I begin to panic.

"Don't worry, it won't kill you like it would most. However, there will be moments of discomfort until it settles." Her assurance lessens my worry about dying and piques it all over again at the way she accentuated discomfort like she was using a nice word to downplay it.

We repeat the dance of steps, her taking one closer and me another step back, ending with her shoulders dropping. "I really didn't need to warn you, did I? You're already so untrusting, even with the little push I gave you to trust me." Her slim fingers wiggle before she kicks the back of Adonis' leg, sending him to his knees, bringing a knife against his throat.

"Don't fight," she whispers against his ear, keeping all focus on me. "I told you those you care about would be in danger. Now, come with me willingly, or I slit his pretty throat."

"Don't!" I reached out, surprised at Adonis' lack of struggle. He has that same vacant look Dora had when she chose me.

"I don't want to hurt him. In fact, I'm willing to bring him with us, but I need you to come with me willingly before the rest of the Gods find you here."

"Fine," I relent, keeping my gaze on the knife at Adonis' neck, watching a bead of blood drip down the bulge in his throat. The sight has me sucking in a breath past the ball that forms in mine. I won't allow him to be harmed or die, not because of me. Not again.

"I promise," I can't get the words out fast enough. "I swear it, I'll come with you."

Swan removes the blade, offering me her hand—a truce. Before I have a chance to take it, her shriek cuts right through me just as an arrow pierces straight through her palm.

"I knew you were a liar!" Artemis yells, sprinting down the alley with her bow at the ready.

With the distraction, I pull Adonis from the ground and hurry toward the river just beyond the alley. We pass the last house, nearing the cliff.

If we can get to the water, we can swim—

I don't finish the thought. My shoulder is yanked back. The river is in sight, only a few steps away, but I don't make it. I fall back, my head slamming against the ground.

"We have to go with her, Kore!"

My mind is in splinters, but my focus is pulled toward my wrists, wailing at how tightly Adonis grabs them to help me up. "Why?"

"I can't be a servant forever, and she can help us."

"We don't even know what she wants. She held a knife to your throat!"

"Because of you! She doesn't want to hurt us. She wants to help you."

I tug, trying to yank myself from his hold, but his grip is too tight as he drags me one resisted step at a time. "Adonis, let me go!" I struggle harder, thrashing myself lower, digging my heels into the ground.

"I'm sorry. I can't!" His features return to that softened plea he's seemed to perfect. "Just come with us."

CRUEL GODS

My argument is on the tip of my tongue when chaos erupts. Black wings fill my vision, flapping against my face and arms. I brace for the painful pecks, but the beaks don't break my skin.

Adonis grunts and jerks as I continue my own jerking motions back, covering my face with my free arm in case the birds change their minds.

It's not the birds who change their attack.

Adonis let's go, but I'm pulling too hard. My foot catches on the other, and although I anticipate another fall, another brutal strike to the head, it never comes.

With a silent scream, I fall over the cliff's edge, hardly getting a breath before my body slams into a wall of water.

For a moment, I'm dazed, lost in the surrounding darkness while the night sky waves above.

My lungs tighten.

I move, swimming toward those twinkling stars, my fingers grazing the surface, when I'm yanked down.

I kick and claw, but no matter how hard I work, I'm stuck, remaining just below salvation. Air right at my fingertips.

Using the last of my strength, I grip the blade I managed to hold onto and cut at the fabric. My legs free, and I feel my foot kick something hard, but the bottom is still too far below for it to be a rock. I don't look down, don't care what it is, I swim faster to break the surface.

The cool night air fills my starved lungs, soothing my aching throat between heaving coughs. I make it to the other side of the river in a haste, clawing at the grass to help me up.

I look back, waiting for something to emerge behind me, but it never comes. I look at the ledge on the other side, but there's no sign of Adonis or the birds that attacked us.

There is no relief, not when the town is looking for me, Swan, and Adonis, too, and I can never forget Artemis and her arrows. I look to the left and see the familiar path home, and then to my right, where the path continues to towns I've only heard of. Neither feels right. People talk of a knowing, an urge, a calling, or intuition, but nothing sparks at the choices before me.

I don't get a moment to consider when a warmth runs through my body, throbbing at my ribs. A mixture of jasmine and hyacinth wraps around me with an after scent of something as sweet as apples and as spicy as that angry cinnamon I smelled earlier. That scent…

A gentle breeze passes, coaxing my gaze to the tree line.

Come, they call to me.

A pull deep in my bones has my knees unlocking, standing toward the uncontrollable lure. My feet move, not taking me left or right, but straight through the forest, well past where travelers roam or hunters lurk, where the ground hardens, and trees thicken. The branches whip past me, but that doesn't stop whatever trance I'm in.

A clearing appears ahead, and my heart sings at the small patch of yellow flowers.

Come, that calling sings again.

I bend down, cupping the strange flower, gentle enough not to pull it from the ground. Its petals open as if saying hello.

Somewhere in the distance, I hear my name, someone calling for me, but before I have a chance to turn around, the world around me spins, fading away.

Chapter Six

DORA

I follow the rapid pattering of Kore's panting and steps through the deepest parts of the forest, deeper than we've ever ventured before.

After the chaos unfolded on stage, the guards thought they could keep me—*me*—locked in one of the temples, but their role requires more brawn than brain. The morons didn't consider the back exit. It was too easy to slip out and head for the forest, knowing that's where Kore would go first.

Per usual, I was right. What I didn't expect was trudging through trees and dirt for an hour, being beaten and battered by branches.

I call Kore's name, but she doesn't stop, doesn't so much as look back. My lungs are ready to collapse, my legs seconds from giving out, when I finally see her stop and crouch. I'm still too far away to see what she's doing, but maybe now she can hear me.

I call for Kore again, breaking past the tree that obscures my view of her, just in time to see her admiring a golden flower as if the entire town isn't searching to murder her.

The laugh that leaves me is painful, a cramp aching both sides of my ribs. I pinch, applying pressure to keep it from spreading, and lower my voice to ask what she's doing.

I don't get a word out after her name. I don't get to suck in another breath, or blink.

Kore vanishes.

She didn't run away, didn't spread wings and fly. She just disappeared. One second, she was there, and the next... gone.

My feet suction to the ground, eyes wide and waiting, fearing I, too, might disappear. After a minute, I take one small step forward, searching for any signs of tree nymphs looking for unsuspecting men. I'm no man, but I don't want to be the exception.

I've seen what nymphs like to do, and it's those images that have me take another look around before making the final dash and throwing myself against the dirt.

My seer gift has saved me too many times to count, something I can't control but don't take for granted. It doesn't matter if I brush against someone in passing, shake their hand, or even swipe away hair from someone's eyes, their past floods me.

I claw at the ground faster, my fingers raking, my arms aching, trying to find a hole large enough that Kore could've fallen through. With every clump of ground I'm able to remove, I'm met with nothing other than torn flowers, roots, dirt, and more dirt.

My breathing grows heavy and labored, but I don't stop. I can't. I won't.

The nymphs aren't the cause for Kore's disappearance, I know that much, but that knowledge does nothing to ease the worry slicing through me or the tears that burn my eyes.

There's too much left unsaid, still so much Kore doesn't know that has been eating at me every day these past five years. The betrayal behind those deep amethyst eyes will only grow with more hatred once she knows the truth, but she *does* need to know. I thought keeping her in the dark would keep her safe, but then I met Swan, and I knew today was the day.

Time stops. The air stills, the hush of the branches quiet. My fingers curl, and that familiar *feeling* courses through me once again. One I've welcomed with every touch that sends it my way.

It always starts the same: the stillness, followed by whatever growing emotion is attached to the visions, usually too quick to make sense of them.

Longing, anger, and desperation switch back and forth with the images that invade my mind: a winged man falling from the sky, a black cat clawing the tree and disappearing just as Kore had, and then a woman with long, kinky hair hiding her face. I see a baby crawling in the grass next to yellow flowers, laughing, a man with raven hair and a crown of fire, staring out into the world, feeling the sun on his pale skin, smiling as if someone were talking to him. The last images are of Kore with vines wrapped around her body, around her bleeding feet. Then nothing.

An entrance.

"This is your fault, Mene," I say, completely spent from the useless digging.

The cat meows in response as she spins in circles, stopping only to peer back at me before spinning and stopping again. If I didn't know any better, I'd think this cat was enticing me to follow her.

Intrigued as always, I ask if that's what she wants, which earns me a loud purr.

I'm not one to take no as an answer, and every leap away from my attempted grasps have been screaming denials that only make me chase her harder. Mene may not allow me to pet her, but if she lets me follow, I won't pass up the opportunity.

I shift to rise to my feet.

A twig snaps.

"She vanished!" a girl screeches somewhere close. With no torch, my only source of light is the moon, which is hardly a sliver with the canopy of branches above me. I'm fully aware of the darkness I'm stuck in, but there's freedom out here, a fresh breeze, and enough space that I don't panic.

"What happened? Where did she go?" a man shouts.

Shuffling feet and snapping twigs close in. They saw Kore, which means they likely see me frozen mid-crouch, contemplating what to do. It's in these moments that all my life decisions come crashing in, and as a bitter taste rises to the back of my throat, I can't help but wonder why I chose a dry wine to drink before going on stage and not the sweet one.

"Dora!" My name is called with the flickering torch just ahead.

They might want Kore, but after the disastrous scene I caused, the search will soon enough be for me, too. I won't endure a long, dark, and lonely punishment while Kore is on the run.

Jumping to my feet, I run. I can't go back to the closet. I won't. Mene leaps ahead of me, hardly an inky blot in the thick of night.

I trust my instincts to follow her, thanking my heavenly stars that she stays close enough for me to see her swift turns and pounces. Without the little beast, finding my way back would have been nearly impossible.

It isn't too long before my surroundings start looking familiar and Mene disappears before I get a chance to catch her. *One day*, I silently promise, making my way to where I was headed before spotting Kore. Nowhere is safe, but the hidden clearing will give me time to breathe and think, to form a plan to find Kore.

As I near our secret alcove, a buttery light dances behind the trees that hide it. I stay light on my feet, avoiding any fallen branches or jagged rocks that would draw attention to my sneaking approach.

I can't imagine how anyone would find our place, where Kore and I go to avoid our lives; my expectations and duties as an upcoming priestess, and Kore's grief and new life as a servant in a town that rejects her so fiercely.

It's at this clearing that I first noticed the way Kore lights up when I tell her stories of the Gods, like the possibility of them being true is more exciting than the fact that they are. It's one of the reasons I study so hard in the priestess' library, so I can bring her a new story to keep her mind away from our mundane realities.

This is *our* sacred place.

I squint to get a better view of the two figures behind the branches. The tall one paces back and forth, carrying a torch, while the smaller one leans against a fallen tree, watching the manic movements. Doing a quick sweep of the area, there doesn't seem to be anyone else.

The taller one turns.

I let out a sigh that I feel to my core, a weight lifting off my shoulders. I've never been so elated to see Adonis.

If it weren't for the golden hair that falls from the hood and cascades down the smaller ones back as she looks back, I would've thought I was looking at Kore with the way this woman is staring at him.

I'm used to seeing girls and older women gawking at him. There's no denying Adonis is beautiful. He just isn't my type. He's too passive and plain. The only personality he shows is when he gives in and teases me, and I do my best to provoke that side out of him every chance I can.

Kore's always too busy being one of the gawkers to notice the way others look at him, except for Meg. The tension between those two is thicker than a noose and just as deadly. A noose I would help measure if Kore asked. Would I like it? No, but I'm loyal, and as I tried to tonight, I would willingly die for my friend, though killing would probably be easier.

The scene before me now, Swan gaping after Adonis, is something else entirely. It's like watching a lion salivating after a deer, or so I imagine. I would say a bird to a worm, but Adonis is much too beautiful to compare to such an ugly thing, and Swan's features are more lioness than bird-like.

"What are you doing here?" I shove through the trees.

Adonis stops his frantic pacing and clutches his chest as if his heart were about to leap out of it. He strides toward me and squeezes my shoulders like he can't believe I'm here, looking me up and down in a way that catches me off guard because it's he who should be looked over. Fresh cuts plot along his face and arms, as if someone had attempted to practice human pin-cushioning. They look red and painful.

"Where's Kore? Are you okay?" He searches behind me, with a million questions written on his torn-up face.

"She's gone." My breath is shaky, but I do my best to explain what happened, choosing my words carefully to leave out any mention of my visions.

While I knew Swan wouldn't react, I hadn't expected Adonis to look at me like I was insane. "What does that mean? She disappeared down a tree?"

I step around him, motioning for him to wait as I stand to Swan's impressive height, pinning my finger to her chest.

"You did something to me." The memory is still hazy, but I do recall one thing. "You sent all those silver lines through me and made me blackout." I fling my arms around the way the silver lines had when Swan whispered into my ear.

She watches me with an intensity I step away from. "How could you see that?"

Oops.

Quicker than I can realize my mistake and what she's doing, her palms cage my head, her fingers pressing into my temples, her voice seductive with the demand, "Tell me how you saw my ability."

Again, those silver lines come into my peripheral, where my hands enclose on top of hers, trying and failing to pry her off.

Unable to control myself, the answer spills out of me. "I'm able to see the past of things I touch. I didn't know I could see abilities until right now."

With a tilt of her head, her lips tighten into a grin, the subtle quiver too quick to be sure it was there. "You're an interesting little squirrel, aren't you?"

Whatever hold is on me releases as her hands drop, my shoulders with them, where they were frozen in place.

"What is that? Manipulation? Oh Gods... That's it, isn't it?" Something snaps into place. "Did you make me choose Kore as the sacrifice?"

Her shrug is too casual for what she's done. "She needed a push in the right direction."

"To die?!" Adonis steps forward, maintaining his distance like a good servant would.

"Yes." Her matching nod shocks us both. "But what I want to know is how much you have seen, and what you know of her."

"I know enough." My chin is high, refusing to recoil or make myself smaller in her presence. There's not a chance I'm telling her anything specific. "Do you know where she went?"

"How would she know?" Adonis' confusion is making this conversation harder, and with his pacing, the tension is even more erratic. "You talk of manipulation and abilities like—"

In one quick motion, Swan reaches for him as he passes by. "Silence."

His face falls into that vacant nothingness, and his steps slow. I can't help but note how eerily like himself he looks, even with the emptiness behind his eyes, that frozen inability to fight off her magic keeping him unmoving. I want to reach for him, to touch his shoulder so he knows

I'm here with him, that he'll be okay, that I understand, but he's too far away.

Ignoring him, Swan confirms she knows where Kore went. Her fingers slide along the chain around her neck, playing with the locket on the end. "I wanted to take her someplace safe, but I don't think there is a place truly safe for her. Depending on where that door went this time, she is either in the safest place she could be or the most dangerous."

My nails bite into my palm. This is my fault.

"Take me there." My voice is harsher and more demanding than I intended, but I'm desperate to find Kore. I have to tell her everything. I have to tell her who she really is and what really happened five years ago.

"Why would I do that?"

This time, it's me who reaches out, grabbing her arms and lifting them, keeping my grip tight so she can't pull away. "Because I can also see these."

Adonis breaks through the stillness, his head angling to see what I'm talking about, but is left more confused at the sight of empty wrists. Only, they aren't empty to those who can see the golden shackles.

"I've seen enough visions to know what a God's prisoner looks like. And I also know how to remove them."

Swan looks at me with doubt, ready to scoff, narrowing her eyes instead. "Prove it."

"How?"

"Who else have you seen as a prisoner?" Her question heightens, seemingly more curious about the answer itself than needing me to prove anything.

"I'm not sure who he is, but he wore a mask. Half a mask, anyway. And then there was a tall blonde woman who looked like you, except her eyes were silver."

Admiration fills Swan's otherwise impassive or amused features, radiating her dangerous, alluring beauty. What this woman could accomplish with a single look...

She tugs her wrists, reclaiming them to brush a piece of dirt from her cloak. "You just get more interesting, don't you?"

"I'm coming with," Adonis adds, leaving no room to argue. The definitive tone in his voice alone is surprising as he's usually one to keep

74

quiet or offer muted comments. "But I don't want to keep spacing out and forgetting things."

"That one wore off rather quickly," Swan muses more to herself. "Our deal still stands."

"What deal?" I glance nervously between them. What could Adonis have gotten himself into? Does he know who she is?

He glances at his feet as he answers, his throat bobbing, "She said she'd get the tattoo removed from my neck if I helped her get Kore to come with us. She said she wanted to help her."

If I weren't so pressed for answers, I would have shoved him and told him how ridiculous he is for doing such a thing. Then again, we're a pot and kettle thirsty for Swan not to leave us dry.

Swan rolls her eyes, clearly as annoyed as I am with his lack of backbone. "I do want to help her. I'll take you both, but you will not touch me again. Do you understand?" She points at me with a look that tells me not to argue and simply agree.

Both of us do so in unison, and I ease, though keeping my guard high. I've heard enough stories and seen enough glimpses of Swan to know she can't be fully trusted, but she can be useful.

"You'll both need more than what you have on your backs." Swan starts back toward the main trail. "We have to take the long way."

"Can't we go where she disappeared?" Adonis asks.

"Unfortunately, mortals aren't allowed through those entrances, and I have no interest in getting lost. They're unpredictable. But I do know where she'll end up."

The drop in her tone tells me all I need to know. She doesn't like where Kore will end up, even less so than wherever she could be now.

"How long will it take to get there?" I hurry to keep pace.

"A few days. We're stopping in Athens first, then we head to Mt. Olympus." She spins back so quickly that I stumble into her. "You didn't see much if you're coming with me willingly."

"I know who you are."

She cocks her head, lifting her finger to twirl my hair. "And that doesn't frighten you?"

I lift my chin higher than before as I move around her to take the lead. "Gods don't frighten me."

Chapter Seven

KORE

Intertwining roots and vines coil around my legs and arms, brittle tendrils rising from the dirt beneath me.

Lifting one foot at a time, I untangle them, and they snap away, cracking and crumbling to dust between my fingers.

That's... odd.

I quickly finish brushing the rest off, noting how tattered my dress is, how tight it clings to my curves, like an extra layer of skin. It's humid, the sweat and blood are sticky, and the tiny cuts from the branches sting. A bath, a tin of salves, and a roll of bandages are just a start of what I need.

The deep breath I take in fills me in a way that clears my head, so much so that I jump to my feet, suddenly aware that something is off. My arms prickle, the hairs on the back of my neck stand at attention. Every part of me is alert.

The forest, the trees, the thickets, the very ground, all of it is either gone or dead. There are no purple wildflowers nor tree trunks growing their strange mushrooms. The branches are spindly and bare, the moon's silver threads beaming through the gaps.

The welcoming flowers I was admiring are no longer here, and neither are the grass or moss, just broken twigs, fallen trees, brittle thorns, and dirt.

I remember falling. But when I look above, all I see are twinkling stars. It's possible I didn't realize just how barren this deep in the forest is when I was stuck in that trance.

I check my forehead with the back of my hand and pinch myself, neither tells me anything except I'm hot and sweaty, and I can still feel pain. I'm almost positive this isn't a dream, but to be sure, I pinch a little harder before starting down the path that looks worn and traveled, leaving a trail of blood to color the otherwise colorless forest.

I could have sworn I heard Dora's voice calling my name before I fell asleep. I must have been too exhausted from nearly dying and running for my life that I collapsed.

I'm torn between wanting to find Dora and never seeing her again. I want answers; why she chose me to be sacrificed, why she was playing Charon at all, and why she didn't tell me. The irony is, I would have felt safer had I known it was her beneath that cloak.

The physical ache riddled over my body is nothing compared to the trust crumbling away.

The reminder of what Pirithous taught me long ago whispers deep in the back of my mind, coaxing me within it: this world is an evil place full of monsters in disguise.

I clutch the black ring around my neck. This and physical pain are the only anchors that keep me from drifting away into that desolate chamber filled with voices that wants to wrap around me, so I feel and think of nothing but the blanketed melancholy. Wine helps, too, but all the adrenaline has sobered me.

A thought strikes me, my feet faltering with the harsh truth. In saving myself, I've likely sentenced another to die in my place.

My hold on the ring tightens, and the skin along my thumbnail bursts. I hiss, drawing in a long breath, my attention settling on my lifeless surroundings. Another desolated place, but one I don't feel numb in, not even with the lack of sound that accentuates the eeriness of the night. No birds sing, no grasshoppers chirp, no flies buzz. The birds that follow me aren't soaring in the sky.

I continue, knowing I have a long journey ahead of me. I may have been in a trance on the way out here, but I was aware of every intriguing minute of it.

Each step is more miserable than the last. The scraped-up arches of my feet are screaming for a break, but I can't stop. I need to get to the clearing to gauge where I am and which direction to go. I can't go home. I won't be able to gather anything before...

I'm not sure.

I've never left, but I know I can't stay.

After a while, I relent and rest against a sturdy trunk, panting from how much energy it takes to limp. My thighs burn, begging me to sit for a few days to heal the chaffing between them. My lips are so dry, I savor the sweat that trickles from my temples onto them.

Snap!

A twig cracks in the distance.

I angle myself toward the sound, straining to see between the haunted trees.

Snap!

I twist to the other direction.

"Hello?" My voice comes out as a whisper, as if even my very skin and bones know not to make any sudden noises or movements.

Snap! Snap!

"Dora?"

Snap! Snap! Snap!

Twigs break from all directions at a quicker pace until a tall, skinny figure emerges onto the trail, too far to see clearly, but close enough that I limp back a step.

The man stumbles forward, stopping to tilt his head to the night sky. Tattered and ripped clothes hang from his lanky figure, with limbs angling in odd directions. Patchy hair falls over his face. His cheeks sink in, his eyes pop from his head, and his mouth hangs open, revealing a row of broken teeth.

My fists clench, gripping nothing while cursing myself for losing the blade.

His head whips back with an interested tilt, bones grinding and popping loudly with the quick movement. His cheeks rise in an attempt to smile.

Not a dream. My head shakes side to side with the brutal denial, the realization that I'm in a nightmare straight from Hel.

The man moves.

I turn and run, ignoring the sting in my arches, pumping my arms as fast as I can to take me farther, faster.

There is no time to think, not when more figures begin emerging from the shadows.

Another stumbles onto the trail just ahead. Its neck cocks and twists as the first had, its head snapping back as if smelling something in the air. That open mouth widens to a disgusting smile before he looks at me.

I blink and he's running straight for me.

There's nowhere to turn, nowhere else to run. My only choice is to sprint straight through one of them.

Something glistens behind the one before me.

Water.

"Dora?!" My lungs ache, but I yell for my friend again. The clearing must be close. If I could just get to that river.

I brace myself, ready for the impact of the decrepit man, when a white shadow flashes by, swiping him into the trees.

I don't dare look over, don't dare look back, as I pass where he disappeared, hoping and praying that whatever it was doesn't drag me into those woods too.

Relief comes and goes as footsteps quicken at my back. I was so focused on the one before me that I almost forgot about the second one behind me.

The steps close in, so close I can feel the brush of bony fingers on the nape of my neck. The slight touch startles me.

My feet tangle.

My palms take most of the impact as my face slides across the dirt.

Before I have a chance to right myself, a cold, rough hand yanks my shoulder and rolls me over. The man is more hideous up close. His skin is sheer and pale, nearly the same color as the bone peeking beneath the rotted flesh. His gaze drops, taking me in, but all I can focus on is his eye, the one that doesn't have a lid. A sight so dreadful I freeze in place.

"No!" I come to. His arms lack muscle, yet he's able to pin me to the ground with enough force to keep me locked in between his legs. His withered hand trembles as he lifts it, grazing his knuckles down my cheek.

"What do you want?" I pant, sinking my head into the dirt to escape the cold touch.

His finger presses against my lips, attempting to shush me, but his mouth won't close, letting out a loud wail that drips saliva from the corners of his gaping mouth.

I stretch my head away as far as I can while his fingers lower until they reach the chain at my neck. Panic floods me as he trails even lower, planting his palm flat against my chest.

For the briefest moment, something light seeps from him, and his face softens. The quick pause gives me all the time I need to wiggle my arm free and slam my fist into his nose as hard as I can. He falls back enough for me to buck and kick him off the rest of the way and scramble to my feet.

"Duck!" I hear. The warning tone shoves me to my knees as something massive flies toward me. The same white shadow that took the short figure down swoops in and tackles the man into the trees.

Whatever it is, I don't want to be next. I don't trust that this quick save was in earnest.

I dart toward the river, and my plan to jump in is quickly abandoned when I see the color isn't blue and the water doesn't run. That doesn't stop me from dropping to my knees at the edge and cupping some to take a small sip, needing anything to wet my tongue.

I take another, and another. On the fourth handful, I spit it out, registering the saltiness I had mistaken for my own sweat.

A croaked whimper leaves my chest, a deep sadness overcoming me, my shoulders drooping.

Why did everyone betray me? Why did my father have to die? Why doesn't Metanira love me? Why does everyone hate me and throw coins at me? Tears pour down my cheeks and into the black river as hurt, betrayal, and utter despair drown me.

Not even the rustling trees pull me from staring at my weeping reflection, sulking further into myself, further than I ever have before. Those whispering questions wrap around my psyche, suffocating me further away, until my hands no longer feel like mine but someone else's, until I'm watching my body from afar.

Someone touches my shoulder, gently urging me back.

I wrench free, needing to focus on the tears splattering into the water, needing to feel the deep aching pain that continues to draw every dark thought I've ever had to the forefront of my mind.

Whoever is behind me doesn't understand, because they wrap an arm around my waist and force me away from the edge.

"No!" I tug and thrash against them. They're so tall that my feet barely graze the ground as they lift me higher.

When I break contact with the river, my mind untethers from whatever sorrowful Hel it was captured in. My heart empties and aches. I nearly collapse in the man's arms at the heaviness that drags me down, until I remember I'm in danger.

"No!" I thrash again, clawing at any skin I can reach, sharp tingles flowing through me with every jab I land. "I can't go back! Please! Let me go. I don't want to die!"

"Calm down, and I'll let you go." The man almost sounds like he's smiling.

I give him one chance to do as he says, having exhausted my strength to fight against the one arm he held me with. My tongue runs along my teeth, ready to bite if I need to.

He releases me, and my knees hit the ground, irritating the unhealed, open cuts.

The man offers his hand.

I knock it away and scoot back. "I'm not going back."

"No, you're not." He chuckles. "But I'm not letting you stay here to die either."

Refusing to let this stranger know how much pain I'm in, I clench my teeth, swallow back a whimper, and rise enough to lean against the nearest tree. Thank the Gods, because my knees buckle at the full sight of him. It's no wonder I couldn't escape his grip. Every part of this man is made of muscle. I don't blame him for displaying every chiseled inch of himself, wearing nothing but a white wrap around his waist. His skin a golden tan. I scan up to the most striking feature of all, deep sapphire gems that inventory every inch of me right back.

His lips tilt, giving me a self-assured grin.

Something moves above his shoulders, hidden by the shadows of the night.

"I…" Holy Hel, the mere sight of this man is stealing the breath from me. "I have to go," I stammer, taking a step back down the trail, finding my breath again.

I make it two steps before he grabs my arm, stopping me from taking another. Where his hand grips me, a shudder jolts through my arm, rattling my bones. He flinches, snapping his arm back as if he felt it too.

"Let me help." Sincerity molds the sharp lines of his face. There's a gentleness about him, a lightness I want to trust. I can't tell if it's an instinct about him, or if he's just unbelievably handsome enough to ignore the instinct not to. I don't even think my instinct is working. All I know is that I'm not going back. I won't let him take me back to die.

He motions to the looming woods still crackling and snapping with heavy steps. "It's me or them, and I do think I'm a little more appealing." His broad grin dimples, making him even more stunning.

I study him closer, trying to decipher his motives.

"I've already saved your life *twice*," he adds without me having to say a word. His natural charm shifts between curiosity and finding something comical. "Do you even know where you are?"

I don't get a chance to think about the bizarre question, not when he centers himself on the trail and spreads white wings that are longer than any normal man is tall. There is a small patch of crumpled feathers, coated in black and gold, that aren't as perfectly slicked and in line with the rest.

His smirk deepens at my shock and awe, the disbelief evident by my slackened jaw that won't close. "You prayed to me tonight. I'm a little hurt you don't trust me."

My head snaps back to him, seeing the sapphire in a new light. "Her— " This can't be real. Gods aren't— They can't be. Sure, I was open-minded to them being real, hoped they were after tonight, but to be in the presence of one?

He bends at the waist in a mocking bow. "Hermes, at your service."

This is a trick.

I limp closer, thankful he stays still while I circle him, trying to find some way for this to make sense.

I reach for where the wings break free from his shoulder blades, pausing before daring to touch them, tracing the connection where skin and feathers meet.

"This is real," I say more to myself as I continue tracing the strange connection, his back shivering when my fingers glide down the velvet feathers.

"Yes." He swivels around, snapping them shut. "Now, if you're done fondling me, I'd like to continue with the heroics and get you out of here before we're attacked again."

A flush rises to my cheeks.

Reluctantly, I nod. My feet ache, unable to so much as take another step, and I did call to him, prayed for his help, and here he is.

"Wait, my friend, Dora. I can't leave without her."

He pinches the ridge of his nose with a hint of a smile hidden beneath. "She's safe. Please forgive me for this, but we really must be going *now*."

Bony figures burst through the tree line.

Hermes moves so quick that I don't even notice I'm in his arms until the breeze cools the parts of my body he's not touching. I peeked over his shoulder, a tremor running through me at the height we're flying, seeing the breathtaking view below.

The woods aren't the only part of land that holds no life or color, but everything. Dirt, haunted trees, and unmoving rivers roll on for as far as I can see. There are homes, marked by the rising smoke of wood-burning fireplaces.

There's no sight of the woods I know, the town I almost died in, or the home I'll never go back to.

"You're okay?" I'm not sure if it's a question or a statement, but I nod anyway. I'm always fine.

"Please, don't take me back," I plead, willing to get on my knees and beg if I have to.

"You have my word." A word I want more than anything to believe, but my trust in others has failed too many times.

He urges me to rest, using his hand to lean my head against his shoulder, promising to wake me when we arrive. I try to fight it, but his shoulder is too warm, and the way he holds me feels like a hammock, cocooning me further into my exhaustion.

I yawn, losing my internal fight to stay awake, and close my eyes.

My mind is dazed when I ask the question I've been too scared to ask since knowing it was Hermes standing before me. If he is real, then so is the possibility of where I've woke up—or didn't.

His answer confirms exactly what I feared. "We're in the Underworld."

I startle awake, still wrapped in Hermes' arms, quickly wiping my mouth to make sure I didn't drool on his shoulder, when I notice small white wings sitting above his ears, immediately flapping as if saying hello.

Hermes smirks.

"Am I dead?"

"No." He chuckles, watching me pinch myself, plotting red blots up and down my arm to see if that somehow tells me anything. It doesn't.

"Then why am I in the Underworld?" I'm quick to accept his word as truth when I have no other explanation as to why everything is lifeless or how I'm flying in the arms of a winged man.

"I believe you came through a door."

That doesn't tell me anything I need to know, like where we're headed and why we didn't go back out whatever door I came through, but when I ask, I'm met with blunt, evasive answers, "someplace safe," and "that's not how it works."

"How do I know you're really a God?"

"You ask a lot of questions."

"I *have* a lot of questions."

"Do you see many men with wings?" His brow lifts, thinking that's answer enough.

"There are many stories that tell of creatures and monsters with wings. How do I know you're not part of the Furies?" An involuntary shudder runs up my spine at the thought of being in the presence of one of the Underworld's torturers, but they're said to be women, so I'm almost positive he isn't one.

"Let's pray you never meet one of them." The fact that they have his beautiful face dropping a smile to convey a look of terror, I silently agree.

84

"And who do the Gods pray to?" With nothing to do but ask questions, I can't stop them at this point.

He sighs. "Dear Mother Gaia, please make this woman stop asking so many damn questions."

I smack his shoulder, mocking offense. I really am asking a lot of questions, but how can I not? If he truly is a God, shouldn't I die or become blind at the sight of him? Shouldn't he be a giant?

"Those beings back there, the ones that attacked me, what are they?"

"Dangerous."

"You're very evasive."

"Selective, not evasive." His pointed look dares me to ask more, and his rising smirk takes my silence as a win.

The silence that stretches between us isn't long before I gently tap his cheek, seeing his eyes droop and feeling his arms weaken around me. "Hermes?"

He nuzzles my palm before his eyes snap open.

"Is it your wing?" I peer over his shoulder to see the damage, but his wings are spread too far for me to see clearly. "Put me down. We can walk."

My body grows heavy at the thought of him carrying me for such a long time. My bulging stomach sandwiched between my chest and knees feels larger than ever.

"I will when we get there." His face twitches, ridding any evidence of his fatigue. "It's not that much farther."

"I'm too heavy. If you put me down, you could rest. I can take a look at your wings. I've wrapped plenty of injuries."

"You're not heavy, and between the both of us," he points his chin from me to him, "we don't have enough clothing to wrap a single feather of mine."

My cheeks heat, but I hold his stare, refusing to look over my torn-up dress that I know exposes too much.

"Just put me down," I urge, annoyed that he insists on being stubborn.

"It's too dangerous," he bites back, hinting that he isn't all smiles and charm.

I wiggle, squirming to annoy him enough into landing. "Let me go!"

All contact is gone.

My screams are silent as I fall from the sky, watching Hermes figure floating above, becoming smaller and smaller by the second. But he isn't laughing like I thought he would be, like he's playing a joke.

He wouldn't let me die, would he?

As I continue to fall my hope dwindles, but then his feathers tighten behind him, darting straight toward me. The impact against his chest rips the breath from me, my heart pounding out of my ribs.

I wrap my arms around his neck, clutching so tight that the feathers next to his ears flutter against my cheek.

"Pick your words carefully." There's no hint of amusement, just a reassuring squeeze that he won't let me go again. I don't care if I smother him; I'm not loosening my hold until we're safely on the ground.

After a few minutes and a few deep breaths, the tension eases from his shoulders. "You looked like a little bat falling from the sky." His breath tickles my shoulder.

"Yeah? Well, you looked like a giant ass with wings."

His loud chuckle makes my own laugh sound strange in my throat. "Most of those who grow up in the mortal realm learn to bow and say pretty prayers to Gods with their useless offerings. You're a bit refreshing."

"Can't say the same. You're living up to your name with your clever words and wings." I bat my eyes at him. "See, I can say pretty words. I think your choosy answers are annoying, not clever." He arches his brow, surveying me closer. "What?"

"You're different than I was expecting."

"Why were you *expecting* me?"

"I'm ordered not to say. He wants to tell you himself." Every hair on my arm stands at attention, and he continues before I can ask who he's referring to. "Don't worry, no one is going to kill you, or torture you, or anything like that. Their deal was very specific."

His face falls like he said too much, biting his lower lip to keep it shut.

"Whose deal?" This could very well be the dangerous God Dora mentioned, the one who makes deals. If I could meet this God and ask for a deal, maybe I could find a way to keep everyone I love safe and secure, never having to worry or think about sacrifices, forced marriages, or punishments again.

It's his next words that have my heart skip, my skin prickle, and my throat tighten all at once.

"All I can tell you is Hades has been waiting quite a long time for you."

Hermes lands us next to an abandoned temple, its circular pillars cracked with pieces chipped away from aging.

I peer inside, finding a dark void, no tables or statues, not even shadows that hint at them.

"What is this place?"

"A door. Like the one you came through. Some items from each veil mirror over into the others, like these doors, but you must know which one to go through, or you'll get lost. And never take a door without knowing where its counterpart is to return. One way forward isn't always the same back."

I seal my lips while he speaks more than he has all night, with a real answer to my question. The sheer amount of words is as surprising as the actual answer itself.

I've never heard of veils before.

Reading my puzzled look, he continues, if only to avoid hearing another one of my questions. He explains how every world is interconnected, like a stack of pancakes with syrup poured over. Each pancake is separate, but they're all on the same plate with the syrup seeping through each one. Hera could be standing next to us in the Heavens, Dora could be standing in front of us in the Mortal Veil, and this temple could be the syrup that remains constant through all. The concept is incredible.

"But I remember falling before I woke up here." I can still feel the air beneath me, the same way I had when he dropped me.

Hermes steps forward, and I'm determined not to stumble back this time as he towers over me, his bare chest meeting my chin.

My breath halts as his knuckles pass over my collarbone, that strange jolt tingling again. He smirks and pulls the golden chain from my cleavage. "You have a key that allows you to jump."

I grab the black ring he dangles between us, securing it back into its place. "How is this a key?"

"Again, with the questions?" He steps back until he settles against a tree, wincing when his wings brush against it.

"Let me take a look."

I can tell he wants to protest, but he stops himself, crossing his arms over his chest and letting me walk behind him to have a better look. "Be gentle. Wings are *very* sensitive."

They jerk when I place a hand above the gold and black tangled mess of feathers stuck together. "Sorry, what is this exactly?"

"Blood."

"It's not red." I can feel his mocking smirk with the hidden question.

"Gods have ichor, the gold you see. Cursed beings have tainted blood, the black you're seeing. Both are mine."

My eyes shoot to the back of his head, where all I see are his short, light curls that hold a ray of sun. I can't help but peruse down his neck to his broad shoulders, down his bare back to where the wings attach.

"You're cursed?"

"All of Zeus' kids are."

I don't know what to say. I have too many questions, but he's easily annoyed with those. I busy myself, inspecting the affected feathers closer.

"Are you petting me?"

I rip my hand away, horrified at myself for doing exactly that. "Sorry, they're really soft."

His chuckle has me internally cringing and wishing I had the knife to cut my hands off to keep from doing that again.

"How——" I stop myself. I want to know how he found me in the first place. Was he passing by? Did he hear me scream?

I take a deep breath, but before I can ask anything, I spot the source of the bleeding. Where one wing is horribly battered, missing feathers, and smothered with the bloody mixture, the other wing is missing a large piece entirely. "How could you fly like this?!"

"Very painfully." He rolls his neck. "But I'll heal soon."

I look over myself. There really is no clothing to use as a wrap.

"You satisfied?" His wings straighten, the left one less so than the right one.

"Not really." I take in the fallen columns again, finding one to rest on. The reprieve from flying eased some of my own pain, but my feet are still torn up and bloody.

Hermes leans against the lifeless tree again, careful to keep his wings from scraping against it. "I'll answer one question before we head through that door."

I'm about to ask why, but the tilt of his head tells me that would be a waste of my one question. "I want a full answer. Not one of your evasive, *selective* answers."

"I'll try my best."

I let out a relenting huff, thinking through the many questions I have, already knowing his responses: Where exactly are we going? *You'll see.* Why did you save me? *You needed it.* What kind of curse do you have? *One that makes my blood black.* Why were all the myths I heard growing up wrong? *How should I know?*

Finally, I settle on one he might actually answer. "How did you find me?"

"I have birds following you." He smiles, knowing he just opened more questions that I need answers to. He's been following me, but why? For how long?

He pushes off the tree, holding his arms out for me to jump into.

"I can walk." Something about being back in his arms stirs things I don't want to think about right now.

The wings on Hermes' ears begin flapping furiously, pattering loudly against his head. His posture turns rigid, uncertainty spilling from his pores.

He pulls me against him, exactly what I don't need. I shouldn't be blushing while he motions me to stay quiet, concentrated on something I can't hear or see. While this is a concerning situation, all I can think about is how soft his skin is and how he smells of fresh air.

Hide, he mouths, pointing to a stack of boulders.

I follow his sharp order, sensing the seriousness in his silent tone, the stark change in his demeanor from playful to *don't-fucking-argue*.

Trying to make myself as small as possible, I rest my back against the large boulder, listening to his greeting, "Hecate, it's been a while."

I risk a glance over my hiding spot to find Hermes back to leaning against the broken tree without a care in the world. I can't see the faces of the two figures standing before him, but I can make out their small and feminine forms enough to know they don't stand a chance against him.

The one dressed in a short, black slip has thick, messy curls falling down her back. The other has dark skin and long, sleek, black hair that glistens wet. She wears so little clothing that if it weren't for the hint of green peeking beneath the woman's hair, I would have thought she was naked.

"Hermes!" The one in the black slip skips toward him eagerly and wraps her small arms around his waist. He hugs her shoulder with a smile that reminds me of when my father would come home from long trips. "It's been too long!"

He holds the petite woman at arm's length, looking her over with concern.

The feisty girl pushes him away. "I'm fine. You see the scar, don't you?"

Whatever scar he sees unravels his unease, and he straightens himself with that assured grin that dimples his cheek. "You can't blame me for worrying, Hecate. It's been years, and I can't risk you not being in control. *Artemis* was shooting arrows at her to collect the reward. His attention switches to the unimpressed woman standing with her arms crossed. "Minthe?"

"Hecate's fine, as you can clearly see. Is she here or not?" Minthe's foot taps restlessly.

I'm practically hugging the boulder, trying to hear everything they say, when something moves next to me.

My mouth opens to scream, but no sound comes out.

"Don't be scared." The man raises his hands to show he doesn't have any weapons.

But neither do I. All I can do is fist my hands and wait, readying my teeth if needed.

Seeing that I'm not going to attack first, he drops his shoulders. "Found her!" He lifts his hand for me to take. "Come on, love, you have nowhere else to go."

My heart sinks with the truth of his statement. He's a big guy, tall, with muscles that press against his black shirt. Hermes can hardly fly; I'm not sure he can help me away from this man.

I peek over to see how Hermes is faring and find no concern at all, but a defeated shake of his head before he palms his forehead. "It's fine, Kore."

I look over the man in front of me again. There is something oddly familiar about him, or maybe it's a trick of the mind to justify taking his hand, his rings pinching my skin as he helps me to stand.

I stumble from my crouched position, unable to find my footing. In fact, everything around me seems to be spinning.

"Shit." The man curses before the world around me falls on its side.

Chapter Eight

KORE

I lie still, my eyes closed, and mouth parted as if I'm still asleep while the others speak freely.

"I told you, she's fine," the woman Hermes called Minthe insists, exasperated at having to repeat herself.

"Kore, I need you to wake up, so I know you're okay." The man sounds distressed. His rings press tightly against my fingers in a refusal to let my hand go. It's hard not to squeeze back to cast his worry aside.

"She's fine!" Minthe snaps again. It's been at least an hour of bickering with no sign of them leaving anytime soon.

When my stomach grumbles, I know it's time to end the charade and face them once and for all, to find out why they took me.

I blink as if I were just now stirring from a dream, flattening my palms on whatever soft, heavenly cloud I'm lying on. And are those furs on top of me? I can't remember a time when my body felt so relaxed and warm.

It only gets better at the sight of the beautiful room, the lavish décor, and furniture. If it weren't for the bed, I would have thought this was an actual home by the mere size of it.

I take it all in, pinching my outer thigh to ensure I'm truly not dreaming this time, hard enough that I wince.

The furs that warm me are black. I can't make out what animal they're made from, but I sink my hands deeper into the plush coat, petting as I would if it were alive. The sheets beneath me are a smoky purple, the richest dye, a unique shade I've never seen before. The bed alone could sleep a family of five, comfortably.

A deep onyx surrounds me. Every piece of furniture is made of it, accented with a complementary shade of gold: the long dresser, vanity, and the chairs that sit in front of the crackling wall-to-ceiling fireplace. A tall, gilded mirror stands in the corner, and I can't think of why anyone would need a mirror so large.

Not even in my wealthiest could I have imagined owning anything this extravagant, and though I am not and have never been royal, I know this goes beyond such a lifestyle.

The glass on the nightstand grabs my attention, and I take it, sitting up enough to drink it down. At the slight movement, pain slams into the front of my skull, throbbing at my temples. My hands shake to keep the cup steady until I'm finished.

No one says anything as I gather my bearings, massaging where the splitting headache feels like it's literally splitting me open. "What—" I want to ask what happened, but words fail me.

When I open my eyes again, working past the blinding ache, I realize there's only one door—the one escape—guarded by Minthe, who looks the part of a guard with her *I-dare-you* scowl, and arms crossed over her chest. I can't look at anything but her eyes. They're larger than any I've ever seen, and her ears curve into sharp points.

Nymph.

She looks as annoyed as she sounds, unlike the man with the rings, who sits in a chair at my side with a mix of distress and relief.

I rest my back against the headboard, immediately spotting what's missing, or rather who. "Where is Hermes?" My voice is hoarse, betraying how groggy I feel.

"Not here," Minthe answers, seeming to relax a little, smiling even. I have a feeling she doesn't do that often.

I look to the man, hoping he'll provide better answers rather than stating the obvious. "Where am I?"

If he says a bedroom...

"Still in the Underworld, love." His voice is soft and apologetic in a way that doesn't ask for trust but promises it, but there's also a wryness about him. "Sorry about your head. I haven't touched a mortal... err, I guess someone as close to it as one could be without being one, in quite a long time. Hecate said your mid-transition, so you should be fine."

93

I filter through all the possibilities of what that could mean, and with the way things are going, none of them are good. I pick at my thumb, hesitating to ask, "What is mid-transition?"

He's taken aback by my confusion. "Do you really not know? Hermes said you knew." There's something about this man that perplexes me enough to stare at him without restraint. He's unlike the men from my town. His jaw is clean-shaven, and his hair is tied at the nape of his neck. I can feel a tug of kindness from him that makes me less anxious, and I can't shake the familiarity in his features and presence. It's like I know him but have no idea who he is.

"I wouldn't be asking if I knew." *Honey, Kore. You catch flies with honey,* I remind myself.

He doesn't balk at my attitude as I expect. Instead, he smiles with pure mischief, rolling one of the many rings with his thumb, and leans back. "A Goddess. You're transitioning into a Goddess."

I bark out a laugh. He can't be serious. This must be a joke that Gods play on mortals. But my laughter dies when I notice the other two don't share my humor. "You're lying?" I look between them, waiting for the joke to be over. "But—How can that be?"

The vial—ambrosia—*A butterfly without wings is a terrible thing. Drink me and become what you were fated to be.*

Sharp pain pinches down my foot. I hiss and pull them in, but they're stuck. Someone's holding them still.

"She *is* still mortal in some capacity, but her feet are almost healed. It seems being here may have paused her transition. Her healing is faster than a mortal but slower than a God." Hecate's unmistakable peppiness comes from over the bed's edge. She pops up, sending her wild, kinky hair bouncing.

I keep myself from overtly staring at the scar that slices from one ear to the side of her mouth. She's stunning in a haunted sort of way. The kind of beauty I see in my withering roses next to the blooming ones at their side.

"Have you experienced any pain yet?" Hecate releases her hold on my legs, looking at me with a wonder that reminds me of Dora. "Extreme heat? Extreme cold? Overall agony? Your body transitioning back to ichor is incredible. I've never met a Goddess that—"

"*Hecate.*" The man stops her babbling with a warning nod.

"*Dionysus,*" she mocks back, drawing out his name, a name I've heard once before. He's the God of wine. I vaguely remember Dora sneaking through my window with a bottle, telling me about a new God that hadn't lived long enough to hold many stories. She said he was the son of Zeus and Demeter, and something about a boat.

"Don't you two have something better to do?" Minthe breaks their banter. "Hexes to break or blood to look at?"

It's then that I notice the opaque vials Hecate clutches in her palms. "Right," she says. "Tell him I'll be late and not to start the fun without me." With a wink, she skips out the door before I can ask her to finish what she was saying about the transition.

Dionysus offers me a weak smile, promising to see me at dinner before disappearing behind her, leaving me with the angry nymph, who demands, "Let's go."

White bandages wrap around my feet, but I'm otherwise left untouched, my dress still clinging to me in tethers. While I'm thankful they didn't attempt to clean me up, I can't help but ache at the thought of the beautiful sheets ruined with my filth.

As I follow Minthe down the hall, I cross my arms over my chest to hide anything indecent. It does nothing for my exposed legs or midriff, and when I look down, I realize I only brought the swells of my breasts high and prominent.

The feeling of being watched veils over me. I look over my shoulders, finding nothing but a long, dark hallway with no end in sight.

I hurry my steps, ignoring that pull to run into the depths of the unknown to catch up to Minthe. Every one of her steps takes me two, and still her long, slender legs take her farther away.

I want to ask her what Hecate and Dionysus meant about transitioning into a Goddess, but something tells me she would be even more evasive than Hermes.

I keep my mouth shut, biting my lip to ensure it stays that way, and study my surroundings. It's immaculate, how a simple corridor can be so vast and long, with no ending in either height or length. The walls are obsidian with crystal droplets hanging above, casting faint glimmers of pale light. Both sides hold what I assume to be doors, though only their shape suggests the thought. One looks to be made of frigid twigs, and another made of glass. The white door we pass is stone that shimmers, and the next burns with a fire that leaves no ash.

The floor appears to be hard, black and white diamond-shaped tiles, but feels of the softest furs I've ever had the pleasure of walking on.

Minthe suddenly stops before a door that trickles water from top to bottom, mimicking a soft waterfall. When I pause, sensing her uncertainty, she looks me up and down, smiles, and motions for me to follow her through the water.

I step through after her, surprised when I emerge on the other side untouched by a single drop of water.

My awe doesn't wane when I see the washroom we stand in is even more luxurious than the one I woke in. The black and white tiles stop and continue with white pearl. Instead of soft furs, the floor is hard and sleek but still warm. In the center is a large tub unlike any I've ever seen, a giant larimar stone glowing with the light blue crystal. Steam rises from the surface, already filled with water.

An arched entrance opens in the back, revealing racks of clothing.

"Take your time. Soaps and oils are over there." Minthe points to the pearl counter covered in vials and jars, then the back. "Pick any dress you like."

When she leaves, I don't hesitate to discard my ruined dress and climb into the tub. It keeps the perfect scalding heat and remains clean even though I watch the filth slide from my body only to vanish.

The blissful moment is ruined when my stomach clenches and grumbles, making me all too aware of how starved I am, and remembering Dionysus saying something about dinner.

Reluctantly, I crawl out and wrap myself in a towel that feels warmed by fire and make my way to the closet that's larger than the washroom. I'm surrounded by dresses hanging in a large circle in order of length and color. There's another gaudy mirror, and a bowl of brooches and clips sits in the corner on a pedestal.

Gods, how I missed the feeling of finery, of soft silks and plush velvets. Desire rises to my chest as I run my fingers along every choice.

If I didn't know I was in Hel, I would have guessed Heaven. The very thought makes me pause long enough to rid myself of it, refusing to think about my predicament. *Wherever* I am is already better than home.

The first year after my father's death was rough. I sold most of my dresses for extra coin, but the elegant ones I couldn't part with hang in the back of my closet, only enjoyed by passing glances and longing, but even those don't compare to the material that slips through my fingers now.

With Dora's help, I realized I needed to fit in with the town, and for the last five years, I forced myself to wear the same awful, rough material they did. My skin was so red and raw from the constant itching that Dora had to rub the soothing salve over my rashes for weeks.

I stop my admiration when it occurs to me, what if they don't fit? They don't have my measurements, and if this is Minthe's closet, there is no possibility they'll fit me. Her hips are curvy, but she is still much smaller than I am. Then again, given how little clothing she seems to wear, this likely isn't her closet.

Still, the urge to find the perfect dress gnaws at me, my dull, lingering headache pulsating with the need. I can't pass on the opportunity to wear something so beautiful. The light hues of the blues and turquoise are lighter than I would typically choose, but considering my only other option is rags on the washroom floor, I can't be picky.

Finding the deepest color amongst them, I pool the dress on the floor and step into the center, slipping it up and over my shoulders before walking to the mirror propped in the corner. There are so many gilded accents around this place, it's almost too much—*almost*.

The dress hugs my body perfectly at the waist, the skirt flowing loosely to my feet, matching the hanging pieces down my arms. I don't know which ones to pin or leave, but this is what I enjoy the most. It's been years since I've had the freedom of ripping, cutting, sewing, and decorating an already beautiful dress to fit my own style. I can't destroy this one, but I'm certainly going to make it more unique.

Taking pieces meant for the hips, I toss them around my shoulders and across my chest, creating an X, and pin the remainder behind my back. Rolling the skirt up to my knees, I pin one side with another golden pin, wishing they were brassier to complement the pale blue, and let the other side unfold to cascade down my leg.

When I'm finished, I look at my reflection in the mirror. The skirt is sheerer than I expected, hinting at my tan legs, but not enough to see the healing cuts from the trees. I twirl around to make sure everything is in place. When I reach my face, I blink and step closer, sure I'm seeing things.

My eyes. Flecks of gold pepper the purple, making them brighter and more vibrant. It must be a trick of the mirror. The crystal light hanging above my head is casting off the gilded edges and reflecting onto me.

Before I can contemplate the obvious explanation or another dress, I turn and leave. The empty hallway continues to beckon me one way, and I realize that I have no idea which direction or which room dinner is in. Taking a chance, I walk to the first normal-looking door and knock.

No answer.

"Hello?" I call.

Again, no answer.

I try the next door with the black knob. *Locked.* I continue through the next eight doors with no luck until I count back to the room I woke in.

It turns out there was no need to count back at all. When I reach it, I trace my fingers along the letters etched into the door: *Kore.*

It looks rushed, like someone quickly took a knife to the cherrywood to be done with it, but it also feels permanent. Hermes said they were expecting me, but for how long are they expecting me to stay?

With no one else around, I slip into the room and rummage through everything, not knowing what I'm looking for. Whoever designed this room shares my love for deep colors and the night sky. Twinkling constellations plot across the walls and high ceiling, creating the essence of sleeping outdoors under a clear night.

Having time to examine everything closer, I notice the dusty residue lingering in unfinished swirls, like someone haphazardly wiped the surfaces only moments ago.

Nothing but blank notebooks and pens fill the nightstands. The vanity holds the basic makeup powders and floral perfumes that I never bothered using back home because they sweat off too quickly.

The dresser holds nothing but nightdresses, and the bed has been changed and remade since I left, with no traces of blood or dirt. I drop to my knees and lift the covers, finding nothing but empty space.

What did I expect? A book explaining everything that happened in the last day? A note that tells me why I'm in the Underworld surrounded by Gods? I've pinched myself enough times to know this isn't a dream or nightmare, at least not a sleeping one.

As I'm about to leave to try more doors, something glistens on the bed. A note pinned to black fabric:

Hecate washed and fixed your dress. Dinner is across the hall, five doors to the left.
-Dionysus.

I lift the dress to see it in perfect condition. How she knew the length and the details like the slit to the right thigh is unbelievable considering I cut it off at the river.

Bracing myself, I take one last look around, promising that whatever happens today, I will find a way to take those heavenly furs back with me.

With nothing left to do but face these Gods and demand answers, *nicely*, I follow the note's instructions and find myself in front of a peach door with a fork handle.

Before I can open the door, footsteps come from behind me.

"About time, Little Bat." Hermes looks exactly like before, no shirt and a white wrap around his waist, except his hair is damp, and his wings are cleaned and bandaged. "Do me a favor?" He holds the door open for me, giving me a crooking grin. "Bring that refreshing attitude to dinner. I'm up for a little entertainment tonight."

"Not sure you can handle my type of entertainment, considering you dropped me from the sky. I'd rather not see what my attitude earns me at a table full of knives and—"

With what little I've explored of the home, I never would have expected the mess that I'm greeted with, or the simplicity of it. It's intimate, with bare walls and a long dining table, and there's so much food that I can't understand how ten people would eat it all, assuming all the chairs are to be filled. The chairs contrast in style and size: a winged-back, red velvet one that looks relatively comfortable sits at the head, a reclined chair to the right where Dionysus sits, and Minthe, across from him, is in a seat that seems made of glass given the way it shimmers. The smile she offers appears genuine as she takes in my outfit, and I consider that I might have misjudged her.

"Kore!" Dionysus calls. "You can sit next to me." He pulls a chair out for me, and with no other offers, I oblige his request, a little wary of his rapture.

Hermes takes the seat directly across from me, offering a reassuring grin. It adds little comfort when my chair is the exact opposite of comfortable. It's taller than the others, putting me on full display. The back curves out in a way that it doesn't make sense to have one at all, and where my bottom rests is only a thin piece of fabric hanging between two pieces of wood.

I open my mouth to insist I swap seats when the door opens again.

The air changes when he enters the room, warming instantly. He looks to be the same size as Hermes, but he carries himself differently—taller, confident, with no hint of that playful charm Hermes possesses.

No one else seems to notice the shift in energy. Dionysus resumes his conversation with Minthe about something I can't concentrate on, while I watch every step this man takes until he finds his seat at the head of the table. He hasn't even looked in my direction, hasn't noticed the stranger sitting at his dinner.

I might have questioned if I was dreaming, might have questioned my sanity, might have questioned my belief in the Gods, but the moment he finally looks at me, I know I've locked eyes with Hades.

Chapter Nine

DORA

Kore's window is unlocked, just as I knew it would be. I hoist myself onto the ledge, knowing the exact spots that don't creak, before stepping down onto the stiff mattress and making for the closet.

Swan keeps watch outside, urging me to be quick before someone comes searching for Kore. It was safer to stop here to gather food and clothes for our long trek ahead rather than risk getting caught passing through town to the House of Prayer, the priestess temples, for a few robes and rations.

Finding Kore's lavish dresses takes a little longer, but necessary, because I would rather sell my soul than wear the scratchy material she wears to fit in with the locals.

There are a few perks of being a priestess in training, one of them being that we, along with the priestesses, are treated like the Gods themselves. Every town wants to clad us in their richest fabrics and feed us their finest food to impress the Gods we serve and speak for.

It's my own personal Hel that I'm forced to hide them under my training robes to appear as simple and pure as the rest.

I eye the violet dress hanging in the back of the closet, the beads begging to be let out of the shadows. My sigh is light but holds enough weight that Swan grumbles again for me to hurry.

It would cause too much attention, the dress. And it had, the night I borrowed it and found myself under a cute boy from a neighboring town, but that doesn't stop my ache to free it.

A throat clears.

Right. The beige one will do. My hips aren't as wide as Kore's, so the material bunches around my middle, but my chest is generous enough that I don't have to adjust it any further.

The curious *brat*, as my mother calls it, can't be contained, though. One look back at Swan has me grabbing one of the burlap dresses and holding it out to her, just to see her reaction.

"I'm not wearing that." The appalled look she turns my way has my internal giggles working my core.

"We can't draw too much attention to ourselves." I straighten my face and shake the rags for her to take, making myself sound desperate for her to understand.

We stare at each other for a minute before Swan shakes her head, knowing exactly what I'm doing. She jumps through the window and is at the closet, faster than I would have thought, without making a sound. "I'll pick my own."

I try not to look impressed while reminding her to make it quick and simple.

Faster than she came in, her cloak and gown are off within seconds. It takes me twice as long to realize I'm staring, only when her grin lifts and she asks, "Have you never seen a naked woman?"

A warm flush colors my cheeks. "Women, yes." I swim nude with Kore all the time, but "Goddess? No."

The peach dress slips over her golden hair and full figure, filling out Kore's dress perfectly. She can't be hidden by a cloak, what made me think a dress would fare any better?

Tossing her a clean cloak and hairpin, I avert my attention to Kore's collection of untouched books.

"You weren't modest before. Don't pretend to be now." She tosses the cloak to the side and picks up the one with Kore's blood.

"What are you doing? You're going to ruin that dress." Gods, I sound like Kore, but she does have a point.

"This one has her scent on it. I'll be able to find out who exactly wants to find her, and I'm not carrying it around all week."

When Swan told me about the reward for Kore, it took everything in me not to find that tree again and dig deeper to search harder for her. Gods, nymphs, sirens, and all creatures will be after her to collect it. Even mortals who know who she is will be able to give her over for anything they wish. Whoever is offering such a reward holds enough power to promise *anything* in exchange for Kore. The question is why?

When I asked, I was met with a muted glance, but I know Swan knows more than she's letting on.

The door springs open, and Metanira storms through, her furious glare aiming right at me. "What are you doing here?"

My tongue suddenly weighs of lead, searching and failing for a reasonable answer. She's usually too drunk to hear me sneaking in.

"Kore ran away, and we're going to look for her." Swan's blunt answer has me questioning what in all the stars is wrong with me because I hadn't considered to simply tell the truth. Lying is as natural as breathing; it always has been.

"She ran away?" Metanira takes a step forward. The hope threaded behind her question startles me more than her presence. "Where? How?"

"She stabbed two guards and ran into the forest, where I believe she fell into an entrance to the Underworld."

I want to strangle the Goddess for being this forthright with a mortal but find myself both admiring her honesty and speechless by Metanira's lack of skepticism.

"If you find her, tell her not to come back," Metanira snarls, her shoulders back with that air of superiority I loathe. "I don't need her tarnishing my reputation any further."

It's hard for me to hate anyone, but Metanira is one of the select few, and hearing her harsh words in person has my nails biting through my palm, deepening the divots I made earlier. "Excuse me," I manage to keep my tone light, though it slips past gritted teeth that reveal my true feelings. "But how can you say such horrid things? She's your daughter."

"No, she isn't. Anything you don't take is going to the orphanage by the morning."

"Do mirrored fates mean nothing to you?" I blurt the words without thinking, the cursed phrase getting her attention—*both* of their attention—Metanira flinches and Swan's head whips toward me.

"How do you know about that?" It's Metanira who voices the question they share.

Having a mother and a Goddess stare at me makes me want to vomit, but I lift my chin and feign confidence, another lie that comes too naturally. "I know about your deal with the Triple Goddess, but it seems you forgot, so let me remind you. Your child's fate is mirrored to Kore's, which means if Kore dies, so does your child. If Kore is tortured, your child equally suffers. If you abandon her, your child will know that rejection. Every. Single. Thing. you've subjected Kore to, your child has had to face."

The color drains from Metanira, her rosy cheeks turn ashen, her green eyes dim, and that superiority levels to that of a mother who was just reminded of the worst mistake of her life. It takes a moment for the initial shock to melt into a cold hatred that ices over her voice. "You know *nothing*." Her hand rises.

I ball into myself to avoid the strike.

"Stop." Swan's calm command stills the room where not so much as a breath is heard.

The blow never comes. I've seen enough visions and have soothed enough of Kore's bruises to know the strength behind that hand, the hand that's now frozen in the air.

"This was rather unnecessary." Swan's head tilts with a concentration as she continues her seductive order, "Go back to crying in your bed and mourn the loss of *both* children. When there are no tears left, you'll go to the orphanage and offer your home to them, and you'll treat them as if you loved them more than your own. You won't *ever* strike another child or let harm fall upon them. Do you understand?" She waits until Metanira verbally confirms, growing still and vacant at the instructions. "Forget we were here."

When Swan releases her arm, Metanira leaves without another word.

Seeing visions of the past is an incredible gift that I thank the Gods for every day, but Swan's ability is breathtaking to witness when I'm not on the receiving end of it.

My heart is still racing as I thank her, keeping a few steps between us.

"I'm not your friend. We just didn't have time."

"If we did have time, you would have let her hit me?"

"Violence is boring." Her impassiveness leaves no room to interpret any real meaning, but it's a statement that lets me breathe a little easier, knowing I'll be spending the next week by her side.

A knock sounds from somewhere in the house. We both freeze, hearing another knock, harder, demanding to be answered.

"Go away!" Metanira yells, her voice thick, her footsteps echoing farther away.

"Open up, Metanira. We're looking for Kore."

Silence.

"Metanira! Your daughter hurt a lot of people tonight. Open the door."

Her sobs grow fainter, trailing off with a click of a door.

"If you don't let us in, we will have to resort to more damaging measures."

A tug on my arm brings me back to the room. Without speaking, Swan motions toward the bag on the bed and the open window, nudging me to go first.

As lightly as I can, I hurry across the bed and hoist myself over the window ledge one leg at a time.

"Dora?" A familiar, pretty face is inches from mine, bewildered as he looks over my shoulder to Swan, then back to me. I offer him a small wave, the same motion that led me under him last week.

Before I can think of an excuse, Swan pushes past me, tackling him to the ground, with her hands wrapped around his cheeks. "You saw nothing. You will climb through the window and report that you searched this house and found no one here. You will forget you saw us. Go."

I jump down before the servant begins climbing in, his pretty face in that frozen trance.

"That really is impressive." Not that I want to find myself iced over with forced obedience again. "But was that necessary? He's a friend. I'm sure—"

"It was obvious what kind of friend he was to you, and we didn't have time for you to sweet-talk your way out of it." She rises to her feet, hunching over to catch her breath.

Even prickled with irritation, I can't stop myself from caring. "What's wrong?"

No surprise, Swan waves me off, straightens herself, and walks away, still panting at a slow pace.

Across the way, we find Adonis changed and pacing near the trail.

"Finally! I grabbed apples, tarts, cheese, and bread from the kitchen. It should be enough." His nervous energy heightens my anxiety, but as much as I worry for Kore, a selfish part of me is excited to finally make the hike to Mt. Olympus. People have climbed it over the years, claiming there are no Gods or palaces, but the myths must come from some form of truth.

Adonis stays two paces ahead of us while I glue myself to Swan's side the rest of the night and well past the rising sun. So far, we've managed to keep conversations to a minimum, not for my lack of trying. I ask any and all questions that pop into my head and tell stories I've made up just to see their reactions, which are annoyed groans from the woman at my side and utter silence from the focused man leading our way.

Adonis' silence isn't entirely unusual. He doesn't speak unless spoken to in front of those he isn't familiar with. A trait I carry for authority, and authority alone.

Throwing his hands in the air, Adonis whirls back. "Is this really happening?" he asks. "I mean, belief or not aside, how does Mt. Olympus help us find Kore? If she's in the Underworld, shouldn't we be going down, not up?"

I can't recall a time Adonis spoke about his beliefs. Everyone knows mine, and it's easy enough to guess Kore's, but Adonis always remains neutral, listening to the stories I tell but never adding his own opinion when Kore and I debate the topic. Kore tries to hide that she isn't a believer by claiming the questions and debate are good practice for a priestess in training, but I've always known and never once judged her for it. The irony though...

106

"Do you not trust me?" Swan answers his question with her own.

"Trust you? I don't even know you."

My mouth gapes, hearing the slight snarl in his voice. He isn't easily riled unless he's losing a game or a bet, or at Kore for speaking harshly toward Meg. I rather enjoy watching him unravel a little.

At Swan's attempt to grab his shoulder, he shrugs away and stalks off.

With a poised smile, Swan shouts, "You'll learn to trust me."

I can't help but wonder if she's ever been rejected. I'll admit I've craved her hands on me since she bumped into me at the market and caught me before I could topple over. I was so captivated by how soft she was that I hardly recall what happened after. And as much as I fear being under her control, I'd risk it.

His little outburst must have been the key to unlocking those tight lips, because she begins explaining veils, how the heavens aren't in the clouds, and the Underworld isn't really under the ground, how they're worlds of their own, layered on top of each other. It's baffling to think Kore could be standing next to me in another veil. None of the books mentioned veils, and a part of me feels betrayed in some way. Books have never steered me wrong.

Adonis doesn't acknowledge that he heard any of it and keeps his quick pace. I know what's going through his busy mind. Myths were becoming reality, and talking about it is unfathomable, like we're kids dreaming up stories together.

It isn't until midday that we finally reach Athens. With every passing traveler, my heart flutters as I offer a small wave and smile, to Swan's annoyance. "I thought we weren't supposed to get noticed?" she mocks me, but I smile and wave all the same.

The fact that I resist the urge to stop and speak with every stranger, to touch their arm and see their story, is an accomplishment no one seems to recognize. The visions don't always come, but that never stops me from trying when the opportunities present themselves. I can't help it. Traveling with my mother and the other priestesses never allowed me to venture far from the carriage or temples. Being with Kore was the one exception, and that was because I lied through my teeth, telling my mother I was convincing Kore into becoming a believer and maybe even a priestess one day. As if I would ever put my friend through what I endure. Kore has her own Hel with Metanira.

When I see the layered city closing in, the alluring chaos of buildings and busy people, I quicken my pace with an extra skip. There are wooden homes built on top of stone structures, connected to brick buildings, which are attached to white temples. It's like a horrible quilt of overlayered patchwork.

Women lean out of windows to hang clothes on lines high above the tight alleys below, and I'm even more in awe at their lack of fear of heights.

I pass Adonis, entering the glorious mess at the mouth. The town buzzes with life around every corner. Women of all ages walk up and down the streets and alleys with little clothing covering their bodies. Kids play games on the sidewalk with coins and sticks. Men walk in and out of buildings, stumbling over themselves, some latching onto a few girls or laughing amongst other men.

I lead us right down the crowded night market, with tables lined along the streets and carts scattered between them.

I inhale the unfamiliar yet inviting aromas of cooked meat and spices. It smells like all the perfumes were sprayed into the air at once and mixed with sweat and lemon. Farther in, I crinkle my nose as the scents thicken with stale meat and apples.

Somewhere close, a soft voice sings along to the slow, sweet tune of a string instrument. When I turn my head, I hear drums off in the distance.

"Dora, please slow down," Adonis calls after me, but I can't. There's too much to see.

I find a table with sticks stabbed through pieces of meat in neat rows. The markets in smaller towns never had cooked meat, only raw, for buyers to cook for themselves.

Another table is layered with tobacco and pipes. A smaller one holds jewelry for body parts I can't imagine jewelry being on. My fingers graze the glistening metal just as I'm spun around by the shoulder, bringing me face-to-face with Adonis. His brows knit with alarm. "I don't want to lose you too. Follow her."

He steers me into line behind Swan, with him right on my heels to keep me from turning back. Unlike Swan and Adonis, who hurry to get out of here, I have a hard time not stopping and gawking at every little detail, which slows us to a baby's crawl.

It's the table of books that makes room for guilt to nestle its way into me. How could I wander a town mindlessly and forget about Kore and the reason we're here in the first place? Maybe my mother is right; my lust for life is going to get me into trouble.

Swan stops before a hanging sign that reads *Hypnos Hostel*. I'm not even close to being tired, not in a city waiting to show its history. Just seeing that lively market has my aching feet numb and ready to walk right back into it.

"I'll get the room. You two stay put." Swan starts toward the door.

"I can pay for a room," I insist, grabbing the sack of coin from my bag.

Adonis snatches the sack from me, shoving it back into my cloak. "Do you want to get robbed?"

"Don't bother." Swan wiggles her fingers. "I can manage."

Before she can so much as look away, I toss the sack that she's forced to catch. "Don't you dare cheat them out of money." I've never sounded so stern. "You may not understand, but this is their business. Their livelihood. They can't manipulate people and get what they want. They work for their money. Pay them properly."

"Huh," Swan tosses the coins between her hands. "I've never had to use these before." With a light chuckle, she tucks it into her cloak and disappears into the hostel.

I move to follow, to make sure she doesn't use her ability on them, when Adonis steps in my way. "What are you doing? Why are you going at it with her? I need her to get my tattoo removed. We need her to find Kore. Your entitled attitude isn't going to help us here."

"I'm not..." I'm at a loss for words at his harsh tone. "I'm not entitled."

"You are. You have no idea how hard it is for me to shut my mouth and not ask my own questions. To stand still and remain passive. You may not understand this, but I'm still a slave that you all call a servant. I'm still marked, and any outburst, no matter how small and in front of the wrong person, could get me imprisoned if I'm not being accompanied by Kore's family."

"I'm sorry, Adonis. I didn't think—"

"No, you didn't, because you don't have to," he hisses.

I hadn't noticed how dark and heavy his eyes were. He rubs them with the back of his hands as if realizing it too.

"I'm really sorry." I swallow the lump in the back of my throat. I hadn't been considering him at all. I never had to before. And calling himself a slave? All servants are paid, making them no longer slaves, but perhaps I've been naïve to think that changed anything.

"No, I'm sorry." Adonis lets out a heavy sigh. "It's not your fault. I'm... I don't know what that woman did to me, but I'm getting glimpses here and there, and I remember Kore looking at me like she was scared of me. And then I have all these cuts." He holds out his arms with the scattered nicks that match the ones on his forehead.

"I remember birds, maybe," he adds, running his hands through his curls with a deep exhale. "I failed her too many times."

"How?"

His head jerks as if he forgot I was here. "It's just... When they said she was set to marry, I felt like I couldn't do anything but let it happen. It made sense that she got to have a better life. And then she was picked for the sacrifice, and I still couldn't do anything. And now she's lost, Gods know where, and I still can't do anything. I'm fucking useless."

I throw my arms around his waist and squeeze, feeling every single word he speaks as my own. "We will get her back," I promise.

My hands start to tingle where they land on his back. My chest thickens and grows heavy, making it harder to take in a full breath. Hopelessness, guilt, and... resentment?

I pull back before the visions begin.

"I don't know what to believe, but I trust *you*. I know you didn't choose Kore at the sacrifice." His fists clench at his side. "Swan grabbed me and somehow made me go with her, and I know she did the same to you. And I hate that we're with her right now. That somehow, we're trusting her."

"She can make you trust her."

He stills. "How do we know what's real? How do we know what we think and feel is real and not her manipulating us?"

"Don't let her touch you." I'm not sure myself, but I can't let Adonis know how uncertain I am. I've been under Swan's influence before and have forgotten about it. The fact that I'm aware of what's happening tells me this is real. "Just think, Kore's probably sneaking into whatever kitchen she's nearby and stealing their wine and chocolates." I chuckle, trying to lighten his mood enough to rid him of the twisted conflict.

His grin doesn't meet his eyes.

"First room on the left," Swan says, dangling a key between her fingers.

Adonis snags it, ignoring her attempts at asking us what's wrong. And for once, I don't answer, giving her a taste of her own medicine.

The room we follow Adonis to holds one bed barely big enough to fit two people if we cuddle together, a small cot, and a washroom without a door. By the time I take it all in, Adonis is already lying on the cot with his hand flopped over his chest and his feet dangling over the edge. Even if he managed to win an argument against Swan or me for the bed, his feet would have been hanging over.

Swan and I eye one another. "I know you want to go." She motions toward the door. "Go ahead."

"I can't." Guilt eats at me for being excited about something while Kore might be trapped in the Underworld, and I really shouldn't leave Adonis alone with Swan.

"Too bad." Swan clicks her tongue. "Athens at night is one Hel of a time." Feigning a yawn, she settles back on top of the covers. "A bouncy little squirrel like you would likely get caught in some trouble anyway. It's probably best you stay put."

It's true. I shouldn't chance getting caught up with a stranger in a town I know nothing about, but I can't stop that itch to look around.

Dropping the bag, I sit on the corner of the bed.

"Why are you really here? And I don't mean the whole *helping Kore* excuse. It's obvious you wanted to find Kore. You wanted her to drink that Ambrosia to help her. You want to hide her from those who wish to use her or collect her as a reward. But *why?*"

111

"Why do you need my motives? Is it not good enough that I'm trying to help your friend survive? That I'm helping your other friend escape slavery? That I'm willing to help you? Did your little visions not show you anything useful, or did they only show you that silly story you graced us with at that ridiculous sacrifice?"

I shift uncomfortably, and it isn't just because of the lumps in the mattress. "I don't pick what I see."

The Goddess doesn't look convinced. "You claim to know who she is, so you can assume who sent me to retrieve her. Yes, in exchange for these to be gone." She waves the golden cuffs through the air. "But by the way you ask questions, I don't think you do know who she really is, or you would know why I really came for her." The challenge she holds as she leans forward raises the hairs on the back of my neck. "Tell me, Pandora, what exactly *did* you see about Kore?"

I shift, adjusting my posture to appear more relaxed, but this is Kore's specialty: ask questions, lean back, and let people talk about themselves. What would she do with someone who doesn't want to talk about themselves and provokes questions right back?

The truth is all I have.

"I saw Gods," I answer. "And I saw you, Aphrodite."

Chapter Ten

KORE

A crown of fire hovers over Hades' tousled, onyx hair, a lock falling above his dark brow. For a King, I'd have expected it to be slicked back or at least brushed, but not him. Even his clothes are strange for a royal, lacking color or any extra adornments that flaunt wealth.

His black tunic opens down the front, revealing the ink across his chest and neck. Where his sleeves roll at his elbows, more ink trails to his fingers.

I can't look away from it—from *him*—completely captivated by the God that could have entire towns worshipping at his feet from the mere sight of him. Hel, I had without even knowing what he looked like. And now, every indecent thought I've had in that temple flickers at the forefront of my mind.

And those eyes… There are no wrinkles like an ancient God would have. How is it they hold both the bright teal of a clear morning and the darkest blue of the night sky, the shallow waters of a stream, and yet the depth of an ocean? The statue didn't capture the vibrant intensity they possess.

I'm too lost in them to realize the glare they hold or notice the way his lip curls in a silent snarl.

Glancing down at myself, I don't find anything out of place, nothing that would earn me such agitation. Perhaps I shouldn't have made the dress so unique after all.

Hermes kicks my leg under the table, pulling my attention away from the glaring King, mouthing for me to eat as he nibbles on a piece of bread.

"You decided to grace us with your presence after all?" Hades' husky snarl matches his appearance. I meet his glare again, confirming his question is meant for me. "I hope you enjoyed your nap while we waited for you," he adds, the dark mirth raising my hackles.

"Says the man who entered last?" On instinct, I squeeze my thigh and bite my cheek hard enough to feel it *pop* and taste blood.

Mind your tongue, Metanira's warnings play as a reminder I'd do well to heed now, if ever before.

At my remark, Hermes chokes on his drink, his shoulders shaking in sync with Dionysus, who covers his silent chuckle.

I open mine to apologize when Hades cuts me off with a single look. "Being *King* is demanding, though I don't owe you an explanation."

My insides are an active war, slicing through the cocooned parts of me that want to stay quiet out of survival instinct, battling to smother the other parts that are bursting free from years of suffocation.

His tone and the subtle twitch under his right eye snap my back straight, refusing to let him intimidate me. "And yet, you just did."

Gods, why can't I just shut up and eat? Smile and say thank you for the food? Be the polite lady I'm supposed to be in line of hostility? But I'm tired of hiding, tired of playing by rules I never agreed to, and I can't deny enjoying the rush at calling out his hypocrisy, both exhilarating and terrifying.

God or not, I've done nothing to earn such distaste from him. It isn't like I came here on my own free will.

I tear myself from his lure, which is harder than it looks, but it seems to break some of the tension.

Throats clear and hands fly in every direction over the table, grabbing from the large spread without a care. Dionysus takes bites of everything before he sets them on his plate, and no prayers or thanks are said before Hermes sips from his soup. There doesn't seem to be a custom for eating, then again, do Gods pray? Hermes joked about praying to Mother Gaia, the mother of all life, but I can't tell if he was fucking with me.

Even though there's a mix of scents, it all smells incredible: the assortment of fish on silver platters, the variety of cheeses scattered about, two large pots of soup, rye and sourdough breads, fruits, vegetables, olives, and nuts.

"Do you not eat?" I still at Hades' voice, his tone forced, suggesting he doesn't want to be talking to me at all.

Before I can search for another snippy comment, Hermes saves me. "She's never been around Gods or a water nymph before, Hades. Let her take it in." His charming grin and light tone should be reserved for those who earned it, not this asshole King.

Dionysus places his second plate in front of me, layered with a little of everything just like I would have served myself. "He's really not as horrible or as frightening as he wants you to think," he whispers at my shoulder.

"Oh? And why would Hades want me to fear him?" I ask as he sets a bowl of soup next to my plate and checks to ensure my cup is filled. His attentiveness is warming me up to him quicker than I would have liked, but my guard remains high. I still don't know or trust any of them.

My focus remains on the food instead of the God I can feel bearing into me, like a hunter assessing if the prey is even worth the stalk.

"The better question is, why aren't you?" Hermes counters, popping a grape in his mouth, watching me with new curiosity.

"Fear should be reserved for what's known. I don't know him; therefore, I don't fear him." I meet Hades' glare once again, the unspoken word hanging between us, *yet*.

My answer isn't a complete lie, it's just, the type of fear trickling inside me isn't something I can pay attention to, or my cheeks will turn as plum as the wine.

"What do you fear then?" Minthe has been so still and quiet, I forgot she was here at all.

"This soup for starters." I spoon the murky liquid, letting the lumps of meat fall back into the bowl with a *plop*. "What is this?"

"Tortoise soup," Dionysus answers, taking a spoonful from his bowl with a hum of pleasure.

Hermes shudders across the table, sending Dionysus into a fit of laughter. "Hermes isn't a fan since he was forced to kill one to make Apollo's lyre."

The winged God pushes his bowl away with utter disgust. "It wasn't any tortoise. She was mine, and I'd prefer if you wouldn't bring it up so casually."

I bite the inside of my cheek to keep from smiling too wide at Hermes' fit, harder when his attention turns to me. "I recommend not telling that one anything you wish to forget." With a quick jut of his chin, he points at Dionysus. "As impossible as it is to believe, his mouth is bigger than his ego."

"You know what's even bigger?" Dionysus reaches beneath the table.

There is no stopping the flush that rushes to my cheeks or my awkward giggle.

"He's talking about his dagger." Hermes visibly struggles not to look amused, failing when he sees me struggling to hold back a laugh that bursts free.

Crack!

The tip of a dagger slams next to my plate, the man holding it sporting a crooking grin as he twirls it and waits for me to express how impressive it is. And it is. This isn't a small blade wasted on a simple slice of a throat. The sharp edge glistens, curving like a snake ready to strike. "Don't let any man tell you that size doesn't matter."

As our laughs die, an ache clenches deep within my stomach, and I spoon the soup around again. I haven't felt these hunger pains in years. Since it doesn't leave a physical mark, withholding food had been Metanira's favorite form of punishment when my father was still alive, favoring the physical ones more after his death.

I've become an expert at squirreling away rations and eating small bits throughout the day to keep from binging myself sick, but with the festival, I had been too busy to eat.

"It's not poisoned." Hades' attempt at assurance isn't promising.

I was so lost in thought, I probably looked as disgusted as Hermes. "I didn't think it was." I let the spoon drop and take a bite of a sliced apple instead, savoring its crisp sweetness.

Hades shakes his head with a knowing, shadowed smirk. One I'm not sure he would be capable of unless it held the dark undertones it does. A sight that has my chest quiver before remembering how disagreeable he is.

"Nothing is poisoned, love." Dionysus leans into my ear. "He's just messing with you."

They wouldn't have gone through all this trouble of bathing me, dressing me, and feeding me just to poison me. If they wanted to kill me, they've had plenty of opportunities, like when I was sleeping, for starters.

Hades stands abruptly, holding his cup in the air, followed by the others. Out of defiance, I cross my arms and watch, more curious for what kind of toast he has in mind, until a foot knocks mine under the table again.

It isn't until I lift my chalice just as high that Hades speaks quickly and in a different language, followed by the others drinking in unison. I hesitate but comply, watching Hades' satisfied smirk lift with every passing second I hold the cup to my lips. My instincts tell me he was just seeing if I would follow orders, testing me.

There is something familiar about the taste, though, like sweet strawberries and honey. *The vial.* The metallic flavor is missing, but there's no mistaking this is ambrosia. I drink until my cup is empty, and before I place it back on the table, it fills again.

My hands shake as I bring it back to my lips, needing more, drinking so deeply I'm practically licking the bottom to get every drop, like my body is starved for it.

"To life and death and those in between, I drink for you as well as for me," Hades says, startling me back to the present, to the world outside of the dry chalice. "It's the original language."

Fucking Styx. "Oh." Regretfully, I place it back on the table, farther away this time, without looking to see if it's filled again. A temptation I don't need. "That's... pretty."

Gods, where's a pillow so I can smother myself? *Pretty?* The phrase was moving, inspiring even, not pretty.

"Can I ask..." I continue while I have the courage, clocking Hermes from the corner of my eye, giving me an *of-course-you-have-a-question* shake of his head. "Why am I here?"

Hades doesn't answer. Instead, he shifts his attention to Hermes, who answers his unspoken one. "She was chosen as the sacrifice."

Clinking silverware cuts through the sudden silence.

"Sacrifice?" Dionysus looks between everyone for an explanation.

"A few towns participate in human sacrifices since the freeze," Hades answers, the tension in his jaw shifting like he hates the taste of his own words. "They believe that's why it ended."

Considering he holds titles such as the King of the Dead and Keeper of Souls, he doesn't appear elated by the brutal tradition that sends more his way.

"And they chose you?!" Dionysus' voice jumps, incredulous with a hidden mirth that lifts the corners of his mouth, while he picks at his plate. It's a familiarity that makes me smile, feeling a kinship with him while I tear a piece of bread.

"I kind of thought maybe that was why I was here."

"No." Hades' reply is sharp. "Tell me exactly what happened."

Everyone looks at me, waiting, but the words are a tangled mess in my crowded head. I'm not sure what he wants, so I briefly explain being chosen, running away from Artemis' arrows, and the vial Swan had given me, omitting any mention of a reward. Hermes jumps in to explain how he saved me from the beings in the forest.

"Do you often drink what strangers give you?" Hades asks on the edge of annoyance.

"So far, it's been *this* wonderful beverage, so I think I'll make it more of a habit." My mocking smile has him narrowing that scowl, and my hands clenching at my impulsive tongue. My body reacted as it always does when I forget myself, but I roll my head as if I'm stretching out a kink to cover up the flinch, taking another drink for show, while equally savoring every second it lingers on my tongue.

If anyone notices, I can't tell, except maybe Minthe, who stares at me a bit longer than polite. The woman is hard to read when she remains so still and impassive.

"Do you know who played Charon?" Hades continues his interrogation.

I shove another piece of bread in my mouth to avoid the question. I can't lie to a God, can I? It's wrong, but giving away Dora feels worse.

"Who was it?" he demands, sharper this time.

Why does he keep doing that? Talking to me so coldly and clipped, like he hates me, making everyone stare at me for answers I don't have or want to share.

After over-chewing, I have no choice but to swallow. "It doesn't matter who it was."

"Tell me who picked you, Kore." My name on his lips makes me pause long enough to curse myself for the unbecoming reaction. One that has me leaning into my agitation just to hide the flush I feel creeping up my neck.

"Shouldn't you already know? I thought Gods knew everything. Or is that just another deceiving myth, along with your kind hearts and polished charms?"

Hermes chokes again on whatever he's eating, covering his silent laughter, something Dionysus fails miserably at with his glossy eyes and rosy cheeks, a laugh that pinches my heart with how genuine and childish it is.

With an exasperated sigh, Hades drops his head and pinches the ridge of his nose before running his fingers through his hair. How the sight brings me more joy is beyond me, but being under his skin feels so damn good, a dangerous place, but one I'd willingly tempt to see him unravel a little more.

"It was her friend," Hermes answers as the wings by his ears flap. "Pandora. Goes by Dora."

A pinch of betrayal washes over me.

"Is that true?" Hades points his question toward me, wanting to hear it directly from the source.

I confirm with a low hum, my glare glued to Hermes, who at least looks apologetic. I really shouldn't care that he outed my friend. We don't know each other, and we don't owe each other anything, but I mistakenly thought he was on my side. My misjudgment doesn't stop me from ignoring Hades to ask Hermes how he knew about Dora.

"I told you I had birds watching you."

"For how long?" I sound as demanding as Hades.

"Long enough." Hermes' smirk leaves my mind spinning about all the things that could mean, all the possible things he could know about me.

"Long enough for what?"

"I told you she had a lot of questions," Hermes tosses the remark to Hades, who looks like he would enjoy bathing in the fires above his head rather than continue listening to our banter.

At the thought, those flames flicker, pulsing with a newfound warmth, but Hermes doesn't seem to notice. No one does. I, on the other hand, savor the warmth on my flushed skin. If there is one thing I love more than pretty dresses, it's heat: a scalding bath, the sun at its peak, the way my body fumes with it after a long run.

"You'll meet with me later," Hades quickly tells Hermes, then stands, nodding toward my full plate. "You should eat," he orders more than suggests. I suppose a King is used to telling and not asking, ordering without question or defiance.

Because my belly is begging for food, I tuck my defiance and refrain from any further remark, taking a bite of salmon.

Hades walks around the table, letting his full frame intimidate the room, or at least me. No one else appears as affected by his overbearing presence.

"Since you have questions and I don't have much time, each of us will tell you a riddle. If you guess it right, you can ask one question. If you get one wrong, the game is over."

He looks unusually pleased, as if I've already lost, probably betting this will end before it begins, but I'll make him regret underestimating me so quickly.

Before we begin, I take a sip of soup. I manage to swallow before my eyes water, and a fit of coughs erupts from my chest. Someone pats my back as I reach for the ambrosia to clear my throat.

"There's too much pepper!" I shout, finally able to breathe.

"Is that not what mortals like?" Minthe tossed her hair behind her shoulders.

"In small amounts." I continue sucking down air.

Dionysus roars with laughter. "You've spent enough time in their veil. How did you not know that?" Minthe scowls at him before shrugging her shoulders.

She did know. Maybe I hadn't misjudged her after all.

A throat clears, and we all looked to see Hades pacing at the other end of the table with his hands behind his back. With the lit iron

120

chandelier above and the candelabras flickering behind him, his tattoos darken, shrouding him with a cunning grace I can't look from.

With confidence, I straighten my shoulders, ready for anything they throw my way.

"Some try to hide, some try to cheat, but time will show we will always meet. Who am I?" Even though his back is to me, I hold the rest of the table's attention, waiting until his focus falls on me before smiling and answering sweetly, "Death."

I've heard this riddle at the market one day, when kids were playing next to my table, trying to outsmart one another, but he doesn't need to know that.

His brows crease. "What is your question?"

"Why am I here?" I repeat the same one I asked earlier.

"Because you fell through an entrance." That pleased look has my hands curling around the chair's arms to keep from jumping out of it.

"That's not fair. That's not a real answer at all. I know how I got here. I asked why. If you're going to evade my questions like Hermes does, at least be smart with your words."

Hades steps come to halt, his head cocking back, but I don't find that same glower he's been giving me all night. He looks... surprised, challenged even.

Hermes straightens himself against the back of his chair, but nothing can break the growing tension between the King and me. "I can be cracked. I can be made. I can be told. I can be played. What am I?"

"You are not a joke." Hecate's small figure skips to the seat next to Hermes, plucking the vine of grapes from his hand, and popping one into her mouth. "Is it my turn? I love this game."

"But I didn't get to guess that one."

"Blame Hecate." Hades raises and drops his shoulders with his small win.

One to one.

Hecate beams as she starts, "What is always old and sometimes new, never sad and sometimes blue? Never empty but sometimes full—"

"The moon!" I shout before she can finish. I've spent many nights staring up at it, tracking the cycles, colors, and closeness. Since I was a child, I waited for the night its size grew so big that it looked like I could run straight ahead and touch it.

Hecate gives Hades an impressed nod, the half-smiling scar making her appear more grim. "Ask away, princess."

I take a moment to think. There are too many questions to ask, but one that stands at the front of them all. "I..." I stammer, unsure if I should bring attention to the reward, but equally needing to know. "I was told there was a reward for me. That people were after me to collect it. I'm not sure what question to ask to get an actual answer here, but I want to know about it. About who would do such a thing and why."

"Oh, that reminds me. I almost forgot." Hecate tosses Hermes a small velvet bag that sounds like coins clinking together.

"Technically, I carried her inside." Dionysus reaches for it, but the sack disappears with a flick of Hermes' wrist.

"Please," Hecate scoffs. "Hermes flew her in from the bone-yard. He didn't jump or carry her in himself because his wings were injured."

Dionysus' jaw moves like he wants to argue, but I cut him off before he gets the chance, "Is that the reward?"

Hades motioned for Hecate to remain silent, his heavy gaze back on me. "Do you feel special for being sought after?"

"No," I don't hesitate to answer. "I feel confused precisely because I am not."

Again, that look of surprise crosses his stoic façade.

"It was a bet we all made long ago," Hecate assures me not to worry. "It's not the reward you speak of."

Those flames intensify once more, and although I'm not sweating, my skin is savoring the warmth a little too much. I'm not cold, but I can feel my body reacting as if it were, peaking in places I don't want to draw attention to, my spine tingling, my breath growing heavy.

"Unfortunately for all of us, you are special." The way the fire flickers above Hades' head makes me aware of just how wrong the statue at home was. It doesn't show the intensity behind the strange blue scowl or the vein that throbs in his neck when he clenches his jaw.

"Leave us," he orders, without taking his hate-seeping stare off me. Knowing we are about to be alone sends a spike of something right through me, something I quickly push down—way, *way*, down.

Too quickly, the room empties, but not before Hermes softly kicks me, *good luck.*

"Play nice, Hades." Hecate sings back before closing the door.

"What is your problem with me?" I cross my arms, feeling a little free now that I don't have a chuckling audience that mistakes my biting comments for comedy.

"You're emotional and reactive, for starters."

"And you're cold and insensitive."

His head tilts with a slight grin that teases the whites of his teeth. "Is that so?"

"What is with the riddles? The dinner? The toast? Glaring at me all night? Is this some sort of game?"

"A test."

"Oh Gods." I toss my head back. "If I have to claw out every answer from you, I'm going to claw your eyes out with them."

"Are you threatening a God? A *King*?"

I scoff, my laugh holding no humor. "You like that title, don't you? You've reminded me multiple times of your position of authority. I'm familiar with men like you because God or King, you're still a man. You thrive off power and reminding those lower than you that you're more important than they are. You're ignoring my questions and enjoy seeing me lost and confused because it allows you to have something over me. I'm not going to play your games, *King*. If you're not going to give me answers, I'll find them myself."

Hades leans over the table, gripping the edge like it's all he can do to keep himself from climbing over it to throttle me. "You're *my* prisoner," he says through gritted teeth. "You're in *my* Kingdom. *My* veil. *My* home. You're eating *my* food and sitting on *my* chair. And guess where you'll sleep tonight?"

My insides quiver, the involuntary images flashing before me. My fists clench as tight as my toes. He can't mean...

"The bed under *my* roof. You've heard of Tartarus?"

I don't have to nod for him to see the confirmation as terror is likely painted on my face.

"Good. Because that's where I could send you. With the worst offenders, Gods, monsters, and mortals alike. I will send you there if you don't behave."

I stand from the chair with enough force that I accidentally knock it back. "What could I possibly be a prisoner for?"

My core trembles with fear, and something else I don't want to acknowledge when that shadowy smirk appears. "I haven't decided yet."

"What's stopping me from running away?" The thought was meant to be internal, but my mouth speaks before I can think straight.

"I hope you try." He shoves his fists into his pockets and settles into his chair, kicking his feet onto the table. "Chasing you would be so much fun." He studies me, like this is a game and it's my move.

I want to comment on how un-king-like he looks, but think better of it. "I..." My mind races. "Can we make a deal?"

"You're in no position to make deals, Kore."

"I don't know about that. You're pretty hospitable to someone you claim is your prisoner. And you happen to know something about the reward for me. I'd wager you need me and whatever makes me *special* for something. And I can easily refuse whatever it is you want from me. Unless we make a deal."

Hades' chuckle is anything but friendly, and it has my full attention. "I could stop feeding you. You're becoming a Goddess, which means you're immortal." He stops, his brows pinching together. "Are you ill?"

I'm in Dionysus' chair, two forkfuls of salmon into my mouth by the time he asks the question. It takes restraint not to use my hands to shovel more food into me before he can make good on his passing comment. "You obviously don't know me well enough to think that's a threat."

"The look on your face, and the food spilling out of your mouth says otherwise." He pauses again to observe how slowly I eat, unaware of the control and effort it takes not to scarf down everything on this table.

He sighs with resignation. "What is the deal you were thinking?"

"I want my friends to be safe. And my... Metanira."

"The ones who betrayed you?" His dark brows crinkle. "Why would you want to help them?"

"I care about them."

124

He appears to be mulling over my explanation while slowly taking in my dress again. When his eyes find my neckline, his jaw clenches, looking away too quickly. "Gods can't interfere too much with mortal lives. I can't guarantee anything."

I bob my head, taking a bite of cheese and popping in a few olives.

"I won't starve you, so you can stop gorging yourself preparing for it." When he looks away, I'm sure it's because he's disgusted. "Hecate insists you learn about your gifts and our histories. Don't mistake my kindness for naivety or weakness, though. If I want you in chains, I'll put you in them. So long as you behave, you can roam free. But you will help me when I need it."

I have no idea what kind of help the God of the Underworld would need from a mortal supposedly transitioning into a Goddess, but with Tartarus being the alternative, I agree. "Of course. But do you have specifics on what *behave* means?"

His lips twitch. "You'll know when you don't."

I raise my hand over the table. "It's a deal then." He accepts it into his own, and I melt from his warmth. "I might not even try to run away."

Every part of me screams to fear this man, but something about him and the way he looks at me with challenge lures out a side of me I thought I could keep hidden away.

His hand tightens. "Don't take away all the fun, little deviant."

Chapter Eleven

HADES

There isn't enough patience.

I take that back. I've had a divine level of patience for centuries, fraying over the past two decades with every year I couldn't find her, and within an hour of having her, the woman shreds my remaining composure with that bladed tongue of hers.

My head falls back to the edge of the steaming tub, large enough to rival a pond, the night replaying on a loop. Every quip, glance, and move.

I let myself take a breath, because she's here. *Finally*, she's here.

A low groan leaves my throat at the dropping heat of the water, hexed to know precisely what I need. But I don't need to cool down, I need to burn away the fleeting thoughts that continue to consume me, no matter my attempts at searing them away, starting with her perched on that ridiculous chair.

It had been irritatingly difficult to look away from her on display, like an offering laid out just for me, one that fell right into my lap.

Fuck. I send my flames to sear away the image of her heated stare, the scowl that could send grown men running away, and put the worst of them on their knees.

Kore is here for a reason, I remind myself, and I don't have time to let my mind wander to unnecessary, *forbidden* thoughts. The years of planning and oaths, waiting for this very moment can't go to waste because she's enticing to look at. Or because I recognize her voice.

Prayers play in the back of my head all day, but I would recognize that voice anywhere. It's usually begging for me to take her, and I'm confident she never meant abduction.

The first few times, I didn't pay it any mind, but something about last year had me paying attention, something about it had me pulled to the door to hear a little clearer.

The pleas had become more vivid with that whimpering voice telling me exactly what she wanted me to do to her. I felt the hesitation behind every word, but she didn't hold back.

There is a reason I threatened her with chains at dinner. I needed to confirm my suspicion, and while she gasped at the mention of Tartarus, when I mentioned the chains, there was a subtle part of her lips, a bob in her throat, and the violet of her eyes turned molten, overtaken by the black center.

The begging I heard earlier tonight had been my favorite, because for some reason, she got off on thinking I was a furious God that she needed to seek forgiveness from.

She has no idea how accurate she is.

It was supposed to be a once-a-year indulgence, listening to that voice, those fantasies painted so vividly for me. It wasn't supposed to be *her*.

My skin prickles at the sinking temperature of the water. I look to the night sky, trying to think of anything else, but even the damn stars are reminding me of Kore's dress. I hadn't recognized it on her at first. Like an inexperienced young God, I had been too focused on the parts that weren't covered by the too-thin material while imagining the curves beneath it.

When I finally realized whose dress she wore, it took every bit of willpower not to toss Minthe out of the room, but I'll never give the nymph the satisfaction of seeing her succeed in getting under my skin. So long as the little deviant ruins them the way she did today, she can wear whatever she wants. I'd give her the shirt off my back to see what she does with it.

The corners of my lips twitch.

The girl is so defiant that she can't even wear clothes the correct way.

My hand flexes beneath the water, begging to imagine all the ways she'll inevitably defy me, to remind me of those dark thoughts I'm certain she never told anyone about, to think of how she crossed her arms and dared to challenge my word with that squinty scowl. It would be an even better sight with my...

I submerged myself completely, willing the water to freeze over and leave me in here until my sanity returns.

She's just a tool. Who she really is remains at the forefront of my mind, a reminder I didn't foresee needing to keep so close. I only pray I get to use her before I inevitably break her.

She's nothing but a tool. My prisoner. A mouthy thing with a tongue so quick and sharp any blade would be jealous.

My hand betrays me, impulsively wrapping around the other traitor hardening between my legs.

One time, I tell myself and immediately think of the way Kore tried to sink into that chair before straightening her back like she caught herself being weak and refused to be so. It was cute, an attitude she'll need to keep to survive.

Every stroke is too gentle for what I'm doing, but I can't stop.

It was the flinch that she tried to hide by rolling her neck and drinking from her cup that had me pause to look deeper into her soul. But I couldn't, and that was even more fucking infuriating.

I can see everyone for what they are; their truth, their core, but with her... nothing. Not even a flicker that told me she was alive. But fuck if that flinch, that *raw* reaction, didn't have my cock jerk. I've never wanted to see someone so desperately, to know what caused such a response while relishing in being near someone unmasked. There's no façade with her. I may not see her soul or her past, but her emotions are painted so plainly on her face, written between the words that roll off her tongue.

My cock can't be strangled hard enough to make me stop now, every tug a sinful regret. It's better than the alternative, following that pull to show her how wrong she is not to fear me. I don't care what that little shit, Dionysus, told her. It might have taken twenty years of searching, but she was never safe from me. Finding her was inevitable, and when that tug in my ribs struck, I knew she had finally been uncloaked, that it was only a matter of time.

Never had I been so angry to be banned from the Mortal Veil, to not be able to grab her and jump back here within seconds. Instead, I reorganized my study to keep busy while Hermes and the others left to find her, racing because of their bet on who would get to her first.

I never considered that she would simply stumble upon my home by herself. Just thinking about her stumbling brings me to the edge.

I searched her face for any signs of *him,* but thank Mother Gaia, she's all her mother. Those huge doe eyes, dark hair, tan skin, but unlike her mother, she has violet eyes and a loose tongue. And curves. The golden chain that disappeared between the swells of her...

My breath grows heavier with the tightening of my fist, my pace quickening.

I hate her. I have to hate her.

In a perfect world, she would have shown up weak and timid, easily bendable, but she has a fire in her that's too wild to control—a fire I have yet to wield.

My abs tighten.

She's too emotional. Too reactive. Too impulsive.

Like with the dress. Did she know how sheer it was? Did she notice that I had to make the room hotter so I could stop staring at...

"Hades?"

I let go, stilling myself and regulating my breathing, both pissed and grateful for the interruption, mentally cursing myself for the sudden lack of discipline.

Relaxing deeper into the water, I call Hermes in, who enters and leans against the doorframe. "Do you remember anything yet?"

"Nothing that I haven't told you before." He shrugs. "All that came to me was Hera telling me to get rid of them. I don't remember placing them in those towns, and Hecate doesn't remember cloaking them, but she said it was definitely her who did. Apparently, Kore has a magic trail or something that smells of her type of magic."

Their lack of memories is grating on my growing impatience. "Why wouldn't either of you have told me about it?"

"We might have. If our memories were erased, it's possible yours were too. We might have all hid her there to keep her safe from Hera's wrath."

I shake my head. There isn't a chance I would have done so willingly. I wouldn't have trusted anyone but myself to keep her safe, if that's even the right term to use.

"It makes sense. Hera's psychotic, and if she found out that I disobeyed her by not killing Kore and Dionysus, I'd be in a cell, tortured, right now." Hermes lifts his chin as if realizing something. "Shit. She's going to find out."

He isn't due back in the Heavens anytime soon, so Hera's revenge will have to wait. If we play this right, he'll never have to return.

"Technically, you didn't disobey her. It may not be in the way she intended, but you did get rid of them."

"You know Hera hates my loopholes. Are you going to tell her the technicality warrants I keep my skin intact?" His face falls before his usual smirk finds its place again. "On second thought, don't say anything. She likes me better than you."

I almost laugh.

It's true. Hera doesn't favor me after I burned her garden to ash for calling me an incompetent king with no morals and necrophilic tendencies. She's behind all the disgusting rumors tarnishing my reputation, and usually I wouldn't have bothered to acknowledge any of them, but she had said it in front of children, Hermes being one of them, and my temper got the best of me.

For as long as I've known Hermes, he has a way of finding loopholes. It's why he's known as the Trickster God, never one to follow rules or orders. It's one of my favorite qualities about him, also why I avoid giving him any demands. The fucker would find a way to disobey it on purpose.

"Why is your friend, Aphrodite, involved? No Gods could see Kore, so how did Aphrodite manage to get her the vial? And talk to her? Why give her any ambrosia before returning her for the reward?" Every thought stumbles out of me.

"She's more resourceful than you think, but she wouldn't have wanted the reward. She's *his* prisoner and wouldn't trust him to pay up." I still don't trust the woman. Being someone's prisoner doesn't always mean you would defy the one holding you.

"Why is she with Kore's friends?"

Hermes' smirk deepens the dimple women bend backward to see. "You're beginning to sound like Kore with all these questions." Knowing to stand down from the look I give him, he holds his hands up defensively. "I don't know exactly why Aphrodite is with them, but I know she won't hurt them." I'm not convinced, but hold my tongue as he continues, "Kore's not *him,* you know. You don't have to hate her, or Aphrodite for that matter."

"I don't like not being in control of this situation." I'm hit with a sudden urge to rearrange my study again.

"Who says you're not in control? You're the one with Kore." That reminder gives me a slim taste of hope I don't often allow myself to have.

Hermes is right. Kore is here. Kore is mine to use, unless she decides to run. If she does, I'll only find her again, and I'll ensure it's me who does just to bring her back kicking and screaming and wrapped in chains. That sick part of me twitches at the thought.

I quickly change the subject to keep the traitor at bay. "I'm sending Minthe to find Metanira a husband." Thinking of that woman possibly being the reason behind the flinches Kore twitches with after every quip—the witty and frustratingly accurate quips—makes my blood boil.

Unfortunately, I'll have to wait for her soul to pass through the Underworld to see everything I can't from Kore's.

Running a stressed hand through his light curls, a gesture I'm all too familiar with, Hermes chuckles. "She's going to have her work cut out. Metanira adopted a ton of those kids from the orphanage today."

That doesn't sound like an awful woman, but my instincts are usually never wrong. "I need you to keep an eye on her. Ensure those children are safe there. And send birds to watch her friends."

"Why?"

"I want to know why Aphrodite is with them. And I don't trust Metanira." I give him the obvious answer. He doesn't need to know about the deal I made with Kore to keep them safe.

I didn't have to offer her a deal at all, but it's important she thinks she has a say in staying here, as if she chose to stay and isn't my prisoner. I made the mistake of dropping the word at dinner, and though fear is what I wanted, Hecate's reminder pulsed through my head.

When you were a prisoner, did you want to help your captor?

131

No, I didn't, and I escaped the first chance I got.

Her attempting to escape plays through my mind, of her cursing me as she runs through the bone-yard surrounding my home, the tattered dress...

"I'm still here." Hermes clears his throat. "You might want to add ice to that pond."

That's going to be a problem.

"I need you to watch Kore too."

"Gladly." I don't like that he agreed so quickly, but I need someone else to watch her that I trust, and I don't trust myself around her right now.

"Don't touch her," I grit through my teeth, knowing Hermes' habits. He's brought back more women than we have souls. The perk of living in the Underworld is that no one *willingly* stays long.

"We both know the questions that would arise if I did that." Hermes pushes off the wall, turning to leave.

Good. He better not forget it.

"Oh, and Hermes?" I call him back. "Tell me if she tries to leave. And if she does, don't stop her."

Chapter Twelve

DORA

Music flows through every narrow turn, the lively market swelling with spilled laughter, sizzling meats, and a cacophony of beating drums, plucked strings, and chants.

I tried to stay put, I really did, but it isn't in my nature to ignore my urges. Once Aphrodite's breathing leveled to a heavy lull, I slid out without looking back.

One hour. I'll only be out long enough to see a few visions and try a little food, returning before they even know I left.

The more I try to convince myself, the easier it is to hear the lie. I'm not sure how I'll part from the life this place breathes.

Everyone moves with such purpose, coming and going from the crowded doors up and down both sides of the street, browsing the tables and carts.

I've heard of taverns through warnings to never enter one, but the unmistakable music and chatter is like a siren song luring me in. Before I can answer the seductive calling, my mouth waters from the greasy aroma, drawing my attention back to the table I saw earlier. I give the short, sweaty merchant a coin and thank him for the charred meat.

Sliding a piece off the skewer with my teeth, juices drip down my chin, and— *Oh, Seven Gods.* The savory spices have me licking the back of my hand after wiping myself clean.

Leaning against the wall, I indulge in people-watching while finishing the heavenly meal, my senses overwhelmed by the flavors on my tongue, the quick-moving town, and the commotion rising with the heat of the night.

I watch as a woman wearing a loose, sheer dress takes a man in an alley and pins him to the wall, kissing down his neck. A small child holding a sticky bun runs from a larger child swinging a broom as a weapon. I find the source of the upbeat music, three thin men wearing tattered chitons sitting along the wall beating boxes with wooden spoons. A cup with a few coins overfills before them, welcoming payment. I drop a few in before heading farther down the alley, tossing the empty stick on the street where I see others scattered.

I make it two steps when a door swings open, missing my face by a hair. A beautiful voice filters out before the door closes too quickly, cutting off the elegant melody.

The men who walked out stumble through the crowd, except for one. He stands between me and the door, taking in my dark cloak, his gaze raking higher until settling on mine with a grin that speaks trouble without needing to say anything. "What are you hiding, doll?"

His friends shout for him to hurry up, but he waves them off without turning back, oblivious to the birds he set free in my stomach.

"Me?" I glance over my shoulder to make sure I'm not mistaken. "You'll have to buy me a drink to find out."

His brow cocks, drawing attention to his shining forehead as he props the door open with his foot. "After you."

The promise of a free drink never sounded so appealing. "And only if you make it two." I duck under his arm and understand why he's glistening with sweat. The place is more humid than outside, the air thick with heat that slicks my skin within seconds.

The man grabs my arm and leads the way through the dark, dank room, passing crowded tables and standing patrons holding mugs, golden liquid sloshing over the sides.

I'm disappointed to hear the singing stopped, but the sound of laughter, piercing banter, and the sight of people tossing dice and playing cards replaces that feeling with sheer giddiness.

As we approach a bar, I see a couple waiting for drinks, speaking with such expressive hands that I attempt to eavesdrop. It's so loud I can hardly hear myself think.

"Two beers!" The man orders, holding two fingers to the plump woman on the other side of the counter.

"Oh, fuck off, Jason." The woman waves a rag in his face, putting a smile on his.

"Come on, Sasha, it's for the girl." He wraps an arm around my shoulder and tucks me against him like we're old friends, smelling of lemon and pine.

Her suspicion sweeps over me. "Why are you wearing that big cloak, girl? You hiding something?"

Jason chuckles at his mirrored question, telling her she'll have to buy me a drink if she really wants to know.

I untie the knot at my neck and slide the thing off, a wave of fresh-*er* air tickling my skin glazing with sweat. "Better?" Without the added weight, I'm not sure if it's a question or statement.

"If I looked like you, I wouldn't be hiding behind anything, that's for sure." Sasha gives me a wink and sets two overfilled mugs in front of us. Jason reaches for one, and she swats him away. "Nah-ah. You said for the girl."

"What is it?" I ask, observing the frothy mug, the foam layered on top of the amber color. "Is this wine?"

The two look at each other with the same confusion I'm giving the drink. It doesn't look like wine.

"It's beer, doll." My middle tingles at the nickname, a much better and more fitting nickname than squirrel. "And you can't possibly finish two, let me take that for you."

Before he can touch them, I toss my cloak at him. "Hold this for me?" I smile sweetly, pulling the beer closer. I take a second to glance at others and notice many taking more than a sip, most of them taking it back all at once.

He gives me that *leads-to-trouble* grin as I tip the mug to my lips, growing more impressed with every passing second I gulp it down.

I am too. This thing is heavy.

I'm fighting for air, but I'm not going to quit. When I see the bottom of the glass, I slam the mug back on the bar, wiping my chin of what little spilled from the sides. I couldn't hide my panting if I tried, so I don't.

As I catch my breath, I understand why they drink it all at once. An icy rush spreads straight through me, making me feel more awake and alert, but my stomach is far too full.

As I reach for the second, Jason stops me with a light touch on my arm. "I get it. You're a badass. You don't have to slam two beers back-to-back to impress me."

"I'm not trying to impress you!" I'm not sure if I'm trying to convince him or myself. I don't *try* to impress men to get their attention, so I'm not sure why I am now.

"Well, *I'm* impressed." Sasha compliments me with a clap before tending to the other customers.

"How did you like it?" Jason asks. "You must, with the way you were going after that second one."

I was too focused on finishing the thing to get a good taste. "It was bitter. I usually drink wine, but—" A loud belch passes my lips, and I cover my mouth, my eyes wide, and my cheeks heat with shame. "I'm sorry."

His head tilts with a soft chuckle. "Beer will do that." His hand drops to the small of my back, pushing the second beer into my hands, and snags another when the couple next to us isn't looking. With a quick nod, he motions and leads us toward the empty seats in the corner.

We make small talk, telling each other the basics, and to my surprise, he isn't from Athens, just a friendly man who makes friends with barkeeps because it leads to free drinks.

"I don't know many priestesses who can chug beer like you." He surveys me again, as if seeing someone new in front of him. I have no idea how he finds more drinks to replace our empty ones, considering Sasha was adamant about not serving him, but I'm not going to question it.

"I didn't take my vows. I was in training, but I left."

"A rogue priestess?" He nods his approval, and it makes me laugh.

On one hand, I'm finally free of the priestesses and the responsibilities that come with becoming one. And that damn closet. Then again, my plan to change the corrupt town from within is now gone. The sacrifice, the orphanage, all of it will remain the same until someone weasels their way inside to make a difference.

"That's probably for the best. You don't strike me as a woman who likes being told what to do."

I laugh harder, truly, for the first time today. "I don't know many who do."

With the growing volume of the room, I lean closer to him, his knee brushing mine. "You'd be surprised. Some people don't like making decisions for themselves. It's easier to follow a crowd instead of starting your own."

That is the exact notion I taught Kore: stay the path, stay alive. The world's a dangerous place for someone like Kore, too willing to speak her mind openly in front of the wrong people, too headstrong and wild in a world that demands order and obedience.

After a few more drinks, my body feels lighter and my restless mind eases for once. Even the drinks taste less bitter and more like a strange honey.

"If you're not from here, why are you here?" I ask him. Something about this man is intriguing, and I want to get lost for a little while. It doesn't hurt that he's pleasant to look at. A man who looks like he's used to getting what he wants with the flash of that unruly smile, a wink of those hazel eyes, or a toss of his brown waves, who's wants are more particular because of it.

"Looking for something, I suppose."

"Not tonight." I give in to the alcohol's hold, brushing my fingers against his. "Let's just... escape the rest and just be."

"That's all I do, doll." He replaces our drinks with the full ones he takes from the men behind us when they aren't looking, an act that would have angered me had it been Swan taking advantage of them.

"To escaping." Our glasses clink, and the beer spills over the rim and onto the sticky table.

The chatter around us disappears as he tells me about his boat and dream of sailing around to all the mythical places that hold magical objects and creatures: an island with a witch, a golden deer, a cave of wonders, the golden fleece. He tells me how his family didn't support his decision, so he ran off to do it anyway, then learned of his father's death only days later. He had saved enough for a boat, but freedom living got the best of him, and the thought of going back felt wrong without his father there.

He speaks as if retelling a story that doesn't belong to him. There is no sadness or longing like someone who lost a loved one. "When I settled here, it felt right, you know? Great people. Great drinks. Even when I think about leaving, something keeps nagging me to stay, like the Fates wanted me here. At this place. At this moment."

Oh. I give him my best pining eyes. "The Fates brought us together then?" I giggle. "That's your line? Was the whole story bullshit or just the last bit?"

He gives my shoulder a playful nudge, that soft chuckle making him appear more suave. "I thought you were a priestess. You don't believe in such things as Fate?"

"In training," I correct. "And I don't like being lied to."

"It's a good thing I didn't lie. But I do believe in signs, Fates, and intuition. If my gut tells me to stay put, I wait and see what it has in store for me."

If that's true, I admire him for leaving home and doing what he wants. Such is the way for men, and I would be lying if I said I wasn't a little jealous.

His smile slowly lifts, coloring me with another flush as he leans in. His lips are so close I could stick my tongue out and lick them, an impulse that disappears when my elbow knocks my mug into my lap, spilling the beer over my legs.

Rather than jump up to clean myself off, my gaze remains on the empty glass. Maybe it's the alcohol that has me feeling brave, but my smile widens as I insist, "Let me get the next two."

He pushes out of my way, and before I can change my mind, I find a small empty spot along the wall and lean against it for a better view of the tavern, thinking of how Jason had waited until no one was watching, timing himself perfectly.

I have enough coin to buy both food and drinks, but I've never been someone who can pass up a challenge. Perhaps it's not that Jason is a man but that he risks to get what he wants. He goes after it without worrying about the consequences. I like that. I admire him for it.

My stomach flutters as I scan the groups of patrons, searching for the perfect targets. Most hold their mugs closer than their coin.

There. Two women repeatedly turn around to watch men play card games at the table next to theirs, leaving their drinks unwatched. I wait a few beats, sensing the pattern.

As the women turn their heads again, I move, my pulse racing as I slide my fingers through the handles and quickly spin to leave, but the glasses are too heavy, my palms too sweaty. My fingers slip.

The women jump to their feet, frantic and covered in beer.

"What the Hel?" The blonde one glares at where I'm frozen, hovering over the table. "Were you trying to steal our beer?"

"I'm sorry, ladies." Jason apologizes, grabbing me gently by the shoulders. "My wife here is blind and got all turned around. Go to the bar and tell them to get you two more on my tab, it's under Lev."

With no other options, I pat around his chest and shoulders, pretending to make sure I have the right man in front of me. He grips my waist and pulls me against his side like I belong there.

I take in a sharp breath as his lemony-pine scent hits me again.

From the corner of my eye, I see the two women studying him with interest, as if his *wife* isn't here at all. I'm about to snarl, but I'm not really his wife, and I'm supposed to be blind.

"Thanks, Lev," they say, winking before they leave.

"Rule one." His whisper tickles my neck. "Have a realistic plan. Rule two," I feel his lips brush against the dip of my ear. "Always have an escape plan. And rule three," His finger crooks beneath my chin and lifts. "*Wife,* never use your real name."

His eyes fall to my lips and mine to his. Warmth spreads along my skin, growing sensitive where his finger traces beneath my jaw and along my spine.

"Do you live nearby?" I don't care how needy I sound, especially when he flashes that *nothing-but-trouble* grin that makes my heart throb.

I shouldn't do this. It isn't like I've never had a one-night stand. I snuck out years ago, too curious to keep myself pure. It was over too quick, so I tried again and again, determined to understand how women find it so pleasing.

This man screams experience. His very presence promises pleasure. "Follow me." His hold drops from my waist to interlace our fingers, leading us toward the exit.

We make it two steps when the room suddenly shifts.

All chatter fades as a low hum spreads through the tavern. Everyone grows still except the woman standing on the table in the center, the source of the light melody. The long braid trailing down her back has leaves swirling in and out as she sways her hips slowly, captivating every single man and woman.

"We have to go," Jason whispers, giving my hand a gentle squeeze.

"Wait, I want to see." I squeeze back, too intrigued by the woman and her soft, elegant humming, the way her eyes remain closed, feeling every note she sings.

A young blonde boy sits on the bench below, playing his lyre. He, too, falls into a trance with his own music. His eyes shut, and his body moves, living within the notes themselves.

Everyone remains unmoved, captivated by the two.

The hand in mine loosens, and when I look over my shoulder, I see Jason isn't watching the couple like the rest of the patrons. His attention is solely on me.

The rhythm slows, easing the room into a sleepy, seductive melody, and I sway to it. Jason releases his fingers from mine and finds my hips. His chest is hard against my back as he pulls me closer, matching my movements, movements I have never made but feel right with the sweet song and man behind me, guiding me through it.

His fingers press into my skin like I'm the lyre and he is the player, and when his lips trace my neck, something inside of me wakes at the connection, like when the visions come, only none appear.

The singing begins to fade, and my heart breaks a little with it. When the lyre plays its last note, the room begins to wake again. The boy and woman jump down, disappearing within the crowd.

"That was incredible."

Jason's breath is hot on the curve of my ear. "What did you like about it?"

"The dancing. The way they both looked like they were stuck in the music like they weren't even aware we were watching them."

"Do you like watching others play?" His voice thickens.

When my belly dips this time, I spin around to lock my arms around his shoulders, taken in by him as much as he is with me. No one ever looked at me this way.

Using the tip of his finger, he lightly nudges my head to the side. "Look."

The couple next to us kiss, gripping each other's hair and waists, bumping into the table. Another couple rips at their clothing, pressing against the wall as another argues in a corner.

A man stands abruptly. "What do you mean you fucked my wife?!" He slams the glass over another man's head, starting a small brawl.

Jason's hold slithers up my waist, gluing my body to his.

"I think something's wrong," I mutter, unable to take my eyes from the chaos erupting in every corner.

"This is why I said we needed to get out of here." His throat bobs with a soft chuckle. "I've been here long enough to see this happen every time those two play their songs. Every night ends like this, people saying things they meant to stay hidden, doing what they probably only fantasized about."

"Not you?"

He shakes his head. "Or you, it seems. Or so I thought, until you looked at me all longingly, like you wanted to take me right here."

There's no stopping the flush that rises to my cheeks. "Says the man whose hands were all over me, asking if I like watching."

"Says the girl who asked if my place was nearby, for what, exactly?"

"And the guy who pretended to be my husband, caressing me all lovingly?"

"And the woman who drank beers and tried to steal to impress me?"

"The guy who offered to buy me a drink in the first place."

"The girl who demanded it you mean."

"The guy—" He cuts me off with a fistful of my hair, pressing his lips to mine. I cling to his middle to steady myself as he pulls my head back and swipes his tongue along mine.

I have no words, which is just as well since I couldn't speak if I wanted to. My thoughts are scrambled into a hazy inferno.

He bends down and quickly lifts me up by the back of my thighs, wrapping my legs around his waist. It doesn't matter where he takes me, so long as he doesn't stop touching me, doesn't stop kissing me.

Maybe following the crowd isn't always a bad thing. No one here gives me a second glance. No one judges. No one is telling me what to do, what not to do, or how to do it.

I could walk out that door right now *if* I wanted to.

My arms lock around his taut shoulders, running my fingers through his chestnut waves as he sets me on the edge of a table.

Moans and groans rise around us, but I remain too focused on the man standing between my thighs, hiking my dress higher before dropping his clothes to the floor.

His muscles dance with every move he makes, and when he pulls me back against him, my body quivers with anticipation.

Again, he tilts my chin with his fingers, letting his tongue coax mine out in a way no other man has before. They were always too stiff and quick, but not Jason. He may have undressed us quickly, but he's teasing now.

While I'm focusing on what his tongue is doing to mine, I don't notice him unpinning my dress until his mouth leaves mine to tease lower, sucking in each bud. His steady hold keeps me from falling back.

"Jason..." His name comes out in a begging whimper when his tongue flicks. A noise that has him done teasing and lining himself against my entrance. Latching onto my lips, he drives into me with one quick thrust.

My moan catches on his tongue.

It hasn't been that long since I was with that servant, but the way he fills me feels like it's my first time all over again.

"Watch them, doll."

Them? I can't take my eyes off him. He could ask me to do anything right now, and I would willingly be an accomplice to murder.

His thumb runs along my jaw, bringing my attention to the rest of the room. Bodies are everywhere, naked, half-clothed, fully clothed. Some women are on their knees, others bent over, pushed against walls, ankles locked around hips. I've never watched others have sex before, and now... now I can't look away. Even the brutality of the few men fighting adds to the dangerous euphoria.

They are all beautiful. Taking what they want. Embracing the moment.

Jason retreats and drives back in, hitting a spot I hadn't known was there, my moans joining the lustful symphony.

Every thrust grows more wild, more demanding.

My hips rock to meet his, replicating how the other women move, how they take control.

When one woman lifts her leg above a man's shoulder, I follow, my back arching at the new depth he takes me. His hand wraps around my ankle, bringing it to his lips. It's so gentle compared to the rest of his merciless grasps and strokes.

My head falls to the side, finding a man who never looks away from where he takes his woman, like he's a sculptor creating his masterpiece.

The allure they have me in is ripped away when Jason cups my cheek and drags my focus back to him. "Eyes on us now, doll."

Every inch of my skin grows hotter; my neck that he peppers with kisses, my nipples his tongue rolls over, the spot he penetrates deep that shakes my core.

I spiral closer to oblivion, watching as he devours every inch of my body, lapping and sucking in places I didn't know were so sensitive.

"Do you like watching me play?" His dark hazels latch onto mine, and I can feel my insides melting, watching where we connect.

"Yes," I answer with a shaky breath.

His groan sends an intense wave right through me as I pulse around him. My hips rotate back into him on their own, pulsing with a need for more.

I'm still in the height of it when he stiffens and pulls out, a warmth coating my thighs and belly.

Both of us lie still, catching our breaths as the moans around the room die down.

"Was that...?" I can't find the right question to ask. I've never felt that spasm between my legs before.

His head lifts from my chest. "What?"

"I mean, I didn't hurt you, did I? I've never... That's never happened before." His brow rises, a look of realization settling over him as he tucks his head back to my chest, readjusting himself.

"Are you laughing?" I lift onto my elbows, suddenly very aware of how naked I am.

He looks at me with a grin that would send my knees buckling all over again if I were standing. "That's supposed to happen, doll."

"Why would no one tell me that?"

He finds a rag and wipes my legs and stomach clean. "I'm sure they didn't want a priestess to get too excited about something she would never experience, and some men are too lazy to get to know a woman's body."

A sigh of relief leaves me and I giggle, the shaky noise giving away just how embarrassed I am. Part of me is angry that this is the first time it's happened, but really, I'm more determined and excited to do it again.

"Wait here," he says, kissing my forehead before pulling his clothes back on and heading behind the bar.

He maneuvers around spent, lazy bodies, some still stuck in that euphoria I was in moments ago.

I take time adjusting my dress back into place, giddy when I see the steaming mug of coffee he holds as he tiptoes his way back. "I added milk and sugar."

I thank him and blow on it before taking a drink, closing my eyes, and moaning at the warmth and bittersweet flavor. When I open my eyes again, he's watching me with a curious expression.

I'm about to ask him about it when a purple dress catches my attention, leaving out the door.

This is my chance.

Dropping the coffee, I hop down and run after the woman, doing my best to ignore the soreness between my legs and the weakness in my knees. I'm still a little hazy from the alcohol and sex, but keep my focus as the need to touch that woman grows with every step.

If Jason is right, and this occurs every time those two play their music, they must be special, lower Gods, nymphs, maybe part siren.

The alley, oblivious to what's happening on the other side of that door, remains livelier than ever.

I pick up my pace before they make it around the corner.

"Excuse me?" I grip the woman's arm.

144

The images come too fast: A blonde man appears next to a river. Irritation. An arrow flies toward me. The man is running away. Hatred. Trees. Lots and lots of trees. A blonde boy and his lyre sit on the grass. Sadness, and then nothing. Pure emptiness like I've never experienced before. Lustful nights at the tavern sprinkle with small moments of contentment.

I pull away.

The woman looks at me with a blank expression as if she doesn't even see me. I can't make sense of the splintered images, but I mean it when I say, "I'm sorry."

The love, loss, pain, hatred, and sorrow that encased me for those seconds were so agonizing that a tear falls down my cheek. No matter how many times I've experienced others' emotions, it always feels just as raw as the first time.

"What happened?" Jason touches my shoulder, and I draw in my hand, realizing I'm still holding onto the woman's arm. "Sorry, wrong person."

The buzz of the beer is wearing off, and the guilt of witnessing this woman's pain weighs on me. Peeking into others' lives has always been a fun hobby. Invading others' privacy never bothered me, considering no one ever knew I was doing it, but there are rare moments when I see and feel too much.

"What's your name?" The blonde boy's question startles us both.

"Dora." The boy takes a cautious step closer. "I didn't mean to intrude."

"Dora?" Jason visibly tenses. "Like Pandora?" There's a hint of weariness in his tone.

"Just call me Dora."

His face sours, a look that has me taking a step back, confused why he would be so angry with me all of a sudden.

The boy's eyes bounce between us. "You're not from here." It isn't a question but aimed at Jason and me with a growing grin that's too mischievous. "Why are you here?"

Before I can think of an excuse to mutter, my mouth opens, speaking without permission. "My friend is trapped somewhere in the Underworld, we think. We're going to Mt. Olympus to save her."

Not again.

I clasp my mouth. "I don't know why I said that."

The boy smiles, and I know immediately who he is without having to touch him. I want to reach for his arm to see and feel everything about him, but I force myself to stand back. Touching a God is what put me in the mess I'm in now, and I'm certain he wouldn't want to be caressed by a strange woman in an alley.

"And you?" He juts his chin toward Jason. "Don't you have another bar to drink empty?"

Jason looks me over, his hands flexing at his sides like he can't figure out what to do with them. "I'd rather be here."

"With Pandora?" The boy belts a bellyful laugh.

"What's so funny?" I ask.

"Oh, darling, do you know the story of Pandora?"

"Of course."

"If you did, you would see the irony."

Pandora's story is simple: the first woman ever created, fell in love, married a Titan, opened a box that led to mass deaths because she was too curious.

Where is the irony supposed to be?

The boy rolls his neck, sensing my confusion. "You at least know the name Pandora is sacred? It's said those with her name are her descendants, forced to live the curse she set forth." With a deep sigh, he waves us over. "Follow me. You too, drunkard."

I don't have to be told twice. This is a once-in-a-lifetime experience I will likely never get again.

I skip a step, following the boy and woman down an alley. Jason stays closely behind me as we turn down one street after another.

We finally stop in front of a tall white temple, the top engraved with the name "Apollo." The God for healing, prophecy, and *truth*.

The very God that led us here.

146

Chapter Thirteen

KORE

I don't wait for Hades to dismiss me from the table before I retrieve my hand and take my unfinished plate to my room to devour it.

Part of me fears he'll make good on his promise and starve me, so I might have grabbed a few extra slices of bread and nuts to hide in the nightstand.

I'm not sure when I fell asleep, coaxed by the soft, warm furs I swear I'll never live without, but when I wake, my muscles ache in a way that feels... good. I lie in bed for hours, reliving the past few days, the conversations and riddles.

No matter how many times I look myself over, I don't see anything that makes me special. Aside from the gold in my eyes, nothing appears different. I'm still tan, my hair is dirty brown, my hips are wide, and my chest is still too full. My feet are healed, though, and my skin is clean of any cuts and bruises.

I don't *feel* different. My fingers are red with irritation from my anxious picking, and the need for balance remains stronger than ever. It's that need that had me provoking Hades at dinner, what had me mirroring the hate he radiated right back at him—*balance*.

Little Deviant, he called me.

I'm tempted to run away just to see what kind of *fun* made his hand squeeze mine with that daring challenge, and his voice drop to that velvety intrigue.

He obviously needs me, so it isn't death I'd face. He also didn't sound too keen on the idea of starving me, though I won't test that theory.

But I wonder, what *does* the King of the Underworld do for fun?

The unsettling feeling of being watched wraps around me. It's what prevented me from falling back to sleep hours ago, and since no one else is in my room, the only thing I can think of is that the stars plotted along the ceiling are little eyes spying on me.

A knock comes from the door.

I bring the covers over my chest, not wanting whoever it is to see that I was too exhausted to change.

Before I can call them in, the door opens and Hermes walks in, hair dripping onto the carpet. "Morning, Little Bat. You ready?"

I'm ready to scold him for being so careless, to tell him that I could have been naked, but the sight of his perfectly sculpted form has me snapping my eyes toward the wall, pretending to observe a painting of a half-naked woman emerging from a river. "Why do you insist on wearing nothing but that wrap?"

"Because Zeus won't let me run around naked anymore." He catches me glancing back at him, and that charming smile quirks up, taking in yesterday's dress when my hold on the covers falter. "Quit staring and change. Dionysus is meeting us in the library after your tour."

I can't leave soon enough. Between the heated irritation thinking of Hades and the entirely different heat Hermes provides, I need a cold bath and possibly a slap in the face to straighten myself out. A need I'm positive Hades would be too happy to help with.

The pale dress I choose glistens, like tiny diamonds, when the light caresses the blue fabric just right. The back cuts into a low V, so I wear it backward to let the high neck cover my back. I rip a sheer piece from the skirt and secure it with gilded, chain necklaces over the open V that now leaves my chest exposed.

It may be a little much, but no one seems to care for clothing here, and by the time I'm finished, I'm too proud to take it off. It's been so damn long since I created anything, since I felt a prickle of pride in my appearance because of it.

By the time I return, Hermes has made himself at home, lying on top of my bed with one hand behind his head and the other resting on top of his toned stomach. I can't fight the urge not to stare like a wanton, needy little mortal.

"You really like making things your own, don't you?" he asks, observing the unique changes I made.

"I do." I twirl, letting the skirt flare. "Dora says it's my way of controlling—" My lips tighten, embarrassed that I open up to him so easily, remembering how he betrayed me last night. "You didn't have to tell Hades about her, by the way. Not when I don't even know what happened. You didn't see her. She didn't look right. She was so confused and…" Guilt rushes in, thinking back to our last moments. I fall into the chair, feeling a Dora-sized piece of myself missing. "And Adonis…" The guilt is consumed by shame. "I ran away, knowing if I stayed, he might get his tattoo removed."

"You'll see each other again." Hermes looks as reassuring as he sounds, though I don't hold the same optimism. I'm a prisoner in the Underworld, with a captor who is sure to catch me if I try to leave. A captor who had even looked pleased to get the chance—practically begging me to try—or maybe that's my own twisted mind playing tricks on me.

"There's no sense in feeling sorry for yourself or them right now. Besides, my friend isn't fond of slavery, so you have my word that Adonis will be getting that tattoo removed without you."

Noting my confusion, he explains that Swan is Aphrodite, not knowing the panic it would cause. I immediately recall the story Dora told us at the sacrifice and how appalled Aphrodite looked when I said I would have blinded her for being jealous of Psych.

"Whatever myths you've heard are probably wrong," he quickly adds. "We spread them ourselves. Mortals believe what we want them to."

"Aphrodite didn't send her son to kill a girl and then kidnap her herself?"

The way his face screws tells me everything without him needing to confirm. "I did say *probably* wrong. Leave it to you to find the one myth that has some evidence to ring true," he softens his voice once more, and grabs my shoulders, crouching so his face is mere inches from mine.

The air stills, and where his skin meets mine, that familiar tingle startles us both, jolting me forward. My eyes snap to where our lips nearly touch, noting the tiny freckle just below his bottom lip.

Without pulling away, those sapphires drag from my lips to my eyes, his voice a little huskier than before. "I promise, I have my birds on them. If I could bring them here, I would, but living mortals do not fare well in the Underworld. I promise if anything looks bad, I will step in."

Still lost in the current that runs between us and unable to speak, I give a slight nod, hoping what he says is true.

His fingers fall to the chains crossed over my chest, his knuckles grazing the skin beneath the sheer material, thumbing the black ring.

When he looks at me again, it takes everything in me not to fall back into the chair. "These are not the dresses I had your closet filled with. Show me which one you've been using."

I keep my distance, needing as much space from him as I can get. When I take him to the closet Minthe showed me, he explains that it belonged to another nymph who no longer lives here, then leads us back to my room.

Obviously not needing the same restraint I do, he takes my hand and guides me straight through the tall mirror. The other side reveals a deep amethyst tub placed in the center, atop emerald tiled floors. The closet holds dresses in various deep colors and cuts, with a bowl of pins of different shapes, sizes, and gems. And lying on top of the chair in the corner are scissors, fabric, pins, and needles.

This is more my style.

What appeared to be a never-ending hall does end after all, leading to steps of what now looks to be a never-ending staircase.

Each floor we pass is unlike the one before it. One reveals a hallway with white carpet that leads to more doors, much like where our rooms are. Another level is a library, which is the tallest room I've ever seen, surrounded by balconies of books connected by ladders. My second favorite is the floor that leads to the room full of paintings, like an art gallery that I very much want to walk through.

The home itself never ends. As we continue to climb, I attempt to hide my heavy breathing, but the restriction itself makes me more winded, while Hermes takes each step with ease. I swear I see his shoulders shaking with laughter when I finally give up and release my unrelenting huffs and pants.

Before I can ask for a break, we stop. The door before us is engraved with *Hades*, the very God barking for us to enter before we so much as knock.

"Why are we here? I thought we were meeting Dionysus?" I was hoping not to cross paths with Hades again; in fact, I planned to go out of my way to avoid him as much as possible.

"Scared of Hades after all, Little Bat?" Hermes gives me a lopsided grin. "Don't worry, with you here, it shouldn't take long."

It's nice to know I'm not the only one who noticed Hades' hatred for me. I'm not sure what's real or what I've imagined when it comes to the callous king.

When we enter, my brows pinch. The room before us is not what I was expecting. Rather than a cluttered mess like the dining room, this one is organized and structured in such a way that makes my head hurt.

Two chairs are perfectly symmetrical before a fireplace with a small table neatly between them. The gray bricks that line the walls look to be the same brick repeated and plotted perfectly. The one wall that isn't made of bricks has rows of books and scrolls that are organized by color and size. The artifacts that are displayed on the shelves are probably organized in some particular way, too.

And then there's Hades. His hands are clasped behind his back as he looks at the books, and though I can't see him, I can imagine the stoic look of contemplation while deciding which one to choose.

With his back turned to us, I take the opportunity to look over his desk. It's massive, large enough for a family dinner. Papers are stacked neatly in one corner, a scroll splays out symmetrical to them too far to read, and a glass with a dark liquid rests in front of the perfectly centered red throne.

"I received an interesting letter this morning." Hades pulls a book and flips through it while turning his attention to Hermes. "I assume you know its contents?"

"I do," Hermes says with a note of apprehension, just as the door opens again.

Minthe enters, strutting straight to the desk, perching herself on the edge. This nymph has no care for modesty, and I understand why. She's stunning. Her top wraps around her chest, exposing her entire midriff, and her skirt is shorter than Hermes' wrap, so when she crosses her leg and begins looking over the stack of papers, it barely covers what it needs to.

The only thing that pulls me away from admiring her is Hades' fists tensing around the poor book. When it groans from the force, he returns it and stuffs his hands into his pockets. The air I didn't know caught in my throat eases, relieved that he didn't snap it in half.

"Who else knows she's here?" He remains deadly calm with a look that demands one correct answer. Hermes' weak shrug isn't it.

I suddenly realize that I don't know what their relationship is. I'm positive Hermes works for Hades, but there's something... *comfortable* about them. It's the way they understand each other through looks alone, answering questions that aren't verbally asked.

And Minthe? She sat next to him at dinner and is now half-naked in his study. They must be more than friends.

Hermes' voice rears back the strange bitterness that flares at the thought. "I've had birds out all morning. No one who came into contact with her has made it back to the Heavens. No one should know she's here."

Hades' head hangs between his shoulders, releasing a sigh that even I feel the weight of. When he raises it to face Hermes once again, Hermes answers the unspoken question, "It wasn't me." His palm covers his heart. "No loophole. No lies. You can order the answer from me right now. I'll swear it on the River Styx. I wouldn't save her multiple times to give her back to the woman who wants her dead."

Hades' shoulders slacken, but even with the crown of fire no longer in sight, I can feel its heat and the anger radiating off the God it's missing from.

Glancing between them, I muster the courage to ask, "Are you talking about me?"

Minthe smirks when I'm only met with Hermes' long, frustrated huff. "She's going to have to go."

"No." Hades turns on his heel and lowers onto the throne, a motion that shows just how calculated and controlled he is in the most mundane things.

The memory of learning about my arranged marriage resurfaces. The way these two talk about me as if I'm not here, making decisions and plans without including me. I step into their line of sight, planting my fists on the desk to get Hades' attention. "Tell me what is going on."

My finger might have flicked a few papers to scatter along the neat surface. *That* he notices.

The color of ocean storm that meets my glare has me pause just to take them in. "Hera knows you're here," Hades says.

His tone indicates I should be afraid, but that thought is replaced with something else when his dark gaze lowers to the chains across my chest.

"So?" I swallow the heated edge in my voice. "Aren't I your prisoner or something? Why would she care about me?"

Hermes and Hades exchange glances I can't decipher.

As they silently communicate, I notice something sitting on the ground behind the king. It's the only thing out of place in the otherwise perfect and orderly study, and I have to squint, blinking repeatedly because it's...

"Is that me?" I ignore Hermes' attempts to pull me back. Hades watches every step I take toward him, making no movement to stop me as I pick the painting up and see my own face staring back at me.

"The hair's too short," I observe out loud.

"And the mouth is closed." Hades' lips twitch like he wants to smile but catches himself.

I give him a vulgar gesture that earns me a rare glimpse at a genuine smile he can't hide, even if it vanishes just as quick. I force myself to look away before I struggle through another uncomfortable encounter with him. "Why do you have a painting of me?" I add more urgency to my question.

Before either can answer, Dionysus bursts through the door, his eyes smiling just as wide as his mouth. "Hecate is tied up, but she'll be here soon." He looks like a secret is ready to burst through him, but upon seeing the painting in my hands, he frowns, throwing his arms in the air.

"You told her without me? I wanted to see the look on her face when she found out we're related."

I spin my head back to Hades, who answers my silent question with a dip of his chin, reaching for the canvas still tight in my grip. When his fingers brush mine, I fail to breathe. A rush of heat sears straight through me, my flesh, my veins, penetrating my bones. It caresses not only my body but my mind, leaving a brand of ecstasy I'm certain I'll never be rid of. It's exactly what I felt last night when I shook his hand, only now I'm not overwhelmed with emotions and the heat of his crown to brush it off.

When our eyes meet again, they linger long enough for me to see the storm behind his darken just before the daylight blues burst through.

"This isn't you." His voice snaps me out of whatever the Hel that was. "It's Demeter." The name comes out as a snarl as he yanks the painting away, taking his cursing heat with him.

My follow-up question is silenced when Hermes' chest bumps against my back. I bite back the sigh and desire to fall further into him. "Your mother."

The words douse all fire that's ignited within me since entering this room. I step away from both Gods to regain control of my body that insists on betraying me at the most inconvenient times. Seriously, though, are they slipping something into my water, or does this transition come with a high dose of uncontrollable urges?

"*Our* mother." Dionysus happily adds, looking like a child being offered a bucket of treats after months of starving.

"No," I shake my head, gathering my composure. "My mother is Metanira."

I hate to burst his happiness, but Demeter can't be my mother. I would have known. My thoughts trail off when I notice the softness that wasn't on Hades' face a moment ago. It isn't pity, but the look startles me all the same. "Metanira is not your mother. Hecate is working on figuring out how you ended up with her, but Demeter *is* your real mother."

My throat feels suddenly tight.

I am not your mother, Metanira's favorite phrase. All the times she said it with those hateful glares come crashing down on me.

My chest begins to rattle with the battered pieces inside shattering into even smaller slivers. The woman I call mother, the woman's love I strived to earn, isn't my mother at all?

"Why?" My thought comes out in a brittle whisper. When my knees begin to shake, Dionysus jumps forward, taking my hand to lead me into the chair next to the desk.

"Listen." When he tightens his hold on my hand, a flood of ease washes through my mind, and a small sense of euphoria fills my veins.

"*Dionysus...*" Hades warns.

I bite my lip to keep from giggling.

Oh, Styx, am I... That can't be right. I only feel this elated and giggly when I'm drunk.

"It was only a little," Dionysus groans over his shoulder, kneeling so he's at my level. "I know how you feel right now. It was a few years ago when I learned all of this myself. Are you familiar with Hera and Zeus?"

"In myths, but I never paid much attention." I didn't think they were real. "Hera has been spiting Zeus' mistresses for centuries, but more recently she's been cursing Zeus' heirs. The ones he sired outside of their marriage," Dionysus continues, "When Demeter gave birth to you, Hera went to Hermes and told him to *get rid of* us."

"Being the genius God I am, I found a loophole," Hermes picks up where Dionysus leaves off. "I did get rid of you two by getting you to the Mortal Veil. Hecate cloaked you, making it impossible for any God to see or sense you. And for the last twenty years, you've been lost to everyone, including those of us who helped hide you because we erased our memories to keep you both safe. We're getting pieces back here and there, but we still don't have all the answers."

The air in my chest dwindles by the second. I can't think straight. This can't be right.

"What about the vial from Swan, I mean Aphrodite? Why don't I have abilities like all of you? Or—" I stop myself from asking why I'm not as beautiful as the rest of them, why I don't have the aura they do. It's not a glow but a pulse, an unmistakable energy that makes mortals seem so dull.

Hades' voice surprises me, when it seems like all he wants is to sit back and watch my reactions to this entire mess. "Gods need two things to live, ambrosia and prayers, both of which you have been without for two decades. From what Hecate says, you were close to becoming mortal permanently. We can all thank Aphrodite for giving you that vial of ambrosia when she did. As for abilities, they manifest with time."

He pauses, giving me time to understand. All the questions I had over the last few days are replaced with new ones, impossible ones I never would have imagined having. "Does that mean… Are you my uncle?"

Hades' laugh booms through the study before he stifles it with a cough. "Gods no. The original Gods were created. We have no relation to each other." He tracks my exhaled relief as I press deeper into the chair, secretly wishing it would smother me. I might have pushed the seat back a little, so it's no longer symmetrical with the other.

Balance.

"How do you know I am Demeter's daughter? Our similar appearance could be a coincidence." I don't believe what I'm saying as I continue rambling, "I don't have abilities like you all. I can barely walk up a flight of stairs. I trip over pebbles. This has to be a mistake."

Hermes glances at Hades, both grinning at each other and chuckling like this is all a joke.

"What are you laughing at? I'm serious. Your Goddess is probably still out there. Instead of focusing on me, you should be looking for her!"

"You're undoubtedly the lost Goddess, deviant," Hades says, tossing the painting of Demeter on the desk as an obvious explanation.

"Why is this so hard to accept? Do you know the people who would kill to be in your position?" Minthe gripes, still quietly leaning on the edge of the desk. "Hermes birds have been watching after you for years. If they say you're the lost Goddess, then you're the lost Goddess." The nymph throws her arms in the air before grabbing a paper off the desk and shoving it into my hands.

I take it, taken aback by her outburst.

"Your *birds* could see me?" I ask Hermes. For some reason, I hadn't considered that he meant real birds were watching after me, but a metaphor for his people or something.

"They aren't Gods, so yeah. At first, I couldn't figure out why they wouldn't leave you, but it makes sense now. I must have ordered it before my memories were erased."

An eerie sense of thanks and violation washes over me when I piece together that it's because of those birds that he was able to save me in those dead woods. "Wait, the birds that attacked Adonis by the river, that was you?"

Hermes' smile rises in answer.

"Thank you," I tell him, then remember all the times birds have followed me all these years. "The one that stopped me and Adonis...?"

Hades' head jerks in a movement that ends with him rolling out his neck.

"You didn't want to sleep with that moron, trust me."

"But you saw..." My throat dries. I was practically naked.

"Read the damn letter." Minthe snaps, motioning to the paper crinkling between my hands.

I do, needing something else to focus on.

Hades, thank you for finding our son and daughter. Bring them to us by the Hunter's moon. All Gods and Goddesses will come to welcome their return home.
-Demeter

I read it over a few more times, still finding it hard to believe any of this is real. Part of me thought maybe I would wake up back in my own bed and with the mother I know, back with Dora and Adonis, and the entire sacrifice would be over.

Dionysus plucks the letter from my fingers to read it over himself. "She'll probably want us to stay. With your *charming* personality, how could she want otherwise?" He snickers, nudging my shoulder.

I stand, no longer able to sit still. Back home, if things were too much, I would sneak out and walk along the forest and river to cool off. Pacing the study will have to do.

I make my way to another table set in the corner, covered in tiny figurines that move around what looks to be neat stacks of maps. An owl figurine stands by itself on one. A swan figurine, a lyre, and a lion are scattered along a second map. The third map is covered in many, but four stand out: a flamed crown, a white bird, a tiny cup, and a leaf huddled together on top of a drawing of a castle.

157

"You're not going." Hades' cold, authoritative order has me whipping back around.

I drop the crown figure onto the table, where it rights itself back to the spot I plucked it from. "What do you mean we're not going?"

How could he forbid me from meeting my mother, my *real* mother? Why tell me all of this to pull it out from under me?

"I said, *you're* not going. Dionysus will be there. He'll offer an excuse as to why you couldn't make it."

"What the fu— "I stomp back and lean over the desk, when I'm cut off by Dionysus. His tall frame blocks my view of the infuriating God behind him.

"Easy fireball." He lightly presses me back into the chair before I can push any further.

I let out a frustrated breath, followed by another. "Why can he go, and I can't?"

"That doesn't concern you." Hades stands over the desk where I had just been, his spicy cinnamon scent invading my nose, and the anger I felt seconds ago slightly dissipates.

"It sounds like it does." I shake the paper that requests *my* presence at him. "Is this what the reward is? Someone returns me to get a reward, right? Don't you want that?"

His head cocks to the side before lifting his chin so he's looking down on me. A *kingly* stance I'm sure he broadens because I push the title on him every chance I get. Everything else about this God doesn't scream king at all, except for the way he orders me around.

My amusement is overshadowed by the thoughts flowing through me. This could be my chance to have a real mother, one who actually loves and cares for me, one who doesn't push or slap me, one who doesn't starve me or arrange a marriage to be rid of me. This Demeter has already searched for me, wants to meet me.

In the corner, Hermes watches the exchange with a growing interest. Whether he is amused or nervous, I can't tell.

Hades' hardened features don't let up until I break the deafening silence with, "Well, I suppose I'll just have to change your mind."

The jerk of his lips, I expected. He seems to be intrigued—less hostile—when I surprise him, saying and doing things he hadn't anticipated, and I knew he was counting on me arguing back rather than relenting to his dismissive order.

It's the way he balls his fists and stuffs them into his pockets that I didn't expect. The pressed outline I catch sight of before he sits back in the chair that has my insides twisting with searing knots.

His hand runs through his raven hair, hair my fingers itch to run through if only to smooth it. "If you want to ensure the soup meets your standards, you can help in the kitchen tonight."

With a bowed head, my spine naturally straightens, molding myself back to the familiar, submissive role. Seeing Hades' toss me a look that's close to a glower, a look that has those tattoos on his neck seem ever so menacing, I shrug the posture off, refusing to be that girl.

"Everyone helps around here. We don't have servants in the Underworld."

"Even you, *King?*" I challenged, despite myself.

When his lips twitch this time, it's wide enough to see the whites of his perfect teeth, the points piercing the bottom one. "King is a bit formal for someone who's *prayed* to me as many times as you have." A cold sweat runs down my spine. "I can't cook despite my lack of trying," he continues as if he didn't just confirm he heard those nights my hands were between my legs. "But I try when I can."

Maybe he hadn't heard me. Why would he hear my '*prayers*' over the thousands of other voices? No, I shove away the thought. He is manipulative. He's just trying to get a rise out of me, put me on edge, make me squirm.

And he won. It's too late to hide the blush I feel burning my cheeks.

He motions our dismissal and returns to the stack of papers on the desk. "Oh, and avoid the gates. The lost souls have been wandering closer, and with her new scent, they'll try to breach them."

Hermes voices his understanding, but I don't. "Lost souls?" I ask.

"The beings that attacked you in the forest," Hermes explains, pulling at my elbow to follow. "They're the souls that won't move on. They're attracted to life. If we go closer to the gates, they'll swarm it. They try to claw their way into living bodies."

"They didn't try to claw into me. It, *he* only touched my chest."

Hades sucks in a breath, the first real reaction I've seen from him, aside from the twitches under his eye or the throbbing vein in his neck when I vex him. "Over your heart?"

"Yes," I confirm, wondering why he's tense. "He didn't feel angry or aggressive. He felt scared, but also hopeful. Is there a way we can help them move on?" The confusion the lost souls must have, roaming the forest, hoping for any sign of life to cling to.

Hades crosses his arms, his head tilting in a way that makes me regret opening my mouth at all. "We?"

He knows what I meant. "You're right. Shouldn't *you* do something to help them move on, *King*?"

"Why are you so confident that I haven't tried?"

"You seem like a man who works on bigger issues, letting tedious things fall to the side. It's easier to ignore issues when you don't have to look at them, but it doesn't mean they don't exist."

His eyes narrow again, this time assessing me with a calculated interest. "Have you played chess?"

I'm taken aback by the sudden change of topic but consider his question. I have seen the boards and pieces but never witnessed a game before. The setup looks like a complicated mess I've yearned to figure out.

"You'll play with me. Here. Every night after dinner."

Minthe's head swivels between us, just as shocked as I am.

What did I get myself into? I was trying to avoid him as much as possible.

"Let's go, little sister." Dionysus squeezes my shoulder.

Before I can get myself chained to the king, I follow Dionysus and Hermes out the door.

"And Kore," Hades calls.

I look back, finding Minthe glaring as Hades says, "That's a lovely dress."

Chapter Fourteen

DORA

The musty air greets us as we enter Apollo's temple. The God himself jumps on top of the center slab and begins rummaging through the laid-out offerings. The crisp bite he takes from an apple ricochets off the sacred sanctum walls.

"Take a seat," he insists, motioning to the chair near his statue further in. I can imagine the last person who sat in the rickety thing, seeking out Apollo for guidance and truth.

The statue depicts what the God should look like; a tall, handsome man. The God I saw in the woman's visions. The boy and the man hold the same light hair and eyes, the same crooked grin, and determined gleam, only I can't figure out how that man became this boy.

With no other seats, Jason crosses his arms and becomes one with the wall, uncertainty and concern set in his stern features, replacing all carefree lightness that disappeared the moment he knew my name.

"Why are you so young?" I ask, testing the chair before putting my full weight on it. "I know you're…" I motion toward the statue, unsure how Jason will react. Mortals say they believe in the Gods, but when faced with the real thing, they tend to scoff in disbelief.

"He knows who I am," Apollo assures, sinking his teeth into the apple again. "We're old friends, aren't we, Jason?"

"He saved my life *once*," Jason explains without any emotion, hinting at how he feels about that fact. Maybe his change in behavior has nothing to do with me after all and everything to do with crossing paths with this God again.

161

Apollo's childlike features light up. "I like to think it's an ongoing effort. Nevertheless, I look this way because of a curse set long ago. One I plan to break soon enough." The look he gives the statue is full of longing. To be a man trapped in a young body is a cruel curse, harrowing when love is involved.

"How?" I ask, unable to hide how eager I am to hear anything he has to say.

My question is met with a shrug before he visibly softens toward the stilled woman at his side. If I hadn't walked in with her, I would have assumed she was another statue.

"Why were you watching Daphne?" He ignores my question to ask his own, sliding his free arm around the woman's waist.

It's odd seeing the two together with such a height difference. It's like seeing a son embrace his mother, except the affection shining from this boy reflects that of a grown man. "You went away when you touched her arm. It was for a second, but I saw it. Where did you go?"

I feel the pull of his magic this time, like hooks digging and latching onto the truths before dragging them forward. The love, agony, and nothingness that had flown through me when I grabbed Daphne resurfaces. "I had visions of her life."

Again, Jason doesn't react, as if such a thing were common to say.

Apollo tosses the apple core over his shoulder. "Did you now?"

A small piece of me hopes that maybe he knows the reason behind this gift. The God of truth must know something, but when I attempt to ask, he ignores the question and asks another. "What did you see?"

I teeter back and forth on the chair as I tell him everything I know about Daphne, making sure to explain that the images don't always make sense. I feel the hooks of his magic ready to pull anything I don't readily offer.

"I see." His gaze slides to Daphne once more, caressing her cheek. She doesn't move from the statuesque position or pull her focus from the wall.

"Do you know what I am?" I try again. I'm confident I'm not a Goddess, but a witch, maybe. I've considered an oracle, but I see glimpses of the past, never the future.

"Like I said, those named Pandora are thought to be cursed. The history of Pandora is tragic, to say the least. One of our greatest mysteries."

"How so?" I listen on the edge of my seat, literally. If there was ever a story I wanted to hear, it's this.

"Do you know why Kronos had Pandora created? Everyone knows she was the *first* woman, but do you really know why?" He continues without me having to answer, "To feed mortal men's desires, or so they say." He chuckles once more at a joke I don't quite understand. "Men couldn't get enough of her, and of course, she loved it. That was until one of the Titans who helped create her became too possessive, too jealous that he didn't get to play with his own creation first. He filled the Mortal Veil with more women and tried to kidnap Pandora for himself, but Kronos found out."

The air in my lungs stills, my heart racing for the woman I don't even know.

"Kronos told Epimetheus he could keep Pandora, but only if *she* agreed to be his."

"And did she?" I ask. My excitement could easily be mistaken for impatience, and when he shakes his head with a knowing grin, I don't bother apologizing. "She didn't want just one man. She wanted all of them."

"She refused him?" I'm not sure if I should feel as devastated as I do for Epimetheus.

Apollo nods, eyeing Jason, whose brows remain pinched as he listens with more intent than I do. "He figured Kronos tricked him, so when Zeus and the Titans went to war, who do you think Epimetheus sided with?"

"Zeus." I should be glad for that because the Gods won the war and now care for and bless mortals. But Epimetheus had turned against his own kind, an act that reminds me of my own betrayals.

"And in exchange for his help in defeating Kronos and the Titans, Zeus gave him the bride he always wanted."

"What about the box?" I've been waiting for him to mention the infamous box.

Jason steps into my line of sight, continuing the story with concentration like he's trying to remember how it goes as he speaks. "Zeus gifted them the box as a wedding present, but Epimetheus knew not to open it. Because Zeus hated the Titans, he knew it was probably another trick of some kind."

"But Pandora opened it?"

"The box opened," Apollo answers. "All sin and disease spread to the Mortal Veil. The war was said to have ended, and Pandora and Epimetheus were never to be seen again."

When he pauses, I know he's messing with me, waiting to see if I'll beg him to finish. I'm not above it, but he continues before I have to. "There are rumors that claim Zeus has them locked away. Others say they're in the Underworld being tortured by Hades. Some say they've been hiding amongst the mortals for too long to remember who they are. And then there are rumors that claim they're hiding someplace together."

"I hope it's the last one." The words are hardly a whisper past my lips. I'm too confused by the twisted ache in my chest. Epimetheus had kidnapped Pandora, had bartered a deal to imprison her with him as his wife after she refused him. I should be livid, but maybe it's because I can imagine Kore's face lighting up at the tragic romance that has me hoping for it, just this once.

"Hopeless romantic, are you?" Apollo's scoff makes the hairs on my arm stand.

My focus on the story fades with a growing concern as the air shifts, and Apollo continues once more. "There was never any record of Pandora having children, but those who have been named Pandora often disappear with no record of death. Seeing that you've preferred the name Dora has probably saved your life. Murderers aren't known for their intelligence after all."

He speaks so surely that I almost don't pick up the word that unsettles me once I realize what he insinuated. "How can you be sure they were murdered if they've never been found?"

I've always despised my name because of its association with the promiscuous woman who doomed all mortals; however, I never imagined that my stubbornness in rejecting the name would save my life.

If anything, I've been warned that my stubbornness in anything would cause the opposite.

"Wishful thinking." The way Apollo's face shifts troubles me even more than his response. He's looked refreshed and eager with every word he's spoken, only now there's a sinisterness that spreads over his boyish smirk and the lazy shrug he adds only throws more weight into pit of my stomach. "You can also see why I said it was ironic that your name is Pandora, and you were throwing yourself at poor doe-eyed Jason here? I'm sure he wasn't your first he one-night stand, nor your last. And look," he tosses his chin in Jason's direction, "he's already following you around. You have your very own Epimetheus." His laughter fills the temple.

"Leave her alone." Jason takes a step, knuckles whitening at his sides. The chivalry alone would have me swooning if the truth of the God's words hadn't stung.

"You brought us here to call me a whore?" I fail to keep the bitterness from my tone. "You could have told me that in the alley. You didn't have to spin an elaborate story to do it."

"No." Apollo hops from the table, pacing one edge of the slab to the other with Daphne following as a dog would its owner. "But I needed to see something, and you didn't disappoint. Why, I don't even think you realize the way you listen to stories is interesting. The way you retell them, too, I'm sure. I'm going to tell you one last thing, and I want you to pay attention..." He reaches the edge closest to me, but rather than turn to pace back, he continues until his knees graze mine. I try not to recoil away as he points to the spot above my navel. "To right here."

I can tell him what I feel in that spot right now. I don't need to listen to anything further to know it shudders with nerves. That shift in the air hadn't been a light breeze that passed but an intuitive tremble to remain alert.

Not even Jason's protective presence stepping between us can stop my rising apprehension.

Run, that intuition grows stronger, pressing against my mind, my limbs, throbbing at my temples. All of it goes ignored once Apollo starts again. "Daphne was the most beautiful water nymph I'd ever laid my eyes on. We fell in love with each other. Everything was perfect for years

165

until Eros went raving mad after Psych. That winged freak shot Daphne with an iron arrow, filled with jealousy. He penetrated her heart with hate for me because he couldn't trust his own whore. He even cursed his sisters' entire line of descendants because of his envy that she, too, found love."

My mouth drops in utter shock to see a boy or even a God speak this way. The visible anger and fury are much darker than when he told Pandora's story.

"If his father wasn't the God of *War*, I would have retaliated. But there we were, stuck with love and hate between us, Daphne and I." He looks right at me and smiles, a sight that has me wishing I had never followed them here. "I'll never let her go. I didn't when I was cursed into this body, or when her father tried to murder me, or even when she turned herself into a tree to get away from me. Can you believe that? The hate you would have to have for someone to turn yourself into a fucking tree for eternity?!"

I glance at Daphne, observing the statuesque woman she's become, remembering the sorrow and nothingness from when I touched her. My eyes burn with tears as Apollo fills in the missing pieces, connecting the images that I saw and the feelings I felt to a thread that makes up her story, *their* story.

"I vowed to take her hate away," Apollo goes on, his temper flaring. "I vowed to take all her pain away. I even found a witch who helped put her back into human form and empty her emotions, but there was a price, as you can see." He points at the shell that is Daphne.

Jason's hands flex, and I can see his feet shuffling closer, sensing the same dreadful feeling I do. But when I reach for him, I'm completely enthralled by Daphne's sudden swaying. She rolls and twirls her hips to the unplayed melody. Unlike at the tavern, I can't look away, can't so much as flicker my eyes to confirm Jason hasn't been caught in the same spell.

"What do you feel, Pandora?"

The spot he touched moments ago roars in answer, starving for more. I don't just want but *need* to keep listening to Apollo's story, to find a new one I can tell him right back. This is my addiction, has always been

166

my obsession. I'm Pandora, and the stories are my box; unopened mysteries I live to unfold.

"Dora!" Jason shouts, but my eyes find Daphne's. The whites of them take over as the center morphs into black slits. "Run!"

Heart pounding in my chest, skin itching to reach for Jason, legs begging to jump off the chair... My body remains still.

Not even the scuffle I sense behind Daphne can pull whatever lure she has over me. I'm forced to watch the dancer's dress slip from her slim figure as her skin begins to shed with it, revealing shimmering scales beneath.

The black serpent bundles itself on the floor, slowly uncoiling and stretching itself taller until those black slits narrow and its tongue tickles the tip of my nose.

A *scream* cuts through the trance, but not enough to break it. It isn't until the serpent snaps her head in that direction that I feel my body again.

I don't dare attempt to find the source of the shriek before jumping off the chair. My legs feel off the second I move them, each step too slow.

I glance over my shoulder to make sure I'm not being stalked, but Daphne is no longer there. I look around, finding Apollo crouching on top of the slab, searching the ground in terror.

I spot Jason, dazed, his head moving, tracking something around the room. Following his line of sight, I see the serpent slithering past the table, through rats scurrying away, like we should be doing.

Jason doesn't respond when I call his name.

As the snake springs toward him, so do I, slamming into his hard body before the beast has a chance to sink her fangs into his chest.

The air leaves my lungs at the impact, and my ribs ache at how hard I struck him, but we don't have time to stop and catch our breath. There's no denying that they mean to kill us.

Righting myself, I pull at Jason's wrist, digging my heels into the ground. "Jason!" I grit my teeth.

He doesn't answer. I pull harder, feeling every muscle work, but he barely moves an inch. He's too heavy. I'll need to—

Something strikes the back of my knees, flinging me onto my back. I wail as pain explodes through my head, where I hit the ground. When I open my eyes, the room sways, my vision spots, and I taste copper on

167

my tongue. But even as the urgent need to get out of here brings me to my feet, I'm momentarily stunned at the sight of a black cat chasing more rats around the temple.

"Mene?"

The scene before me grows clearer as I blink away what I swear is a hallucination. The rats are still there, and instead of finding the cat, I spot Jason tackling Apollo, his fists meeting the God's face in a repeated rhythm without mercy. "Go!" he barks in my direction.

I hesitate, refusing to leave him alone, but I wouldn't be much help either.

I turn to do what he says, just as something hot and wet slides down my cheek. When I wipe it, I find my fingers covered in sticky, black, crimson goo.

I look up, meeting black slits.

The giant serpent flings down. I roll away just in time, and it slams against the floor.

With it disoriented, I move to jump on it, to claw at its eyes, but the black cat beats me to it, slashing at the beast's face.

Apollo howls, hunched over and holding his ribs, watching his lover being mutilated.

"Let's go, *now*." Jason hauls me up by my elbow, not letting go as we exit the temple and take alley after alley without talking. Eventually, music fills our ears, and people pass by the streets ahead. The market is just as lively as when we left, with the sky lightening ever so slightly.

We slow to a walk, pausing to listen for any following footsteps.

"I should thank you," Jason says between breaths. "I haven't had a night like this in a long time."

"You mean almost dying at the hands of a God and his serpent lover?" I look at him, baffled by his calm, nearly elated composure, but I'll take this over the cold and stoic man from the temple. "Happy I could be of service."

"You have to admit it was a little thrilling. We didn't die, and we have one Hel of a story to tell." For some ridiculous reason, his simplification of what just happened lightens the mood. The way he does it with such ease probably means he's been through something similar before, a story

I very much want to hear. "Look, what he said about you and the whole Pandora story—"

"It's fine, really." I stop him. "He wasn't wrong, so I can't really be upset, can I?"

"Men blamed Pandora for sleeping around or opening a box, but no one ever looks at the one who created her or the box." He pulls me in and wraps his arms around my shoulders, his words startling me more than his sudden returned lightness. "I'll be your Epimetheus any day. The pining part, not the kidnapping part. Although I have a feeling I wouldn't have to."

I chuckle against his warm chest, realizing just how right I was about that *nothing-but-trouble* grin. I have never met a man like him, who thinks the way he does. I didn't feel any judgment from him either, except once.

"Why were you angry when you knew my name?"

When he pulls back enough to get a better look at me, a flash of distant sadness crosses his face. "I knew a Pandora once. Like Apollo said, she disappeared. I guess when I heard your name, it brought me back to that time." By his tone alone, I know his past is filled with more than a few unpleasant memories. "I want to see you again."

"I'd like that." I mean it. "If the Fates will it."

Our time, our agreed escape for the night, is over. With a heavy chest, I offer him one last smile and start back toward the hostel.

"I'll will the Fates to my demand," he calls back. "I'll see you again, Pandora," he promises.

And for once, I don't hate my name.

Chapter Fifteen

DORA

With the hostel room swallowed in darkness, I shuffle my feet along the floor until my toe stubs against the wooden bedpost.

I catch my bottom lip with my teeth before I can groan too loudly, holding my breath while slowly lowering onto the bed.

Silence is the loudest noise of all, I recall Kore grumbling when I slipped into her room after a night out. It had been so late, I hadn't wanted to wake her, and sneaking back into the House of Prayer was always a risk.

Waiting a breath after settling under the thin blanket, I keep my voice low, "I know you're awake."

"Did you have fun?" Aphrodite's whisper holds a hint of levity that nestles a seed of guilt in me for leaving Adonis behind. I keep one eye on him to make sure he hasn't stirred as the night replays. I met a God, but not just any God; Apollo is an Olympian heir, the son of Zeus. He's said to be a beautiful, gentle, kind man with golden hair the sun could envy, identical in every way to his twin sister, Artemis, except her hair is said to be wild and black, like her spirit. The two of them are rumored to be inseparable, but there was no sign of the wild Goddess there, and the boy I met wasn't gentle or kind either.

My chest grows heavy. My books have failed me again, and because of it, I almost died. A God I had studied, had prayed to... They say Hermes is the trickster God, but Apollo had tempted me with stories, had lured me into his temples to feed me to his lover, to *kill* me.

I swallow the thickness building in the back of my throat, wishing I had water. "I had an experience."

I don't consider myself a spiteful person. I was taught to be unbiased of others' actions, that it's the Gods who judge and deal fates, but who judges the Gods?

Aphrodite shifts, propping onto her elbow. "You're not one for passing comments."

The fact that I'm stuck beside this Goddess instead of Kore is more upsetting than anything; frozen in trances, forced to speak, or being attacked by a serpent.

I miss her immensely. If Kore were here, we would have explored the town, tried new food, and drank past the rising sun. Although I likely wouldn't have met Jason.

"This town is livelier than what I'm used to."

Aphrodite's eyes narrow as if she can see the night replaying in my mind. "You live up to your name, don't you?" Seeing my mouth gape, she flashes a smile and continues, "I'm the *Goddess of Love*, I'm not shaming. I encourage. Intimacy is—"

"I've already been called a whore tonight. I really don't need you to advocate for my impulses." An ache pulses against my temples as the loss of adrenaline weighs me down, and I really don't want to talk about my lack of control when it comes to attractive men.

"I knew you were naïve, but I didn't take you for a prude. We all need to eat, squirrel. There are those with larger appetites, some more selective, others not so much. Never be ashamed of your voracity or palate."

I lift my head, pinning a glare where she lies on the other side of the pillow partition. "My appetite is satiated." *No, it's not.* "My palate is simple." *Is it?* "And I'm not ashamed." *A little ashamed.*

I'm too exhausted to move, my body begging me to roll over and rest, but Aphrodite is speaking with such piqued interest, I can't pass on this rare moment. "Why are you interested?"

"I was merely curious how a training priestess fares in a town full of mayhem. You don't disappoint." Her perfect smile dims. "I don't believe you would have gone through with it. Becoming a priestess, I mean.

You're not the kind of person who can be tied down to anything or anyone."

"Because my name is Pandora that means I must be just like her? Or is it because you know me so well after a day?"

I don't know what comes over me, but I'm tired of being called a whore, tired of being compared to a woman simply because of my name, and as much as Aphrodite is accepting of my urges, I'm not. I despise myself for being so weak to my curiosities.

Her mouth parts to say what I'm sure will be an insult, taking me by surprise when she simply shrugs and says, "There's a lot your kind doesn't know about me."

I want to laugh and tell her everything I know about her before prying her for more, but exhaustion wins out. When my eyes begin to close, I force them open for a moment longer. "I know more than you think," I add through a deep yawn.

I know the true vanity behind the woman lying next to me. The lengths she has gone through to be known as the most beautiful Goddess—*being*—of all time.

"You should rest, squirrel."

"Stop calling me that."

"I will when you realize why I do."

I would roll my eyes, but they are already closed.

"Good night, monster."

The silence is deafening, and I finally understand what Kore meant. So much is said in the quiet of the unspoken.

"What did you call me?" I can feel Aphrodite's stare bearing into the back of my head when I roll over.

I have no idea where that name came from, but Aphrodite doesn't know that, so I mimic her. "I said good night, monster. And before you ask, no, I will not tell you why I called you that until you guess why."

Uninterrupted dreamless sleep comes not a second too soon.

I pull the blanket over my head to hide from the blinding sun. My legs tangle in the sweat-soaked sheets, holding them hostage. The restraint...

I kick harder, thrashing until I get so worked up, I throw the covers off and yank, unraveling myself free.

With my eyes still adjusting to the morning light, I knit my brow when I feel I'm wearing clothes. I never slept in clothes. Like the sheets, they're too suffocating.

Thud! Thud! Thud!

Someone pounds on the door.

I groan loud enough so whoever it is will take the hint and leave me be. It's too early for morning prayers.

When a masculine voice demands I open up, my eyes widen, taking in the room that isn't mine. The cot is empty. The spot beside me holds nothing except the covers I just threw off.

No matter how long I stare at every corner, neither Aphrodite nor Adonis jumps out to explain that this is all a joke.

The pounding on the door grows more demanding, as does the voice behind it.

"I'll be right out!" I snap.

Moving as fast as I can, I wipe myself down with soap and water before putting the sweaty dress back on. I place what I hope covers the cost of the room onto the counter in case Aphrodite used her manipulation on the poor man for a free night.

When I open the door, I flash the waiting man a quick smile before pushing past him, continuing down the streets with hurried steps as he calls after me. With no sense of direction, I ask a few passing people if they've seen anyone matching Adonis and Aphrodite's description, with no luck.

I never should have left the room. Then again, why didn't they leave when I was gone last night? Why wait until I was back in bed?

I speed up, looking down every alley and into every building I pass. With the sun just breaking the horizon, most of them are empty.

"Shut up! She wasn't that pretty. You don't even like blondes." A woman whines from the group passing ahead of me.

"Like you weren't looking at the man getting the tattoo removed from his neck?" a man barks back.

"I don't even understand how a man who looks like that could have ended up as a servant. Unless it was a different kind of servitude." The second woman winks at them, and all four of them laugh, bumping into one another sluggishly.

"That woman didn't have the mark," the second man adds. "Do you think she bought him?"

"You were looking at her awfully close to notice that."

I run ahead and grab the man on the shoulder. "Where was this?"

He staggers, looking hungover and a little agitated to be interrupted.

"What is it to you?" The first woman props her hand on her hip, her eyes narrowing where my hold remains on the man's shoulder.

"She's my sister," the lie comes quick, but they don't look convinced. I reach for the woman in what's supposed to be an attempt to plead, but when she moves to pull away, my grip on her arm tightens, the images coming too quick to stop them. This woman's life is a mess: lust and late nights with both men, jealousy for her friend at her side, nothing of Adonis or Aphrodite. If I weren't so concerned for Adonis, I would indulge them with breakfast, just to see how they all interact together.

"Get off her!" The man rips me off the woman.

I apologize, cursing myself for not having more control over my gift, but no amount of practice ever helps. The visions show what they want, not necessarily what *I* want or need.

"Please. Where did you see them?" I shove the entire bag of coin into the man's chest, and he glances inside with a widening grin. I can understand the woman's infatuation, even my belly does a little flip at the sight. "We saw them getting a tattoo removed by some kid, and then again headed outside the city, about an hour ago now, maybe two." He motions toward the forest.

I give them my thanks and set off, making it a few blocks when I spot a horse being tied to a post.

"Excuse me," I call out. "Can I borrow your horse?"

The man mutters curses behind his back as he continues tying the beautiful mare.

"Excuse me?" Never have I been dismissed with such hostility. "It's urgent—"

"No, you cannot have my horse," he shouts over his shoulder. "Are you dull?"

"But I need it."

He turns around, already starting to give me a piece of his mind, when he stops mid-curse once he sees me. His messy auburn hair and graying beard sway back and forth as a breeze picks up, peering up and down the streets. "You alone?"

I know that sinister tone, the drop in voice, the shifty eyes.

Ignoring his question, I push mine. "Can I buy it?" I reach for the coin bag and drop my hands, realizing I just gave it all away. Priestesses don't usually need money, so I hadn't thought twice about it until now.

The man crosses his arms, waiting to see what I have to offer, which is nothing but the dirty clothes on my back.

He takes a step closer. "You can still buy him if you don't have coin. But it would be a while until he was paid off." His mustache curls with his lips, and when his fingers graze my arms, desire fills my senses. "How bad do you need this horse?" He doesn't finish the question before the images flash before me: women pleading, men drinking, and guns pointed at others' backs. They play in loops until his finger lifts, and they suddenly stop.

"I'm betting you'll want your usual?" A large woman pulls him inside the building, leaving me with disgust and the phantom feeling of his grimy touch.

"Oh, come on, I was having fun," he whines.

"Get inside jackass. She's my cousin, and I need to talk to her *alone*." I'm beyond glad to hear that familiar voice, to see Sasha's pudgy, smiling face.

The man shoves past her with a stumble. "Another cousin, huh?" he spits, continuing inside.

When he's gone, Sasha holds something in her hand, motioning for me to take it. "It's best to stab first and ask questions later."

I unwrap the cloth to find a small blade cradled inside, a gift that feels like an omen. "Thank you?" I hope my grin shows more appreciation than I sound. "But I could use a horse."

Her cackle is wide enough to reveal the backs of her teeth. "I learned the hard way that this is the first thing you need." Her leg lifts to the wooden post to reveal a collection of scars, some more brutal than others.

"That one is small, but so are you. Men will try to take advantage of that, but us girls need to look out for each other." She grabs the knife from my palm and rewraps it before pulling on the neckline of my dress and shoving it between my snug cleavage without an ounce of shame. "Jason must like you. He usually leaves before the songs start."

A warmth fills my cheeks, and I can't stop the smile that rises. "It was quite a night." One I'll think about often.

I eye the horse again. "Can you help me get on? I've ridden before, but I can't recall how to get on without a step."

Sasha cackles even louder, accepting what I plan to do with or without her help. "With that grit, you'll be needing that blade sooner than you realize." She drops to a lunge and slaps her thigh, letting me use it as a step. Once I'm settled on top, she circles the animal in the direction of the woods.

"Remember, stab first."

"Questions later," I finish, offering my most sincere gratitude. I pray I won't need to use it. Then again, with the way things are going, I have a strong inkling that I might.

I find Aphrodite and Adonis walking without any sense of urgency, long after my bottom grows numb and my arms ache from trotting on the horse for hours.

I call out to them, pressing the animal faster, but the two don't bother acknowledging my approach. It isn't until I wield the horse to block their path that they slow their leisurely pace.

"Why would you leave me?!"

Aphrodite claps, drawing each one out slower than the last. "That was faster than I thought."

Their clothes are the same as the night before, which means they didn't want to wake me by taking the time to change.

Adonis takes an awkward step, his slight sway catching my attention, the way he nods off like he's asleep while standing.

Swinging off the mare, I stagger toward him, caressing his cheek into my palm. The way his eyes droop without being able to look straight at

176

me riles a feeling that's starting to become too familiar at this point, pure outrage.

"I am a woman of my word." Aphrodite rubs the back of her head, motioning for me to check his. Sure enough, the nape of Adonis' neck is bare, no servant mark, not even a scar.

"That doesn't explain why he's out of it!" I snap, attempting to wake him gently by patting his cheeks. It would be easy to slap him out of this, but I'm not sure if it would help or hurt him. "Or why you left me."

"Apollo's healing tendencies are a bit *unorthodox* at times. We also had to use alcohol." She wiggles her fingers. "And a little of my own specialties."

A tremble runs through my legs at the mention of the God who almost killed me. "Is he your friend?"

"Apollo?" Aphrodite puzzles over the question. "I'm surprised you think I have friends."

"You're right. That was a stupid question." I shift my focus back to Adonis. "Is he okay to walk? Is there anything that will help him?"

"From personal experience, walking it out is the best way to get rid of that little shit's healing methods." I don't try to hide my creeping smile at her snarl.

Without a way to put Adonis on the horse, I swing myself over after a few failed attempts.

"I knew you'd be resourceful enough to catch up," Aphrodite adds, her fingers fiddling with the locket around her neck. "But if you didn't, I assumed you would have found yourself having another eventful night. Maybe convince another God to take you to find Kore. Apollo did seem more agitated than usual. Did you run into him while you were out last night?"

If Apollo hadn't tried to kill me, I would have taken offense to the comment as Aphrodite intended, but the question gives me an idea. "I think we need an agreement. A more *permanent* agreement, in which you swear never to leave or lie to me again."

Aphrodite looks momentarily stunned as if she were persuaded by her own abilities to remain still. "The kind of deal you want needs balance. What do I get in return?" Her concern is palpable.

"You ask me as many questions as I ask you. I won't speak to you again until we have something that makes me feel like I can trust you." I see the opening I leave for her to remark how perfect that would be, sure she'll take the opportunity, but no sly remarks come. Instead, she looks to be considering my words.

"I swear on the River Styx, I will never lie to you or leave you *again*." Her hand raises between us. I take it into mine and repeat the phrase before either of us can change our minds.

When I'm finished, I wait as patiently as I've ever been, unaware of what to expect after making an unbreakable, soul-binding oath. It's a concept I've only read about in books. Would it even work between a Goddess and a mortal, or whatever I am? Children swear on the river all the time, and nothing happens when they go back on their oaths.

Just as I'm starting to consider that this might be silly after all, a sharp warmth spreads where we're still connected.

Aphrodite retrieves her hand, cradling it against her chest with a frown. "Happy?"

I look mine over. Nothing looks different. Other than the settling warmth, nothing feels different. "Tell me your name is Kore."

"I will not and cannot lie to you."

"Try," I insist. "How else do we know if it worked?" I motion that my lips are sealed and stubbornly cross my arms.

She huffs, knowing I won't say anything further until we have some sort of proof that this worked. "Fine."

Adonis leans against the horse, pale and looking as if he's going to be sick at any moment. "I don't feel well."

I brush his head with the back of my hand, feeling his skin burning up.

"My name is Kor—" Aphrodite drops to her knee, her teeth clenching together, groaning in what sounds like agony. A cut begins to open down her palm, spilling liquid gold, exactly where mine begins to tingle.

"My name is Aphrodite!" she yells through gritted teeth.

My hand stops tingling as Aphrodite's cut slowly seals itself back together, leaving a pink scar on her otherwise perfect skin.

"Are you happy *now*?" She lifts her palm, displaying proof that the River Styx oath worked. A marking not even the Goddess's healing can mend.

I regret pushing her when pure delight grins back at me. "Your turn."

"You're out of your mind," I screech, taking the horse's reins into my hand to set the pace. "Besides, we need to get Adonis help. He's burning up."

Aphrodite strokes her pink scar with a pout. It's so full of sorrow that I almost feel bad. That poor thing has probably never had anything imperfect about her. "It's the magic working its way out. He'll be fine in about an hour." Her eyes flash to mine. "Don't you want to see what will happen if a mortal betrays their oath?"

Oh, Gods do I. And damn this one for knowing it.

"This isn't because of you," I state, looking down at her. "It's only fair."

She gives me a knowing look before grabbing the waterskin and pouring it over Adonis' head, helping him drink from it while I take a breath.

My nerves are a wreck, confused if they are supposed to be excited or scared, but I'm grateful Aphrodite isn't completely soulless, though she is still an untrustworthy, manipulative wench. I had no idea what would happen if either of us went back on the oath, but Aphrodite does, and she still wishes to see me suffer through it.

"My name..." I take another deep, shaky inhale. "My name is Kor—"

Fire spreads, consuming every inch of my being: my head, my legs, my belly, my arms. I try to open my eyes to see who's sliding a knife up my hand, but they're sealed shut.

The searing pain is too deafening, too blinding, to hear what Aphrodite is yelling. All I can focus on is the slow slice of an invisible blade cutting up my wrist.

Thud!

A blaring white pain strikes my head. Am I on the ground?

I'm thankful something else hurts to take my mind from my wrist, even if it is only for a second.

179

Pressure pushes against my chest. Quick slaps shoot across my cheek with sweet relief.

"Dora!" Another *smack* on my cheek.

My eyes fling open.

"Say it! Dora! *Pandora!*" Aphrodite grips the neckline of my dress and slaps me hard. "Say it!"

"My name…" I take a deep breath, mimicking what I said moments ago, "is…" the exhale empties my lungs, "Pandora."

Everything stops.

There is no lingering after-pain. The burning, the knife, all of it vanishes.

I reach for where the back of my head throbs, but I can't move my arms with Aphrodite straddling me.

"Get off." I wiggle to free myself, but the look on her face stops me. I follow her gaze to where black and red liquid puddles on the ground at my side.

"Oh squirrel, I know exactly what you are."

Chapter Sixteen

KORE

The week passes agonizingly slow, days filled with reading about the God's histories until the words on the pages look like a language I don't speak. If I'm not reading, Hermes provides verbal lessons as he chaperones me to and from every room.

We're currently on our way to Hecate's workspace for another failed attempt at deciphering my abilities. Aside from immortality, they expect me to be agile, strong, and quick healing, with the possibility of morphing into an animal and manipulating at least one of the natural elements.

From there, the possibilities of what I possess are endless. Some Gods have the ability to manipulate minds, others can speak to animals, while few, like Hermes, can fly. Very rare Gods have prophetic gifts, and even fewer can heal others.

So far, agility has been my strongest asset. I can run faster than Dionysus, which impresses everyone except Hermes, who laps us ten times over. I climbed a tree with ease, only to learn too late that the climb down was the challenging part. But when my body thudded against the ground, I sprang right back up, barely feeling the last branch whip me. And as everyone reminds me, I have a quick tongue and wield it well. It's the impulsivity I need to work on. The timing of my *clever quips*, as Dionysus calls them.

Hecate assured me that the rest will reveal themselves at a slower rate because of the Underworld's inability to support living things.

"If Hades would let me go to the Heavens…" I press, but no one ever agrees to help me sway him. Hades' word is final—according to them anyway. I plan to continue pressing the issue with him directly, but he hasn't been around since I learned that Demeter is my mother.

Every breakfast or dinner he doesn't attend leaves me disturbingly disappointed. I can feel his dark, overbearing presence in every room, every hallway of this castle, but when I look over my shoulder, he's never there. When I make the hike up those stairs, his door is locked, even though it was he who insisted I join him every night for chess. I feel like a fool with every step back to my room.

My father had been a leader, so naturally, I know how busy and taxing it can be, yet he still made time for me every night he was home; always showing me new recipes or how to plant the new seeds he brought back from his recent trips.

Hades isn't my father though. He is a king. A devastatingly beautiful, manipulative, cunning king, keeping me as his prisoner.

Lovely dress. His comment replays in my mind with different tones: teasing, mocking, angry, judging. None of them sound as sincere or enticing as he had last week.

How can he go from calling me a deviant, in that deep, suggestive voice, to forbidding me from meeting my real mother? Then to complimenting my appearance?

"You're quieter than usual." Hermes nudges me as we descend farther down the steps. My legs and calves no longer burn from the constant ascending and descending of our daily treks.

"Oh no." Whatever look I give him causes his head to tip back with a plea to Gaia for patience. "What now? I already told you Dora and Adonis are fine, I gave you three books on curses so you can try to figure mine out for yourself, and I ate that apple pie you made even though I despise hot fruit." I bite my cheek to keep from laughing at the memory of his disgusted, faux smile while he begrudgingly swallowed every bite. "Let's not forget carrying you to bed when you fell asleep in the library."

How could I forget? My cheeks flush remembering my hazy, half-asleep, needy hands pulling his arm around me and forcing him to snuggle. Considering I woke up alone with the phantom feel of his arms around my waist and his chest at my back, I figured I had dreamt it or made the entire thing up.

"Do you know why Hades hasn't been around?"

His brow lifts with that amused look I know too well. "Are you not having fun with me? And here I thought we were heating up after you pulled me into your bed last night."

I gape at him, searching his face for any hint of lying I know I won't find.

"Don't worry, Little Bat, you were a gentleman." His wink sends me into further shame, and swearing off late-night wine with Dionysus. "Hades is taking time to catch up on a few things. Sentencing mortals, torturing murderers, and whatever else kings do. I'm sure he misses you just as much."

"I don't miss him." I attempt to assess my fingernails to prove just how uncaring I am. "I'm just trying to figure out how to fit his chess lessons into my busy schedule. And since we're on the topic of your curse..." I take the opportunity to detour the conversation away from my gnawing thoughts on the riddle that is Hades, "Care to tell me about yours yet? The book I found stated something about wings being hereditary, so I assume that can't be it."

There's no deciphering the weary look he gives me, and I nearly fall in shock when he says, "It's been a blessing in disguise."

I bite the inside of my cheek a little harder, knowing full well he'll shut right back up or toss me some flirty, joking remark if I show any hint of glee that he's answered one of my questions.

"How is a curse a blessing in *any* way?"

His pace slows during the last stretch of the hallway, bathed in an amber glow from the candles hanging overhead. I fully expect him to brush me off with his usual evasive remark or ignore me completely, but his hand hesitates over the handle. When he turns back with those sad eyes, my heart cracks a little.

"I get to see unbelievable places and meet unforgettable people, and..." He takes a breath, a light curl falling over his brow as his chin meets his chest. "I fell in love."

My head spins. I'm not surprised he's been in love, but I can't ignore the prickle of fury knowing someone caused the hurt in those deep sapphires. I'm overcome with a growing need to find this woman to see if hers holds the same loss and longing. And if they don't, maybe there is something that can be done to ensure they never hold anything except precisely that.

"With who?" I ask, but like the door now behind us, the conversation closes.

In the back of the very hectic, very crowded basement—a room I can only describe as a witch's wet dream—Hecate leans over one of the many vast cauldrons, too entranced with whatever she's mixing to notice our arrival.

Delicately, we tiptoe through the maze of books splayed and scattered on every surface. The clutter in this room hurts my head in the same way Hades' orderly study does. There are cabinets, shelves, and tables lined with a variety of jars filled with liquids, herbs, spices, healing salves, and bones in murky water. Some are neatly together, others toppled over, and a few have colorful smoke emitting from the uncorked vials. There are mortars and pestles with whatever Hecate had been working on, though I'm positive I see last night's stew in one. The walls are decorated with insects splayed out, pinned recipes sloppily written, and notes covered in gibberish. The smells almost gagged me the first time—like rot and musty herbs.

Hecate jumps back with a squeal. "Oh stars!" She grabs her chest, her panicked breaths growing eager. "You're early, come, come! It's not a complete image, but I was able to find something, *finally*, about Metanira's past."

I'm fine with anything that doesn't include me attempting air, weather, or water manipulation again, all of which left me red-faced, gasping for oxygen, with a lingering headache only a long nap or a little wine helped alleviate.

Using the stool on the other side, I step up, catching myself on Hermes' shoulder when I almost topple over. The legs aren't even, but I'm too anxious to see what Hecate found to find another one.

Keeping my hold on Hermes' shoulder, I peer over the cauldron's lip as the witch swirls the dark, murky liquid while muttering words I don't understand.

I listen to her broken song when a strong scent of cinnamon and earth surrounds me, a smell I can't quite rid myself of, not even after I soak and lather with the apple or vanilla soaps. I often wonder if it's the scent of the Underworld, like how the woods smell of pine or cedar, but together make up the scent of *the woods*, or how the sea smells like salt but also distinctly like *the sea*.

The three of us watch vehemently as the liquid stills, slowly shifting into an image of a young Metanira, swollen belly and caked in mud as she runs through a white field. The ripples change, revealing her kneeling before a cloaked figure. "Please, please, I made a mistake. Celius is wonderful, but I—I can't give her up." She cradles her bump. "Please. I'll do anything. Take back the deal. I don't care about the wealth or security anymore. I want to keep my baby!"

To hear her plea and see the tears streaming down Metanira's face is more than startling; it's disheartening. I've never seen her so broken or heard her so pained. To see the strong, self-assured woman I know in such despair crumbles a small piece inside me.

The cloaked figure's reply is inaudible, but by the hopelessness on Metanira's broken face, I know whatever this being says isn't what she wants to hear.

"Take care of who?" Metanira's voice holds the tiniest sliver of hope. "Take care of the girl and I'll get my baby back, but for how long?" *Silence.* "What does that mean, mirrored fates? They'll be connected?" *Silence.* "No, please! I'll do it. I understand."

The cauldron turns black.

The lack of fire crackling on the logs has nothing to do with how cold I feel.

"We think…" Hecate explains what I already pieced together. It's clear that Metanira made deals that ended with her having to give up her baby and take care of me.

It all makes sense. Metanira resents me for taking the place of her real child, always waiting for the day the cloaked being returns with her baby.

You have no idea what I gave up for you. The sneer and hate in Metanira's eyes were always real, not a drunken emotional outburst or some misplaced malice. When she said she had never loved me, she meant it.

I was always a transaction. A burden.

"I'm sure Celius didn't know." Hecate attempts reassurance, but that thought hadn't even occurred to me. I've been so focused on one false parent that I haven't considered that Celius isn't my father.

My heart falls deeper than I thought imaginable. *Did he know? Would he have cared?*

There is one question I'm too afraid to ask out loud, let alone think of. Celius is my father. Nothing will change that.

Swallowing the thickness that threatens to make me a permanent resident in the Underworld, I settle for a question that won't leave them staring at me with those pitiful eyes. "Who is the cloaked figure?"

It's not just Hecate's stirring that stills, the witch's entire body freezes over. "I'm not able to say." Her eyes don't meet mine.

This must be the God I think it is then, the one Dora told me about.

"No one you want to cross paths with." Hermes shakes his head rapidly, not realizing he only confirmed my suspicions.

"That was the Triple Goddess, wasn't it?"

Hecate's jaw drops, the smiling scar growing white as her cheeks grow red. The only time I've ever seen her this furious was when she couldn't mix the belladonna fast enough for some curse she was trying to break.

"Don't." Her voice shakes. "Don't *ever* search for this being, Kore. You have no idea what the cost is to make these deals. You watched Metanira give away her child only to regret it. *Nothing* is worth calling upon her."

I feel Hermes brush the small of my back, warming the very spot he holds. The tension in my shoulders vanishes, and the angered quip I had ready on my tongue releases through a long breath that eases out of me. Whatever intrigue he's feeling flows through me, replacing the heartache and irritation I held only seconds ago.

"Ooo, are we looking at pasts?" Dionysus breaks the remaining tension as a stack of books plummets to the ground behind Hermes, who isn't near me at all.

I turn back, finding nothing behind me except a chair covered in an old blanket and dusty books.

"You little…" Hecate pins Dionysus to the wall with her glare.

"I'll clean it later, witch. I want to see my little Spitfire's past." Dionysus tosses her a small vial that he confirms is siren tears, and her temper sizzles away as she bounces on her toes with sheer excitement. She quickly forgives him, but not before demanding he clean the mess.

Hermes and I give him *good luck* salutes, knowing just how particular the witch is about her things she claims are organized.

With all seriousness and caution gone, Hecate beams and zooms around the room, looking under tables, behind chairs, opening books, tossing things behind her back that she doesn't need. "Hermes, you're strong, can you bring a new cauldron over to the table?"

"I'll do it." Dionysus pushes Hermes' shoulder to keep him from helping, and I have to use my palm to cover my laugh. The three of them never fail to entertain me when my mood sours, which is becoming less frequent.

Hecate's gaze never breaks away from him as he moves the cauldron without a struggle. It isn't until he drops it and tosses her a ladle that she finally turns away and measures everything precisely.

"Help me stir." I take her offered ladle, listening to her instructions. "Think about what you want to see."

Not wanting another moment from the past, I focus on my friends, hoping to see where they are now. Another thing I mean to ask Hades about, if he ever shows himself.

Again, we all focused on the changing void. The image that appears through the rippled liquid shows a laughing Dora and smiling Adonis sitting by a campfire with Aphrodite. The scar along Dora's arm gives me pause, but she looks good otherwise. Adonis still has bird scratches along his arms and forehead while eying the ravens in the trees beside him.

Hermes gives me an *I-told-you-they-were-fine* look.

"One more day and we'll be in the Heavens." My ears perk at Aphrodite's voice, a sound that's just as seductive without actually having to be in her presence.

"And you're sure Kore will be there?" Dora asks, noticeably being pulled between excitement and concern.

"In time." Aphrodite's focus remains on Dora as she continues, "It's inevitable. A friend, a long time ago, prophesied Kore becoming what she was always fated to be there." Her gaze hazes over as if in the distant memory. "We just have to ensure—"

The images disappear, muddying into a dark brown.

"What happened?" I stir faster, trying to bring them back. *They just had to ensure what?*

A broken gasp leaves me at the new images that appear, my insides knotting, weighted down by what feels like the chains Hades threatened to keep me in.

Metanira's messy yellow hair spreads over a pillow, next to *him*, the man who churns my stomach, who brings bile to the back of my throat. Seeing him without a shirt on, that sick grin, those drunk nights he stumbled into my room come flooding to the front of my mind.

"Do you think Kore will come back?" Pirithous asks, stroking Metanira's arm.

"If she's smart, she'll stay away."

Hecate whispers something to Dionysus, too low for me to hear, or maybe it's the ringing in my ears that drown them all out.

"That's too bad. She was good help."

"Does it look like I need help?" Metanira snaps. "If you wanted Kore, you should have taken her when you had the chance. I gave you enough opportunity while Celius was away."

"I never wanted Kore, Metanira. I already explained that it was a misunderstanding. She came on to me, and we punished her for it. I've always wanted you."

The entire room fills with the rage my body trembles with, my skin is burning, like it was just set on fire.

Pirithous strokes Metanira's cheek, and her hand falls onto his, revealing the matching gold rings. "Besides, we agreed she'd marry Theseus. Why would I want to tarnish my cousin's prize?"

Metanira remains unconvinced. "Have you found your servant? I really need more help with those damn kids."

"Meg is still missing, and if you ask me, they were better off at the orphanage."

It feels as if I swallowed barbed wire and every sentence they mutter adds a new layer. Metanira has the orphans? And Meg worked for *him* all this time. And Metanira *married* him?

Pure acid burns higher up my tongue, too much to swallow down.

Pressure pulls at my waist, and before I know what it is, I'm emptying my stomach in the bin before me. The emerald tiles tell me I'm somehow in my washroom, and the white wings fanning my sweaty skin tell me it's Hermes holding my hair and rubbing circles on my back.

"Get in the tub."

I lean against the wall, wiping my mouth with the back of my hand. "I can take care of myself."

"Of course you can." He pulls me up by my shoulders, setting me onto my feet to follow his orders. "Now, get in the tub. I'll be right back."

When he leaves, I undress and move as fast as I can into the steaming water. I don't care to think about how we got here. I'm just thankful no one other than Hermes saw me this weak.

The water steams, hotter than usual, but it's exactly what I need. If I can find a way to make it boil to singe away the memories I thought I'd ridden myself of, I would gladly soak in the scorching bubbles and let it melt my skin along with them.

When the door opens again, I hug my knees against my chest, sinking deeper into the bubbles. "What are you doing?!"

Hermes drags a chair next to me, holding a cup of water and a plate of food. "I told you I'd be back. Knowing you, you forgot to eat this morning so you could jump into those books."

I give him an unamused look that makes him laugh. I definitely didn't forget to eat, and certainty wasn't in any rush to read more about the Gods and their violent histories.

I take a drink of the water before grabbing a piece of bread drizzled with oil and crushed tomatoes, one of my many weaknesses. I'm still reeling from what I saw and heard to fully appreciate the savory treat.

"We need to get those children away from Pirithous and Metanira. They're..." I stop before saying *abusive*, which would only lead him to press further. "...neglectful."

Hermes must see the terror written on my face because he leans over the lip of the tub and tilts my face to his, a motion that cools the water a few degrees.

"I have birds, Little Bat. I know how *neglectful* they can be." His eyes soften. But his birds were never around *inside* our home. "Hades had Hecate put a protection spell around the house and each of the children. As for Pirithous, Hades didn't have any influence over their marriage. He originally wanted to find her a husband but ultimately didn't want another mortal to keep eyes on. He ensured Metanira had enough riches to keep herself safe, which means she chose to marry him of her own accord. I have my birds on constant watch, and no one has made a move to hurt any of those children."

His assurance and the bread ease my nausea enough to breathe a little lighter. I don't like the thought of the children there, but knowing Hades held up his end of the bargain makes me feel better about being his prisoner if it means they're all safe.

"How did you know I was going to be sick?" I ask, watching him pick through the fruit.

"I've seen that look many times before." His smile doesn't mask the faint somberness in the back of his voice.

"You make a lot of girls sick?"

His laugh is light, shaking his head at my teasing remark. "Not me."

"Who?"

"I can't say."

"Can't or won't?"

"Can't."

I squint in thought. His curse must be tied to his words, being able to say or not say certain things. "If I guess, can you tell me?"

He takes a bite of the salted cheese, eyeing me as if I'm looking for trouble. "I'm afraid not everything has loopholes."

"Nonsense." The bubbles thin, and I'm suddenly aware of how naked I am mere inches from him. If he only looked down into the water instead of focusing on the plate, he would see my peaking nipples between the fading foam. "Nothing is absolutely impossible."

His head angles like he wants to look over, but stops himself as the wings on his ears give a soft flap against his curls. "Times up, Little Bat. You need to rest."

He hands me the rest of his cheese before moving to lean against the counter, crossing his arms and ankles.

190

"Can you leave?" He easily dodges the cheese I throw at him. "You don't have to babysit me, you know. I can manage a bath without you, and I think I can even get myself to sleep."

"You sure? You couldn't last night." His wry grin only makes me wish I had something else to toss at him. "Besides, Hades put firm instructions to watch you at all times."

Of course he did.

"Should I tell him that you left me alone to get water and food?"

The spreading curve of his lips leaves me breathless, a feeling that doesn't go away when I follow what he points at. A black raven is perched on the windowsill, cawing in greeting.

"Did you watch through him?" I splash water in his direction, not even landing a drop near his feet.

Hermes tosses me the towel from the counter, forcing me to rise out of the water to catch it before it lands in the tub.

His dimple deepens. "I don't need the bird."

Chapter Seventeen

KORE

Pirithous' breath smells of wine. The sweat slicking his body reeks of the musky odor. He stumbles, catching himself on the edge of my bed, lingering, watching.

His eyes travel from my exposed neckline, down to where the blanket bundles at my waist.

I should have gone to sleep instead of staring out the window at the black birds lining the tree and rationalizing the sudden slap I earned earlier.

"Look after her for me?" My father had said as he packed the carriage to leave, yet again.

"Of course," I told him, glancing over my shoulder to where my mother was scolding Adonis for something I couldn't hear, glancing our way. "I'm surprised you're leaving again so soon. You returned only a few weeks ago."

I wasn't really surprised at all. His trips grow more frequent, regardless of the amount of wine he has to sell.

He squeezed my shoulder, "I'll be back before you know it, Bug. I'll bring you back something special like always."

I waved him off as the carriage rode away.

"What did you tell him?" Metanira stepped beside me.

"Nothing, I swear."

"It better be nothing. You know what would happen if he ever found out."

"I said, I didn't say anything." I clenched my teeth with immediate regret.

The sharp sting lingered as I stalked toward my room with heavy breaths, cupping my cheek to hide the red swelling as I passed Adonis in the hallway.

Now, it's the middle of the night, and Pirithous is drunk, sitting on my bed, his hand grazing where my leg is stretched beneath the blanket.

192

We both look.

I attempt to yank my leg away, but he's quicker, gripping it steady at his side.

"You're in the wrong room," I whisper.

"I came to see you. I was having a chat with Adonis earlier, and he said that you two have never... been together."

"Of course not." I glance at the door, watching the soft light coming through the crack at the bottom to make sure no one walks by and overhears him. "Please, you need to leave."

"It's just, you've been so good not telling your father about your mother and me." My stomach sours at the memory of finding the two of them together. "You can keep another secret, right?"

"You're drunk."

"True, but in my drunken mind, I've had a thought. See, you have this secret about me and your mother. If it comes out, who does that hurt? I'm not married. I'm just a young man being berated by an older woman. Then, of course, I have that lovely secret you trusted me with. And as I said when you told me, I swear I won't tell anyone your father is a nonbeliever, but sooner or later, I'm not so sure I can stay motivated to keep these secrets."

I shake my head, disbelief burning my eyes. We're friends, or we had been before I found him with Metanira.

He adjusts himself with a smirk that makes me sick. I want to yank away, to pull myself back as his hands slither higher, but my body freezes.

If anyone found out about him and my mother. If anyone found out about my father...

My heart pounds against my chest. I want to hide. The thought consumes me as I look down at myself without feeling connected to my own body. It's like I'm not here at all, watching at a distance, from a safe pocket inside my mind.

My eyes fly open.

The feeling of his hands all over me makes my skin crawl. I throw the covers hard enough to hit the vanity across the room, knocking over the untouched perfumes.

My feet carry me like a distant memory, remembering my need for space and fresh air after those horrid nightmares. They take me to the lower level, down mazes of hallways, lined with more oil paintings and sculptures than there are artists, until finally leading me to the massive entry doors.

I fling them open, the cool night breeze filling my lungs with the deep inhale. I let it consume me while I take in the horizon, the stars glistening in the night sky that lightens from black to a dark shade of blue, indicating that the mortal veil is experiencing daylight.

That had been one of the most fascinating concepts I read about: the Underworld is ruled by the moon, the Heavens by the sun, and the Mortal Veil by both, each created by one of the three veil makers: Selene, Helios, and Chaos, respectively.

Walking over and peering over the cliff, I see where the diamond gate cuts through the lifeless bone-yard to keep the lost souls from entering the property. It's too far to see clearly, but it looks to be chiseled into sharp edges that point away, warding off any unwanted intruder. The rainbows that the diamonds cast in the light make for a strange greeting.

Farther below, woodsmoke from chimneys rise from other homes. From this high up, I can see the rivers and paths snaking in all directions with no end in sight.

This is how I imagined a cave to feel—dark and dreary, and yet, my awe can't be explained with words. It's a place of melancholy myths and unknown wonder. Any normal person would see this darkness and think of death, but all I see is the flicker of life, an unseen pulse.

I can't help but wonder if this is what Psych saw and felt when she peered over the cliff before jumping. I take another step when a sharp tug in my ribs causes me to hiss and spin around.

This way. My sights fall toward the back of the castle where that instinct urges me to follow, but I'm momentarily captivated by the sight of the home I'm a prisoner in. It's out of a gothic romance: dark stone slick with shadows, sharp spires claw at the sky, and windows that drink in the stars.

Hermes had showed me around, but when he brought me outside, it had been too brief to really take everything in.

As I start down one of the twisting paths, there isn't much to see. Dirt and tangled twigs litter the ground, and there's a forgotten statue crumbling away, unless it's supposed to just be legs.

That pull tugs harder, willing my feet faster. If I wanted to stop, I probably could, but my curiosity rises the farther I go, stumbling down the slope, stepping over more rotted bushes and around dreary trees.

When the ground levels again, it isn't long before my breath is stolen at the ghastly sight before me.

Behind a tall iron gate, with rods that come to sharp points, jutting toward the moon, lies an enormous, decimated garden.

I rush toward it, my fingers fumbling, faltering to open the squeaking arched entryway. I make it inside when that pull that brought me here stops, my knees landing on a carpet of wilted rose petals. I take in the scenery, the withering plants, lifeless trees, and flowers left unbloomed.

I know the Underworld can't provide anything but death, but seeing someone's attempts to prove otherwise... My heart splinters for them and the Underworld, never being able to grow or hold the beauty of a garden, to perfume this veil with fresh scents. I realize now that the dried herbs and flowers in every room around the castle provide what this garden can't, a hint of life.

I ache even more for the person who attempted such a thing, the disappointment and heartache they must have for failing.

"What are *you* doing here?"

I remain rooted in place, clutching the dusty ground at the sound of the voice I've been waiting to hear all week.

Twigs snap under his approaching footsteps.

When I peer up, Hades glares down on me. His brow rises, but there's a dark humor in his eyes, one that has me acutely aware that I'm on my knees, jaw dropped before him.

"I, uh..." I stumble, scrambling to my feet. "I needed air."

He looks exhausted. His onyx hair is tousled, his eyes darker and heavy from lack of sleep. Even tortured, he's devastating to look at.

"I can go if I'm bothering you."

"No," he says quickly, looking around at the desolation. There's a hint of defeat in his features that I never would have thought he was capable of. "You're not a bother at all."

His comment softens a part of the shell I've become since waking up, but also leaves me too stunned to say anything else.

That arch in his brow lifts higher. "Your tongue isn't as sharp as usual. No smart remark about how I'm a bother to you?"

"It's hard to be a bother when you're not around. If I didn't know any better, I'd say you were avoiding me." And suddenly I find my voice again, only to sound bitter at his absence.

I peer deeper through the grounds, wondering where he came from and why he's out here, but the shadowy exhaustion in his face makes me ask, "Do you not sleep?"

His chuckle is light, and I'm glad to see he doesn't stifle it as usual. "I forgot about your incessant need to say whatever is on your mind with little concern for those you speak to."

"And I forgot you were so uptight." I cross my arms and turn, stalking off and cursing myself for being so easily swayed by a bit of kindness. The man clearly holds only contempt and wants nothing to do with me.

By the lack of twigs snapping, he doesn't follow, and for some reason, his silence leaves me as glum as our surroundings.

I try to ignore it by putting as much distance between us as possible, by admiring the rest of the garden and guessing at what was planted, but he's too deep under my skin to ignore.

My steps slow, but I don't stop. I have every intention of leaving him behind, but like a splinter, there's no way to get rid of him unless I pick back.

I turn around, ready to ask him, once again, what his problem is with me, but my mouth seals shut before I get a chance.

The flex in Hades' jaw, the way his dark gaze rakes over me, searching for something, makes me realize my mistake.

I'm still in my night slip.

"What the fuck happened to your back?"

My knees weaken and the lump in my throat tightens, threatening to suffocate me, and none of it is because of the hot rage radiating off him or the balled fists he stuffs into his pockets.

He takes one step forward, stopping himself from taking a second. "Who did that to you?"

I fall back against a tree, clinging to the bark biting into my skin that's keeping me from escaping into my mind. "It's nothing."

"Now is not the time to lie to me, Deviant."

196

"It was my fault. I..." My vision blurs. How could I have forgotten? I'm always so careful and particular about what I wear.

"Breathe." His palm is warm, pressing against my cheek, the other beneath my chin. It's so fast that I hadn't even seen him walking toward me to make the contact. "Why are you panicking?"

"You weren't supposed to see, no one was supposed to see." His face is a blurry mess, but I recognize the look he's giving me as one I found on myself long ago. "Don't pity me."

"I'm not pitying you, but I want to know why you would protect someone who hurt you." There's a need in his voice that I don't understand.

I'm not protecting anyone. I just don't want to talk about it, ever, especially with him. I may not wear them like a badge of honor, but I earned those scars.

"What do you care? I'm only here so you can use me, right? I'm fairly certain captors don't usually bother getting to know their prisoners."

His eyes narrow, and the skin beneath the right one twitches. "Adonis?"

"What? No, of course not. He's—We're friends." I hadn't thought about him at all until I realized Hermes had been the one who stopped us from doing more than just fondling. Thinking back to that moment now, I'm glad he did.

"Friends that fuck?" I gape at his brazen question while he continues studying me, waiting for my answer. I'd say patiently, but the look on his face says what little he has left is thinning.

"That's none of your concern."

His jaw ticks, not one for being so easily dismissed.

"The man from the cauldron?"

"How—You weren't even there."

His hands drop, returning to his pockets. The lack of his warmth makes me shiver. *That* he takes notice of.

In one quick motion, he pulls the shirt over his head, tossing me the heated cloth.

It isn't the shirt that catches my attention, but what it was covering. It's not just his neck and arms that are covered in ink but his entire torso: dark swirls, ravens on his shoulders, symbols I don't recognize, and two snakes peeking out from his waistband that have me turning my head, averting my eyes to keep him from seeing the flush that burns brightly in my cheeks.

Heavens fucking sin.

"I was there. You just couldn't see me." When I peer up again, he's gone, and something grabs my shoulder. I turn, but nothing's there. A tap brings my head to the left, and a second later, he appears before my very eyes.

I yelp, my feet tangling on the vine beneath me, my arms flailing. Before I fall, he grabs one, yanking me hard enough to bring my cheek against his chest.

The scent of cinnamon clouds my head.

He's so warm.

His steady palm brushes against my lower back, and I let out a shaky breath.

It was Hades who calmed me in Hecate's room, not Hermes.

"Now, Little Deviant," He speaks with a tranquility that sounds forced, like he struggles to maintain control over such a delicate tone. "Tell me why you would protect the man who did this to you."

I yank my arm from his, pulling myself from whatever hypnosis he has over me. "I'm not protecting him. I deserved every lash he gave me."

A deep growl ripples from his chest. "If you don't tell me, I'll have Hecate show me."

I would rather he put me in chains than let him see any part of my past with Pirithous.

"Because I didn't let him fuck me, okay?!" I throw his shirt back in his face, regretting it immediately when another shiver runs through me, but I'm too angry to care. "If I had, then no one would have found out my father was a nonbeliever, and he wouldn't have been the sacrifice. He would still be alive, and it's my fault he's not."

I don't back away or fight when he seizes my hand, his heat instantly stopping my teeth from chattering and my body from shivering.

The instant warmth does nothing for the shudder that spreads through my bones or keeps the words from leaving my lips. Now that I've started, I can't seem to stop.

"You want to know why I have these scars so desperately? Because Metanira finally saw what he was doing, what he forced me to do, after she went to bed. Of course, she didn't believe me, so she let him whip me for being a liar and accusing him of such horrendous sins." A bitter laugh leaves me, one I never would have believed belongs to me, but a raving lunatic. "Then, when my father was sacrificed, I received more of these lovely lashes because I dared to cause a scene by crying and begging for them to stop."

Hades' face remains unchanged as my skin and bones fill with his rising heat and the fury behind it.

"The last lashings came when Pirithous tried one last time. I remained too still and uncaring for him. He said he'd rather cut his hands off than touch something so dull and lifeless."

Those last words have Hades' hands clenching again, releasing when he realizes he's still holding mine. It probably would have hurt if I didn't favor the gut-burning pain it brings. It's the relief as it eases that I crave too much. The anchor in it. The reminder that I have a body I don't need to escape from in this moment.

I'm second-guessing if I said too much to the man I know so little about. A man who's holding me prisoner and has promised to put me in chains if I don't behave.

His fingers tighten once more. "You feel guilty." It sounds as if he's asking and answering his own question. "I won't bother telling you that it's not your fault. You won't believe it until you learn it for yourself. But I will promise he'll suffer for what he did."

I want to ask him what he means, and tell him exactly what that internal balance inside of me demands as payment. But my lips remain unmoved as I study the laughing skull tattooed on the back of his hand.

"You said you're only here so I can use you." He pauses, contemplating his next words. "You're not wrong, but I'm all about fairness, so, in the meantime, I can offer you something in return."

"What?"

"Use me." I'm met with a wry grin. "Let me burn away your scars."

"You want to burn me?" I balk. "Are you ill? You think I'd want to burn after being ripped open?"

His head drops, observing where our fingers interlace, where he warms my entire body with that single touch. When he takes a step closer—his chest inches from mine—I take in just how tall he is, how dark and depraved his aura radiates. Power and body, he's impossible to ignore.

My mouth dries, feeling the heat releasing from his chest.

Flashes of what I imagined in that temple resurface, and it takes every part of me to swallow the heavy breath so he can't see how he affects me.

When his eyes catch mine, I find a look that entraps my soul, and words that test my sanity. "You could use me in other ways."

His stare drops, tracking the part in my lips that let out the remaining breath I have.

It isn't the warmth he sends coursing through me that has my core warming to the brink of boiling and my skin burning a shade past crimson.

My back hits the tree again, forcing out a soft whimper. "What about Minthe?"

I cringe at the resentment in my voice, but he only chuckles, a soft sound that makes me smile, even more so at his answer. "I'm not with Minthe. Or anyone for that matter, if that's what you're concerned about."

When his palm grazes my lower belly, I melt at the touch, and I know I'm agreeing to whatever he has in mind. He doesn't need to ask, and he doesn't.

"Tell me what you want." My toes curl at the needy demand.

"I…" If he means it, I won't miss this opportunity. "I want all memories of him gone."

"Consider it done." He drags my hands above my head, pinning them with something I can't see. "We'll start replacing them now."

Replacing?

What's running through me is hard to decipher. It isn't fear, but something close to it, something that has my chest rising and falling rapidly, my core clenching. This is too close to last year's *prayer*.

He steps back and looks me over. A tickling warmth starts where my toes graze the ground, rising slowly up my ankle, around my calf. Like a snake slithering, the heat finds its way above my knee. Tightening around my thigh.

That soft burn follows Hades' gaze to where the slip lifts from the new position.

If this were anyone else, I might panic at being restrained, at being looked at and touched so intimately, but I've dreamt of this, dreamt about *him*.

My skin savors that flame as it coaxes my eyes shut. I force them open to watch him, the concentration between his knotted brows, his fingers dancing as he controls the flames like a marionette, and the pressed outline I saw in his study.

The tips of my breasts tingle as if he'd flicked them with his own fingers, and my head flings back when it feels like he pinches and tugs.

My mind dazes as my entire body awakens, a tremor of sparks bursting through me.

"You're *very* sensitive, Deviant. I haven't even started and you already—"

"You made me." The accusation has that devious grin tilting.

I don't get to catch my breath before the thin fabric singes away, the slight breeze cooling my naked body.

My wrists jerk, instinctively wanting to cover myself back up, but the look on his face stops me.

He takes one step forward, before righting himself back in place, maintaining his distance.

The flames find my sensitive nipples again. This time, the pinch is softer, matching the ones running along my neck and spine.

Desire fills me in ways it never has before, but it's too soft. His flames drop from my spine to tickle my upper thighs, teasing, refusing to go where I need them to.

The grin that plays on his lips tells me he's doing this on purpose. He somehow knows exactly what I crave and refuse to ask for.

Why can't I be normal and enjoy this gentle touch? What I want is too embarrassing, too depraved.

"If you don't tell me what you want, I'm not going to give it to you."

"But," I whimper. "Hades, you said—"

He takes a few steps forward without backing away this time. He's so close I could kick him if I push off the tree, which is what I want to do right now, but I feel too weak to try.

"Hades…" I writhe against the restraints, a movement he focuses on before dropping his attention to my breasts. His tongue coats his bottom lip, and for a second, I think he's finally going to touch me. But when he lifts his hands, his fingers dance instead.

The flames come alive, licking along my neck and teasing my over-sensitive nipples. Every inch that isn't touched by the flame is cold and aching for it.

"I'll give you exactly what you want. I'll swear on any entity you believe in." He pauses, drawing out every word. "I'll give you *exactly* what you want. You only have to tell me."

My shoulders sink. "I need…"

His chest rises and falls with an unsteady rhythm. I can see the restraint he holds on himself, the need and desire, feeling them as if they're my own.

"*Words*, Little Deviant."

The demand, the restraints, the flames, it leaves me a melting mess at his feet. I don't care if it isn't normal to love the things he's doing— the teasing, the neediness, the subtle depravity. When he urges me to speak again, I can't hide or lie.

"I want more!" I resist the urge to bite the inside of my cheek. "I don't want soft and gentle. I want to be sore and bruised." My stomach flips at the admission, but I can't hold my tongue, not with him so willing to give me what I've craved. "I want the ruthless *King* to use me."

His control over the flames disappears, and for a second, I regret letting him get to me, for allowing him to pull out the twisted side of me I wanted to keep hidden forever.

When I chance a look at him, I see the blacks of his eyes as he makes the two steps to me. "Fuck it."

The moment those inked hands grab me, my body melts into his and comes alive all over again.

His mouth replaces where the flame had been. He kisses, licks, and sucks my sensitive flesh before his teeth sink into my neck. His name slips past my lips again at the sharp sting.

202

His thumb slides across my nipple before tugging it between two fingers. He copies the motion with the other one before bending down and taking it into his mouth, his teeth and tongue working simultaneously, leaving my suspended body trembling and open for him.

There is no controlling my moans, not as his flames continue to roam between my legs, leaving kindling that lights the second they leave. Or maybe it's his hands. I can't tell where one ends and the other begins. Everything is so warm.

My knees would have given out if it weren't for the restraint around my wrists. That, too, is growing in heat. Either he's losing more of his control, or he knows I live for that scorch. I can feel the sweat begin to drip down my forehead.

His fingers dig into my thighs, promising bruises, as he lifts me. My legs wrap around him on silent command, giving him the access he needs.

"Mine to use?" His breath tickles my ear before nipping at the lobe. Where his fingers hover, I ache and throb with anticipation.

Yes! I nod, straining against my confined wrists, needing to touch him, the tense ravens on his shoulders.

His brow cocks, and I know he won't touch me until I say it out loud.

With a groan, I give in, allowing him a point in this stupid game. "Use me," I don't recognize myself as I finish the word I know will get a rise out of him, "*King*."

A low groan vibrates from his chest as he brings his mouth to mine, sliding a finger into me. His teeth catch my lip on the moan, pulling out to add another finger, cursing with me when he fills me even more.

I continue to moan against every swirl of his tongue and nip of his teeth, every drive between my legs and circling of that spot that sends golden stars across my hazy vision.

When I nip back, that firm control he holds disappears. He takes his fingers from the nape of my neck to the crown of my head, taking a fistful of my hair and pulling, opening me up even more.

The only sense of control he has left is the hand working between my thighs at a worshipping pace, one that's meant for me. It isn't slow but deliberate.

Savoring the burn at the back of my scalp and the flames digging into my thighs, my mind muddles between reality and believing this is one of my fantasies.

Euphoria spreads throughout every sensitive inch of me, as I unabashedly call his name as if I were dying and in desperate need of a God to save me—the God of Death and Souls, the one he's coaxing from me now.

When he releases my hands from above my head, they naturally wrap around his neck, my fingers lacing through his messy onyx hair as I come down.

"Kore." His ragged breathing is a song against my ears.

When I open my eyes, I cup my mouth to keep from gasping.

As much as I don't want to leave his warmth, I untangle myself from Hades' hold and drop to the ground, scooping the purple wildflowers blooming beneath my feet. It's hard to tear my attention away from them to take in the rest of the flourishing garden, now filled with apple trees, lemon trees, orange trees, roses, lilies, chrysanthemums, tulips, raspberries, blueberries, strawberries, blackberries... It's endless.

A bird caws, and Hades slides his shirt over my head, reminding me that I'm naked.

When I look up, I find him taking in the garden with pure fascination. A lightness softens his hardened features as he closes his eyes to inhale the fresh new scents. He quickly stiffens once more when he senses me watching him. "You're still not going to the Heavens."

I lift from the ground, adjusting the top to make sure it covers me before poking his inked chest. "That has nothing to do with what just happened, and don't you dare try to make it into that." When he doesn't say anything, I poke him again. "Besides, you heard Aphrodite in those images. It's inevitable."

He gives me another challenging look, those eyes sharpening with a glimmer that doesn't wipe away that lingering smolder but accentuates it. "Is that so?"

I give him my own *your-move* glare, that he accepts by grinning wide enough to show his teeth. The very ones that were nipping my lips and teasing my neck.

204

My body doesn't understand that now isn't the time to melt in front of him, because it warms back up, about to do just that.

Until he disappears as if he were never here.

The beautiful miracle that surrounds me should have me beaming and filled with happiness, more so because it's in the Underworld, but all I can think about is my next move against the God who left me alone after making me feel so alive.

A raven's caw brings my attention to the branches in the tree he ravaged me against.

Hermes.

Chapter Eighteen

HADES

P
lease, don't—I swear, I didn't do it."

The begging and lies fuel a deep laugh I didn't realize I needed, a release that won't lead to self-hatred.

"It was an accident. I swear!" The man pleads. They always grovel with their falsehoods but never for forgiveness, scrambling to save themselves.

"Really? You swear? My sincerest apologies for misunderstanding what I witnessed myself." I drag the blackened blade along the ground next to the soul lying limp below the hanging boulder, its steel pulsing with the lives it's claimed, eager for this one. "I must have misunderstood the young woman before you, begging you to leave the room. It was an accident that your disgusting hands were all over her body after she pleaded for you to stop touching her?"

As I taunt the worthless worm of a man, I'm not thinking about his repulsive past but rather a certain deviant that came undone on *my* hands. She hadn't pushed me away nor told me to stop. There was no look of fear or hatred, not the sick and twisted kind anyway. I searched for every way out, but for some reason she begged for me to continue, whispered my name with that sultry plea, fought against the restraints to touch me.

I didn't plan to touch *her*.

The flames were supposed to be the only extension of me that was lucky enough to feel her curves, to lick her soft skin, but that whimper and need in her lust-filled eyes had me crumbling at the sight.

I lost control.

The need to cleanse her of every bad memory of that lowlife scum, *Pirithous*, and her *friend* Adonis, and any other senseless prick who touched her, fueled the only restraint remaining in me to not take her entirely. Selfishly, I want those memories replaced with myself, and not just the ones she asked me to get rid of.

I want her to be all consumed by me as much as I am by her. Even now, I can't focus on the tortured soul before me, because of *her*.

"Why?" I ask the pleading man, needing to know. "You could have found a willing woman. Why touch the one that didn't want you?"

"I—It was an accident. Pleaaaa... I beg you—" His cries fall on deaf ears. This isn't as satisfying as I thought it would be. I need the real one to ask why *he* touched *her*.

Stabbing and leaving this man for dead would be easy, maybe a little fun to dismember him while he continues pitying himself, but it isn't his cries I want to hear.

He does cry out, though, as I cut a small line down his cheek, his blood seeping into the blade—Requiem, I call her—that binds his soul to Tartarus. "This rock is going to land on you when you least expect it." I stand from the crouched position, watching the man struggle against his shackles with terror flooding his every nerve. "*Maybe*."

Rather than leave to think about the Goddess plaguing my mind and testing what thin patience I have, I jump to the one room with the one woman who can talk my ear off long enough to get me out of my own head.

"Hades! *Oh*—" Hecate's excited greeting drops, seeing my hands stained with crimson blood. "That's the fifth one this week. Are you going mad?"

Her head would blow if she knew exactly how many I tortured just today. I wave her off, perching myself on top of a stool in front of the fresh flames, letting the heat refuel my stores. "Mad as one can be here."

Hecate dashes around, gathering the usual to make the tea I need to sleep. "I love torture as much as you, but this is excessive for either of us. Are you sure you're not going a little mad? You know, Kore said something the other day about going mad here. She said if she has to read another book about a war Ares took part in, she's going to gouge her own eyes out with the daggers she makes from the paper."

I chuckle at the imagery. The only things I want removed are those violent scars on her back.

"*Hades*," Hecate warns as my hands fill with flames. "I've never seen you this untamed."

I grunt, taking back the tea in one shot. Before sleep can take hold, I tell Hecate everything that took place in the gardens, not withholding any information. If I considered anyone a friend, it's her, and Hermes, but his curse prevents us from sharing too much. Hecate, on the other hand, has been by my side for centuries. She knows me well enough to know the exact weapon I need to torture with, depending on my mood, so telling her about the intimate details of what happened between Kore and me is easy. I know too much about Dionysus as it is.

I still can't figure out how Kore found the gardens. I had gone there to stay clear of her, to avoid all temptation, and then all of a sudden, the little deviant was there, kneeling before me.

Hecate's usual eagerness fades, making the scar on her cheek appear longer and happier than she is. "That... I... Here? That's impossible." Usually not one for a lack of words, Hecate paces back and forth, biting her nails in broken thought. "You have to keep enticing her."

"Absolutely not." Touching her again would only further complicate what I need her to do for me.

"She's fueled by lust. Until she has control, that's how she can access her gifts."

My head aches, and I let it drop into my hands. I need her to have complete access to every depth of her abilities, but putting myself in the position to lose control again is risky.

The week away did nothing but test my ability to stay undetected by her and everyone else. I planned to keep my distance, focusing on sentencing and wrangling the lost souls with Charon until I could get a grip on myself, but when I saw her sleeping in the library with books scattered all around her, the crease between her brows like she was having a nightmare, I was enamored with a need to know what it was that caused it. That was just the first time.

Since then, she hadn't noticed me walking behind her in the hallway while she bantered with Hermes or sitting across from her in the library as she laughed so carefree with Dionysus. She didn't feel me watching her struggle to sleep or squirreling away food in case I did plan to starve her. I even followed her and Hermes to this very room when I heard her ask about me, seeing the way her cheeks pinked and how she bites the insides of them when she thinks she's said too much. When I saw her grow irate with Hecate, I couldn't stop myself from reaching for her. I hadn't expected my touch to calm her.

My favorite moments were when she tried to persuade the others to help convince me to let her go to the Heavens. The determination of the little deviant is strangely erotic to witness and has my wrist sore at this point.

Hecate stops pacing to grab a book and thumbs through it mindlessly, making every flip of the page sharper than the last. "If you don't want to, I'll tell Hermes to do it. He'd have no problem turning our little princess on. He even slept in her bed the other night."

My head jerks at the comment.

When Hermes found me carrying Kore to her room after finding her asleep in the library for the third time, I handed her to him like I couldn't care less. I didn't want to hear the asshole point out what I already knew.

I should have known Hermes would ignore my *one* request not to touch her.

"Maybe it's you who needs to learn control." She nods to the fire building in my palms again.

I release the flame before pocketing my fists. The witch isn't wrong.

The door opens and closes, and by the way Hecate snarls, I know it's Minthe behind me.

"Your mortal pet is begging to see you. She says she can't stand to be around Eris, Hypnos keeps *accidentally* putting her to sleep, and Moros is standing guard to keep her from running off."

"She's not a prisoner, so why—" I run my hands through my hair, ignoring the urge to rip it out. "Never mind, put her in a room up here until we can find her something else."

Minthe taps her foot, unfinished, every single one pressing on my nerves. "Why keep Kore here and not out there like the other mortal pet?"

I turn, leveling my growing frustration with the nymph. If I were the ruthless, careless being that everyone thinks I am, I would have banned

209

her from the Underworld long ago. "The mortal isn't my pet. She's an indefinite guest until I say otherwise. Kore will stay where I want her to stay. Neither concern you." I angle my head back to Hecate. "I'll help Kore myself."

The witch grins, already knowing I would agree. Before I leave, I conjure a book directly into her hand. "Make sure she gets this. If it comes from you, she'll read it. It's time she starts understanding why she's here."

I thought I had more time to ease her into her new reality. She was to learn about the past, her abilities, and ally with me before I needed her. But with Demeter's call and Kore's persistence for defiance, I'm not sure time is on my side.

I jump back to my room, where I slump onto the mattress, ready to drown myself in nightmares.

Instead, I dream of amethyst eyes and the sharp tongue of my enemy's daughter.

Chapter Nineteen

DORA

I dump a bucket of water onto last night's fire while Adonis finishes watering the horse, and Aphrodite gathers our drying clothes from the branches.

A sharp sting tears a hiss from me. I clench my teeth and jerk back, seeing the sliver of wood that snagged my knee, the trickle of black blood dripping to my ankle.

Touched by evil, that's what Aphrodite said I was.

Only after enjoying my panic-riddled spiraling questions did she explain that the term comes from those who fear the primordial beings who possess the marking: Furies, Titans, monsters, witches, and true oracles.

My monthly blood has always been red, and any cut or scrape I've managed has only ever scabbed over crimson. Whatever caused this change came recently. Either I hold some suspended primordial-like blood that's revealing now, or, most likely, I'm cursed.

It wasn't Apollo because, as Aphrodite explained, he's a prophetic God, who was cursed but doesn't have the ability to curse. Having the burden of living on greed, he dragged me, who came all too willing, to the temple to feed off mine. If I had listened to my instincts and left instead of listening to his stories, I would have been safe from him, though not necessarily the serpent.

I look over the pink scar that slices from my palm to my elbow, wondering if perhaps it had been the oath that triggered the change.

"One more day, right?" Adonis asks, leading the horse back to our campsite. "I can't sleep another night on the ground or eat another gamey rabbit." His steps are lighter, and he smiles more, now that the tattoo is no longer on his neck. A tiny spark of the rare, playful Adonis replaces the old passive one I knew and the hopeless one I've become acquainted with on this journey.

Another week and he might stop standing so statuesque all the time.

Aphrodite nods eagerly. She, too, has relaxed more as we passed the week walking along the river, no longer peeking over her shoulder every few minutes. Even her voice holds less snark as she pressed us about our relationship with Kore.

I still don't trust her, but since we can't lie to each other, my walls slip a little when we get lost in conversation.

As we start on our last trek up the steep mountain, my eyes catch on Aphrodite's golden shackles. Unable to hold my tongue any longer, I ask, "What did you do to end up as a prisoner?"

Her glare pierces straight through me, replacing all progress we've made over the week. "Does one *need* to do something to become a prisoner?"

Adonis tenses, falling back to my side. "She didn't mean it like that." His unspoken words are written on his face: *Dora doesn't understand.*

My ego shrinks to the size of a pebble. "I may not be a servant or a prisoner, but I can empathize. I simply wanted to understand what we could be walking into. If you're a prisoner, what does that mean for us? Will we be prisoners too?" I'm rambling now, but I can never stop once I start. "If you murdered someone, I guess I'd want to know how and why, but also why would they let you free? If—"

"*Dora.*" Adonis nudges my shoulder, a faint smile tugging past his warning glance.

"*Adonis.*" I nudge him right back with my own failed attempt at a stern glare, leaving us smiling at each other like idiots.

Aphrodite takes us in with dimmed amusement, and I can see the stubbornness melt away the moment her shoulders drop, and she begins fixing our bag on the horse. "*Very* few can even see the shackles, and even fewer are aware I'm a prisoner. *He* likes it that way, so you'll be guests in my facade of a kingdom. It's small but quaint."

As hard as it is, I don't press the topic any further. Had I not noticed the quick flinch in her hands as she finished untying and retying the knot, or the slight quiver in her voice, I might have, but I've seen the signs of trauma before and know better than to poke a lion.

As we continue in silence, I pass the time daydreaming of what Aphrodite's kingdom could possibly look like, imagining the enormous palaces, menageries, and gardens. I imagine it has an airy feel with a sea nearby.

Adonis' newfound confidence has no such restraint because it isn't long before he asks the exact question I want to know. "Who imprisoned you?"

To my surprise, Aphrodite's mouth opens to answer, quickly shutting at the sound of voices calling behind us. Without stopping, we glance at one another before peering over our shoulders. Three figures close in, their walk brisk and direct.

"You will obey my commands, and you will not leave my side by any means." My body freezes over all at once, barely feeling the gentle touch of Aphrodite's fingers pressing against my wrists. The Goddess visibly softens, seeing the shell that becomes us. "You'll be aware and remember everything, I promise." Squaring her shoulders, she turns to the approaching figures cloaked in white, whispering back one last time, "Stay still and silent."

I see the panic in Adonis' eyes, but I can't reach out or say anything.

"Well, well, well, if it isn't Aphrodite, and…" The woman removes her cloak, revealing her pin-straight pale hair cut to her jaw, elongating her skinny neck that showcases the points of her ears. "Pets," her voice heightens, flashing me a look that makes the hairs on the back of my neck prickle.

"If it isn't low-level sea scum Princess Pallas and…" Aphrodite mimics her head tilt to look over the woman's shoulder at her followers.

The taller one removes her cloak, revealing a body that could match a man's strength with ease. Her hair is darker than blood, braided down her back.

The shorter one is the exact opposite: dark skin, short and petite, with barely any curls kissing her scalp. Her most striking feature is her thick lips with one freckle below the crease.

"Pallas and her what?" The larger woman dares Aphrodite, who dwarfs them all while still managing to keep her head held high, letting her silence answer for her. Her specialty, I've learned.

The masculine woman's attention falls to me. If I weren't already frozen, her cold assessment would have glued me to this very spot. "Is this her?"

"No," Aphrodite answers, examining her fingernails, a gesture I've only witnessed Kore do when she's feigning uninterest.

The large woman takes another step, attempting to use her size to intimidate Aphrodite. "You know we can sense her here. I'm surprised no one's taken her from you yet. Do you really think Zeus will give you freedom in exchange for her?"

"It's not her, sooo, no. As Pallas so accurately noted, they're my pets, Athena."

My chest flutters with elated terror knowing the warrior Goddess is before us. How Aphrodite is standing her own, *bantering*, against a woman who aids Ares in war is incredible—daring and borderline suicidal, but incredible, nonetheless.

"Is that right?" Somehow, Athena manages to broaden her shoulders even more, shadowing Aphrodite with her impressive build.

"This is easy to resolve," Pallas interjects, separating them with her bony arms before stalking in my direction. When she reaches me, I can't coil away as she hooks her finger under my chin, and takes a deep, long inhale through her nose.

At the light touch, I attempt to pull an image, anything to make this unpleasant passing useful, but she drops my chin before anything comes.

Pallas turns her nose toward the horse at my back, her massive aqua eyes flickering back to me one last time before grabbing Kore's bloody cloak and holding it in the air. "It's not her. It's this."

"So, you did have her. And you lost her?" Athena boasts triumphantly, her chuckle strong enough to make me shiver. "When I heard about the homecoming, I knew it couldn't be you who would bring her to him. It'll probably be Ares or Hermes." There's a hostile bite as she speaks, her icy stare falling to Adonis before sizing me up again. "I suggest you keep your pets on a tighter leash than Zeus keeps you."

"Worry about your own pet, Athena. It seems yours is getting a little too comfortable in charge." Aphrodite motions toward Pallas, who whistles and lets out a confident snicker, the tension in the air physically thickening the longer it draws out.

It seems everyone is waiting for the next harsh remark, all eyes bouncing between Aphrodite and Athena.

It's Athena who makes the next move.

Smack!

Her massive fist strikes Aphrodite across the face, blood spraying the grass, not gold as I had seen before, but black. "You're lucky you're under Zeus' protection."

Being frozen and aware is almost worse than not being aware at all. I scream for my body to move, to help the Goddess I've come to know, but my limbs remain unchanged and deaf to my commands.

Aphrodite angles her anger toward the short woman who hasn't moved. "What are you looking at?"

"Medusa doesn't speak," Pallas says, knocking her shoulder against Aphrodite's from behind, only to circle back around. They are like a pack of wolves playing with and circling their prey.

Medusa remains stoic, covering her head with the white hood, content to stay the quiet observer.

I'm not as content. Pure hatred blooms for this woman who can just stand by and watch as another is beaten, more so than the ones making the physical blows.

I'm forced to watch as Pallas stalks back to me, her head tilting with a sickly interest. "I kind of like this one." Her hand smells of the salty sea as she strokes softly down my cheek. "Can we have her?"

Aphrodite sucks her bottom lip between her teeth, looking up to Athena, clocking the warrior Goddess' glare burning into the back of Pallas' head. "Maybe later."

No, I silently cry as Pallas' pleased smirk lifts at the promise.

"Let's go," Athena demands, pulling at her skinny friend's shoulder.

"Come on, 'Thena, she'd be perfect with the other priestesses." The *sea filth* wraps a lock of my hair around her finger, bringing it to her nose for another whiff.

"I said, let's go," Athena shouts.

Pallas surrenders, but not before whispering in my ear, "I'll see you soon." Her soft lips brush my cheek before sauntering away with a wink.

The two grab Medusa's arm and vanish, just as Kore had, right before my eyes.

215

With the tension gone, Aphrodite releases a deep breath. Her lip drips with blood, but the cut is already healed. "I release you."

Adonis runs to her first, pulling her to the river's edge to clean her face. I fall in step behind them, feeling the need to bathe away that woman's salty stench from my skin.

Aphrodite glances at me, looking me up and down as if to check if *I'm* unharmed. When our eyes meet again, I'm ready to burst with questions and stories about Athena. The Goddess was every bit how I pictured, massive and mean, built and bitchy, with a smug aura of a know-it-all.

As brazen as Aphrodite is, she didn't deserve to be abused or belittled.

The one question I want to confirm is at the tip of my tongue when Aphrodite nods, reading it on my face. "Zeus."

Zeus is her captor.

Zeus set the reward.

Zeus, King of all Gods, wants Kore.

None of us speak as we continue up the river. The horse pants alongside us because we all refused to weigh the poor thing down and didn't have the heart to leave him behind.

The trees grow sparse as we climb higher, the breeze chillier. It's hours later when I notice the change in color, the burgundy and ambers settling into the greenery, the fallen leaves.

Oh, sweet Styx.

"You'll be thankful to be in the Heavens. If you ask nicely, I might even let you stay until the freeze passes." Aphrodite confirms my fear. I had been too young when the freeze took over the Mortal Veil, but I heard rumors and read how cold and barren the earth grew, and how many people died and suffered.

Adonis passes me a look that mirrors my alarm.

"It's best not to dwell on things you can't control. You should be thinking about the homecoming. Your friend and her brother have been lost for twenty years. And if they're letting in sea filth like Pallas, I can assume this will be the largest gathering of Gods yet."

We all pick up our pace, having abandoned our sweat-slicked sandals that gave us blisters in places I didn't realize blisters could grow.

"What if Hades doesn't bring Kore?" Adonis asks.

When Aphrodite told us about her prophetic friend seeing Kore become what she was fated to be in a clearing near the Heavens, my instinct was not to believe her. Then I remembered our oath to never lie to one another. It's what she *isn't* saying that has me fearful for Kore.

"Hades can't enter the Heavens. And knowing him, he's likely to keep her in the Underworld for as long as he can. I have a friend who will ensure she's there to finish her transitions."

Adonis rubs the back of his neck, a habit he's formed during the long days of walking.

I can see his relief almost more than I can feel my own, knowing that our visit to the Heavens won't put us in Hades' path. Not even my aching curiosity piques for the death God. Some things and beings are best left unknown.

That's what I tell myself anyway because I refuse to think about the stories and myths I know about him, how it's said he abducts women and uses them until they die, and then even more after. The real fear comes from his methods and bloodthirst for torture.

But I won't let myself think about that, not while Kore is still there. Something Aphrodite said she confirmed through *the birds*.

When I spot the top of Mt. Olympus in the distance, I rush toward it without waiting for the others, ignoring the sting in my feet and ache in my legs. My fingers tingle to touch the ground, the trees, the—

My feet slow, my head jerking in every direction. That flicker of joy dissipates.

The clearing is empty. There's nothing but grass surrounded by the same changing trees we walked next to all week, and a few toppled pillars.

Adonis catches up, his excitement faltering just as mine had. I didn't expect palaces or kingdoms right away, but maybe a bench, or a tiny home for visitors, or something.

We're too busy taking in the emptiness to notice when Aphrodite begins whispering in a language I've never heard.

"What are you doing?" I ask.

Two golden chalices appear before her. She quickly bends to grab them and hands us each one. "It's your first time, so you must drink for the veil to drop."

217

I reach for it, my fingers inches away, when I still. Everything stills. Pressure builds in the back of my head, as if visions are trying to reach me, but they're blocked.

I step back, suddenly uneasy. A sense of deja vu rushes through me followed by distant screams begging for me to leave, *immediately*.

I take another step back. "This isn't right."

"Have you forgotten your oath never to leave me?"

No. An urgent panic rises higher in my pounding chest, suffocating me, promising death before taking that chalice.

"You're being quite ungrateful. You demanded I take you to Kore, which I am. I removed Adonis' tattoo. Pallas wanted to take you with her, but I didn't let that happen. I swore on the river Styx for you to trust me, scarring my perfect hand, swearing not to lie or leave you again. In fact, I remember saving you at Metanira's house from being captured by that servant, who was most certainly going to turn you in. And I even stopped Metanira, who tried to hit you. So, tell me, Squirrel, why in all the veils are you so untrusting of me now?"

"Dora, we came all this way." Adonis reaches for me, but I jerk away before he can touch me.

"Something's not right. I—I can feel it. I'm not supposed to be here." Every inch of my skin tingles to not so much as touch the earth beneath my feet, to run away from this place, as far away as I can.

Run! A small voice in the back of my mind screams.

Aphrodite's lips lift so slowly that I think time stops for a moment.

"On the contrary..." She juts her chin toward Adonis, giving him a signal I don't understand. The next thing I see is him rushing me, slamming me to the ground. "This is exactly where you were always supposed to be."

Aphrodite leans down, tucking my hair from my face. "Drink," she sings, lifting the cup to my obeying lips. "It's not ambrosia, not that it would affect you anyway." The liquid trails warmth down to my aching stomach.

Aphrodite returns to the center of the clearing and continues what sounds like a prayer.

When Adonis releases me to take his own drink, I sprint for the tree line, finding everything beginning to shift. The moon disappears, replaced with a bright blue sky. The trees change back to a lush green, making me realize just how orange and red they were before.

What looks like a cluster of temples appear all around us, their entrances crumbling and cracked at odd angles except for the one right in front of us. It bears two large white statues of a bearded man with a seven-pointed star hanging from his neck, holding a raised silver gate.

With a soft touch on my shoulder, Aphrodite's whispered cadence freezes over me, "Follow me."

Chapter Twenty

KORE

The sound of pattered knocking wakes me from the deepest sleep I've had in years. Whoever is behind the obnoxious noise has a book to the head coming their way.

"Come in!" I shout, reaching for the one laid out next to me.

Dionysus pokes his head around the door. "Are you decent?"

I'm about to toss the book when I notice which one I have. It's the one I had been reading when Dionysus walked in on me *indecent* last night.

I found it to learn more about Hades, to use whatever I can against him in whatever game it is we're playing. But as tired and angry as I was, I couldn't stop thinking about his flames licking over me, how he restrained me with them, the way he watched my every limb writhe and listened to my every moan. His demand for me to say what I wanted, and how he gave it to me the second it left my lips.

Replaying the night in my mind wasn't enough. I tried to mimic what his fingers had done. I could practically hear him next to me whispering exactly what to do, how to circle and flick my fingers, when Dionysus barged in.

Hiding the flush I know is creeping up my neck, I slide the furs higher, asking what's so urgent that he had to knock for ten minutes straight.

He drops onto the vanity chair, picking through the floral scents and untouched makeup. "You weren't at breakfast or in the library. I figured you were sick or tried to escape." He gives me a worried look. "You do look awful."

I change the book for a pillow and launch it. He catches it before it hits his head. "Oooh and cranky," he teases, tossing it right back. "You must not have finished."

I ready the book this time.

"If you hurry up, I'll make you breakfast." He holds his hands up in defense, but the book is already dropped at my side. I don't need any further encouragement to rush to the closet and put myself together.

As I wash up, I catch the bruises on the sides of my thighs and hips. I drink in the sight, a dark, satisfying pride flickering as I trace them. *I allowed this.*

I snip the citrine-colored dress in the right places to hide the pretty reminders, stretching the sapphire bangle to sit along my thigh, matching the sapphires I pin in my hair.

When I reemerge from the mirror, Dionysus' whistle makes me blush. It's one of my favorite designs so far, inspired by the daisies and bluebells I saw in the garden.

He conjures two cups, passing me the one filled with my favorite wine.

"Is it bad to drink this for breakfast?" I don't wait for his response before sipping the sweet grape.

"Not if I join you." He lifts the cup to his lips. "Besides, it's the afternoon."

I nearly trip over his words. There isn't a day in my life that I can recall sleeping in after the sun rose. Then again, there is no sun here.

I think back to the garden and wonder if it will continue to thrive without the daylight, wondering if it was me who had caused it to bloom. Hecate said I would feel when my magic appeared, but I had been so lost in the moment with Hades' fingers—

I swallow the growing heat down with wine, refusing to think about last night with my brother walking next to me.

After shaking my head to physically clear it, I ask him how he found his abilities.

Something deep inside, deeper than my veins or bones, lights up. I had felt that kinship tug between us before, but this time it has me studying him closer.

On the surface, we look similar, with the same round eyes and dark wavy hair. But his height towers me, and where he's hard with muscle, I'm soft, where I swallow myself with timidness, he grows with confidence, and where I giggle with embarrassment, he roars with laughter.

If I weren't already looking at him, I would have missed the strange darkness that passes over his face. "It was under extreme duress, and I was lucky to be mid-transition when it happened, or I would have killed that poor girl."

"What kind of duress?" I pry for more, too curious to leave it at that.

I follow him through the spotless, white kitchen, helping him gather fresh bread and cheeses as he continues telling me how he was kidnapped by pirates for ransom. He falls into a distant memory when he mentions the annoying woman tied up with him, *Ariadne*. He whispers her name like it's a secret, and continues to explain how they were restrained for days before the crew realized there was no place for them to escape in the middle of the sea, and there would be no ransom if they died of starvation. They dined that night and drank wine like it was the water they desperately needed.

It physically pains me to watch him mangle the bread against the counter, slicing it into thin pieces. I watch from the corner of my eye to ensure he doesn't cut his finger, a habit I formed from too many incidents with Dora. The girl could cut her finger with a spoon and mistake salt for sugar in less than five minutes.

Dionysus ignores my keen observations as he waves the knife up and down his body, explaining the heat that overcame him that night, followed by the freezing pain. The crew tied him back up, believing he had a plague, then proceeded to drag a kicking and screaming Ariadne to the bunks below.

"I wanted them to rape each other instead, or jump over the boat and drown themselves, anything to get them away from her. You can imagine my surprise when they all threw themselves overboard. I knew instantly—I could feel that I made them do it."

"What about Ariadne?" I ask, hoping the poor woman wasn't hurt. "You said you almost killed her?"

He holds his hands up as an explanation. "She untied me, and when I tried to help her stand, she fell into a deep sleep that I couldn't wake her from. By the time she woke again, I'd already changed every cup of water into wine, and I figured I must have done something similar to her, so I stayed away." He sighs softly, dropping the knife, and giving me those round, sorrowful eyes. "It's what happened when I tried to help you stand that first night. You're a Goddess, but you were also depleted at the time, and I must have forgotten myself."

Remembering my own pounding headache and grogginess, I'm relieved that the girl woke up at all.

I finish plating the grapes, pop one in my mouth, and ask how he learned control.

"I accessed them when I was in a state of fear, so I used that fear to call them up again until I could control it better." He refills my glass with an impish glimmer behind his eyes. "Do you want to play a drinking game?"

I stumble down the tilting hallway with my arm threaded within Dionysus' until we make it to the enormous library, a room I never thought I'd seek out on my own so often.

Untangling myself from him, I run across the entryway and leap onto my favorite plush chair that swallows me whole. The high ceilings and the tower's airy beauty still take my breath away. Every level is lit up by what looks like tiny stars or glowing drops of rain that reveal tiers of unlimited books and scrolls.

Feet pad down the hardwood floors, too quick and light to be Dionysus.

"Are you two the idiots who conjured these plates of mushed bread and cheese with bites taken out? And the grapes?! They're everywhere!"

My giggles are followed by Dionysus'. We are indeed the idiots, or rather, I am. It took a lot of alcohol, which I was forced to drink after every failed conjuring attempt. With every grape, cheese, and bread I finally made disappear, it was Dionysus' turn to drink. It turns out conjuring makes me hungry, and the cheeses are creamy enough to die for.

"I smell a witch with too much salt in her cauldron," Dionysus slurs, plopping himself onto another bed-sized chaise. "Come on, Hecate, have a drink with us."

Hecate leans over a railing. "You think I would drink with you again? You had me out of my slip before I had a chance to get a refill. And you, princess," Hecate points her small finger at me. "You're lucky you're family with him or you'd be out of yours too."

"I only have eyes for you, wicked witch," Dionysus calls back.

"You're really going to seduce Hecate in front of your sister?" Hermes' voice sends my stomach to my feet and a heated blush to my cheeks. I can't forget the birds that were in the garden last night, and I'm not naïve enough to think they weren't his. I cover my face with a pillow, peeking over the top to find him leaning against the post behind me.

His head cocks to the side. "Are you drunk, Little Bat?"

Absolutely.

"That's my fault." Dionysus chuckles. "I wanted her to try using her abilities without being so in her head."

"And?"

Too elated by my accomplishment, I angle myself so I don't have to crane my neck to tell him, "I conjured plates!"

Hermes gives me a proud, dimpled grin and nod of approval.

"Conjuring is wonderful, but what do you think about mind manipulation?" Hecate squeals, skipping toward us. She looks even smaller than she is with the high shelves behind her. "It's rare and probably won't work, but since he's already drunk, we can try it on Dionysus. His mind will be weaker than it normally is."

"Why don't you toss a few back, and we can have a go at you?" Dionysus moves to grab her, but she scurried out of the way just in time to jump on my chair and crawl under the blanket with me. "I had a book of prophecies sent to your room, tagged with ones I want you to read through. It's hexed to add new ones, so don't be alarmed if it grows." She bites her lip on the last word, her cheeks rounding with an eager tint.

She knows.

"Sorry, we've been friends for centuries. He tells me everything."

My mind clouds with what it could mean that Hades told Hecate anything about us. *What* exactly did he tell her? I had wanted to tell the witch about everything what happened in the garden, with the flowers and Hades, if only to make sense of it all. I've grown so used to gossiping with Hecate while she works on her witchcraft. But Hades telling her—

It means nothing. He told me to use him. He felt sorry for me and maybe a little guilty that he was going to use me too. I can appreciate the balance. Him leaving me half-naked and alone after reminding me I wasn't allowed in the Heavens tells me all I need to know. It was a one-time lack of judgment on both of our parts.

I hiss when the skin around my thumb breaks.

I can feel Hermes' attention on me again, but it's Hecate's touch that startles me. It's getting easier to stifle the flinches when everyone grabs, pulls, and pokes me all day. I've come to learn that Gods have no sense of boundaries.

Realizing Hecate's nails aren't going to dig into my skin, my shoulders untense as she swirls her long nails along my arm, gently tickling and giving me goosebumps. It's innocent enough, but the soft caress is surprisingly titillating.

"You can tell me all the details tonight. After Hermes and I deal with a pet issue. But first, try to connect to Dionysus and get him to say this." Hecate cups her hands around my ear to whisper.

My face crinkles, and Hermes snickers, hearing everything as always.

Hooking one leg over the armrest, Dionysus motions and mouths, *Show me what you got.*

As much as I don't want to, I repeat Hecate's phrase in my head over and over, but Dionysus remains silent. I have no idea what I'm doing, but I use what we've practiced during our other trainings, concentrating on the object I'm attempting to manipulate, Dionysus in this case. I'm about to repeat myself one last time when I feel that kinship connection light up, pulsing between us like a heartbeat.

Want it.

His mocking grin slips as we study each other.

You have to want it.

It isn't his voice exactly, but a feeling—a knowing. I focus on that beating connection again. I *want* him to say these words. At the thought, a new sensation builds as I continue repeating the phrase with genuine intention behind it, the tendrils of my mind caressing that connection.

"No matter what I say, I don't last long in bed," Dionysus repeats before belting, "That was one time!"

"It was the only time." Hecate flings her head back, her uncontrollable laughter penetrating every corner of the vast room.

I sit up straighter, my thoughts sobering. "Did you feel that?" I ask him.

"Feel what?" Hermes eyes flicker between us.

"We have a tie." Dionysus takes the words from my mouth. "It's like a beating, invisible rope we can tug back and forth."

"I could feel what he was trying to tell me, not hear him, but I just knew it," I try to explain.

Hecate gasps, stilling her laughs. "That's beyond mind manipulation. That's—you're soul-tied. Do you know how rare that is? Not even Apollo and Artemis are soul-tied, and they're twins." Her excitement is infectious.

I don't even have to ask what it means for her to continue with a growing elation that I feel, "There are few ways souls are connected. Those who are soul-tied are bound to each other in a way that no one has been able to explain except for a beating, knowing connection—a push and pull, a tug, a tie, a tether of some kind. You should be able to feel one another and access each other's abilities for yourselves. I don't believe you can use it on others, though. It's a personal tie. Then there's fated mates, cursed fates, mirrored fates. There's a book around here someplace. I'll send it to your room. But soul-tied is the rarest and the one we know the least about."

She glances between us with a new interest, like she's seeing us as one of her insects stored in those clear vials. "You both need to practice opening and closing that tie at will, or you'll end up a drunkard." She points at me first and then Dionysus. "And you could end up growing flowers from your ears."

Hermes asks what it felt like, like he, too, is trying to understand something.

"It's hard to explain," Dionysus starts. "It's like—"

"Like an extension of myself," I finish, finally able to place that deep bond. It isn't like the pull I feel with Hermes and Hades, where my body and mind are at constant odds.

226

I seek what I imagine is a beautiful, colorless string and tug. Dionysus pulls right back, his very essence strumming through my veins.

"I can feel her emotions as if they're my own."

"She's an empath," Hecate says with a wonder that once again reminds me of Dora. "I had a feeling."

"She's *very* happy." Dionysus chuckles right before all connection snaps away. He pushes himself to the back of the chair and plants a pillow over his lap.

Hermes' laugh booms throughout the tower.

"Shut up." Dionysus' entire face reddens, his head lolling back. "I just pulled too much."

I glance between the three of them, confused.

"Oh, my Gods." Hecate covers her laughter, understanding something I don't.

"Will someone tell me what is happening?"

Hecate is too lost in laughter to answer, her cheeks bursting with color, folding over herself like it's hard to breathe.

"It means you turned your brother on." Hermes bends at the waist with his own unruly laughter.

"That is not what happened!" Dionysus shouts.

I sink deeper into the cushion, too embarrassed for both of us. I had been happy a moment ago, but not *that* happy. Now, I'm just disturbed. Can he feel my emotions all the time? Had he felt me last night?

"I'm sorry, I didn't mean to," I offer weakly. It's meant to be an apology for his unbecoming reaction, but I'm more than sorry if he feels me at all times.

"It wasn't you!" he says, finally relaxing. "It's like with my gifts. I can make others feel good, but too much can make them act out of control. I didn't will them to, but it happens. When I pulled at your happiness, I took too much."

"You really don't have to continue," Hermes' face sours, but there is a lingering amusement on his lips.

"Please do!" Hecate interrupts. "I need to know everything if we're going to understand her."

The air is suddenly too thick.

I sway as I stand, excusing myself. Crossing to the back of the library, I climb the steps two levels up and stroll the aisles for new books I can barely read the spines of.

Between my mother ignoring me and a town that only snickered behind my back, I'm not used to so much direct attention or having so many people around me at all hours of the night. And with a constant chaperone hovering over my every step and people barging into my room whenever they feel like it, I'm easily suffocated at a moment's notice.

I take in a long, deep inhale through my nose and release it through my mouth.

As I reach for a white book, someone pulls it before I get a chance to.

"Curses?" Hermes flips it a few times between his hands before handing it to me. "I thought you'd be searching for a book on how to perfect your garden in the Underworld."

An unusual ache tugs in my chest and I'm not sure if it's me, Dionysus, or a feeling I'm sensing from Hermes. All I know is I'm mortified at the possibility of him seeing me and Hades last night. So much so that I turn on my heel and head back down the aisle. Avoiding Hermes today had been my top priority, right next to avoiding Hades.

"Wait," he cuts me off before I can round the corner and dash down the steps. "For one, you are not climbing those steps drunk. I'll take you down. Second, why aren't you more excited? The Little Bat I know would be dragging us all out there to see it."

Did you see? I want to ask. I search for any hint that he saw or knew about me and Hades, but all I find is a concerned cocked brow.

"I, um…" I swallow a shaky breath. "I don't really know how I did it." I've been thinking about the garden most of the day, trying to figure out how it bloomed. I know it was me. I know it in my bones. But every time I try to look within, to put myself back in that moment, it only brings me back to Hades.

"You take after Demeter. She has the ability of harvest too, but not even she can grow anything here."

"Has she tried?" I go back to the shelves, pulling a book I'm certain has the word "*Deal*" in the title.

"Once. Hades was desperate to find a way to bring life here, but nothing came of it. The Underworld is impenetrable. Not even his fire can burn the trees."

I flip the pages, considering what he said. I may have sobered a little, but I'm still too drunk to multitask.

If this is what Hades wants from me, to bring life to the Underworld, that should be easy enough once I figure out how I did it. But something nags at me. There must be something else he wants, or he would have thrown me back in the forest and demanded I find a way to bring those withered trees back to life.

A thickening uncertainty rolls off Hermes, and he looks up and down the shelves, like he wants to say more but is unsure how to. "Can't or won't?"

He glances back at me with a small smile, his shoulders visibly dropping as his mouth parts to answer.

"Hermes!" Hecate calls from below. "We have to go!"

He takes a step, his chest brushing mine. I'm sure he can feel my pulse rising. It doesn't matter if I'm thinking about Hades or the gardens, or about the book in my hand, his closeness always affects me this way.

Our bodies move in sync. He lifts me bridal style as I wrap my arms around his neck. He doesn't move right away, and suddenly the wide aisle feels too small for the both of us. It's like the very air he wields is sucked out of my lungs when his eyes drop from mine to where his fingers pull at the sapphire band around my thigh.

A current moves between us, one that snaps away when Hecate screams his name again.

We're back to the first floor within a blink. Hermes sets me down and leaves with the witch without looking back, leaving me with a snoring Dionysus and a hunger I can't satisfy.

My stomach groans in response. There is one hunger I can alleviate.

Orange cake sounds phenomenal, and I know just where to get that orange.

I'm turned around, wandering rooms I've never been in. They're filled with colorful tapestries, an array of simple and gaudy furniture, thick rugs before empty fireplaces. It all appears to be a giant storage for junk if I'm honest. Nothing is layered with dust, but there isn't much life in them either. It only further reminds me how empty the castle is. There are no servants or other guests who pass through the halls.

I turn down another corridor. This one I know. It's decorated with beautiful oil paintings leading all the way to the arched entryway I make my way to, the room filling me with a breathless awe.

Every inch of the walls, including the high ceilings, is covered in more intricate paintings, depicting scenes from myths I heard about growing up. All hold incredible detail, giving me a greater appreciation for such artistry. I can see the different shades of blue in Hades' eyes in the painting of him sitting on a throne of bones, and every muscle that builds Hermes in the art that depicts him flying across the sky. Hephaestus' mask looks like actual metal in another, and Ares' helm appears soft enough to touch as he carries a sword covered in blood, framed with what looks to be that very sword cut into four pieces.

More art is lined along the floor as if there isn't enough room to hang them, even though one wall is left nearly empty, except for the one canvas perfectly centered. It's the only one with a chair in front of it.

I don't sit, choosing to stand to study it closer. The image is truly breathtaking, and the painter who wielded the brush has more talent than I knew one could possess. There are so many different textures, it looks like actual sweat dripping down Kronos' forehead as he's struck with Zeus' lightning bolt in the war of Gods and Titans.

I cross my arms, admiring the work, though it's harder through tipsy eyes.

"What are you doing here?" That phrase flips my stomach, but it's Minthe's voice, sharp and clipped, not Hades. The very sight of the glaring nymph, her hands on her waist to emphasize her distaste for crossing paths, has me wishing I hadn't sobered up so quickly.

Actually...

I reach for that bond with Dionysus. Unsure what to do, I caress it like I had earlier, tapping it, gripping it, but I don't feel anything except the essence of the bond. When I pull it, a rush of euphoria floods me, warmth spilling into my veins, coursing through my belly.

230

I feel the cold glare drilling through the back of my head as the nymph repeats her question louder.

"I heard you," I say. If this were any other being, I would have answered, but she speaks with such animosity that I go back to studying the painting.

If Minthe wants to get a rise out of me, she isn't going to get it. The thought of making friends with her left the moment I realized she had played a joke on me by leading me to the wrong washroom to dress in someone else's old clothing for reasons I still don't understand. It had been the only time I saw a genuine smile on her face, which tells me all I need to know about her.

"Do you think those dresses make you pretty? You're still a prisoner Hades keeps around because he has to, not because he actually *wants* you."

I spin around, the movement causing me to sway and catch myself on the wall. "I don't know. Hades seems to think they're *lovely*." I see her memory jumping to the same one I anticipated.

Her lips tighten as she stalks toward me.

The rush, the swift movements, it's too familiar. I startle, bumping into the lone painting. I turn to catch it, but it's too late. I fall back just as the frame's gilded edge strikes my forehead before cracking on the ground beside me.

Minthe jumps back as if I were set on fire. "I wasn't going to hit you. This arrived for you." She tosses a letter to the ground. Her eyes roll to the ceiling when I offer an apology with a giggle I can't contain. Whatever I pulled from Dionysus is making me delirious. "Never apologize for your honest reactions. It makes you weak and a victim, which doesn't make you special. We're all victims of something."

Agreed.

"And stay away from Hades," Minthe adds. "He may have been waiting years for you, but—"

The air in the room shifts, and the scent of cinnamon that follows me everywhere wraps around me again.

"But what?" Hades asks, picking up the broken frame. His attention shifts from the canvas to Minthe with a look I can only describe as loathsome. "Hmmm? I'm sure Kore would like to know what you were going to say. I know I do. I've waited years for her, but… What?"

231

I audibly swallow, thankful I'm not on the receiving end of that cold stare and harsh tone.

He's cute when he's mad.

My hand clasps over the giggle that wants to weasel its way out.

The nymph doesn't look phased, crossing her arms—her armor shielding herself from him. "I'm reminding her of her place as your prisoner and that you're a busy king who shouldn't be bothered by her pining and little girl tantrums."

Hades drops the painting with disinterest to help me to my feet. I grab his hand, noting the crinkle between his brows deepening when my giggles finally burst free. His arm wraps around my waist to keep me from toppling back over.

"It's you who needs a reminder of your place." He tells her, but his storming eyes don't leave mine. "I'm sending you to the Mortal Veil to pick up a little present. When you bring it back, you can go to the Heavens for intel. After that, you can help Charon wrangle souls from the rivers, and then—"

"I get it," Minthe cuts him off, radiating with anger.

"Great. And Minthe," A sinister smile lifts, and when he tears his gaze from mine, I feel colder than the ice in his voice. "If I find you disrespecting Kore again, I'll send you to Tartarus."

A cluster of butterflies riot in the pit of my stomach.

I'm at a loss for words long after Minthe's footsteps fade back down the hall.

"Tartarus?" I try to shake the alcohol from my head to sober up, but the last laugh is unstoppable. "You can't be serious?"

"You drunk is quite a sight." He gives me a crooked grin and wipes my forehead with a wet cloth he conjured. When I attempt to take it from him to do it myself, he holds it out of my reach, making me look like a toddler jumping after a toy. Eventually, I relent and let him bandage me up with a delicate touch that surprises me.

"She doesn't speak for me." He finishes fixing me up with one last brush of his thumb along the bandaged cut, and picks up the gilded frame again. I don't even bother asking why I needed it when I heal faster than I ever have before. "Why do you insist on protecting those who mean you harm?"

232

"You should be flattered to be on the list." The laugh I thought I'd hear doesn't come. Instead, when that dark aura returns, all lightness I had with the jest suffocates in its presence.

"I suppose you're right." My insides twist at the implication, uncertain if he truly means to harm me or play on my words to mess with me.

I watch him closer as he eyes the painting a little longer before magically fixing it and placing it back as if it had never fallen. "But if the time ever comes where taking up for me means your life, you do what it takes to survive." His sincerity is unsettling. It's like he anticipates such a thing will happen.

As he speaks, his attention never leaves the scene painted on the canvas, and I can't help but ask, "Why is this painting alone on the wall?"

He motions for me to sit in the chair.

Still a little drunk and lightheaded from the strike to the head, I oblige, watching as he circles to the back and leans over, his breath hot against my neck as we observe the painting together.

"This is the moment everything changed. Zeus killed Kronos and took over as King of the Gods, fulfilling the prophecy that he would die by his last creation. The painter of this one was a mortal prophet who painted rather than spoke or wrote what he saw."

He pauses, letting me take in the prophecy before us. What the painter must have seen and felt as he made every stroke, knowing he was capturing a moment that impacted the future and lives that crossed over three veils. It isn't about the painting, but the painter.

"Kronos knew about the prophecy and the painting long before he even created us, but once Zeus was finally made, Kronos panicked and sent him to live amongst the mortals, hoping he'd never find out who he truly was."

"But he did," I finish, having read this part in one of the books. "He strategically divided the Gods and Titans."

"But Zeus didn't know about Kronos' curses he put into place upon this exact scene. It's the war that hasn't ended."

I turn to ask what that means when his lips brush mine. It feels like the lightning from the painting has come to life and is sparking straight through the slight touch. Those cold eyes are gone, replaced with the

233

warm midnight ones I lose myself in. The hunger in them falls to my lips as they part, his throat bobbing.

Neither of us moves, and when rushing footsteps pound down the hallway, neither of us pulls away.

"Hades!" Hecate's panicked calling catches both of our attention enough to look. She runs straight to him, her eyes wild. "Thanatos is here."

At that name, Hades straightens himself, taking all the heat with him. "Where?"

She hesitates, looking over at me apologetically. "He's asking to see her." Her small body shakes with unease, while Hades is the perfect image of calm.

"Well, Little Deviant," he turns to me, and I've never felt such livid malevolence, "it appears Death himself would like a word with you."

Chapter Twenty-One

DORA

I come to from another dreamless night, surrounded by brown furs and plush pillows. Pulling them higher, I wrap myself deeper in their comforting warmth.

Seven Gods.

I fling up in a panic, remembering the Heaven's gates opening before everything became a blur of forgotten images. I recall riding in a carriage, passing an ocean, and walking down a hallway, feeling overwhelmed with a sense of fear and familiarity.

The room I'm in now feels oddly familiar too with its simplicity. It's too similar to the temples I grew up in, where everything was kept white, clean, and pure. The only sense of self I had was the dresses I hid in my closet within the piles of robes.

Something about this room sends a cold chill along the back of my neck, and that urge to leave screams louder than before.

It isn't the lack of a vanity, the missing hearth, the cold, open floor, or even the scarcity of light wavering from the lone sconce in the corner.

It's the echoing silence of a breath that isn't my own.

I push away the covers, regrettably when a chill slams against my legs. I rub my arms, and the white slip that cuts above my pale knees does nothing for my prickled legs. I'm about to grab the furs to wrap around my shoulders when my eyes fall to the iron gates behind the bedframe.

My senses heighten and I grip the bars, pulling and tugging them back and forth, side to side. They don't budge or so much as whimper against my tiresome attempt to open them.

"Hello?" I call upon seeing a similar cage across the hall. "Adonis?"

Swallowing hard, I call the name of my captor, but it comes out as more of a whimper. "Aphrodite?" The pink scar remains a reminder that the Goddess can't be too far away.

"It's no use," someone grumbles.

I press my head against the bars, looking up and down what little I can see of the dark corridor, bordered by more iron-grated prisons.

"Who's there?"

"Your friend isn't here," the woman answers. "Not if your friend is a *he* anyway."

"Who are you?" I shove away that flicker of hope that someone might be able to help me out of this cell. It's more likely to be another prisoner than a guard I can persuade into releasing me.

"Someone who's been here a long time." The stranger sighs, and I can feel the despondency behind the heavy breath.

I press against the wall where the voice seems to be coming from, asking where they are and how they got here. Before they answer, the blush stone beneath my fingers shakes, pulling me in to reveal images of a young blonde woman with puffy eyes, pacing the cell, leaving and returning, aging over the years into a withering old woman. As she ages, the crying becomes less frequent, her shoulders round in, and her mannerisms grow stiff and stolid.

When I draw back, my entire being fills with impassive stillness, like the wall itself. Witnessing the past through inanimate objects always leaves me depleted and distant, void of human emotions for hours, sometimes days.

The revelation of who lies in the cell on the other side is enough to spark new motivation to find my voice.

"Psych?"

The broken gasp that answers me is followed by shifting movements from the other side. "Do I know you?" she asks. "Did—Did Eros tell you of me?"

My heart tugs for this woman and the hope she holds after all these years.

When I told the story of Psych and Eros at the sacrifice, I wanted to see Aphrodite's reaction, to spot any signs of guilt that would point to the story ringing true. And when she said she would keep Psych locked away, yearning to see Eros again, I didn't want to believe it. The cruelty of it was too evil to be true. Hearing Kore's hypothetical tragic ending allowed me to think that it had been a silly, albeit horrific, jest.

But here she is—Psych—the beautiful woman who disappeared long ago, now Aphrodite's prisoner.

I apologize, "I've heard of you from rumors and myths. How long have you been here?"

The woman's chuckle is soft and farther away as the bed creaks from the other side. "I lost track. It should be any day now, though. I've done everything she asked. Eros is going to see how I proved myself. He will forgive me for betraying him." She rambles on, "You need to trust those you love, you know? You can't have love without trust. No matter what anyone else says, you need to trust yourself and..." Her voice falls off. "Another test. This is just another test."

Not following what she's talking about, I begin pacing my cell, looking for anything that can help me escape.

"I did all of it. I filled the jar with the five rivers of death, plucked the feather from a dove, and collected herbs from a woman who turned me into a pig. I unknotted a rope and burned it, so it never tied again. I filled the sand timer one grain at a time. He'll come back for me. I know it. I *know* it."

Metal groans with loud clinks of moving iron. A short, bent-over woman in a thick, oversized, beige dress comes into view on the other side of my cell.

This is the oldest woman I've ever seen. Her withering face looks like a melting candle. What little hair clings to her scalp is ready to shed at any second. Her hands contort with arthritis.

She presses herself against the iron to get a better look at me in the midst of finding nothing to help my escape. It doesn't help that the room holds only a bed with furs and a chamber pot in the corner. "She favors that friend of yours. Handsome, but not as handsome as my Eros."

"Where are they?" I rush toward the bars, but Psych pulls back in time to avoid my touch. If she's a prisoner, then how is she able to get out of her cell at will?

Psych's laughter starts low, becoming more hysterical at a joke I didn't hear. "Aphrodite has a bad habit of bringing mortals back here to play with. You'll be here until she grows bored of your friend, and then you'll be next."

It's the next day when Adonis comes, sliding a platter of food below the cell bars. His hair is wet and slicked back, and the scent of lavender and lime permeates the air around him. His face is freshly shaved, and his ragged clothes are replaced with new ones that make him look regal.

I fall to my knees at the door, greedily taking a bite of everything, starved for food and the need for him to tell me what's happening.

"You'll be out of here soon. Aphrodite said this is for your own good until she can ensure it's safe."

"Safe from what?" I ask with a mouth full of beans. "You're the reason I'm here." I remember him tackling me to the ground, letting Aphrodite manipulate my mind into following orders.

"I panicked." He gives me an apologetic frown. "I didn't want you running away. You want to find Kore, don't you?"

His words strike me like an ice bucket to the face, but it's his tone, the shifting of his eyes, and the slight lean in his posture that's even more odd. I've never seen him so relaxed and rigid all at once. "Do *you?*" I'm not sure where the question comes from, but it has me thinking more about our last week together. Something's changed.

"Of course." His posture straightens, his chin pointing toward my food in silent suggestion. "But you're here right now, not Kore. I'm doing everything I can to make sure you're safe."

The passive Adonis I once knew is disappearing before my very eyes. "We can't trust Aphrodite. Not fully. She may not be able to lie to me, but she can omit things. Like whatever is going to happen with Kore. There's more to it than she's letting on."

"I know," Adonis agrees.

"Then help get me out of here. Is there a key?" All the begging and attempts at manipulating Psych into telling me how to open my cell failed. I've pinched, pulled, and yanked every bar, but it never budges.

He shakes his head. "She's scared of something. If she doesn't want you out until it's safe, I'm not risking it."

I balk at him, but before I can retaliate, he grabs my hand between the bars and squeezes. "*Trust me*. I'll get you out, and we'll find Kore."

As upset as I am at him, the sight of his head lowering angers me more. "Is she hurting you?"

He lifts his chin, hardening his features in a way only a servant can perfect. "I'm doing what I need to."

Psych's laughter fills the hallway. "I'm sure you are, handsome."

He pulls away from me, his cheeks flaring with every broken cackle made by the hysterical woman in the neighboring cage.

"I'll be back with more food later," he vows before walking away, ignoring my pleas to stay.

I fall back into bed to the sounds of Psych's manic laughter, no longer feeling bad that I *know* Eros will never come for her.

Chapter Twenty-Two

KORE

I pace my room, determined to mold a permanent path with every neurotic step and sharp turn. What could Death possibly want with me? The very concept that Death is an actual person, one that isn't Hades, is unfathomable. But that person, that *being*, wants to talk with me?

A smart girl would acknowledge Hecate's wringing hands and Hades' stiff shoulders as a sign and listen to their warnings to stay put until they say otherwise. A sane girl wouldn't be leaving her room and climbing the stairs toward literal Death.

I'm not going to walk in; that would be asking Hades to put me in chains and lock me up for good, but I do drop to my hands and knees and lean my ear against the small crack beneath the door of Hades' study.

"She's nothing. Just a low-level Goddess that fell here and doesn't want to leave." Hades' comment is distant but clear, and I hate that it carves right through my chest.

"Mhm," an unfamiliar tone hums, unconvinced. "That is her garden out back, is it not?" I can feel the seedy darkness seeping from the room, my bated breath clinging to me, waiting for Hades to answer.

The silence prickles at my nerves.

"Hear anything interesting?"

I turn, startled at how close that voice sounds. No, how close it *is*.

Hades' hands tuck into his pockets, his head cocked to the side while taking in my position on the floor with a growing tilt of his lips. His tongue slides over the bottom one, and I follow his gaze to where the band around my thigh slipped, his fingerprint bruises on full display.

My mouth parts, but words are lost on me.

Then, like in the garden, he vanishes.

The door opens, and with a shake of his head, Hermes offers his hand to help me from the floor. "You know if a horse can't learn to trot on command, it gets put down, right?"

Wiping any dust from my silk dress, I stride past him into the room. "Sounds like a trainer issue."

Hades settles behind his desk, tracking where my eyes fall to the dirt on his cuffs, quickly wiping it away to remove any evidence that he revisited the garden.

"Sit." His voice is harsh, leaving all hints of amusement he had in the hall behind. The demand has my knees shaking to follow orders, but I don't lack enough control to make a fool of myself. With Hermes leaning against the wall, I'm forced to take the only open chair on Hades' left, pulling it a few inches away before sliding into it.

Dionysus silently chuckles from where he sits next to a nervous-looking Hecate, her knee bouncing in a chaotic rhythm with her fingers curling at the hem of her slip. When he grasps her leg to calm her, that dark presence in the room thickens, making it impossible not to notice the man a seat over.

Thanatos.

His wings splay out behind him. They aren't feathered or leather, but swirling, moving shadows, calling for my attention. When I do look into the void, their hold on me releases.

Not yet, a chilling whisper penetrates the edge of my mind.

Thanatos reminds me of Hermes in the way of complete opposites. Both are shirtless, but where Hermes' skin is golden, Thanatos pales with an assortment of scars along his slender form. Where Hermes appears primed for the Heavens, Thanatos is the epitome of what I previously imagined the Underworld beings to look like, with black fitted bottoms, long white hair, and darkness that physically surrounds him.

His head tilts, observing me right back with colorless, milky eyes. "You have interesting eyes, darling." He closes his and inhales through his nose. "And scent." His voice is deep but soft, like a mother coaxing her child to sleep.

"*Enough,* Thanatos." Hades' nostrils flare, the authoritative command causing me to shift in my chair, scratching at the flush creeping up my neck.

241

Anyone on the receiving end would have shuddered, but Thanatos remains unaffected while keeping his attention solely on me.

"You look at her any longer, I'll jar your eyes and gift them to her."

Hecate gasps at him like she can't believe he would talk to Thanatos in such a way. I can though. I witnessed an identical threat to Minthe not an hour ago.

It's the cobalt flames that dance along Hades' fingers and the violent promise in his eyes that he didn't have with the nymph that has my curiosity dangerously close to tempting his control to see what he'll do.

Thanatos' lip twist, dragging his assessing gaze from me, at a painfully slow pace toward Hades, an ancient tension suffocating the air, one I feel in my bones. "The dead are restless. I've never seen this many souls wandering about aimlessly. It's... unsettling."

Hades agrees, "I'm aware."

"Then you're also aware that little garden is not the only thing growing? The woods are no longer decayed, and the town is blooming with life." Thanatos turns those white voids to me. "What are your gifts, darling?"

"She's not your *darling*," Hades speaks before I can answer. "And you don't need to know anything about her gifts."

"Life is growing, and the dead won't rest. We both know she's not a mere harvest Goddess." Hades doesn't reveal any indication of what he thinks of Thanatos' accusation. Unlike me, who watches their predatory poise grow more lethal with unabashed fascination. "I can feel another of her gifts right now."

"What gift?" I ask before Hades can even think about cutting me off.

Thanatos' smile deepens, two sharp, pointed teeth taking my focus. If this is Death, he isn't handsome in the typical sense, like Hermes or rugged like Hades or Dionysus. His beauty is tied to the lure of fear that tells you to run away as it pulls you in closer. His bleak eyes promise a forever home amongst the shadows behind him, a comforting welcome that called to me before that *not yet* whispered against my mind.

I repeat my question louder. He might look blind, but he isn't deaf. With the way he looks at me, I'd be willing to wager that if he has a gift other than stealing souls, it's patience. A predatory level of patience.

Hermes' shoulders tense at my raised voice.

"Needy one," Thanatos assesses with a calculated squint. "And quite demanding. Someone who knows what she wants. Sneaking up here to listen to meetings without permission." His hairless brows pinch. "I'll teach you everything you could ever wish to know about your abilities if you work with me."

"No." Hades pushes off his seat to stand, the room heating with his growing power. The hearth ignites with flames. His very presence and posture demand that his word is final.

"I can teach you things they don't even know how to teach you." Thanatos ignores what I can't, his promise drawing me back from the rising heat.

I'm not trying to ignore Hades' stare, or Hermes' hand on my shoulder, but I'm hooked in Death's lure. It's just us, alone in our own private conversation within the widening cavernous shadows, and the rest of the world melting away.

"What makes you so certain?" I ask.

I can physically feel a pull to look at Hades, to give him my attention, to allow him to control this conversation as I don't even know the being before me, but I'm stuck, entranced by Death's every word.

Hermes squeezes my shoulder. "*Kore.*"

The shadows back away as a ball of cobalt flames suspends between us. I breathe a little easier with them gone, but another part of me longs for them to find me again.

It takes all my strength to shift my attention to Hermes crouched at my knee, his face covered with worry. "Trust me. You can't work with him."

"It's nothing like I had you do, Hermes."

Thanatos is cut short by Hades, whose voice is sharper than a blade's edge. "I said, *no.*"

Everyone in the room turns rigid, stuck in a war of power between the King and Death. The shadows darken, the fire brightens, both of them filling the air with a silent rage.

The soulless glare Thanatos turns toward Hades is chilling, his tone an even-keel and measured grace of someone who's carried the weight of authority for too long to stoop to impulsive reactions. "You might be King here, but remember whose home this really is and the deals in place.

If you want her to stay, then you'll allow her to work with me. You wouldn't deprive her of her full *low-level* Goddess potential, would you?"

I realize then, exactly what Thanatos is, *who* he is. As if I need another reason to look at him with even greater awe. "You're Divine."

All attention turns to me, but mine is stuck on the Divinity—not a God at all.

Thanatos' head snaps back to me. I was wrong to assume he wasn't one to betray his emotions so rashly. The muscles in his jaw work as he looks at me with that damning expression. "How did you hear of such a term?"

The question strikes me as odd. The term isn't uncommon, mortals just believe it's synonymous with Gods.

I tell them about the book I found in my attempts to read more about the prison I agreed to live in. The Underworld's ancient royals were called Divinities, beings that were neither dead nor alive. It was a single page, but I remember because the book had pages torn out, keeping me from reading further about them. The last sentence mentioned the Divine Death and his soulless eyes that caught the attention of his Divine wife. That was where it left off.

Thanatos' nod is slight.

"I'll work with you," I say before Hades can disagree on my behalf.

There is an obvious power struggle between the two that seals with forced, unwilling respect that I can possibly use to my advantage, a move against Hades, or something that can help me get to the Heavens. All I can work on in time, but one thing still unsettles me.

"But I want to help the lost souls move on," I add, leaving no room for arguments. I can't forget the hope clinging to the bony man's body over mine. If I'm the cause of their unrest, I'll find a way to help them.

"*Ah*—"

My cry pierces my ears, ricocheting off the walls in my mind. I claw at my head as Thanatos' shadows penetrate my mind again, deeper this time, wisping around.

It's Dionysus who moves first, tackling him to the floor, straddling him with a fist around his pale neck. His dagger is at Death's chest, pinching against his heart. "*Let. Her. Go.*"

The initial pain subsides, leaving a lingering, dull headache.

244

You feel guilty. Purposeless. Thanatos' lips don't move but I can still hear him. *Who is Celius?*

"Get out!" I scream. It's too much, too invasive. Whatever he's doing is pulling emotions I refuse to acknowledge, ones I tucked far, far back to keep the voices away.

When his shadows finally vanish, I let out an icy breath. My raspy gasps are silenced with Dionysus' even heavier panting. There is no killing Death, but if anyone could, it might be Dionysus with the sheer determination on his face.

Knowing my brother could end up the one dead by the end of this, I pull at our connection, softening his features instantly. His head cocks back, glancing me over before removing his blade and climbing off the Divinity beneath him. "Hurt her again and I'll find a way to kill you myself."

Between Dionysus and Hades' threats, I'm not sure he would attempt to.

Righting himself as if nothing had happened, Thanatos smirks. "I was only testing a theory. I didn't harm her, but I was able to breach her mind, which means she's weaker than she should be."

"If you want any deal with me, you'll stop right there." I rise from my seat to meet his chest, poking the indent where Dionysus' blade scratched. "Guilt, purposeless, weak, or not, I want to help the souls. And you're not going to talk about me as if I'm not here. Or invade my mind without permission, that I most certainly won't be giving you." I cock my head, narrowing my eyes right back at him. "Do you understand?"

Thanatos looks to his right, where Hades is now standing and watching our encounter with his hands behind his back, again leaving nothing as to what he's thinking. "She's already a better leader than you, even with all the anger and confusion seeping from her."

Hades' jaw ticks, but he also holds the tiniest glimmer of something I can't name. "Prove you can teach her gifts, *without* harming her."

"Fair enough." Thanatos motions me closer, taking my hand into his bone-chilling one. I hesitate but follow his lead, facing him as he turns his palm up next to mine, a black mist swirling withing it. "Think of something living besides a person. It could be a bug, a dog, a deer, anything."

An image forms, and I nod.

"Close your eyes and focus on the energy in my palm. Feel for it but continue thinking about the living thing."

I do as he says, biting back a gasp as a lick of heat tickles my calf and crawls up my thighs. I scrunch my face, trying to stay focused on Thanatos' instructions, even as the growing heat builds inside me, along with the curses I have for Hades for fucking with me.

With my eyes closed, I find the mist floating before me only it's no longer black but deep red swirls dancing just inches away.

The *feeling* of the mist touches my skin as if it were begging to bathe me like the flames that find their way between my legs. "Pain?"

I clear the thickening in my throat when my voice comes out breathier than I intended.

"Good," Thanatos encourages, oblivious to me internally melting before him. "Now take it."

"What?" Hecate screeches. I ignore her, focusing on the ball of pain and begin pulling it in. It's somehow both physical and emotional, like a burning, searing cut mixed with an agonizing, grieving loss.

My breath hitches.

The lick of the flames burrow between my legs while a warm grasp wraps around my waist like they're Hades' hands keeping me steady. Embers run slowly down my neck as if it were his tongue.

It's a frustrating mix of arousal, fury, and focus.

I wince, biting back a whimper as that searing pain, both physical and emotional, and the sensitivity making my legs weaker intensifies. Using every bit of strength I have not to get lost in either, I refocus on bringing that mist within my grasp.

"Now, mold it into that living image, and then release it."

I revel in the pain longer than I should, letting it burn my palm before that sweet relief eases through me.

The flames vanish, and my thighs clench together, the loss leaving me on edge, like a breath is stolen just as I inhale.

Hecate chokes on words that sound like a mix of gasps and prayers.

I open my eyes, finding a red, wispy butterfly flapping above my open palm.

"That wasn't—She can't be," Hecate stumbles, searching between me and Hades with a concern that has me swallowing hard and taking in the others.

"Energy manipulation," Hades says, keeping his calm composure though his brows pinch. "She's a Siphoner."

A collective mix of confusion, awe, and disbelief hit me at once, something I wouldn't have questioned when I first arrived, but these beings aren't easily rattled.

"What's wrong?" I look around, finding only Dionysus sharing the same confusion I have. "It wasn't that bad."

"They're concerned because it's a rare gift bestowed solely on those who can handle it. Those who can balance both light and darkness. Life and death." The room dims as Thanatos' dark wings take over the empty space above us, collecting the red butterfly back into itself. "You can give or take someone's pain, misery, even happiness, but you cannot keep it, or it will drive you mad. Any being, including *Gods*, can overburn themselves into a darkness that is nearly impossible to come back from. I felt you hesitate to release that pain, but even a masochist like you needs an outlet to let the excess go. I funnel mine into the void, the shadows you see. You funnel yours through creation."

A part of me hurt seeing the butterfly I formed disappear. I did that. I used pain and loss to create something beautiful and living, as fleeting as it was.

"May I ask, why a butterfly?" Thanatos' question hitches with curiosity.

I'm not entirely sure how to explain the intuition that whispered to me, so I offer a shrug and say it was what the pain wanted.

His shadows return, back in place of long wings, offering me his hand. "We have a deal then. You work with me, and I'll teach you more about controlling your siphoning abilities."

"And we'll help the lost souls move on," I add. This is more important to me than learning any skill. I don't want to ask about Celius, nor do I want to confirm the fate my decisions led him to, whether he's lost or moved on. At least I can try to help someone. Right some wrongs.

Before I can lift my hand, Hermes places his on top of mine. "She will do so until she wishes to no longer work for you, and she won't do anything she doesn't want to."

Thanatos' smile isn't friendly. "Of course," he agrees.

Hermes steps back, and though he's hesitant to do it, he nods his approval.

Without looking to Hades, I take his hand. "We have a deal." A dark mist forms around where we're joined together.

Thanatos gives a curt nod toward the king and vanishes within the mists, leaving some behind to scurry into the dark corners.

The lingering cold that frosts my fingers doesn't warm when he's gone, not even when Hermes grabs my wrist, lifting it high to show an inky marking of a black butterfly beneath my palm. "You just made a deal with Death."

That should scare me, but it doesn't. It was intoxicating.

"Everyone out, *now*." At Hades' sharp order, everyone disappears, not even bothering with the door, as they vanish without another word—*jumping,* another thing I need to practice.

That emptiness Hades left me with grows irate at the sound of the crackling hearth, the flames teasing and taunting me.

"*Deviant...*" His testy voice is a seductive calling, his gaze dipping to the slit that reveals the sapphire bangle around my leg. "Why is it so hard for you to listen?"

He rounds the desk and leans against it, crossing his arms over his chest. The slight movement lifts his shirt, teasing the serpent markings.

My mouth waters at the sight, and my thighs clench together again, needing some sort of friction to finish what he didn't.

"Is there something you want to say?" He licks his lips, and I'm done for. I had curses at the ready the moment he touched me with those flames and even more when he took them away, but all of them disappeared the moment he rounded the desk.

Maybe it's the adrenaline of facing Death or remembering Hades' threats toward the being for simply looking at me, but I can't deny what my body craves, can't refuse that flutter deep in my ribs, pulling me toward him.

"How long does your offer stand?"

The blacks of his eyes replace the midnight blues, giving away what he's thinking, *finally.*

He waits, knowing exactly what he's doing by not answering, the way it makes my heart pound faster, my skin heat, my insides knot. He lifts his hand and those flames that live to please flicker across his palms. "As long as you ask for it."

I don't realize I'm walking until my arms wrap around his neck. "Then please, finish what you started?"

The fire in the hearth grows wild when my lips seal to his, melting into them.

His arms wrap around my waist, running his fingers down my back, my ribs, digging into my spine, caving me into him like the shadows tried.

If he wasn't holding me against him so tight, I would have fallen from the headrush.

My mouth opens for him when his tongue demands access. Every curl and clash has me craving more.

Why is *this* so easy, so natural?

He pulls at the laces in the back of the dress.

I tear myself from his hold to help, "You have to——"

"I know how to unlace a dress."

His dark chuckle has my already heated core steaming. "I'm sure you do, *King*, but not mine."

I pull the string that ties just below my breasts—not along my back like most—unlatching the pins in place that allow me to dress myself without assistance.

With one last pull at the lace, the dress falls to a pool of citrine at my feet, but it's him I watch as he tracks every movement, his eyes raking up every inch of me in the thin slip.

I step into his space, his skin molten fire against mine. "It's really distracting when you're using flames to fondle me while I'm trying to focus."

His laugh ripples against the curve of my neck. "Get used to it. Your abilities are accessed through lust until you find a way to control them." I take a step back, but he pulls me right back in, leaving not a breath between us. "I'm not done."

His dominance has me throbbing and bracing myself on his shoulders. The bowl of dried petals on the desk pops with bloomed jasmine and roses, giving me away. "I'd say you aren't either."

His crooked grin has me helpless, willing to bend and waiver to whatever command he gives me. Should he ask me to throw myself into the fire right now, I'd be on my hands and knees crawling for it.

A soft moan rolls out of me as Hades pulls my arms behind my back, sealing them with the flamed rope. His need to restrain me is equally arousing and pissing me off. I want to touch him. My fingers itch for it whenever he's near.

I pull my wrists, but the flames tighten, arching my chest toward his face. Not a second later, the slip disintegrates, and I can't help but thank the God for not burning the dress at my feet.

His name is a curse on my lips when he brings his around the tip of my breast, sucking and teasing them both quickly, before flipping me over. Putting my front against the desk, and him at my back.

With this new position, I can't move, can barely turn my neck to see him.

"Do you defy me for fun?" I quiver at the deep and raspy voice against my ear and nod.

"*Voice*, Deviant." His fingers crawl beneath me and pinch my nipples.

"Yes!" I cry out, that spike of pleasure pulls at my core with the sweetest burn. There's something about the twitch under his eye and the way they darken with every opposition that arouses something in me, resembling maddening obsession—a need to see more, to see his hands slip into his pockets, not because of a need to restrain himself from reprimanding me but ravaging me in other ways.

In *this* way.

"Do you think Thanatos can teach you things I can't?"

I want to say, of course, he has the siphoning ability I have that Hades doesn't, but as he leans harder against me, pinning me between him and the desk, I know that's not what he's talking about.

That sick part of me needs to see his reaction. "Maybe."

He lets out a guttural growl, his fingers finding that spot between my legs that quivers for them. I'm building fast from his earlier teasing.

As his lips and teeth graze my neck, my breath dips, my sanity with it. The only thing keeping me from falling over is the hold he tightens around my neck, sealing me to his hard chest.

"Spread your legs." He orders, tapping his foot against mine. It readily complies.

250

I slump forward when he releases my throat and palms my hips. His fingers dig in as he pulls them back, so I'm flush against him.

The feel of the pressed outline I've only glanced at has my insides trembling, my mouth watering.

"Don't move."

He places something on my back and around my legs. A bowl of dead plants drops in front of me, and then he's gone, leaving my entire backside missing his warmth.

When I attempt to lift myself, I can't move. My body is sealed against the wood, and my legs are restrained apart. "Hades?"

The flames lick the back of my thighs. "I'm right here."

I can hear the sound of the chair moving, followed by a drink pouring.

The humiliation of being tied up and bare, completely exposed in front of him while he sits back with a drink has me calling for him again.

"Yes, Deviant?"

"Untie me." I struggle against the rope with no success. If anything, my wrists are starting to ache from how tight they continue to seal.

"Not until you bring those flowers back." I hear him take a sip of whatever he poured himself. "Don't pretend you don't enjoy this. I can see how much you do from here."

I try again to close my legs, embarrassed by my body's betrayal, but the flames keep them secured in place. "This—Hades, this is…" *Obscene, sordid, depraved.*

A sharp sting slaps across my ass. I hiss, sucking in a breath as it strikes again, replaced by a soothing warmth.

"Don't try to talk yourself out of what you like, Deviant. You can't lie to me when I know your darkest fantasies."

How… I groan against the table as another sting comes and goes.

"I may not have been able to see you, but I heard you *begging* for me."

My groans turn to heated panting as another sting rocks me forward. *He knows.*

I can't lie to him, not when I feel my body's reaction pooling between my legs, not when he heard all my sick thoughts, the details—this very one, only it was on the offering slab with the chains someone left on it.

"You knew this whole time?!"

His deep chuckle has me squirming again, my wrists wailing in response.

"You can beg me more after you bloom those flowers." His flame trickles down my spine encouragingly, driving away all the shame and anger that spike at his words.

"Feel for them like you did that mist. It will feel like an extension to yourself, like an extra limb."

Another sting has me hissing against the desk. The burn soothed away too quickly.

"*Deviant...*"

I turn my focus on the flower as the flames lower, settling exactly where I need them.

My hot breath steams against the wood, and the fire in the hearth roars at my moan, nearing the ceiling. The shadows in the room begin to darken. It's an erotic dance between light and shadow, as if they, too, are tempted by the other's danger to their own existence.

"*Focus.*" Hades' velvet order is too far away.

His flame strokes that spot that has me writhing against the desk, and I prop my chin up to do as he said, focusing on that damn bowl.

It's hard. All I can think about is how alive my body feels. At the thought, a spark of gold appears in the center of the withered flower.

Now what?

I reach for it, but my hands are still trapped behind my back.

"The flower is an extension of you. It is you. Call to it." He takes another sip, the glass rattling against a table.

Every movement he makes puts me more on edge, waiting for him to come over and replace the flames with his hands, his mouth...

The fire circling my clit slows. The sting comes down harder, but this time he doesn't soothe the burn. He isn't going to let me finish until I do exactly as he says.

All my focus goes to the golden light, shining brighter than before. I call for it like I had for the pain in the mist, like I had when I reached for and grabbed Dionysus' connection. This time, a string flies out, connecting directly to my left shoulder. I strum it, mentally, feeling a tickle at the connection.

My breathing grows heavier with the small amount of magic I use, and the flames quicken, building me back up.

The petals in the bowl bloom, a rose unfolding before me.

One moment, I'm sighing, relieved that I had done it, purposely this time, and the next, I hear a glass shatter and feel Hades against my back.

His fingers slide into where the flames had teased, pulling out to sink in another, filling that aching need. His unhurried speed only makes me weaker, useless against this damn desk.

"Is this how you imagined me coming behind you?" He whispers against the shell of my ear, pumping in sync with every bit of his hardness grinding against me.

"Please, let me touch you. I want—"

He releases my hand, guiding them so my arms aren't so tight, knowing what I want. My fingers fall into the thick onyx at the nape of his neck just as his mouth finds mine.

"Do you know what I want?" His teeth graze my jaw.

"Hm?"

"I want to taste you, Deviant."

My stomach flips over itself. His alluring words always surprise me, how he knows exactly what I want and need. He had heard me all these years telling him my darkest fantasies, but this... I never imagined, had never thought to.

I want him to use me in whatever way he wants. "So, taste me, *King*."

My skin will be bruised tomorrow from how hard he spins me around and lifts me onto the desk. The neat papers scatter along the floor, a mess on top of the dress, pinned beneath his dropped knees—a sight I want imprinted in my mind forever.

He doesn't wait to throw my legs over his shoulders and glide his tongue along my slit in a slow, drawn-out flick. It's cold against my hot skin and seeing him on his knees for me makes my belly quiver.

A shaky breath falls out of me.

I hate myself for never fantasizing about this. I'm positive my imagination wouldn't have been this good.

He draws out another slow lick until he's at the top, sucking that nub into his mouth.

A groan leaves his chest, and I curse his name like it's my favorite prayer.

His eyes lift to mine, the storm of blue freezing me in place. I don't know when he removed his shirt, but seeing my legs draped over the ravens on his shoulder, the laughing skull holding me steady, I can't look away.

The way he tongues up and down me, circling around my clit before flicking it...

It's slow and deliberate, just like his fingers. Like he's savoring every second.

"*Fuck,*" he groans. "Your cunt is addictive."

My arms are too weak from his words to hold me up any longer. My back hits the desk, and my head flings back. Naturally, my feet lift to the edge, but he holds one tightly over his shoulder, trapping it against him. I can feel the wry smile against my skin.

His fingers dig into my thighs, and when he grazes his teeth before flicking his tongue over that spot again, I'm done for. My hand falls into his hair, my back arching off the desk, seeing the stars this veil has coveted.

He keeps my hips still, feasting on me like the starved God he is, until I'm begging him to stop.

I want to return the favor, but the second he's gone from between my legs, my panic takes over. "Don't leave. You don't have to talk, just... please don't leave this time."

Being bent over in front of him, naked, begging, and aching with need, is nothing compared to the humiliation I feel asking him to stay with me. But I can't handle him vanishing away like he can't get away from me fast enough.

Completely spent, I can't argue or fight against him dragging me from the desk and into his arms without a word. Exhaustion has me nuzzling into his chest as he jumps us back to my room.

He drops me on the bed and flips me over and then begins to rub something warm along the stings in soft circles that settle me too deep within the furs to move.

When he's finished, he continues to surprise me by pulling up a chair and crossing his ankles on top of the mattress.

I look at him closer. Seeing the messy hair tousled from my fingers gives me a sense of power over him. Like I earned a point in the strange game we play.

His fists don't clench in his pockets as usual, either; they lie limp on top of his lap, his head hangs back, and his eyes close with the same exhaustion.

It isn't fair to ask him to stay when he clearly needs sleep, but selfishly, I want him nearby. "You didn't know Thanatos was Divine, did you?"

He shakes his head with a low laugh. "When you said Divine, all I could think about was how *divine* that dress looked on you." His grin falls. "But no, I didn't know. All the books before I came were destroyed. Thanatos is the only being with any memories of what it was like here before Kronos put me in charge. I've heard the term, but it was a myth, like the siphoning abilities you both have."

I think about this for some time while watching Hades' head fall back against the chair. I consider telling him to lie on the bed, it's big enough, but his eyes are already closed, and something tells me sleep doesn't come easily for him.

Something else is eating at me, though. "Why are you so insistent on harming people because of me?"

I'm ready to let sleep take me, sure he didn't hear me, but when he answers, I'm left wide awake.

"*For* you, not because of you."

Chapter Twenty-Three

DORA

Psych lingers near the doorway, hunched over and waiting, while I soak in the lukewarm porcelain tub. Being a prisoner isn't as bad as I anticipated. Adonis brings me food every morning and night: cheeses that melts on my tongue, bread so soft I could sleep on the loaf, and meat so juicy my mouth waters just thinking about it.

Psych escorts me daily to and from the baths, even though I never go anywhere except back into my pretty cage with the blossom-toned walls, warm bed, and flickering light that refuses to die.

In my one attempt to flee, I found myself pounding on a locked door at the end of the hallway, with an impatient Psych at my back waiting for me to tire out, which I had in a matter of minutes.

The washroom is immaculate and easily my favorite part of the day. The chandelier hangs above me, casting rainbows along the cream-colored walls as the sun twinkles against the diamond teardrops. The room holds four additional porcelain tubs large enough to fit three of me, and the soaps smell as lovely as Adonis with his new aroma of floral and lime.

Today is different, though.

When I woke, tight chains were wrapped around my wrists, restrained to another chain snug around my hips so I could hardly move. The dim light did nothing for my rising panic. I might as well have been back in that closet, drowning in darkness, only my fists couldn't pound against anything, and my cries earned me more cackles and ramblings in place of the calming voice that's saved me from that darkness too many times to count.

I must have blacked out from hysteria because when I woke again, Adonis was carrying me down the hall, muttering apologies for the chains, explaining that they're to keep me from touching things that Aphrodite doesn't want me to, which means I'm finally leaving the cells.

Adonis stayed long enough to help me work the dress around my new accessories and lower me into the tub, turning his head when he needed to. He didn't so much as blush when he helped me wash my hair. Psych had come to dismiss him, leaving me struggling to work the soap down my legs and back.

With my arms wrapped around my knees, and the water growing colder, I think of Kore, praying she isn't being restrained and held prisoner like I am. She's willful to a fault, with a mouth that will get her into trouble if she doesn't hold her quick tongue. I taught her how to read body language and facial tics as if they were their own stories, something to keep her silent and observant, but her fiery spirit can't always be contained.

Aside from building myself up within the priestesses, watching after Kore has been my sole purpose these last five years, a calling I willingly answered, and one that I'm currently failing at.

Guilt-ridden, I bow my head, close my eyes, and begin a prayer to Hades, asking him to be kind to Kore and forgive her for anything she might say that might upset him. It isn't that I've never prayed to Hades, it's that I've only done it once, five years ago. I'm not too proud to admit that the God scares me. Not even my abilities show me anything about the Underworld or its ruler. He is a complete mystery known only by myths. Horrid ones at that.

My chin remains tucked to my chest, my body shivering from the chilled water.

"She's waiting," Psych interrupts, impatiently tapping her foot and motioning for me to get out.

For someone who has waited decades, if not centuries, to reunite with her old lover, completed endless and impossible tasks, and lived in a cell for just as long, the woman is easily restless. At least she's somewhat helpful, drying me off with the towel, knowing my struggle with the chains.

I wait until I'm dressed to ask, "Why help the woman who lies to you? You know she never plans to reunite you with her son?"

"You lie!" A light scowl deepens the wrinkles around Psych's eyes. "She's helping me. The Goddess of Love needs me to prove *my* love is endless and can withstand any trial. You'll see." She falls into the belligerent whispers about tests and showing everyone.

I pity the desperate old woman. It would be so easy to grab her shoulder and attempt to will the images to show themselves, but I'm not interested in seeing Psych's past. I'm much more interested in seeing what will unfold.

The halls are as exquisite as I imagined, with the rose and carnation wallpaper, and continuous floor-to-ceiling mirrors that reflect the bright sky from the opened windows along the other side.

The salty scent of the sea wafts in with the light breeze, refreshing compared to the musk in the cells.

As we pass the hallway of mirrors, I peer back at myself and the long teal dress trailing behind me. It would be beautiful if the rattling chains didn't out me as a prominent prisoner. Not that anyone notices.

Those who pass hold the same downward gaze with their hands clasped in front of their identical scarlet attire, refusing to make eye contact. They don't appear to be servants with the elegant fabrics clinging perfectly to their bodies, and the diamond and pearl jewels around their necks, but they all hold themselves in the same subservient manner.

One man lifts his head and opens his mouth as if he wants to say something but thinks better of it and returns in line with the rest, but not before flashing a quick smile.

The tingling in my hands wants to reach for him, for all of them. Maybe it's good I have the chains because I would gladly make a fool of myself to see how they ended up here.

A set of double-wide doors swings open as we approach the end of the hallway, revealing an empty great hall filled with more delicate, airy designs. Rather than tables long enough to seat over a hundred guests, this vast room has numerous circular ones for smaller groups to mingle more intimately.

It's exactly as I imagined. This entire palace is as if Aphrodite had seen the images I thought of and designed it as an exact replica just to mess with me.

I find the Goddess perched on one of the tabletops. The mere sight of her makes me stumble a step. The cream dress shimmers with gold, cutting down her chest to showcase the gilded necklace she never takes off. The straps slide past her shoulders, revealing her glittering collarbone, and the skirt slits well past her hip, where Adonis' hand rests on her knee. The diadem centered atop her head makes it appear like he's seducing his queen.

I'm not sure if it's the clothes, the fresh shave, or maybe being isolated for days, but the beauty between Aphrodite and Adonis could rival one another. And I could have drunk in the sight longer, had Adonis not snatched his hand away at the sound of our approach, a notable blush running up his neck.

"Welcome home." Aphrodite spreads her arms wide in greeting before waving her wrist at Psych, her voice curled of disdain, "Leave us."

Psych obeys without so much as a nod, the doors clicking closed behind me.

I take the seat next to Adonis, my chains rattling with every step.

"Did you enjoy my gift?" Aphrodite's face lights up and dims just as fast, seeing the confusion written on mine. Her head cocks toward Adonis, who doesn't meet her heavy stare. "I guess I'll have to send another."

His jaw ticks, remaining silent.

"Nevertheless, Adonis has convinced me to let you two attend the homecoming to find your friend."

I don't miss the slight shake of his head at the term *convinced*.

"Wonderful," I reply. "And what do you get in return?"

"It's done. It doesn't matter." Adonis answers for her, quick and sharp.

She side-eyes him with a soft scoff. Whatever is going on between them is filled with tension that has me watching them a little closer, and paying attention to Aphrodite's words for any clues as she continues, "Unfortunately, it is dangerous for two mortals to mingle amongst the Gods. What if you find yourself alone with Pallas again? I don't think she'll let you leave next time." Her smile lifts, and she pauses to let me remember the skinny woman's bony fingers along my cheek and the promise to see me soon. "You'll go as my pets, which means you aren't to leave my side."

I hold up my confined wrists as high as the chains allow. "What about these?"

Her smile widens as if she'd been waiting for this question. "You said you knew how to remove them. I don't see the problem here. Tell me what you need, and I'll get it for you."

A miracle is what I want to say. "From what I read and—"

"Forget what you read. It's wrong. I thought you saw something?"

"The vision I saw showed a liquid being poured over them, and as I was trying to say, the book I read mentioned siren tears and water from a death river."

"That's a myth," Aphrodite drawls, bored. "I thought you might be useful."

"My visions don't lie."

"Then you're too dull to understand them." She stands with such force that I could have sworn I heard the table crack. "There has only been one person to ever leave Zeus' gilded shackles, and she hasn't been seen in centuries. I can't believe I thought..." She shakes her head, "Never mind. This was a waste of time."

The dismissal leaves me baffled. Surely, she wouldn't have dragged me through the woods for days and held me prisoner only to ignore me.

"What's going on?" I ask, convinced I'm missing something.

With a frustrated sigh, she rubs her temples and walks toward the exit. "I'll let you two catch up. You have five minutes. Your gift will be in your cell when you return."

When the door closes, Adonis reaches for me but changes course and rests his hands on the table. "I don't think getting out of those shackles is why she brought you here. I think she needs us here for something else."

"Like what?"

He looks around before leaning in closer with a voice that rivals a whisper. "Something to do with Kore. She doesn't say much, but she keeps asking about her, simple things like how she grew up and what she likes. I've been thinking about how she used me to try to get Kore to come with us. I think she sees you as another opportunity. This whole homecoming thing is an excuse to dangle us in front of her."

It makes sense, but the only way to get to Kore is to play along and attend the homecoming, especially with my own prominent shackles keeping me from moving freely.

"What about you?" I ask, needing to know we aren't in any immediate danger. "Is she hurting you?"

He leans back, and I catch the deep exhale, the way his eyes flicker from mine to his hands that he rubs together. "Nothing I haven't experienced before."

I reach to touch him, but the chains catch, and I'm forced to drop them back to my lap. "Tell me."

"I'm fine, really."

"Adonis," I plead for him to tell me what happened. The isolation these last few days has left my mind wandering to the horrible things Aphrodite could be making him do, while also giving in and thinking about the horrors Kore could be experiencing with Hades. It's a miracle I don't dream, or they would be filled with images of those very fears. As dull as sleep is, it's been my friend and savior in that cell.

His head hangs with resignation. "You can't tell anyone. Not even Kore."

Without hesitating, I promise. It isn't my preference to hold secrets, but Adonis needs me right now.

With one last swift exhale, he fixes his attention on the flowery wall beside us. "We're taught everything in the orphanage. We're taught to cook, to clean, to fish, to farm, to hunt and skin animals..." He cuts short, his jaw working the words before speaking them, his voice quivering enough to catch my attention. "To *please*."

I'm thankful he isn't looking to see my face crumble.

"They call it an orphanage so no one knows what it really is. There are more adults being bought and trained through there than anything. They use the kids as a front, claiming they're waiting to be adopted when

261

they're really training to become dutiful servants. It isn't until we come of age that we're taught everything. *The Last Right*, they call it. Women would come so we could practice, teaching us what to do and what not to do. Not all men know how to please their wives. Not all men can give their wives a child. It's our duty to ensure the household is taken care of in every way." He chances a glance at me, his jaw tightening as he continues, "The husbands don't know. It's one of the highest-kept secrets of the orphanage. Aphrodite—"

"You don't have to," I rush, hating that I can't reach him. "I understand." It kills me to stop him, but he doesn't need to relive everything for the sake of my stupid curiosity.

"I am thankful that you truly don't." He clears his throat and moves like he's physically ridding himself of the haunting memories. "But what I'm doing with Aphrodite, I can handle. I don't feel sorry for myself, and neither should you. It's ingrained in me to serve and follow orders, and I do it well." He winks, but I don't find any joy in it.

"Dora, it's fine. You asked, so I told you. If I have to play servant a little while longer so you can find Kore, I will."

"We." I look at him again, seeing that same avoidant look he had in the cells on the first night. "You said so *I* can find Kore."

"I meant we." His curls sway as he shakes his head at the mishap.

Liar.

It doesn't matter why he's lying; I'm not going to stand by and watch as he sells his body to a Goddess, for me or for Kore. Chains or not, I'm going to find Aphrodite and barter for some other deal.

There is one last question I can't leave unasked. "Meg?"

When I touched Meg's shoulder at the market, explicit visions branded into my mind, horrid enough to make me cry in the back of Hades' temple. It was the only time I had ever entered, knowing it would be empty so I could wail alone.

"We grew up training together."

My heart shatters for the two of them and every other person in that orphanage. "Adonis, I'm so sorry."

I knew about the abuse and corruption in the town, but I never would have thought it went to this extent.

"It's not your fault." He offers a weak smile. "Besides, she's not there anymore."

My ears perk. "What do you mean she's not there anymore?"

The distance between us is too great in so many ways. If he were closer, I would try to brush against him, not that he needs my comfort, but it would make me feel better.

"A Goddess, or nymph, or muse, or something, stopped by earlier. I didn't see them, but I heard them speaking with Aphrodite. They said Meg is in the Underworld, with Kore."

Chapter Twenty-Four

KORE

Nights pass too quickly, bringing Dionysus' leave for the heavens closer and my time to convince Hades to let me join him thinning. Hades remains grim and forbidding at my every attempt to discuss the matter, and our *training* suspiciously increases with me bent over the desk and tied up, his palms replacing those flamed strikes to my ass.

Perhaps Thanatos was right when he called me a masochist because that hasn't stopped me from pushing the topic and reveling in the persistent *punishments* the King provides, coaxing my gifts out with every crude whisper against my ear, every curl of his fingers, every bruise he leaves behind.

Or maybe it's how he ends each night with his head between my legs and my fingers in his hair. The prayers he writes with his tongue feel like a curse, a hex that brings me back hours later, tethering me to him for more. I can't get enough.

Chess, on the other hand, is the price I pay for seeing Hades on his knees. I didn't think it was possible to hate something so fiercely. Every move I think of Hades is there, ready to take any piece I strategically put into play.

"You have a mortal mind," he told me when he took three pawns, both bishops, and my queen before I had a chance to steal anything besides one of his pawns. "You focus too much on the immediate next move and not the long game."

He's not wrong. I've never been one to consider the future. I've never had anything to look forward to.

264

The games have grown longer since. He doesn't rush me, though, and I can't tell if it's because he enjoys the silence while I concentrate on studying his moves while planning my next five, or if he truly holds all the patience this veil has.

He only startles when I move my queen out of pocket, which I continue to do just to see his puzzled squints, not even bothered when he inevitably snags it away.

My abilities have strengthened with the long nights spent in that study. Not only can I bring flowers back from the dead, but I can manipulate trees, flowers, and herbs to move at my command. I even earned a full grin from Hades when I wrapped a vine around his wrist, which he snapped away and returned the favor with his flames.

There's more, though, I can feel it. Like kneading bread, knowing it still has to rise.

"You're not focusing," Thanatos reprimands me from the other side of my room, his tall, sickly form leaning against the mirror with a feline grace.

I slump over the bedpost, mentally exhausted from pushing past his mental block. "It's too thick. I can't push down a damn brick building with two small hands."

"Then use something bigger." He crosses the room and hands me the glass of water from the vanity, giving me a look of disapproval I want to wipe from his emotionless face. For someone who carries so many feelings and emotions, he rarely shows any.

I'm mid-yawn when my door opens and Dionysus struts in without knocking to mark the end of our practice. Before Thanatos vanishes, he presses his ability into me. I attempt to build the mental wall, but he steps right over, mining my mind and pulling out the nearest emotion, anger.

Fucking Styx. Wrath will be coursing through me over the next hour, already fracturing what little elation I had at my progress to build a wall at all.

Dionysus visibly shivers once the Death Divinity and every shadow he brought with him disappear. "I don't know how you spend hours with that thing."

I shrug. "It's only unpleasant when he's inside me."

265

At his gaping mouth, I backtrack and clarify, "Inside my mind." I reach over my bed for the sole purpose of throwing a pillow at him for thinking such a thing. And it would have struck him, if Hermes hadn't appeared, taking the soft blow to his chest—bare and golden as always.

The sight of his crooked grin almost makes me smile until the happiness flees, replaced with the anger Thanatos brought forth.

I walk straight to Hermes and shove my finger in the center of his chest. "Where have you been?!"

His grin doesn't drop. "Aw, did you miss me, Little Bat?"

"No." I cross my arms, throwing an internal tantrum. There's no denying the loss I felt in his absence. Every morning, I expect him to walk through my door to chaperone me, but Dionysus comes instead, not that I don't enjoy his company. Dionysus has a way of making everything a little brighter, and it's not just because he brings me wine.

Hermes gives me a look that tells me he doesn't believe the blatant lie. "I've been here. Just not *here*."

I seal my lips, hoping that my lack of response will convince him that I don't care enough to pry, and lace my arms through Dionysus'. "Well, we were on our way to steal some of Hecate's weird herbs she likes to hide behind the cauldrons. You should probably get back to whatever has been too important to so much as have breakfast with us."

Hermes crosses his arms over his chest. "You expect me to believe you are capable of stealing?"

"Better than you." I scowl back at him.

"I once stole a coin from a man's hand while he was holding it," Dionysus boasts. "I'm better than either of you."

"I took a woman from a man's hands." Hermes' sheepish gloating has my anger flare even more, enough to drop Dionysus' arm before my tensing can give me away.

"You guys are insufferable. I'm sure you're both awful at thievery." I don't believe that for a second. Hermes wouldn't be known as a trickster God if he weren't good with a sleight of hand, and Dionysus has that charm about him that could get him out of any situation. Hel, even Hecate has a soft spot for him in her own *I-hate-you-but-please-keep-me-company* sort of way.

"Do I sense a game?" Dionysus squeezes my shoulders, a little light of happiness seeping through. Whatever this game involves will undoubtedly end with someone drunk, Hades annoyed, or one of us needing Hecate for healing. Possibly all three.

"No abilities," I state the first rule.

They both grunt in agreement, Dionysus with less enthusiasm, though his face brightens with a thought. "We take something from Hades' study without him knowing."

Great, so he wants to try the impossible. Hades is meticulous about that room. Everything has its place, including me—preferably bent over that desk.

"Kore has an advantage there." Hermes' pacing picks up in thought. "I would say Hecate, but Dionysus has an advantage there as well, and I work closely with Minthe."

"Great, let's do all three," I say before I can start pressing him for more details on his relationship with the vile nymph. I also want to prove them wrong and need every chance I can get.

"Easy, Little Bat. That fire is what got you into the deal with Death." Hermes' sight drops to the butterfly marking on my wrist. The tension between us thickens whenever my deal with Death is brought up. After Hecate scolded me for hours on my irrational decision to tether myself to Thanatos, she explained Hermes frustration is because he despises deals and anything that ties someone to obedience.

"It's a game, not a huge life-altering decision." I twist my hair back within itself as if preparing for battle, a battle I plan to win.

"Prize?" Dionysus twirls his rings.

"A favor. Whoever steals the most valuable items receives a favor that must be given by the others." Hermes looks like he already had ideas lined up.

"That's a bit bland, but don't think I won't make you regret it. I could use a wingman with those Muses."

I roll my eyes but agree. The smiles they give me tell me this isn't going to be easy.

Hades lifts his head, narrowing his eyes on the three of us as we enter his study. "What is it?"

"We don't know." Hermes points his thumb in my direction, insisting, "Kore wanted to come here."

"She said she has something she wanted to talk to you about," Dionysus adds. "It sounded serious."

They stride straight through and begin pacing the corners of the room, not-so-casually admiring the hearth and maps, leaving me to face Hades alone. I bite the inside of my cheek to keep from cursing them out loud.

Well played.

I look for any sort of inspiration as to why I would interrupt him outside of our usual meetings. "I—um…" It dawns on me that we always met in the study. Besides the first night, he never dines with us or joins us in the library. "Why don't you leave this room?" There is misplaced venom in my voice, and as the question comes out, the furious talons latch on and refuse to let anything other than anger pass.

Leaning back, Hades interlaces his fingers to rest beneath his chest, allowing those tattoos to tease beneath his sleeves. He gives me that look I know is piqued curiosity from the slight rise in his dark brow to the tilt of his head. "You came here to ask that?"

"Yes!" I toss more rage in his direction. "You shouldn't brood alone in your study. It's unhealthy. I don't even see you eat!"

Too reactive.

"Sure you do." A shadow of Hades' smile appears at my unreasonable frustration. "Last night, I believe you watched me eat—"

"It must not have been a memorable moment," I cut him off, feeling the other two presences halt to listen in.

"Would it help if I ate slower?" I can't so much as process what he's insinuating as his eyes fall to my center, raking their way back up to meet mine. It's the flicker of his tongue over his teeth that has me so weak in the knees that I have to grab the edge of his desk to keep from dropping and returning the favor. "Or, perhaps you want to join me for breakfast from now on? Make sure you're *satisfied* with my eating habits."

The lust building in the back of my throat is hard to swallow, and there isn't anything I can do about the throbbing between my legs.

Inaudible whispers followed by a throat clearing reminds me of the two at my back, and why I'm here in the first place. "I'm not much of a breakfast person, so you'll have to ensure you're satisfied yourself."

I tear my gaze from his darkening grin to pace around the desk, running my finger along the dark wood. He would miss the papers on his desk, and the only other thing within reach is his mug, that he usually fills with pure black coffee, like a psychopath. I splashed milk and sugar in it once to see if he'd notice, but all he did was glance at me before finishing it with a wry shake of his head. My mug that's usually filled with hot chocolate or wine is next to the chessboard on the other end of his desk, next to the first rose I bloomed here.

"I'll stop by your room to get you tonight."

"What?" I turn back, but not before dropping the black queen into a shallow pocket at my hip. With that done, I consider what he said. Why does it feel more intimate than anything we've done here?

Hades tracks where my eyes dart to the edge of the desk. "No lessons," he says, reading my thoughts. "But you will bring that chess piece back before our next match?"

A pang of embarrassment has my hands shaking as I pull the glass piece from my pocket and slide it toward him, refusing to look him in the eye. "What are we doing tonight then?"

This time, his reaction shifts from amusement to one I've witnessed when he wields his flames, specifically when he molded a horse from the hearth and sent the flamed beast around the room. "You'll see."

No amount of anger can stop my smile, not even my teeth biting my lip to keep him from seeing the anticipation that stirs in my chest.

Before that fury can steal this moment, I stalk out of the room, the two Gods following closely behind.

"Who's next?" I ask, tightening my question to hide the emotional war wreaking havoc on my insides.

Dionysus' booming laugh fills the stairwell, reaching the soaring ceiling. "I thought you would be better, Kore."

"She still has time." Hermes comes up beside me, taking each step down at my leisurely pace. "Really, though, a queen piece? You of all people should know how particular he is about the setup of that game."

That's why I chose that piece to steal. Hades sets the chessboard by touching every single piece, making sure each one is perfectly centered inside its square, and does the same after every match. Of course, he would notice a piece missing.

Hermes runs into me as I turn at the bottom of the steps, spinning a long and thin, silver whistle. "Think he'll notice this missing, too?"

Hermes' jaw pops wide open. "How did you get that?"

"I'm not giving you pointers." Rather than tucking it back in my pocket, I tie it safely next to Celius's ring around my neck.

I spotted the whistle when we first walked into the room, but I wasn't sure how to grab it off his desk without him noticing, especially when his eyes never left me. So, I found a reason to touch his desk, even if I did want to crawl into a hole and hide from the embarrassment of getting *caught* stealing.

Hermes holds out his palm with a chunk of glowing emerald. Dionysus reaches behind his back to reveal a book.

"I won this round." Hermes flashes us a smug smirk while looking between all three items.

"Says who?" Dionysus counters. "He reads this book all the time. It's more valuable than that piece of rock or a dumb whistle."

"The whistle was on his desk, where all the important things are. This has to be valuable to him." My words have me thinking things I shouldn't.

"Mine has actual value." Hermes steps in front of us to lead the way to the bottom level.

We make it to Hecate's room, where I quickly return the favor by telling Hecate that the two wanted to ask her about a specific healing herb. The witch was still talking long after I snagged a vial of sleeping serum and a bag of the strange herbs Dionysus told me about.

On our way to Minthe's room, Hermes showed us the book Hecate had been writing in when we arrived, and Dionysus showed us the ring she never takes off. I'm certainly losing with my useless vial.

Our last stop is Minthe's. Her chambers are a mess, with clothes flung all over the floor and a vanity covered with perfumes and used makeup. It's as beautiful and elaborate as mine, but where my room is accented with gold, Minthe's is emerald.

I don't know Minthe as well as the others, but the room doesn't fit the calculated, vexing woman I've gotten to know. I would have expected something closer to Hades' study, neat and clean, so particular, it's infuriating.

The only thing that makes sense is the giant tub that's just as large as the one Minthe tricked me into using that first night. When I ask why it's so large, Hermes explains that being a water nymph without water is like being a mortal without food, or a God without ambrosia. It even tunnels straight to the nearby hot springs and lake, allowing her to swim freely.

We all agree to keep our stolen items a secret until she returns, so we can see if she notices any of them missing. I'm not sure if the beaded necklace I found under her bed is any good.

With the day nearing its end, Hermes leaves, once again, to wherever he secretly flies off to, this time taking Dionysus, who stole the herbs I'd taken from Hecate.

Lying in the scalding tub, I examine the silver whistle between my fingers, soaking a little longer in the apple scents to rid my skin of the lingering anger Thanatos left me with. With most of it gone, my stomach is in knots thinking about tonight and wondering why Hades would have the whistle on his desk. I've never noticed it before, and I know every inch of that thing.

I lift it to my lips and lightly blow.

Nothing.

Harder this time, I try once more, but again, no sound comes.

Odd. Maybe it broke and he meant to mend it.

I freeze, the air in my lungs with it.

Hot breath warms the back of my neck, too heavy and too thick to be Hades.

I wait, the panting ragged and quick. Slowly, I tilt my head toward the ceiling, spotting long, drooping slobber falling to my shoulder.

And a giant helhound looming above me. Its eyes are solid black like its fur. Its ears curve to points like dark horns. Its teeth drip with salivated hunger, teeth sharp enough to rip my throat with one bite.

I remain frozen in place, hoping the lack of motion will bore the thing into leaving.

Its head cocks as if hearing my thoughts and finding it funny, its tongue hanging out the side of its mouth.

Oh, fucking St—

"Cerberus!" A feminine voice calls from behind the beast, "What in all Hel?"

To my surprise, the beast doesn't lunge for my throat. Its tongue laps down my cheek before jumping over me and into the tub. It spins, water splashing everywhere as it continues its loving assault.

My head falls beneath the bubbles. I push at its chest, but the helhound is too heavy, lapping at the water, its nails scratching along my hips.

The weight suddenly vanishes. My vision is too distorted within the water, but I can feel someone pulling me out and laying me on the floor before draping a towel over my shoulders.

I cough, spraying water onto the dark green tiles. I'm too busy fighting for air to make out who's calling my name, and when I look up, my ears are ringing too loud to care.

The woman before me shouldn't be here, with her golden hair that falls loosely down her back, and her attire that's no longer that of a servant, but an elegant pale lilac dress that makes the hateful green in her eyes pop.

"Cerberus!" Meg calls. The beast ignores her and runs straight for me with its tail wagging, flipping onto its back, its belly in the air at my feet.

Hermes crouches to my level, lifting the whistle between us. "I didn't think you'd blow it, or I would have taken it back."

My attention is still on the woman I thought I'd never see again. "What are you doing here?"

"I woke up here. You?" Meg looks about as pleased as I am to cross paths. "Come to find your dead daddy?"

Pure rage clouds my vision. All I see is the gold hair that I want to wrap around my fist and the tub I want to drown her in. The vision alone is enough to settle the rage just below boiling, to ask, "Are you dead?"

She shakes her head, not offering any words.

"Why aren't you back home then?"

"I made a deal with Hades."

My ears prickle at the mention of the God I've become close with, the God who failed to mention that he made a deal with another woman.

272

I hadn't seen any sign of another person living in the castle. How and when did she arrive?

"What sort of deal?"

Meg crosses her arms in answer, *That's none of your concern.*

I eye between her and Hermes, realizing I have no idea how or why they are in my washroom.

"I was with Meg, helping her handle Cerberus, when you called him with this." He lifts the whistle again.

That's where he was all week, with *Meg?*

Something inside me jerks like it always does with Hermes. Our connection is like a tide, drifting closer with every laugh, shared story, or subtle touch, but drifting farther away the moment we part.

"Hades sends me to check in on her when he can't," he further explains.

When he can't? I tighten the towel around my shoulders, still dripping wet on the tiled floor.

Feeling a familiar thickness enter the room, I insist they leave me alone so I can ready for tonight. Hermes promises he'll be back to talk, to which I tell him not to bother. I'm about to get all the answers I need.

When the helhound refuses to leave my side, Meg saunters over to Hermes, drops one hand to the beast and the other on Hermes, smirking as she interlaces their fingers before they all vanish.

"I know you're there."

Revealing himself, Hades sweeps me into his arms, walks us back through the mirror, and gently tosses me onto the bed. I sit up as he pulls the vanity chair to the edge of the mattress, rolling his sleeves to his elbows and untucking his shirt. Every movement slow and calculated.

I can't take my eyes off him. The all-black attire matches his combed-back hair that I want to run my fingers through to mess up. There's a grim look in his eyes as he turns to me. "Ask."

I bite my lips, refusing to sound jealous.

In one step, he reaches me and grips my jaw, parting my lips with his thumb. "*Ask.*"

It isn't a demand or order but a plea that has my heart stutter. I glare straight through him, ignoring the gnawing, sinking feeling that tells me to hide safely in my mind, to hide from the feelings this God pulls from me with a single touch or glance my way. With him, I don't want to hide from any of it, not even as the sense of betrayal cuts me wide open.

"What you do with Meg isn't my concern. You kept her hidden for a reason. Who am I to be privy to a *king's* business when I'm only a prisoner?"

"Is that how you want to do this?" His grip on my chin tightens and his arms shift, giving me a view of a shining red fabric, sparkling behind him on my vanity. He follows my line of sight before waving it away.

"Change of plans." He releases his hold on me to interlace our fingers, something he favors when he's not teasing the rest of me, and I can't deny that I enjoy it too. It's a simple touch but comforting, something that says more than I think either of us ever will. "Close your eyes, or this will get unpleasant."

At his warning, I do just that. And that frightens me even more, because when did I start trusting him so freely?

The air shifts, picking up a light breeze, and the bottom of my core spins. The smell of cinnamon, roses, and apples surrounds us. The mattress beneath me disappears, replaced with Hades' arms.

"Open."

A bright light blinds me, keeping me from opening my eyes right away.

When they finally adjust, I gasp, stunned at what I find.

A sunset paints the horizon, with light golden rays peeking behind violet, gray clouds, as if rain will come at any minute. A patchy mix of dirt and grass rolls on for as far as I can see.

Hades places me on my feet, and I notice the towel has been replaced with my silk, scarlet slip.

"There's no door and no place for you to leave. If you want to be stubborn, fine. But we both know you're not simply my prisoner." He shrugs his shirt off before grabbing something long and pale from the ground as he continues, "Meg arrived the same day you did, except she appeared in the middle of town where Eris found her and brought her to me." He drops something small and round to the ground and lines up the white stick—not a stick, a bone.

"I saw her life and what she had to go back to, so I offered her a deal, which she took." He swings the bone behind his back and whacks the small ball, sending it flying into the air toward the enchanted horizon. "A mortal is useful here, so long as they're under protection to keep them alive. There is nothing more than that. I was sent to see her once because of the lost souls hovering near her. I had Minthe bring her to the castle to ensure she remains safe until we solve that problem." He chances a quick glance at me before swinging the pale bone behind his back again, bringing it down to strike another small ball. I try to track where it goes, but can't follow once it's lost in the sky.

"There's no sex, or anything close to it," he continues without taking a breath, "There is no me and Meg. Hermes is looking after her now in another wing because he told me of your issues with her. You think I want her insulting you about Celius?" At the curl of his lips, I know what he's going to say before the threat comes out. "I'll send her straight to Tartarus if you want me to."

"No!" His ridiculous need to harm people who insult me should be alarming, but I have to bite my cheek to keep from smiling. "I'll keep my distance."

Relief floods me at his hasty explanation, more so that he felt the need for it, but it also thickens with uncertainty. What are we to one another if not prisoner and captor? If not king and guest? I haven't wanted to think about it, had never considered any other option, because what is a low-level Goddess to a God like him?

"This is your home." He steps toward me. "*She'll* keep her distance."

I force myself to look up from the jagged bone to the God holding it, to the snakes slithering out of his waistband, to the birds atop his shoulders, to the smoldering, self-assured grin watching me take him in.

No matter how often I see him this way, it leaves me breathless and needy to touch him. I have to clench my hands at my sides so I don't.

"I realized during your visit that you don't know what I like to do." His dark features in the light make him appear more menacing—forbidden—and my initial thoughts of towns bowing at his feet at the mere sight of him still hold true, only now that thought sends a jealous fire burning through me, and not in a pleasant way. I don't want anyone else on their knees for him.

"Outside of the study, that is." He lifts the bone between us. "Do you want to try?"

"I'm not touching that." My arms recoil into themselves.

"It's only a bone." His chuckle is light, and he says it as if he's had this conversation many times before. "The soul has moved on. Whether to a new body or to whatever afterlife they were given, the bone was just part of a vessel for the soul that's gone. It's cleaned up, obviously."

The laughing skull tattoo on the back of his hand catches my attention, falling to the bone it holds. The vulnerability he's offering stirs a need to understand, not the game, but him. "Alright, show me."

I grab the bone between my fingers, finding it hard and surprisingly smooth, not slimy or as gross as I expected. Whatever reaction shows on my face has Hades' head craning back, his throat bobbing with a throaty laughter.

Seven fucking sins, I love that sound.

"What you want to do is hit the ball to the tree over there." He points toward the sunset and line of trees in the distance before grabbing another bone and taking a stance on the other side of the white ball. Like before, he swings back, this time slowly while explaining every motion. Even through slowed and detailed instructions, he sails the ball toward the trees, landing just short of them. He curses under his breath, setting another one on the ground.

"Come here." He waves me over and steps back, spins me where he wants me, and wraps his arms over mine. I have to fight the urge to push my ass against him or make a comment that would cause him to wrap me in his flames.

His hands cover mine, making us one while he walks me through every movement again. When I swing, the ball barely moves a foot. I try again without him, and this time it goes a little farther.

As much as I miss Hades at my back, it's easier to move without him. I get a few good swings in before he sits on the ground in front of me to watch, which only hinders my concentration. The next few attempts to hit the ball, I miss them completely, and his throaty laughter returns.

I like seeing him this way, relaxed and carefree, his arms hanging over his knees, focused on something mundane and laughing.

"Do you dance?" he asks as I line the ball up, realizing now that it's a hardened eyeball.

I would have gagged if his question hadn't made me pause. "Never. I'm not very coordinated."

The bone in my hand disappears.

Hades jumps, disappearing to reappear in front of me, wrapping his arm around me with one hand at my waist and the other taking my hand into his.

"I didn't think kings danced."

His shadowy smirk is gone, replaced with a lightness I didn't think he was capable of a few weeks ago.

He takes one step, and we begin to move. His lead allows me to not think or worry about the steps, and I don't even care that there isn't any music.

"I've never danced either," he admits.

For some reason, maybe it's his question or how he takes charge, but I want to dance with him, I want to be good at it.

As we turn and twirl, he spins and dips me, while telling me about the helhound, Cerberus, that he is harmless to those he trusts, and that he wasn't worried about the beast liking me because Cerberus likes deviant little things. He had the whistle on the desk to introduce us later, and he did, in fact, notice that I stole it.

Time feels different here, like no time passes at all.

He asks me about my life back home. There isn't an end to his questions that send me through every emotion possible as I answer every one; happy to talk about Celius, confused and angry to tell him about Metanira, and both elated and sad to tell him about Dora and Adonis, the latter causing Hades' grip to tighten.

When he asks what I liked to do there, I realize that I don't know. Baking, running, swimming, drinking, and gardening had all been ways to escape and kept me from sinking further into my mind, disassociating, a problem I don't have here.

When I ask about him, he tells me about Kronos, who was his creator and father figure, even though they didn't share a blood relation. He tells me that he trained his entire life to take over the Underworld with no other choice, that it needed someone Kronos trusted to sentence mortals without judgment, and how the crown hides his soul to make those judgments. I can see how easy it is to keep prying. I want to know everything about him, but there is still one question I need answered before anything else. A question that lingers between us.

"Why me?" It's a question of many in one.

I'm not sure if he'll answer or give a simple remark, and I'm worried he'll stop swaying and twirling me around, but when he glances down at me again, he looks... distant. I feel the tension building in his shoulders beneath my palm.

"The prophecy isn't written anywhere, but I remember it as if I had just heard it:

> *The King of the Underworld will unite with the Bringer of Death—*
> *of which roses wilted will bloom again;*
> *When shadow and light dance but willing to part,*
> *will their fated song bring forth an end,*
> *will a cycled curse replace another,*
> *when the seventh blessed child of his enemy ends the life of the other.*

My mouth drops in awe at the pretty verse. "A riddle, but how does that answer my question?"

He doesn't get a word out when I flinch, pulling my hand away at the touch of rippled skin.

He catches my hand before it can retreat too far and places it back over the long-raised scars hidden beneath the black tattoos.

"This was the first one." He drags my hand over his heart. "It was a stab to the heart to see if I could die. And then the slice of the neck to see if I could bleed out." He keeps his hold tight on my fingers as he continues through every scar. "The whips lasted months, but he had healers come in so he could start fresh again. He thought I was a spy for Kronos, so he had to be very thorough to ensure I wasn't. He tried snake venom, poisons, knives, whips, swords, starvation, hanging, drowning, any torture you could imagine for years."

My eyes water for the man before me, my chest shattering for every touch of pain he felt, every whip and stab that left the tattered skin my fingers trace. With every ridge, a piece of me slices away, even more for the ones that don't leave proof of the long mental torment I know lingers beyond.

His chest rises and falls too calmly against mine.

"Who did this to you?" My voice cracks as I look back up to hatred that isn't meant for me.

"The enemy from the prophecy." His body stiffens. "The reason you're here."

I feel his heart pounding as fast as mine while my hands remain interlaced in his, both of us refusing to let go.

"Your father. Zeus."

Chapter Twenty-Five

KORE

Perched against a full-grown weeping willow, I flip through the book of prophecies, wrapping my head around what Hades told me.

Zeus is my father, a God, but not just any God, the King of all Gods. I'm not a low-level Goddess at all, but a princess, and according to Hades, I'm the seventh child destined to kill Zeus—his enemy from the prophecy.

I don't understand how. I couldn't possibly kill a man I've never met, let alone an immortal God. But then I remember the feeling of Hades' scars, the raised reminders that are so much like my own.

There aren't words that hold enough weight for the anger that consumes me. Every page I flip shakes from too much force.

It all makes sense now, why Hades looked at me with such disdain when we first met, why he was so harsh and cold.

It infuriates me that he kept me in the dark for so long, that he knew who my father was and didn't say anything.

It feels... *violating* in a way that he had been peeling back each of my abilities to pinpoint which one to hone to make the final blow to Zeus, crafting his own personal weapon.

I know there's more he isn't saying, more plans and schemes I'm not privy to, but the look on his face when I told him I needed space nearly broke me. He jumped me back to my room and said, "As someone who has lived centuries, there is only so much I can tell you in a day." Then he left before I could respond, though words were lost to me. They still are.

I came to the garden, my sanctuary, to scurry through the prophecies, searching for anything else that could help me decipher his riddles. Perhaps he's wrong, and this seventh child isn't me at all. Maybe I don't need to be a pawn in a game I know nothing about. I don't know the players, the rules, Hel, I don't even know the board it's played on, or if it's a game of cards or dice with no board at all.

The breeze picks up, flipping the pages uncontrollably, stopping abruptly on one titled: *The Birth of Persephone.*

The hairs on the back of my neck prickle. I look around, thinking I'll find Hades, but the scent of cinnamon doesn't appear, nor does his warmth.

I look back at the book in my lap. Like the rest of the margins, the page before me is jotted with scribbles that aren't entirely legible, but above the title is clear: *The Bringer of Death.*

I resettle against the tree, focusing on the familiar words from Hades' prophecy.

The Birth of Persephone

Created from Death and Desire
Fury and Divinity
A butterfly without wings is a terrible thing to be

Used for vengeance and revival
The dance of Flame and Shadow
She'll emerge into what she's fated to be

Mirrored, cursed, soul, and mated
Suffering and sorrow, cast crimson sight
To mark the gifts of death and life

Neither dead nor living
Through balanced being
Persephone will reign and begin the reaping

My thumb drags along the poetry, a heavy ache chipping at my chest for what they spell out so clearly. I'm just a small piece of the prophetic story of Hades and Persephone. *Their* destiny.

When the seventh blessed child of his enemy ends the life of the other.

Part of the prophecy I recall from Aphrodite's vial: *A butterfly without wings is a terrible thing to be.* Had the Goddess known my fate? That I'm intertwined in the Persephone and Hades prophecy? That I'm just an afterthought meant to kill Zeus?

For someone so used to bringing back life, I feel like mine was sucked away, only I don't know when it was revived over the last few weeks. The familiar sweet sting of loss burns worse than before because I hadn't realized I was looking forward to tomorrow, and the next day until now.

Why does tragedy fill my heart in such a way that normal romance doesn't? The emotions, the intensity, the raw purity of them that hold their impact as invisible scars on the heart, a story forever etched in place.

Something falls from the bottom of the book, a folded paper landing on the side of my lap. I pick it up, recognizing it as the letter Minthe gave me in the art room.

After making the deal with Thanatos, I'd forgotten about it, partly because I can't think of one person who knows where I am, let alone someone who would write to me.

When I'm done reading it, I regret not doing so sooner.

It changes everything.

It gives me an opportunity I didn't have before, only accepting it now means something else entirely.

My head jerks toward the shifting trees where the unmistakable sound of snapping twigs draws my ears. I call out a soft hello, hoping I'm not about to relive the night I arrived in this veil.

Instead of a broken, bony man contorting his limbs, a smaller, much shorter figure pokes its head from behind a tree on the other side of the diamond bars.

It doesn't say anything as it cranes its neck back to peer up to the top of the divide with a look similar to confusion. It's hard to tell with the melting skin falling down its face, revealing the skull beneath its dripping flesh.

A thickening emptiness and sadness radiated from the lost soul, one that mirrors my own.

"I'm Kore." I gently place the book to the side and inch my way to the back of the garden. The soul's large, round eyes meet mine with a curious tilt. "Do you have a name?"

Its jaw lowers, letting out a low humming garble.

"Are you trying to talk?" In answer, the soul nods. "Do you know how to read?" Its head shakes.

My mouth screws to the side with a thought. Squeezing my arm through the gate, I wave them forward. "Give me your hand."

The soul looks at me wary, eventually placing its cold flesh into mine. I search for any flicker, a sign of that golden light behind the dead child. If my gifts can bring the dead plants back to life, maybe I can restore this child's body from desolation.

Closing my eyes, I focus. The light is dim, hardly there at all, and I let part of my own light flow from my fingertips.

There's nothing but that flicker of sadness that weighs heavier as the second's pass.

"What are you doing?" My eyes fly open at the sound of a little girl's voice, finding her still decomposing within the tattered, ripped tunic. It doesn't matter that she doesn't look any different; it's a blessing that the girl can talk at all.

"I was trying to—Never mind." My fingers pulse where the light fades. I may not have fixed the girl's body, but at least we can communicate.

"Do you know where my mother is?" She looks around, searching through the trees. "We were, um… I don't remember."

"What's her name?"

"I don't remember."

"What about how you got here?" I cup her hand a little tighter, but the poor girl's bones are so fragile I feel them grinding together. I settle on a gentle brush of my thumb along a patch of skin that isn't terribly burned.

She leans into my touch. "I don't remember anything. I was walking through the trees, and then there was a weird tingly feeling that led me here, and I've come back every night since."

I explain feeling the same pull to this very place, but any further questions leave us both without any answers. The girl doesn't remember anything about herself, not her name or how long she's been here. There's a never-ending burning sensation along her skin that hurts her bones.

I come to the conclusion that maybe she had burned to death with the way her skin appears melted and singed.

"You're not usually the one who comes here." The girl looks around again before dropping to the ground to settle in for a longer conversation. Because our hands are still tightly connected, I'm forced to follow, crossing my legs comfortably.

"Before this place was so beautiful, the dark one would try to plant things. Now that everything's become colorful, he comes here even more, always sad while he picks at bread."

She must be talking about Hades, but sad? I've seen him show a variety of emotions, all quick and measured, but none of them were ever sad. Hearing about the bread isn't a surprise. He never eats.

Looking at the blueberries nearby, an idea comes to mind. "Help me?" I pick the fruit, having the girl follow by plucking strawberries from the other side. We fill the time with stories, and I tell her the one Atlanta told me about her mother, the boy, and the lion.

The girl looks at me in wonder as I move on to the Psych and Eros tale, followed by Narcissus, and before I know it, the girl is snoring on a bed of grass.

Behind the burnt, rotting skin is a sweet girl looking for her mother, and I'm flooded with a need to help her. An opportunity that fell into my lap an hour ago.

After collecting the fruit, I look at the girl one last time. "I'm going to call you Macaria." A name I saw, fittingly, scribbled in the book of prophecies next to the inscribed words, *Blessed Death*.

I smack Dionysus' hands away from the bowl and continue pouring strawberry filling over the cooled cinnamon bread. He and Hermes have stolen most of the strawberry lemon tarts while my back was turned to grab the fourth batch.

The scent of Hecate's musty herbs overpowers the fruit and spice, and I don't miss the way Dionysus squints and sways as if he's seconds from falling asleep.

"You need to be more careful in that garden," Hermes mumbles through a full mouth, swallowing before adding, "With Thanatos coming around, the Furies have been flying closer than usual."

An icy shiver quivers beneath my skin. Had I not spent a day stealing, I could have admired the beings, except none of the books mentioned whether they torture petty thievery done in good fun or just the malicious kind.

"I'm sure I'll be fine." Unlike how Dionysus looked when he came in, pale with an aura of disgust and sorrow. When I pull at our connection, he pulls back, *It's nothing*.

It clearly isn't nothing, but I don't want to push the topic while he's nodding off, catching himself on the counter when he stumbles over. Before he can hurt himself, he grabs a strawberry treat and runs out the door, fast enough to avoid the spoon I toss at him, striking the wall instead.

With him gone, the kitchen swells with a heavy tension. "Why do you bother with all this? It's not like Hades can't make food for himself." There's a bitterness in Hermes' usual playful persona, one that has me biting my tongue to come to Hades' defense. Now isn't the time.

"You seem to be enjoying my efforts." Glancing at him, I find his jaw set and his brows drawn while he rubs the back of his neck. A nervous tic I'm sure he's unaware of. Most usually are.

There is so much I want to say, so much I need him to explain, but my lips remain sealed, unwilling to ruin what we have, which my first question will undoubtedly do.

"Why do you think he's helping you, Kore?" I'm taken aback by the sharper edge in his tone and the use of my name rather than *little bat*.

"What is your problem with me leaving him food?"

"Nothing." His shoulders noticeably slump. This time, when he steps close enough to touch, my fingers don't itch to.

"It's sweet that you care. It's sweet that you knock on my door every morning when you're done getting ready, so I don't have to find you. You find books about the Muses for Dionysus because you think it's funny

285

to egg him on to find a Goddess to date. You clean up after yourself, even though Hecate's workroom is already a mess. And you made this deal with Hades to keep your mother and friends safe. Everything you do is for other people, and that's going to get you hurt." His breath is heavy, like it's hard to speak, and so is mine. I can hardly think past the tenderness tremored within his words, the warning threaded at the end.

Instead, my mind presses with something I pieced together too late, that question I need him to answer. "Why didn't you tell me you're my brother?"

He startles back a step as if I'd grown a second head, visibly shaken by my change in topic. "How— He told you?!"

My scowl answers for me first. "*You* should have."

"Kore, it's—" He stops himself, eyes searching, mouth bobbing like he can't find those carefully chosen words to explain. His hand covers his chest as if it had been struck. "I can't—"

"You can!"

He moves past me, heading for the door. I grab his arm and spin him around so hard that his shoulder stubs the wall. "You knew we were related, and you didn't say anything. We were… We were so flirty."

As fast as he walked away, he closes the space between us and cups my cheek, looking down at me with those sad sapphires. "I—"

The door burst with giggles, interrupting whatever he was about to say. We both step apart like we're caught doing something we weren't supposed to.

Minthe and Meg's smiles drop.

I clear my head, thinking of where to send all the treats before any more go missing, keeping one in my hand. The conjuring ability is now as easy as picking a book from a shelf.

"What are you doing here?" Minthe asks, her smug face a twin to Meg's.

Not in the mood and finished with what I came to do, I push past the two more aggressively than I intended, but not before turning back to tell them with every ounce of honesty I have, "I hope you two suffer."

With a newfound purpose, I let the pull deep within my ribs lead me down an unfamiliar passage, narrow and hardly lit enough to see. The stairs take me lower than I knew the castle went, the air thicker and damp, bearing none of the vibrant paintings.

As comfortable as I've grown in this place, the sconces, few and far between, are grim, twisting that seed of unease when pleading voices begin echoing through the daunting shadows.

"Please. You don't understand."

My ears grow more alert as my path brings me closer to the rising voice.

"Please. I didn't mean to. She tempted me. She came to my bed. I would never have killed her. My wife... she did it. I swear it. She killed that woman and then me. Please, I beg you. I have a son."

My pace slows as a small arched entryway reveals the backs of a waiting, silent crowd, facing the God sitting on the throne before them. His presence, calm and stoic, holds no hint of emotion, and I can't stifle the shudder it causes.

I don't fear Hades, but it's this look that reminds me how different I am. My body can't differentiate the difference between trepidation and desire, that titillating thrill laced with an anticipated unpredictability.

The soullessness behind his eyes, the lack of the sharp ocean and midnight blues I love, are replaced with a black void I can see from the back of the room. I can feel the cobalt flames that blaze over his head.

My gaze falls to the three men to his right, their heads bowed in black robes.

"You think you deserve to live again?" Hades holds himself with a muted coldness, giving no care about the conversation or pleading from the man kneeling before him.

"Yes, yes, absolutely." The bowed man lightens with hope.

"No."

"What?" The man lifts his forehead from the floor to look at the King. "But—But I have a son. His mother killed me and that poor woman."

"Do you see why we brought him to you?" One of the robed men turns toward the throne.

Hades' nod is slight. "He lies. He raped and then murdered his mistress, and then his wife killed him. The woman was his wife's sister. Let the Furies have him. We have hungry guests to feed."

When all three black-robed men wave their hands, the man vanishes, his pleas cut off.

"I'll hear one more." The authority in Hades' voice sounds like the centuries-old God he is and not the young king he appears to be.

His lure brings me closer, but a brightening sconce catches my eye, and I return to my hiding spot within the shadows.

"But sir," one of the robed men presses. "We have over a hundred more." He motions toward the crowd of people that I now realize are very much *not* alive. The woman standing in front of me has a knife protruding from her ribs, and another man is covered in blood from deep gashes down the side of his face. All of them have a visible glow around them, so slight that I missed it at first. It's different than Macaria, who's trapped inside her physical body.

Hades' unyielding mask tilts toward the robed man, daring him to argue. The flame above his head grows, and a wave of heat kisses my skin as a collective groan leaves the dead.

Everyone's attention turns to an older woman being ushered to where the pleading man disappeared. "This woman sold each of her children to the highest bidder, pretended to be an elder woman to gain women and children's trust, and then kidnapped and stole them. The problem we're having is—"

"No," Hades cuts coldly. "Obliterate her."

"Yes, sir."

Again, the three wave their hands, and the woman disappears without muttering a single word.

A second later, Hades flicks his wrist, and everyone vanishes, leaving the empty throne room warmer than it was when it was full.

When Hades' crown disappears, so does the hollowness behind his eyes. His entire body slacks on the throne as he begins massaging his temples.

I should leave before he notices me, but I'm stuck watching him, taking in how vulnerable and exhausted he looks. It's so different than when we were in the sunset room, where he held a glimmer of tranquility. The sight alone draws me forward.

"I was wondering if you were going to run away or make yourself seen." All the coldness is gone, replaced with amused caution. He watches my every step while I take in the simplicity of the room. It holds a despairing energy without decor along the dingy gray stone. There are no tapestries or tables, no candles or chandeliers. The only source of light comes from the hanging, gothic chandelier. The only heat lingers from the crown that is no longer here.

I make my way up the steps and take in the throne he's on. It's made of iron and holds no cushion, no ornaments, nor any designs.

It's not fitting for a king at all; at least not this one.

The iron beneath my fingers is cold as I drag my hand along the armrest.

His fingers wrap around my wrist. "Ask."

It isn't lost on me that he doesn't ask how I found this place or how I knew he was here. That pull... I can't explain it, but it's tethered to him, and I have a feeling that he feels it too.

"I know what you do, Hades." I run my fingers through his tousled hair, and his eyes close, savoring the feeling just as much as I am. "I know what you are, *who* you are."

The hand that captured my wrists loosens, and when his eyes open, there's a flicker of surprise. "You don't care that I sentenced a man to be tortured?"

"You saw what he did, didn't you?" I know his ability is seeing others' lives and souls, seeing who they really are at their core. It wasn't until I saw him slacken in the chair that it dawned on me the extent of what he witnesses.

He answers by pulling me onto his lap, and I cradle the blueberry tart, so we don't smush it. "The judges do most of the sentencing, leaving me with the more challenging cases that require my specific gifts."

Naturally, my arms wrap around his neck, thankful the crown isn't here to hide his soul from me. "I'm sorry you have to live through that."

"You don't ever need to apologize to me." His fingers brush a lock of hair that falls over my eyes, tucking it behind my ear. "Besides, it's not so awful when you enjoy punishing the wicked." He places a gentle kiss

289

along the back of my wrist, and when that sinister smile lifts, I can see the truth behind it. "There are necessary evils in this world, Kore." His eyes flicker to mine, assessing my reaction. "I am one."

He won't apologize for it, nor do I want him to.

The contrast between the soft kiss and the dark words on his lips has me shifting in his lap, his hand tightening on my thigh. "I knew that before I met you. I hoped that the myths weren't wrong. So, you don't need to warn me about evil when I prayed you were real my whole life."

It's as if the entire world stops when he looks at me. That ache in my ribs strikes so hard it jerks me forward, and the way his chest flinches, I know he felt it too.

His eyes fall to my lips, a breath away from his.

Before I can change my mind, I hold out the treat, plucking one of the blueberries into my mouth. "I know you don't like to eat."

He doesn't hesitate to take a bite, his tongue brushing against my finger suggestively, chewing slowly to savor every second. Only he could have me wishing I was a damn tart.

I want to throw the thing and do what I should have a second ago, but I'm running out of time, and if I don't ask now, I'll only get too distracted. "How were you going to have me kill him?"

Hades stills, his narrowing eyes betraying his concern as he finishes swallowing. "I knew you were a key. You might hold a blade to his chest, or you could affect someone who would. Prophecies are riddles." His answer is clipped, and if I had to guess, I'd say it's because he regrets telling me about Zeus more than he hates not knowing exactly how I'm supposed to kill him. Something shifted between us after he told me, and it scares the Hel out of me. We were always walking a tightrope, only now it's more like balancing on a razor blade, where one step in either direction promises pain regardless.

His answer doesn't help, but it doesn't change what I want, what I need, before everything else does.

Grabbing the treat, I toss it over my shoulder, watching him track it with a frown before looking back at me with a new intensity.

I don't need my gifts to know what emotions and desires run through him when I shift to straddle his waist. It's in the way his eyes darken and fall to my parted lips, how he grips my hips and grazes my spine. Every time he does it, I melt against him and now it no different.

I lean into him, nip that part of his ear that makes him groan, and whisper, "Please—"

Before I can finish, the room shifts. Hades hovers over me, his arms on either side of my head, caging me into the sheets that give away his spicy scent. We aren't in the study, but in his room, on *his* bed.

He doesn't let me take it in before he kisses me. It's soft, teasing, and tastes of the very cinnamon he smells of, with a hint of blueberry.

I've never possessed the control he's mastered. A burning desperation spreads through me, pressing me to lift his shirt over his head, and he finishes by tossing it across the room.

When my palms fall to the raised scars along his back, I can feel him tense before he assaults my lips with his teeth.

I understand now why he's always restrained me. I chalked it up to his need for control, and while that is most definitely a part of it, it's deeper than that. It's like how I never wanted anyone to see the scars on my back, he made sure no one did by covering them with tattoos and ensuring I never touched his skin, only his hair.

The fact that he's letting me now means he let go of some control, enough to allow me to touch him without stopping me, what I've yearned to do since the moment I saw him. I wanted to know if he runs as hot as his flames, and he does.

His kiss deepens, growing more demanding, his tongue dancing with mine.

He can't get close enough. My head spins, dizzy with desire, lost in the thumb that strokes my neck, the teeth that nibble my lip, the fingers sliding between my legs.

"I want *all* of you, Hades." There's no hesitation, no stutter or shame this time.

When he pulls back, I see a hunger rising, demanding to be satiated, swearing to devour me entirely, and promising to leave no pieces behind.

"There's no going back." His voice thickens. "If I have you, I can't promise I won't drag you from that bath to have you again or take you over the dining table before you take a bite of food. I'd fuck you awake from those nightmares, so if you don't want that, this is the one time I'd suggest you keep your mouth shut."

My core trembles, but I can't think of how he knows about my nightmares right now.

To prove just how much I want and *need* him, I knot my wrists and hold them above my head. He follows the movement, and that sinister smirk returns, mirroring my own. "Can you fuck me to sleep too?"

Instead of ropes, flamed hands hold my wrists against the headboard while more incinerate our clothes. For the first time, both of us are bare, in more ways than one. The realization has my eyes fluttering, my heart racing.

When he lifts back onto his knees, I see every inch of him: the markings where the snakes continue down his waist and thighs, his corded muscles rippling, hints at the raised scars hidden beneath the black ink. Beautiful describes most Gods, and then there's Hades.

When he strokes himself, my mouth waters, jealous not to be that hand. Feeling it grind against my thigh is nothing compared to the sight before me, that bead glistening off the tip.

Gripping my knees, he pushes them out to the side.

"This is your last chance." His chest rises and falls with the same anticipation. "I won't be gentle."

His voice alone takes me deeper, has me writhing against him in desperate answer. "*Good.*" I nip at his lip and when I pull away I see a bead of ichor—gilded black. "Don't hold back, *King.*"

At the last word, he sinks into me.

My breath catches in my ribs at the pressure that has us both cursing. He grabs my chin, and my eyes flutter back open to find a look of disbelief and surprise staring down at me. "*Kore…*"

I know he's thinking of all the ways he defiled me in the garden and over that desk, questioning himself how he didn't know. "Does it matter?"

The fullness between my thighs is too much to breathe right. Slowly, he pulls out, reawakening that sweet sting.

I think he's going to leave, to tell me I'm childish for never having sex before, but he drives back into me with a harshness that makes my eyes roll back, a moan so loud I'm sure the entire castle hears.

"No." He doesn't look away as he retreats and presses in again, my legs shaking with every newfound depth. "But you made a mistake letting me have you. Letting *only* me have you." Another harsh thrust draws a moan that even I find intoxicating. "Because I'll be all you ever know."

He drags my knees higher, his tongue trailing down my neck to that spot that leaves me breathless until he's whispering in my ear, "And if you thought you were ever leaving, think again." I can hear the smile in his voice. "Because you're *mine*, now." His words send a shock straight to my core, but he doesn't stop. "Every twisted, broken piece." He kisses my cheek. "Mine to use." His tongue laps up where a tear fell down the side of my cheek. "Mine to own." When he fills me again, he brings my face to his. "Do you understand?"

He doesn't move, waiting for me to say the words out loud.

"Yes." A step forward on that razor blade, the tightrope that has me sliced and bleeding.

"Yes, what?" A dark lock falls over his brow. "Say it, Kore. Whose are you?"

"I'm yours." His teeth sink into my neck and I feel the skin give way as he sucks as if tearing out my soul to claim as his. "Every broken piece."

His thrusts and grips become unrelenting with my answering moans. The harsh way he fills me, the restraints keeping my hands from touching him, his grunts, I'm done for. The orgasm that hits me is harder than any of the ones before, and I ride it with his name on my lips.

Hades finishing is something I could witness forever. It's me who caused it. A moment there are no walls or guards up. A moment of no schemes or worries, just pure ecstasy.

"You sleep here from now on." The furs I love appear above my head, but he doesn't stop to let me grab them before he's flipping me over, tying my hands behind my back, and driving into me from behind.

He brings me to the edge of sanity, complete dazed madness as he fulfills every silent promise to devour me in every possible way all over again.

I want to demand he return the promise, demand that he vows to be mine right back, but the prophecies sought another for him, and I don't have the heart to tell him this will only be one night.

CRUEL GODS

I'll be gone the moment the sleeping tonic I stole from Hecate kicks in.

Chapter Twenty-Six

APHRODITE

Adonis' sun-kissed curls remind me too much of my old friend, Hermes. One of the prominent few I tolerate, and one I must keep secret. Hades is the only one who knows of our agreements, and only because he witnessed our exchanges through a mortal who tragically died. Now we keep our meetings to a minimum and primarily through birds.

I graze my finger toward a curl when Adonis lifts just out of my reach. Holding in a sigh, I roll onto my back. "You're going back to her?"

"She's my friend," he says, throwing the tunic back over his head. "You don't have to keep her locked away as a prisoner."

"She's unpredictable. I can't have her touching everything around here." Dora has already seen too much. If she manages to so much as touch this circular bed, the wall-to-wall vanity, the feathered pillows on the chaise, even the clawed tub in the next room, she could see things that would ruin everything we worked so hard to plan.

"I can't imagine what it's like for someone to touch what you don't want them to," he retorts with enough sarcasm to make me laugh.

"That's not the same."

His head lowers at the malice in my voice, naturally going back to the years of the obedience beat into him. Remembering the tattoo was removed, he rights himself, lifting his chin with a glare meant to scar. "All you women in power are the same."

"What is that supposed to mean?" Modesty isn't a concern of mine, so when the blanket drops to my waist, I don't bother covering my breasts that spring free. Instead, I lean against the headboard and raise my chin right back to him. "Are you telling me that you didn't want to be with me? You didn't seem to mind last night. In fact, if I remember correctly, it was you who had your head between my legs and told me how sweet I tasted before fucking me slower than an illiterate writes poetry."

His eyes lower to my breast, and my skin comes alive, remembering the gentleness of his coarse hands. Most men are too rough, pulling and yanking, but not him. I had forgotten sex could be so tender and kind.

"I've learned to make the best of a situation." As subtly as his lips lift, they harden just as fast. "I never could refuse a lonely woman."

The jab lands as he intended. But I'm not letting this man belittle me, not in my own home, not after everything I've done and been through. Servant, king, God, or mortal, all men are the same.

"Dora has been lonely in those cells. Is it her you want? Is that why you've tried to deter all the gifts I sent her way?" I roll onto my knees, watching him take in the soft sway of my chest. "Those men weren't ordered or manipulated to want her. They volunteered *enthusiastically*. One of them even succeeded. Did you know that?"

His gaze snaps to mine.

It had been fun taunting the squirrel to give in to her urges. Of course, I had to be selective about who I sent her way because of her ability, but I really do want Dora to enjoy herself.

Every man who came back unsuccessful had said the same thing.

"She sent word that she would refuse them until you were free of our deal." The tightening in Adonis' jaw, that vein that throbs in his neck, almost makes me laugh again. He really has no idea who he's up against. But as much as I take him by surprise, he perplexes me even more. "I may have instigated our little get-togethers," I continue, "but I never forced you into anything. I don't know what game you think you're playing, or *who* you're playing, but Dora gave in after I told her there was never a deal and you've been free this entire time."

I pull him in by his tunic, and he stumbles forward, his hand grazing my jaw, another gentle touch that tempts me. "I hate you."

I feel the truth of the word hanging between us.

When he angles his head, lowering to give in once again, I lean out of the way to whisper in his ear, "*Self*-hatred looks bad on you."

Done with the conversation, I shove him back and scowl, giving him a *What are you waiting for* gesture while motioning toward the door.

To my disappointment, he doesn't argue or look back before stalking out. "I'll be in the cells." The *slam* of the door makes me jump.

He's going back to Dora.

I'm not jealous, not because of Adonis anyway. It's Dora's lack of awareness, the *newness* of her, how she doesn't hold the centuries of memories that I do, how she reminds me of a friend long ago, but is also nothing like her—*Pandora.*

The Pandora. Just thinking about her slices away at my insides, bringing forth memories I would rather forget.

I shake my head and remind myself that they aren't the same. Dora and Pandora *are* different.

Maybe throwing Dora in a cell wasn't entirely necessary, but the retribution felt too damn good, and once I started, it was impossible to stop. I only wish it were Pandora.

That day will come. Until then, Dora will do. That need to right what Pandora did long ago is too strong to ignore.

I ready myself for the day, fresh with an idea that may not right everything, but will sure as Hel make me feel better. The same can't be said for Dora.

Every step I take, each one slower than the last, draws out my entrance, allowing them to sit in anticipation.

Cross-legged in front of Dora's cell, Adonis shoves a plate of food through the opening, his eyes narrowing at my approach.

"Hello, Darlings," I greet them, stopping to peer into the lavish prison. I wanted Dora to be stressed, not tortured, so I might have made her cage a little more comfortable than the others, particularly Psych's, whose bed is basically a rock and an old dog towel.

If looks could kill, Dora's might have if I weren't immortal.

Perfect.

"I see my gift wasn't successful at calming you. Would you like another?" I smirk. "Maybe female? Or has Adonis lent his services?"

Adonis stands abruptly. He's tall, but not enough to cower beneath the vaulted ceilings. "We're just friends."

His need to remind me of that fact eases something I hadn't realized was building, something I hadn't felt in centuries, and need to control before any more people die. On instinct, my fingers thread the locket around my neck. *Never again.*

Clearing my throat, I face Dora to do what I came to do. "Adonis made it very clear that he doesn't want you down here, but I can't have you touching everything with that wicked gift of yours, so I had a friend make you something." I bring the white gloves from behind my back. "You'll wear these at all times."

Dora grabs them reluctantly, sharing a puzzled glance with her friend.

"You're letting her out of the cells?" Adonis' levity is more than I care for.

"She can stay here or move to our room."

"Our room?" Dora rises to her feet, darting her scowl between us, piecing more of the puzzle together.

I'm not sure why the girl cares, now that she knows he's been with me of his own free will. Maybe she's still hung up on the idea that he's Kore's.

That was never going to happen. I internally chuckle to myself.

Besides Hermes' birds watching over her, I had my own set of eyes on Kore. If I could see it, how could Dora not notice the resentment he holds for her? The placated grins at her face and tired sighs when she turns away. The way his shoulders tensed whenever he did anything Kore said or asked for.

I don't doubt that he cared for Kore, but his feelings are more complicated than either of them realizes.

"Once you let me put these on you, you'll be free to walk around anywhere you wish. But you will sleep in *our* room."

Being the eager squirrel she is, she threads her hands through the bar and lets me slide each of her fingers into the slips.

When I give her my arm as a silent offering, her glare lifts into my second-favorite expression, pure curious joy. The childlike eagerness that will most likely get her hurt worse than it already has.

She doesn't waver to grab onto me with utter concentration, her brows knitting. "Nothing," she huffs, those blue eyes casting a look of betrayal. "But I can't always control it."

"I trust my friend enough." I unlock the cell and wave for them to follow. "Hurry along, Squirrel. I have a job for you."

Psych waits for us at the top of the steps with a bucket and sponge. "Adonis is going to watch you wash the floors."

"Me? Why? They're not even dirty." Their hurried steps slow.

Spinning around, I give Dora my best judgmental glance over, watching her squirm beneath the look. "Have you ever cleaned anything in your life?"

The embarrassment is written all over her puffed cheeks, and her lack of response is answer enough. It's evident from the way she talks and gawks at strangers that she grew up with a certain privilege.

"That's what I thought." I face Adonis. "You are not to help her. If you're hungry, Psych will help Dora fetch food for you. If you're thirsty, they will gather water for you. If you're bored, they will sing or dance or entertain you in whatever way you wish. But you are *not* to help them."

"I am not your servant." Dora's hands fist at her side.

There she is.

"No, but you are his. And considering I'm being so hospitable, the least you can do is clean. If your friend needs something, are you saying you would not help? Are you so used to being loved and obeyed that you can't extend a kernel of kindness to him?"

"Aphrodite," Adonis sneers, silenced by the dismissive flip of my wrist.

"I have things to attend to. It's time you feel how the other side lives." With a turn on my heel, I whip my hair and walk away, knowing the wispy ends struck her face.

Spending the day watching her in misery is all I want to be consumed by, but I can't forget my oaths. All the happiness I just built vanishes the moment I walk out my door.

My insides twist as I close in on the clearing, the specific spot where all veils cross together, one of only a few locations where any beings can enter freely without the curses Kronos set into place.

With my gifts limited by the shackles and running late from messing with Dora, I don't get the chance to hide within the fallen debris before the screams start. Not that being here early would change anything for the poor woman.

As quickly and as quietly as I can, I crawl under a splintered, wooden door to hide, covering my mouth with my shaking palms to keep my breath calm and silent. No matter how many times I do this, it never gets easier.

He comes into view. Even kneeling, his massive figure is taller than most men, a feature he takes full advantage of. He's the reason mortals believe Gods are giants, or that they'll turn blind with one look upon them.

Keeping my eyes averted from the vile scene before me, I take in the rest of the clearing. It's empty aside from the screaming woman and Iris, *his* other messenger.

Fucking Hel, where is Hermes? I don't have the same deal with Iris as I do with Hermes, which means I'll have to use extra precautions.

"Please, I didn't think—" The woman cries as her body flattens on the ground, already exhausted. This *Godly Lesson*, as he calls it, never lasts long, but the God has his way of pulling the soul to the edge of the body, to the brink of Death.

His large hand wraps around her neck, scooping her up so her back is against his chest. "You will now, though." His cruel laugh makes my skin crawl, feeling the thunder behind the hideous noise. "Who am I?" he asked, continuing the abuse.

"Zeus," the woman pants, tears streaming down her plum cheeks. I close my eyes as bile rises to my throat.

"Who are you going to pray to every night?"

"You," she cries out, "Zeus."

He finishes with a grunt and another boasting laugh. "Take her back. Make sure she doesn't spread that nonbeliever bullshit again." He considers for a moment, then adds, "Let this one keep her tongue."

300

Iris lifts the woman's limp body in her arms and flies into the Mortal Veil. It should only be a minute, and then I can follow them. Usually, *he* leaves first, and I'm able to make the trade with Hermes or use my gifts on Iris.

Why *isn't* he leaving?

"Did you miss me, Aphrodite?"

My heart plummets.

No! He disappears from my view, and my pulse rises to my ears. A tremor rocks through my body.

I snap my gaze from left to right, trying to see where he went, but all I can see are trees, low-hanging branches, and the door I'm under.

I grit my teeth as his meaty hand wraps around my ankle. With a harsh yank, he drags me from my hiding spot, sticks and rocks scraping up my back. I bite harder, refusing to cry out at my ripping flesh, the sharp pain that's nothing compared to what's about to happen.

"Don't you have enough pets to satisfy you?" He laughs. "I've even let you go into their veil to have fun. I understand why you like them. They're weak and their minds are easy to meddle with, but I always thought you liked more of a challenge." His *tsk* grates the inside of my ears as he grabs a handful of my hair.

Before I can open my eyes, his knuckles shatter my nose, my eyes watering at the *crack*. "How about this time, I'll let you run, but if I catch you—"

"No!" I gasp for breath, my vision blurring, my mouth filling with tangy blood I'd rather choke on than play his games.

"No? I'll take what I want right here just fine, but I'll make sure you don't enjoy it this time."

Never have I enjoyed his brutality, but that doesn't mean it can't get worse. If there was anything he taught me, it's to never underestimate an opponent *and* know when to stand down.

I heightened myself, steadying from my knees to my feet, but the blow leaves me shaking and unsteady. "Good, Little Monster." That fucking name... "Now." I take in a raspy breath. "*Run.*"

I don't have to be told twice. I turn and sprint as fast as I can toward the Mortal Veil. The one place he, nor any of the Olympian Gods, can step foot in.

I'm nowhere close, and I don't make it far before Zeus appears, lifting me up by my throat, my feet coming off the ground.

"That was pathetic." He rips my dress away without touching it.

My heart races even faster as his fingers zap my neck, sending the electric current straight to it.

"Go ahead and scream. No one will hear you out here."

With my chin held high, I spit, coating his repulsive face in my unglamoured blood, hot and black. He has a face others worship, but one I curse with every breath.

Thunder roars through the billowing clouds.

I won't scream for him. I never do.

I tighten the cloak around my shoulders. I'll burn it when I get to my room, but at least Zeus left me with it this time. Neither of us wants anyone to see the lightning burns, the evidence that he touched me. "*If I so much as see a hint of these marks, I'll make you regret it.*" In public, he treats me as if I don't exist, never so much as looking my way.

The walk back to the carriage is excruciating, and I'm too drained to jump. Fortunately, the horses know where to go. My home sits outside of Zeus and Hera's territory, as far away from their kingdom as he would allow, nestled right along the ocean. Some might consider it cruel or self-deprecating to set my home where I look upon freedom, but those people don't see the hope in such a thing. The anchor.

The rest of my kingdom, if it can even be called that, is where those who are lost reside. Those Zeus or Hera deem unworthy, usually Goddesses Hera caught staring at Zeus a little too long, or released prisoners with no other place to go.

The ride back runs straight through the main road, but I can't check in on anyone this time, not even the one who bangs along the carriage, demanding an audience to discuss Ares' army intruding onto her property.

I can't even roll my eyes properly. Ares' army is constantly intruding into my territory to get my attention. That's nothing new.

As much as I want nothing more than to give in to the exhaustion, the fear someone might find me in this condition keeps me awake and feeling every bump agitate my battered body.

"Excuse me!" Psych calls when I walk through the door and shuffle past the kitchens. "Who are you? You can't be here."

"It's fine." I clear my aching throat. I might not have screamed but clenching my throat to prevent it is just as painful, only it was my pride I got to keep. "It's me."

Straightening my stance, I bite down the pain in my ribs to appear like my usual self.

"Can she be done?" Adonis asks.

"Yes." I turn and head toward my chambers before either of them can see me, calling back, "Sleep somewhere else tonight. I'll see you in the morning."

I make it to my room and shut the door. The first thing I do is flick my wrist to light the hearth before tossing the cloak into the hungry flames. Another flick and the mirrors flip around to keep me from seeing what he's done. I made that mistake the first few times.

"What happened?" Adonis stands in the doorway, raking his gaze up and down me, taking inventory with a horror I once held for myself. My instinct is to cover before he can fully take me in, but the cloak is already incinerated.

My jaw aches from clenching it so hard at my mistake. How did I not hear him following me?

His arm lifts as if he wants to run toward me but isn't sure if he should. His hesitation hurts more than anything Zeus did.

"A reminder," I say, stepping into the washroom and kicking the door shut behind me. Screw him if he thinks he can look at me like that, like he wants to take me into his arms and make it all better, then stop himself. He's the most indecisive man I've ever met. I hate myself more for that flicker in my chest before he doused—

The thud I expected doesn't come.

Looking back, I see Adonis pushing through, flexing where he caught the door with his hand.

"What happened?" His question is as distressed as his gorgeous face.

Not again. Never again.

303

Ignoring him, I lower into the tub, wincing with every cut and scrape that submerges. Not one part of my body doesn't hurt—my skin, my bones, my soul.

My blackened blood drips down my legs from the tiny cuts from the thin branch whips. My ribs are bruised, possibly broken. The purple marks from the lightning spasm, plotting up and down my arms and around my middle, where more slashes penetrate even deeper. My shoulders jolt every few minutes. The after-effect of too many bolts.

"Pour that bottle in here." My magic is drained after moving all the mirrors, and if he insists on staying, at least he can help.

I grit my teeth as the healing waters work their magic. The stinging and searing tell me it's working.

Adonis follows orders quickly, grabbing my hand when he's emptied every last drop into the tub. I attempt to pull away, but he squeezes a little tighter, and I don't have the energy to fight anymore.

I take a deep breath, submerging my head below the scalding water, and scream.

Hurrying toward the throne room, I fix the tie around my waist. Psych interrupted my healing to inform me that Iris was here with a woman.

Not another word was said before I grabbed a robe and was out the door, demanding Adonis stay put.

He's been hovering since the moment he walked in and saw my injuries. I'm not entirely ungrateful, but no one likes pity, and I really need him at a distance right now. The push-and-pull game he's playing is giving me whiplash, and the last time this happened, I was put in these shackles.

Iris' wings are tucked back while she waits by the throne with the woman Zeus had screaming in the clearing, lying at her feet, still bleeding and bruised.

Without speaking, she hands me a letter.

The birds saw this one. I had help altering her memories to get to you, but you'll need to wipe them both.

There's no seal or signature, but I don't need it to know it was from Hermes. I only wonder who he trusted enough to help him.

I crumble the letter, noting how Iris sways on her feet like she's drunk. Whoever it is was sloppy.

Placing my hand on the messenger's temple, I concentrate to carefully alter and place the memories I want her to have, persuading her mind to remember the horrid scene in the clearing, followed by her flying the woman back home and returning to Zeus. It never matters that I don't know what their homes look like.

"Remember," I sing, sealing the permanent demand. "Go home and forget you were ever here. Sleep for two days and remember what I showed you." Iris walks off, leaving the woman panting at my feet.

If I didn't need to look strong for her, I would tumble right over with her, not caring if I slept on a hard floor for a few days. The healing waters did nothing for my exhaustion or aching muscles.

"Please, Goddess, I..." she mumbles, her eyes wide with fear and more pleas she can't find, her feet kicking her body farther away. The poor thing is worn out, terrified, and confused, not to mention traumatized.

Crouching to her height, I soften my features, pushing back a lock of hair from her tear-covered face. "You're safe now."

"Who—who are you?" Her naked body shakes with terror or from being cold, probably both. I slide the robe off and drape it over her shoulders, making sure to wrap it tightly to cover her up.

"Aphrodite, sweetheart." I thumb away more tears that fall down her cheeks.

The woman doesn't stop panicking. "I—I, please, I am not beautiful. Not as you are." She stumbled back even farther. "I've never laid with a man willingly."

They always stutter and look at me as if I were the one who brutalized them, as if I'm going to continue where Zeus left off.

"I am not what they made you believe I am. I'm going to take care of you."

Disbelief falls over her. "You're not going to kill me?"

"Of course not. I love all Kronus' creatures." Except for the one occupying my home for the last few decades. All the Gods claim I have pets, but I only ever had the one, and it isn't one I love. No one truly knows that story either, not even that little squirrel who thinks she does. Psych isn't a wronged woman who lost the love of her life, and the wench deserves worse than being a mere pet in my cell.

The woman's heaving slows.

"Do you want to remember what he did to you?" I ask her.

"No." Another cry catches in her throat.

"I'll help with that too." None of them ever wants to remember. If they do, they eventually beg me to make them forget. "First, we need to get you into a bath. Can you walk?"

"I—I think so."

I put my arm around her waist and start toward one of the many washrooms.

Movement catches my attention from outside the doors, and I could have sworn it was those sun-kissed curls. Something sours in my chest. I don't want anyone to see me this way. He saw me vulnerable enough in the tub, but if he sees how I am with this woman, he'll think I'm soft— weak.

I'm not weak. I've endured Zeus more times than I can count and lived to continue my own strikes against him.

Not one soul knows what I've already begun to bring him down. With the help of an alliance that I hoped I didn't need, Kore should be here soon enough to get started.

Chapter Twenty-Seven

KORE

Tearing myself from Hades is far more difficult than I anticipated. Not because I'm leaving the warmth of my favorite furs, or because of the satisfying ache between my thighs. It isn't that his heavy arms cradling me into his heated chest are too tight to slip from.

It's knowing that I'll never return, knowing that last night had been our one and only night together.

I look up at him one last time, brushing a dark lock from his eyes, admiring how at peace he looks when he's asleep. His jaw isn't clenched but relaxed enough to let his mouth part. His brows aren't set in that suspicious scowl, and his fists aren't balled.

"I'm sorry." My voice is hardly a whisper as I press my lips to his. I don't expect his forgiveness for dosing him with the tonic, but I do hope he'll understand why I had to leave. Soon enough, he'll forget all about my bleak existence in his long immortal life.

Slipping out of his possessive hold, I grab his discarded top and slide it over my head before hurrying to my room. I gather everything I need, ripping pages from each book and tucking them safely beneath the simple dress I change into, ignoring that aching pull back to Hades to follow the one that's telling me this is the right decision.

No one passes me as I follow the hallways and leave out the front door, and it isn't out of luck. Hades' tart wasn't the only one that contained Hecate's sleeping tonic. I knew Dionysus and Hermes wouldn't be able to resist stealing as much as they could while I wasn't looking, Hecate received a plate of them, and I might have *forgotten* a few in the kitchen for Minthe and Meg.

The journey down the mountain starts easy with the worn trail to follow and the map in my hand, but with the newly grown trees, there are now paths that aren't on the map I stole from Hade's study. Following the perimeter will take longer than I planned but it might be my best option.

"Where are you going?" Macaria asks from the other side of the gate.

"I'm meeting a friend." Without stopping, I follow the diamond wall. "Do you happen to know where the opening is?"

Macaria beams as much as one can with a face that's melted and scarred with burns. "This way!"

The back of my legs and knees work as we descend the slope, some paths steeper than others. I lose her a few times but eventually find her and soon enough she tells me we've made it.

At first, I think she's mistaken. The wall that separates us isn't different from any other we've walked next to thus far, but then I see it. The latch. Since the souls can't touch the gemstone, I supposed an intricate door wouldn't be necessary.

I reach for it.

My fingers hang in the air, inches from freedom.

"What are you waiting for?" Macaria asks.

This should be my time to boast that I found a way to the Heavens, that I won whatever game Hades and I have been playing all these weeks, but...

I look over my shoulder at the dark, grim castle, holding people I've grown to know and care for. A prison I hadn't expected to find safety or comfort in—a home.

"Yeah, what *are* you waiting for?" I know that voice without having heard it.

I rip my longing to shreds and turn back, facing what's ahead and not what I'm leaving behind. "Ares?"

He has a warrior's face that's meant to intimidate with a mere glance upon it, chiseled in a way arms and torsos are, the way *his* are. I'm starting to appreciate the variety of physiques Gods have. The most comparable is Hades but Ares has a look about him that warns me from tempting to get under his skin.

He answers me with a slackened grin, a gesture that looks odd on him. Like even he's uncomfortable making it.

"Kore, I presume?" He sounds as unimpressed as he looks taking me in. "You got my letter then. I didn't think I could trust that slimy nymph." He glances at Macaria. "Who's this?"

Her eyes narrow, curling into herself while looking him over. "Macaria."

He dismissed her by looking away and clasping his hands behind his back with a grunt.

Seeing the fall of the girl's jaw, I unlatch the gate and step between them. "Don't be rude. She's just a little girl."

My ears ring from the haste decision to stand up to the God of War. His reputation fills books on his successes of destroying people, his precise strategies to crumble kingdoms, the hands that crush skulls, and knives that butcher senselessly.

When he simply says, "Fine," and starts down the path, I let out a heavy breath, thankful he can't be bothered with my motherly need to protect Macaria's feelings.

"There are wards in place here, so we have to go on foot for a day," he calls back.

I move to follow, stopped by small fingers interlacing through mine. She gives me a gentle tug, and I lower so she can whisper into my ear, "I don't like him. You shouldn't go with him."

If he weren't my only way to the Heavens, I wouldn't be pushing away that same gnawing feeling to stay put.

Her hairless brows pinch together, filled with tension and worry no little girl should have.

I give her the biggest smile I can and promise that everything will be fine, forcing out a laugh like I'm not riddled with the same anxieties. When she doesn't ease, I give her hand a squeeze. "What if I promise you'll be able to move on if I go with him? That what I'm doing will ensure you'll be free? That the pain will go away."

"I'd rather you stay."

"What if I promise to come back?" The lie comes too easy, and I hate myself for it when I see her wariness slip.

"Tonight?"

"One day." It isn't a complete lie. When I die, my soul will have to pass through here.

Ares whistles, calling me like a dog, earning him a shadowed scowl from Macaria.

"Please be safe." Her sentiment gives me deja vu, putting me back in front of my favorite orphan, Atlanta, only this time I know my life is about to change forever.

"Do you remember your name?"

Her smile lifts like it were a gift that I gave her one. "Macaria."

"Don't forget it. When I return and ask where you are, I want everyone to know where to send me."

Tearing away from another person it aches to leave, I hurry to catch up to Ares, who doesn't have the patience to wait any longer. "How long until we're there?" I hold my head stiff and straight to keep from looking back again. "I'm not sure how long it will be before they wake up and notice I'm gone."

His brow lifts. "It sounds like it might not be a coincidence that everyone is asleep?"

I lower my head to avoid admitting what I've done, which he accepts as answer enough.

"As I said before, a day. Hades is remarkably private and paranoid, and the wards keep anyone from jumping in or out without permission. Once we pass them, it'll only take a few minutes to cross over to the Heavens."

The way his jaw tightens when he finishes and his focus remains forward as he speaks, I can tell he isn't one for casual conversation. That doesn't stop me from trying, if only to push away the dark thoughts that grow louder with every step away from the place that's felt like home. *How did I think this would end? I wasn't meant for things like love, peace, or family, not when I find comfort and familiarity in grief, tragedy, and solitude.*

"Did you walk here every day?" I pull out of that dark basement in my mind, remembering his letter. He had written that he would wait outside the gates every night until the day of the homecoming for me, knowing

310

Hades had no intention of letting me leave. I don't care that he's probably only helping me to collect the reward for himself. I have my own game at play now, and so long as I make it to the Heavens, nothing else matters.

He nods. "Favor for a friend." His clipped answer tells me he isn't happy about it.

My own experience in these woods comes to mind. It's easy to forget when they're now so full of lush grass and thick branches of green leaves. "What about the lost souls? Did they attack you?"

His gives a quick toss of his head over his shoulder, to the knives strapped down his back. He has the gall to smile, a sick glimpse at the man I've read about. Someone who finds satisfaction with slaughtering poor souls like they're low hanging branches in his way and not lost and confused beings who need help.

"I prefer quiet company."

A pulsing hatred blooms in the pit of my core. I keep my mouth shut, knowing there's no arguing with a God like him. While I might fuck with Hades, Ares doesn't strike me as someone who likes to be pushed to his limits. He doesn't strike me as someone who lets another person so much as test his patience.

We remain silent amongst the trees without any signs of lost souls. When we near a town, Ares steers us away. We're too far to hear anything, but I'm able to catch broken glimpses between branches, and the haunted town is a sight to see. Buttery lights bath the streets, and the buildings are decorated with beautiful stained-glass windows. It doesn't seem to be overcrowded, with only a few strolling about.

It's out of fear for others that I follow Ares' lead, and remain hidden, not wanting whatever he did to the lost souls to happen to whoever is unfortunate enough to catch sight of us.

As we pass through trees amongst even more trees, I use my gifts to grow small flowers to busy myself. *Idol hands are Charon's calling,* I remember the mortal saying and giggle to myself.

"What is your gift?" I ask. "Mortals call you the God of War. What does that mean exactly?"

"I go to war."

I want to say *no kidding*, everything about this man screams war. From the lean muscle under the leathers to the weapons strapped to his back and hips, the lack of hair, the stern face, and the cold exterior. He's certainly not one for talking.

I open my mouth to try a different technique, but he cuts me off before I get the chance. "Unless you want to attract the unwanted attention of those—*fuck*," he snarls, shoving me against a tree with his arm over my chest. His head tilts, tracking something in the sky.

"What—"

He shuts me up by pressing his palm against my mouth, pulling my head against his shoulder to flatten us closer against the trunk. There's no panic in his movement. It's calculated urgency that comes with experience.

Everything stills except the beating in my chest and the flexed pec against my cheek as he shifts even closer, sandwiching me too tightly between him and the rough tree at my back. With the angle of my head, I spot his eyes narrowing on something above, following it as a predator would its prey.

"The little pet has finally come out to play," a screeching voice calls in the distance. I try to peek, but Ares' hold is too damn suffocating to let me take so much as a sip of air.

"She holds fear," another, deeper, voice says.

"And something... *dark*," a third one giggles. "She did something naughty."

From the corner of my eye, I see something like wings flapping between the canopy of branches.

"We've smelled you for weeks." The deeper one whimpers like she's in agony. "Poor Megaera could taste your jealousy and..."

Another giggle bursts, louder this time. "And thievery. And lies. And deception." They all inhale deeply. "And is that the essence of murder?"

Ares' hold doesn't falter, not even as the three figures dart toward the ground, landing gracefully on their feet. Before their wings tuck in, I see they aren't feathered like Hermes or shadows like Thanatos, but dark leathered wings like a bat, dark veins and bones webbing throughout. Their skin is as black as their wings, their eyes, a golden yellow, their hair is thick and matted down to their naked hips, covering their bare chest, and when they smile, I see the rot around the sharp, pointed teeth.

Furies.

"Awe." The middle one tilts her head to the side. "Such loving brotherly affection, protecting your sister from us. You do know Hades is going to find a way to murder you when he realizes you stole his favorite pet."

Ares releases me only to shove me behind him as he takes a step toward the beings. Rounding his shoulders, not bothering with words, his features display the image of brawn and opposition.

I shudder.

I would have dropped to my knees and pleaded for forgiveness for crimes I didn't commit to save myself from whatever promise lies behind those eyes. My jaw aches from where his hand held me steady, I can't imagine what they could inflict with real purpose.

My focus falls back to the three beings, who don't look the least bit affected by the unmistakable threat his form possesses. Between the four of them, I'm not sure who I'm most intimated by, the God who promises pain and destruction, or the Furies who guarantee it.

The Fury on the right giggles and sticks her forked tongue out. "What? Are we not what you expected?"

"Tisiphone, don't play with the food."

I swallow back the panic at being called food and answer, "Not at all. You're much more *appealing* than I imagined." It isn't exactly a lie. The lack of torturous, spiked whips does make them more pleasing to look at.

The one in the middle laughs, not getting one step closer to me before Ares side-steps between us.

"Alecto," Tisiphone sings their leader's name.

The differences between the three is subtle, Tisiphone is taller and slimmer. Alecto stands shorter and thicker, in the middle, and the one on the left, Megaera, has a spasm in her face every few seconds like she can't blink enough.

"I think we have company," Tisiphone looks to the sky just as white wings fall between us. Hermes trembles the ground where he lands next to Ares, widening his wings to block me from their view.

Shit. I look to the sky, through the trees, behind me, to the side, waiting for that scowl to bury me six feet under.

"Don't be such a sourpuss, Hermes. We want to see her," Tisiphone whines, so close to stomping her feet.

There's an obvious tension between them that I can't look closer at when the shadows darken and that familiar whispering intuition glides along the breeze, *Go to them.*

My heels dig into the ground, but that calling continues until the need to go to them consumes me, latching onto my every thought stronger than Thanatos ever has.

With a trembling hand, I touch Hermes' shoulder, returning all the assurance he's given me. "It's fine."

"It's not," he snaps back. The dark circles under his eyes give away how tired he is, and that glare is full of a warning that reminds me of Hades.

Go to them, that urge is more demanding, a gut-churning feeling that tells me if I ignore it, something terrible will follow.

I not only don't have the strength to fight it, but I don't want to. My intuition is all I have, and if it's telling me to go to these beings, however dangerous they are, then I will. It's what led me here, to finding out the truth of who I really am, what my purpose is.

Lifting Hermes' wing, I crawl beneath it and feel his protective hand on my back as I take a step closer to the waiting Furies.

"You're brave." Alecto clicks her tongue. "Do you know who we are? That we could feed off the evils you've done, leaving nothing of you. Not even a soul."

My throat struggles to clear, drying as I muster the courage to reply, "You're assuming I've done evil things."

"Oh, darkling." The leader tilts her head to the sky and lets out a throaty cackle that has the other two following, creating a chorus of warning laughter. "We've all done evil things."

"Can we have a taste?" Maegera's screech comes out as a light whisper, her eyes twitching rapidly, followed by a lick of her lips.

A trickle of fear creeps up my spine. They can't mean to really eat me.

I start to retreat, one foot catching on the other. Hermes grabs for me, but Alecto is there first, yanking me out of his reach.

314

The Fury spins me around, pressing my back against her naked body with a long, curved fingernail pointed at my throat. "Nah, ahh, ahh Hermes. You're familiar with how our poison works. Let's come to an agreement."

The unmistakable spicy aroma invades me, like my mind is so weak it's reaching out for the one thing that can comfort me at the thought of dying.

"Your deal with Hades involves you keeping your hands off what's his, and she," Hermes points his head toward me, "is his." Bitterness wraps around his last words, and I'm not the only one who notices. Ares' head cocks to the side, studying us. The first movement the God has made since Hermes showed up.

"You think we can't smell him on her," Alecto scoffs. "We only wanted to have a little fun." Her nail drags up my throat and around my chin, tucking a piece of hair behind my ear lovingly. "Do you understand your selfish curiosity got you in this position, pet?"

"I believe it was yours," I say too quickly, biting my cheek enough to wince before the burst of metallic lathers my tongue.

I can hear Hades' warning in the back of my mind, *They like fighters. If you don't want to get hurt, I suggest you bite that lip a little harder.*

Hermes' face holds nothing but the same warning, a complete contrast to Ares' high chin that carries his twisted grin.

"Oh, she's delightful," Tisiphone squeals next to us, practically jumping on her toes. "Now I really want a taste."

The suspended pause is palpable, no one daring so much as a wrong breath with the threat scratching back down my neck. If it weren't for the mention of poison, I would risk fighting my way out of Alecto's hold, but I know Hermes enough to understand when even he's scared and pissed.

"What Hades doesn't know won't hurt us," Megaera rasps with sheer exhilaration.

I draw in a breath before I'm clawing at Alecto's arm, failing to stop her from slicing her nail along my shoulder, the icy sting burning straight through me. She wipes her palm across the cut before pushing me into Hermes. His arms wrap around me, and I clutch him back just as tight.

From the corner of my eye, I see the other two Furies come to their leader's side, her hand covered and dripping with a mix of crimson and black blood.

In unison, their heads snap to me, their voids narrowing. "I knew your scent was curious, but this is impossible."

"Leave us, Alecto. You got what you wanted," Hermes warns.

"Am I cursed?" I ask no one in particular, pushing from the safety of his hold.

"That is not—" Alecto tries, cut off by Hermes, his shout loud enough to shake the trees.

"Leave!"

"You know better than to think we take orders from your kind, messenger boy. Just like you know that we're aware of the horrors you've inflicted, and that we could feast on you for eternity. Does your little bat know that?" The tilt of Alecto's head has me questioning why I ever stepped closer to her. She's the personification of terror. "Tell me, Hermes, do you know how Hades came into possession of this creature he calls a pet?"

Before I can so much as blink, I'm back in Hermes' hold, his arms caging me against him protectively—*possessively*.

"You *do*. Interesting." Those golden eyes lock back onto mine, a glimmer of something… like wonder, like she's witnessing a miracle for the first time. "I should have known from the eyes. We'll be seeing you soon, darkling," Alecto promises before shooting into the air with Megaera right behind her.

Tisiphone lingers, bending at the hips to stare at me closer without risking Hermes wrath. Giggling, she clasps her hands, those sharp teeth gleaming rot with her rising smile before peering behind us. "We didn't mean to scare the poor thing." Looking around Hermes' shoulder, I find Dionysus pale and frozen in place as the last Fury shoots up after the other two.

Relief doesn't come when they're gone. If anything, the beings were keeping me from facing the repercussions of what led the Gods here.

"What is wrong with you?" Hermes' accusatory tone spins me around to face him. "Have you learned nothing? You can't trust like that. Look at Dionysus. That is how you should be acting. He stayed behind me, shut his mouth, and looked terrified. You can't challenge beings like them."

"I wasn't scared." Terrified and intrigued are better descriptions for how my insides were split into both wanting to run as far away from them as my feet would take me and wanting to invite them to dinner to listen to the stories they have to tell.

Gods, I'm starting to sound like Dora, a trait I have come to understand more and more since knowing Gods were real.

"Then you're an idiot," Ares says. "Everyone should have a sense to fear ancient ones like them."

A curved dagger appears in Hermes' palm. One I recognize as Dionysus'. His chest widens as he stalks toward the God of War with enough force to shake the ground. "What the fuck do you think you're doing, Ares? You took her?"

"How did you know?" I look between him and Dionysus, noticing the exhaustion on their faces. I had done everything right.

"Know what?" Hermes' jaw ticks. "That you left? I know what Hecate's sleeping tonic tastes like, and so does Hades. How do you think he sleeps every night? This one's herbs countered it." He points the knife toward Dionysus before righting it back to Ares. "Or do you mean how we found you? The trail of flowers was a hint, your pull with Dionysus..." he trails off, and I search the trees again, the air, my heart stilling as I wait for the wrath that is sure to come my way any second.

In the same breath Hades claimed me as his, he had told me I was never leaving. What will he do once he finds out that I did?

"He's not here. I said he knows what it tastes like. I didn't say he got to the antidote in time." Hermes dips his chin. "We left him behind to get you." A pinch of betrayal on Hades' behalf surges through me, even if I'm the cause of it. "He told me long ago not to stop you if you left, so I'm technically following orders."

Dionysus clasps my back and says the words that make me sigh in relief to no longer be alone with the silent warrior. "We're going to take you to the Heavens." It doesn't stop the stinging guilt that Hermes' words evoke.

Ares steps into the blade, not caring that it cuts into his chest, "I get the reward."

"You get to stay out of Tartarus." Hermes lowers the weapon, handing it back to Dionysus. A second later he's holding a vial. "I knew we'd need this."

"You're going to want to squeeze, Spitfire." Dionysus clasps my hand.

Before I can ask why, the pain in my shoulder sears again. Dionysus cries out with me as I tighten around his hand, feeling his knuckles pop in the center of my palm while Hermes pours the rest of the vial over the cut, still dripping blood.

"It will heal quickly. Unfortunately, some cuts do scar Gods."

"I have enough not to care," I say through clenched panting.

Dionysus and Hermes glance at each other, but neither press for more.

"This will get rid of their venom, but you might have some side effects, like extreme cold or hallucinations," Hermes explains. "My home isn't far from here. We'll stay there until it passes.

The house is small but comfortable enough for the four of us, if someone sleeps outside or on the small dining table. Dionysus runs straight to the one bedroom, already knowing exactly where it is. It doesn't surprise me one bit. Dionysus and Hermes are closer than even Dora and I ever were.

Hermes gets to work, lighting the hearth and grabbing as many blankets as his arms can hold before piling them in front of the growing fire.

"I really think I'll be fine. I don't feel cold. We should go before Hades wakes up and finds us," I insist, to which Ares nods his agreement from the porch.

Hermes is already holding a dagger, ready to threaten him again, when Ares tells us he'll take watch outside and slams the door.

The fact that the God of War didn't put up any arguments makes me uneasy, and the way Hermes repositions the couch to face the door tells me he feels the same.

"I can't believe you followed that..." He gets lost in his words like always as of late. "You have no sense of fear, do you? Ares is a fucking monster." His teeth grate as he drops onto the sofa and rakes his hands through his hair. "I've done regrettable things, but I don't have a choice. Ares chooses to do those things and does it with a fucking grin." His eyes are toward the ceiling as if he's watching specific memories that sicken him.

As I step toward him, his scowl falls to the long scar along my shoulders, softening ever so slightly. "I've been nicked by each of them and trust me, you got lucky with Alecto."

I don't tempt changing the topic back to Ares, to pry for specifics. Not only have I read enough to understand, but I've never seen Hermes so stressed, so enraged and unsteady.

Thinking he needs space, I fall into the mountain of cushions and covers piled on the floor before the fire.

With my lack of fight, he visibly relaxes and places his hands behind his neck, crossing his legs at his ankles. The rapid rise and fall of his chest notably slow with every long exhale.

"You hear that?" Snores ring through the home. "That's what happens when a God is terrified. And drugged."

I wrap myself tighter into the blanket, trying to hide myself from the guilt that consumes me for betraying them.

"I'm sorry," I say it so lightly that I'm not sure he heard it. As my mind begins to drift, his face becomes a blur.

Our argument in the kitchen replays in my mind. I want to finish it before we never get a chance to.

"I watch you sometimes," I slur. Am I drunk? The pull between Dionysus and I isn't pulling or pushing, but the room begins to spin as if I've had a few bottles. "You hold too much in," I continue.

"You have no idea," I hear before my head hits the pillow.

When my eyes open again, my body shakes with a frozen shiver. I clutch the blankets tighter and tuck my knees to my chest.

Fucking Styx. How long was I out?

I peek over to Hermes. His eyes are closed with his wings wrapped around himself. *Lucky bastard.*

As if reading my mind, a wing rises, long enough to curve against the ceiling before slowly lowering and tucking beneath me. The feathers tickle at first, but the warmth is immediate, yet a chill still lingers.

"If you don't stop shivering, I'm crawling to the floor with you."

"And how would that help me stop being cold?"

I watch him over the couch's edge as his lips curve, all anger from before gone. "Do you want to find out?"

His wing pulls me in a little deeper as he crawls to the floor and tucks himself under the covers, wrapping his arms around my waist and letting his warmth surround me.

"As someone who chooses his words wisely, I'm sorry I can't find a way to tell you what I need to."

"Does this have to do with our last conversation?" He nods. "I have a theory."

"Maybe we shouldn't speak about it yet."

I yawn, my head floating too far away to listen clearly or hear the caution in his voice. "But I want to know why you pretend to be..." The words stick in my throat.

"Pretend to be what?" His fingers drag up my spine, that jolt between us stinging every spot he trails. His free hand finds my cheek, tilting my head so we're fixated on one another. "Why do I pretend to be what, Kore?"

"My brother." It comes out as a whisper. "I know you're not really my brother."

When I berated him in the kitchen, I was hoping he'd tell me the truth. I saw the difficulty he had not confirming nor denying it, but I know, deep down, I know. My connection with Dionysus is that of the soul, my bond with Hades is of something I'm trying to forget, and that jolt I have with Hermes is right there with it. Not to mention that he knew who I was and continued flirting with me in a way no one would with their sister.

His chest deflates, letting out a weighted breath and words that confirm my suspicion. "You can never repeat that again."

I move my arms from his chest to around his waist, settling more comfortably. "I know."

He places a tender kiss on my temple. "Sleep, Little Bat."

Hades' voice plays through my mind. Not just his voice, he's here, sitting on a throne. His raven hair is still a mess. He isn't stiff or cold like

I had seen him there before but relaxed with his legs kicked out in front of him. The muscles on his toned stomach are on full display, but it's his grin that holds my attention, remembering all the promises he demanded from me, how that mouth was all over me just last night.

I look down and see I'm in the scarlet nightdress, feeling his flames tickle up my legs.

My fingers grip the hem, a movement he tracks. "You thinking about me, Deviant?"

Always, I almost say.

"Always?"

"I didn't say that."

"You thought it, and in here, we're connected. You can't hide from me here."

I bite the inside of my cheek, embarrassed that he'll know all the crude thoughts that pass through my mind.

"You're thinking about my tattoos and scars." Hades stands from the throne, taking each step toward me without any sense of urgency.

"You're thinking about mine, but I don't know how I know that."

He stops, looming over me a whisper away. "Like I said, we're connected here." He traces the scar along my shoulder. "They're going to be punished severely."

"For hurting your favorite pet?" I try to sound more vexed, but I can't deny the heat that rushes to my core.

"You're angry that it didn't bother you."

"I'm not a pet."

"That you were *my* pet is what didn't bother you."

My belly coils, tightening at the insinuation that I'm *his* anything. Our banter is a song I want to write and listen to forever, but that thing in my chest stops itself, my mind quickly righting the impossibilities. I can't be his anything.

We had our one night.

I want nothing more than to straddle him on that throne or spin around the room to a tuneless dance, but even in this dream the guilt pierces me too deeply, keeping me from enjoying even a dream.

He cups my cheek, a loving gesture that breaks me. "I'm so sorry." My knees weaken, dropping hard to the floor.

321

"For what?" His seductive tone is replaced with apprehension as he wipes away my tears. "I've imagined you in this position many times, and as much as I love seeing you in it, I need you to tell me what's wrong."

I choke on a sob, forcing myself to peer back up at him. "You aren't— You're meant for someone else. The prophecies. You and Persephone... I have my purpose and— It was the only way."

"Slow down." He bends to my level, his elbows resting on his knees. "What was the only way?"

"I couldn't stay knowing you were hers. And what Zeus did, I—" My head shakes, gripping his arms to steady myself as I tell him, "I gave you sleeping tonic so I could sneak away to the Heavens."

The room erupts with fire. Cobalt flames lick every inch of my skin, but it doesn't burn.

His hold on my cheek falls to my throat, squeezing tight enough to keep me steady and my eyes captivated in the blazing fire within his. "*Where are you?*

The room shifts.

My eyes open, still groggy, still dizzy, but enough to see a lit hearth and familiar tattooed arms wrapped around my waist.

I let out a breath. I'm still dreaming, safe in Hades' arms, in his bed.

I pull his face to mine, kissing him hard. "I'm sorry," I say, waking him up.

His kiss is softer than ever before, deeper, slower like he's savoring this moment with me.

"Kore." His whisper is too soft to hear, his arms wrapping around me, pulling me in tighter. Even his hands are softer, sliding around my skin with a natural control.

I'm not ruining this one with useless confessions.

With a moan against his lips, I beg the way he likes, guiding his hand between my legs.

He doesn't nip at my lip like he usually does or tie my wrists behind my back or above my head.

There is no heat or fire at all, it's all him.

His fingers run up and down my center, unhurried, before circling that spot that has me rolling my hips toward him.

322

I shouldn't have left. I could be in his bed instead of having this damn dream that isn't giving me enough. The way he's fondling me, instead of pinching or tugging at my nipples is too soft.

There are no zaps of tortured pleasure. It's like this dream is torturing me for betraying him.

I need more.

Climbing on top of him, I drop my dress to bunch at my waist, and I ride his fingers. My teeth catch his lip, hoping he understands what I need without having to beg any more.

He always gives me what I want, so long as I ask, so why is he being so timid now? Fuck, even his mouth on my nipple is too kind, his tongue rolling over each bud slowly.

Something tugs at me to stop and I push it away, continuing to climb, finding my own rhythm. It tugs harder, *demanding* I stop.

I reach between us to replace his fingers with the thing I know will give me what I need when a harsh pull at my rib has me crying out.

His mouth finds my neck, and he moans my name, but the voice is wrong.

My eyes snap open, finding Hermes beneath me, eyes dazed and skin flushed.

I tumble off, kicking back to get as much space between us as I can until I feel the hearth behind me. "I didn't mean to."

The lust on Hermes doesn't wash away, and he does the one thing I wouldn't expect, sliding his fingers into his mouth, licking each one clean with a *pop*. "There's no evidence that anything happened."

"I—" My throat dries, the sinful sight leaving me speechless. When his eyes lower, I realize I'm still naked and hurry to cover myself with one of the pillows.

"Hallucinated?" He grabs his heart with a jested smile. "I figured when you called out Hades' name."

Hades.

"We have to go. Now!" I jump to my feet and fix my dress, explaining what happened in the dream that didn't feel like a dream at all.

Hermes is quick to understand and rushes to wake Dionysus while I catch my breath, my mind racing at what just happened.

"That was interesting," Ares' voice slices through the silence, and I jump back, clutching my chest to stop my heart from jumping out of it.

"Gods, how long have you been there?"

His face gives away nothing. "Funny, neither of you thought it was awkward." He stands from the table, making his way to the door. "I have a feeling I will be collecting that reward after all."

Chapter Twenty-Eight

KORE

After hours of walking and glancing over our shoulders, we make it out of the wards and vanish to a clearing. The place is scattered with junk, shattered mirrors, broken doors, crumbling columns, and burned books.

"What is this place?" I ask, taking in the mess. With the pines and elms surrounding us, it feels like a place that was meant to stay hidden.

"It's the crossroads," Hermes answers. "All veils interconnect here. It's one of the few entry points that don't change. These doors will always lead where they're supposed to."

Dionysus' whispers pull my attention. He looks to be in prayer, his head bowed, chanting to himself like Hecate does into her cauldrons. Before I have a chance to ask, Hermes, beaming with pride, adds, "He begged to be the one to open the door."

A massive, gaudy gate appears with two large statues on either end, showcasing a bearded man I know immediately must be Zeus. He doesn't look anything like the statues back home, where his features are softer, playful even. These statues depict a powerful man who doesn't want anyone to enter his veil. His strong jaw holds no hint of a smile, and his eyes bear no light.

At the sight, my insides tremble and not in the way Hades makes me quiver with that confusing mix of fear and desire. If this is a replica, I admit, I'm terrified to meet the God it resembles.

Don't, a voice that mirrors Hades sounds so close, my head darts in every direction to find him. The painful plea behind that word has me certain it can't be him but my own mind playing tricks on me, attempting to sway me from this decision.

I catch Ares watching me, taking me in with an interest that makes me step closer to Hermes.

The gates rumble, and I see the moment he spots my hesitation, that flickering question if I'm doing the right thing when I hear Hades' voice again, giving me the ultimatum to stay put or he'll make good on the promise of putting me in the chains when he inevitably drags me back.

Any other time his threats would have been my sole focus, but with the warrior barreling toward me I can't think of anything but the determination in his eyes as he grabs my wrist and yanks me forward, dragging me through the gates. My wrist wails in response, my whimpers drawing Hermes' and Dionysus' attention, the latter already reaching for his dagger.

We're on the other side within a few steps, but before I'm able to take in our new surroundings, my vision spins with that familiar dip in my stomach, my gut churning with the forced jump.

Someone grabs my elbow and when we stop, I yank from Ares' hold right as Dionysus releases his hold on me to slam his fist to the God's nose. "Don't touch my sister again." Another slam to Ares' jaw.

Hermes steps beside me, holding Dionysus' blade, probably saving his life. There isn't a man who cut Ares and lived to talk about it.

With blood dripping down his chin, Ares' points his twisted grin at Hermes. "Just me? What about—"

Hermes takes one step and jabs Ares' throat, sending him hinging at his waist to catch his breath. "No one wants to hear you talk."

I'm speechless, an unexpected sensation rising at the violence I don't flinch from. Weeks ago, I would have but now... Now I want to incite my own pain onto him. I want Ares' blood dripping from my fist for touching me, and it isn't because of my drive for balance.

Hermes whispers something in Ares' ears while Dionysus inspects my wrist, cradling my hand into his with the softest touch, cursing under his breath when he notes the red fingerprints. Again, those images of Ares' blood on my skin instead of his fingerprints flash through my mind.

They disappear the second I notice where we are. There is no moon and there are no torches lighting our surroundings, there's no need when the sun is high in the sky. The very air is different here, lighter, and yet a little harder to breathe.

And then there's the palace. Hades' castle is nothing compared to the enormous, multi-pillar, golden home before us. I've never seen a building so big, so white and blinding. It's exactly how I've imagined the Heavens.

Ares leads the way, but it's Hermes I follow inside, admiring every detail. The vaulted ceilings look like they're made of the sky itself, pink clouds with golden rays. The silence is graced by the sound of flowing water. A peaceful music I could listen to for the eternity I now have.

I avert my eyes as naked, gilded women pass us in the halls. Dionysus holds no shame, his head craning after every passing one.

Every detail of this place is immaculate, from the granite banisters my palm slide along as we climb the spiraling stairs, to the chandeliers that don't hold flames but jewels for the sun to shimmer off. We pass dozens of doors with the familiar sounds of those in the throes of ecstasy.

The chambers we enter nearly takes my breath away. The wall directly across opens to a balcony, letting in the fresh, sunny breeze. Dresses are piled on the four-poster bed. The vanity holds enough makeup and perfumes for a small town.

"You have ten minutes." Ares turns to leave.

Hermes stops him by cutting off his path. "Until what?"

"Zeus has been *impatient*." The looks between them are a silent conversation I can't decipher. "He'll know they're here, and with the festivities dragging on all month he's grown bored. The sooner they've made their appearances, the sooner this can all be over."

Hermes relents and agrees, telling him to wait outside.

With a curl of his lip, Ares doesn't bother shutting the door before propping himself against the frame.

"You heard him." Hermes points me toward the washroom. "Ten minutes."

"But," I look around the room, at the dresses on the bed, "I didn't bring anything. I can't just wear someone else's clothes."

"Why the fuck not? You've been fine doing it in the Underworld?" Hermes tosses me a blue one from the top.

Being here, being thrusted into this veil, this home, these chambers, ordered to hurry, the tension... The reality of what I've done comes crashing down. I hadn't thought to bring clothes. It's such a simple step, and yet I was so focused on the bigger picture that I hadn't thought about what it takes to get there. Hades is right, I have a mortal mind, too focused on what's in front of me, the immediate next move, that I didn't stop to think.

"Zeus keeps these rooms stocked with extra clothes for those who lose theirs," Hermes explains. "So, you don't need to worry about asking for permission."

"Actually," Dionysus waves his hand, and a pile of red and black appears on the bed. When he turns to me, he holds a glimmer in his eyes, a proud one. "Hades and I," That pride dims, "we worked for days making this dress for you. He planned to take you through the town while I was here. And when I returned, we were going to show you my memories through the cauldrons, so it felt like you were here with me." He lets out a bitter laugh. "He made me swear not to do anything fun, if you know what I mean."

I recall seeing the ruby dress on the vanity before Hades got rid of it and took me to the sunset room because of my jealous tantrum. Seeing as how that tantrum is what led to me finding out about Zeus, learning Hades' prophecy, reading Persephone's prophecy, and realizing my place is here, I'm not sure if I regret it or not.

I take the material between my fingers, finding it soft and shimmery, feeling a new ache in my ribs as I head for the washroom.

I don't take time to admire the glass tub or smell the soaps before I quickly rinse myself and hurry into the dress.

When I come back out Dionysus is cleaned up. His hair is tied at the nape of his neck and he's wearing a long-sleeved ruby top that matches my dress. When he lifts his head from where he's fixing his dagger in his waistband, his eyes widen and he lets out a long whistle. "I have no words."

He takes my hand and spins me, twirling the sheer skirt, the shimmer from the tiny diamonds plotted perfectly. I can't help but wonder what it would look like under the moon.

"If you weren't Zeus' daughter, Hera would probably murder you." Hermes leans against the doorway, back from wherever he left with Ares. He, too, cleans up nicely, but I much prefer him outside of the crisp white attire he wears now. This Hermes is one I don't know, the clothes making him appear more uncertain and stiff, whereas without them he's charming, surely, and free.

Since our encounter with the Furies, or maybe it's because of Ares' presence, he's become a ghost of himself. There's been a permanent concern written on his face, even when he licked me off his fingers. The ones that are now itching his jaw and making me blush from the memory.

It's not his comment that leaves my mouth dry. "Is this too much?" The last thing I want is to anger Hera, who's already ordered my death. What will she think about my return?

"It's perfect." My head is already faint, but when Hermes licks his lips, I just about topple over. That jolt between us stings without even touching, and the way his eyes snap to mine, he feels it too.

Clearing his throat, he asks, "Ready?"

No. I nod, lacing my arms between the two Gods.

With a vague, weak plan, I lift my chin and step toward my purpose.

Chapter Twenty-Nine

DORA

Nothing removes these gloves. It doesn't matter if I soak them, use a knife to pry them off, bite them with my teeth, pray to every God I can think of, they're stuck like a new layer of skin.

Aphrodite smiles with that nefarious glint whenever I throw a fit about them not coming off. "I told you, you had to wear them at all times, so why are you trying to remove them?"

I storm out of our room to do the chores she assigns me for the day, or rather, makes Adonis assign me since I'm *his* servant and *not* hers. There is little solace in that fact.

And yes, it's now *our* room, as in all three of us, for reasons I still can't quite understand. It isn't like we're going to leave, not without Kore, so why keep us so close?

Weeks ago, I would have been thrilled beyond belief to be in the presence of a God, let alone sharing a room with one. Now, it's grown tiresome.

Aphrodite purposely goes out of her way to make my time here as miserable as possible. The chores, the gloves, forcing me to share her bed, making passing comments that lead me to ask questions she never intends to answer.

At least she stopped sending men my way. I slipped once, but it was only because I needed something, someone, to rid my mind of that night with Jason. With so much alone time it was all I could think about, besides the constant need to escape. It hadn't worked, and now I'm plagued with scenarios in which I have them both. Jason's voyeurism and the new man's talented tongue.

I roll onto my side, adjusting the pillow lightly so as not to wake Adonis at my side. His brow creases and I reach to rub it out, hating that look on him. After everything he's been through, how he was raised, he deserves peace if only in sleep.

How he's managed daily chores for over two decades is beyond me. Even the silk sheets irritate my knees where they're bruised and sore from kneeling on the hard ground to scrub them. My skin feels wrinkly under the permanent gloves after washing hundreds of dishes daily, taking longer than it should because I can't stop gagging at the horrid smells.

At my touch, he visibly softens, and I think about how different he's become these last few weeks. I can't figure out why he wanted me to believe Aphrodite used him for sex. Maybe he feels guilty that he was free and I wasn't. It reminds me of the servants here. At first glance, that's what they appear to be, but when the shutters close, it's like they wake from a trance, eating, laughing, and dancing. No one is a hollow shell, and their servant attire is replaced with an assortment of different styles.

I've been observing and listening around the great hall, practicing my lip-reading skills to search for the stories I crave. One woman was sold by her mother to a group of men for a small patch of land and a lamb. Another was thrown in as a wager by her husband for cockfights. One of the men had no memory of his past at all, but he knew he had a wife he missed dearly, though he couldn't remember anything about her. I even approached a few to ask how they got here, but to my surprise, they all gave me the same bewildered expression before explaining how Aphrodite approached them to live with her, with all the food, friends, and happiness they could ever want. No catch.

That doesn't sound like the Aphrodite I've come to know. There has to be a catch, some ulterior motive, or maybe the Goddess really is so lonely that she's resorted to stealing mortals to keep herself company. Why else would she keep me and Adonis to warm her bed?

Just thinking about the Goddess has her bursting through the door, tossing clothes on the vanity before yanking the duvet clean off us. Her

331

eyes shoot between Adonis and me, latching onto where his arm drapes over my hip to pull me against him, muttering about how cold it is.

I could have laughed seeing the envy write itself through her scowl but stories about the death that follows that look have me pushing him away and shaking his shoulder to wake him.

He shoots out of bed with apologies I'm not sure are for me.

Before he shuts the washroom door, Aphrodite places a hand on his chest, her face too impassive to read. "Everything will take place tonight."

I sit up, my pulse quickening, taking in Aphrodite's appearance with this new information. The white dress leaves nothing to the imagination. Two thin pieces of cloth drape over her shoulders, down her chest, and meet below her belly button where a diamond jewel pierces it. The material meets in the center and drapes to expose and accentuate her hips and thighs that are decorated with diamond jewelry. The gilded bracelets are covered with the same diamond bangles and match the one around her neck and diadem placed on her crown of golden braids.

Two black boxes wait in her hands. "I have a gift for both of you."

Any other time, and from any other person, I might have been elated to receive a gift, but Aphrodite's last gift took away my visions.

Adonis doesn't hold the same hesitation. He uncaps his box and holds out a shining diamond necklace that matches the one I find in mine. "It will keep you both safe while we're there."

"How?" I step out of the bed and examine it closer. The diamonds glisten in the morning sun shining through the window. It doesn't look special. Then again, neither did the gloves.

Adonis puts his on and the way he does it without question only solidifies that he fares much better here than I do, and I'm not sure if it has anything to do with him sleeping with Aphrodite. When I tried to convince him that he didn't need to, he told me to leave it alone. Since then, he's kept closer to her, following her if she leaves a room, studying her with a newfound interest.

When he drops his arms, I swing my head toward a gleaming Aphrodite. "Is this a collar?"

She bites her grin. "Everyone will have servants, or pets, or wives, or even husbands with similar collars. If everyone knows you're mine, they can't take you for themselves. If you're in danger, rub your finger along it and I'll know."

She takes the gift from my hand, and I don't reject her help as she walks to my back and lifts the collar to my neck. The need for such a protective gesture only reminds me that I know nothing about the Heavens or the Gods who occupy it. Everything I've read could very well be wrong and knowing Pallas will likely be in attendance doesn't ease any of my concerns. I can't be sure the sea nymph won't take the chance to steal me this time.

As unsettling as it is, Aphrodite is the only being I can trust. And as if proving her point, she tugs at the diamond necklace to confirm it isn't too tight.

"And the gloves?" I hold out my hands, but Aphrodite shakes her head. "Please?" I'm not beneath begging.

"If they find out about your gift, they *will* take you. It's too dangerous."

"But it could help."

"I said no. I'll remove them when they need to be removed," she snaps.

Adonis tenses.

We've had our arguments and bickering, but Aphrodite never loses her temper, not without that sly flicker which doesn't flash over her deadly stern stare she cuts me with. "This is my territory, Dora. Do you understand me? You will do as I say." *Dora.* Not squirrel.

I swallow the fight in my throat and nod.

The palace Aphrodite takes us to is immaculate, a place one could dream up and still never create anything so grand and opulent. I could stay here for eternity and never tire, possibly never take in everything it has to offer. There's never been a place I wanted my magic to sing to me more.

But I don't get a chance to take in so much as the drapes before we're slipping behind a group and making ourselves unassuming in the corner of what I overhear is Hera's garden, the sun as low as it sets here.

Aphrodite explained the importance of blending in. Mortals aren't prohibited, but Gods play cruel games that she didn't elaborate on, and her seriousness puts me on edge enough to heed her warning and attempt to be on my best behavior.

Rather than mingle, I stay put, taking in everyone, from Gods to Goddesses, and nymphs to creatures I can't place. Some have horns, wings, webbed fingers, and scaled skin. There are some I know of, like the centaurs with their half-mare lower body, a cyclops with one eye, a satyr with its goat-like legs, all creatures I couldn't imagine being real, and yet here they are, mingling with one another in the Heavens.

Gilded women pass with trays, offering a variety of drinks and food, but my attention is on the flowers emended at every turn, in neat rows as if someone had painted them there in perfect order. A smile plays on my lips thinking of how Kore's head will spin when she sees them.

Something about orderly things, especially in a garden, has always irked Kore. She lets her flowers bloom where and how they want, cuts up dresses to fit her own style, and bakes treats with flavors that don't usually pair. That was until Celius died, and I taught her to blend in. Be a sheep in the crowd and the wolf might not notice one of its own dressed as the prey.

I continue my search for her familiar frown. Adonis must have been doing the same because Aphrodite grabs us both and says under her breath, "Stop acting like mortals. Do you see anyone else gawking?"

Rather than take the suggestive question to peek once more, my gaze lands where her hand rests on mine.

"Relax. I am not manipulating you." Her eyes hit the sky with the dramatic roll. "As you two have once warned me in your veil, you don't want any attention. Trust me."

"How are we supposed to find her without looking?" Adonis' posture remains statuesque, his hands behind his back, a habit that will probably help in this situation.

Aphrodite stops one of the gilded women to hand us each a glass, keeping one for herself. "You won't need to look."

Unable to help myself, I gaze from one being to another, noticing that Aphrodite had been right when she mentioned the collars. A man speaks to another, both of them with women standing at their backs with collars

334

around their necks, one blue, and one green. Another woman stands near them with a man collared in yellow. Two collared women giggle around a table with the same silver necklaces. The colors and accessories are clear markers as to who they belong to.

Aphrodite waves us to follow her near an apple tree to put us in view of the entryway. "What is your plan when you see her?" She swirls her untouched drink.

We talked about this, of course. We need to get Kore to the clearing where Aphrodite's friend prophesied her to fully transition into her true self. After which, we'll take her back to Aphrodite's home, where she will be safe from whatever Aphrodite fears and refuses to talk about.

As for me specifically, I'll wait until we're back at Aphrodite's to tell Kore *everything*—all the lies and secrets. That's where my plans end. I have a feeling once Kore knows the truth, I'll be sent back to the Mortal Veil, alone.

Adonis clears his throat. "We'll tell her to follow us."

Aphrodite doesn't look convinced.

"We'll rub our collars so you can use us to lure her back," I finish for him, hoping it doesn't have to come to that. I don't take pleasure in fooling Kore that we're in danger, but if that is what it takes to make her safe, we can apologize later, adding it to the prominent list.

Aphrodite swirls her drink once again, notably relieved that I don't argue or attempt to persuade her into another plan. "While we wait, why don't you ponder on your end of the bargain, Squirrel."

There doesn't seem to be another being amongst us with any sort of shackles aside from the collars, and it dawns on me how strange it was that Aphrodite lives so freely as a prisoner. Bold and brazen, with her own small kingdom to rule over.

I doubt very much that the answers to removing the shackles will be written in a book, at least one accessible to me any time soon. I look between the crowd and my surroundings once again, wishing I could pull everyone into an individual dance, their stories playing as we sway. I could spend all night practicing my focus to draw out specific images from them.

"Your knuckles are turning white." I follow where Aphrodite motions to where I hold my glass. My pale skin loosens around the stem, nearly dropping it when I realize the gloves are no longer suffocating me. "When did you do this?"

"You were right. It could help you here, and I figured if there was ever a time for you to practice control, it should be in a life-or-death situation."

The threat should bother me, but I'm too relieved to feel anything but pure gratitude as I wrap my arms around her neck.

Too quickly, she pushes me off. At first, I think it's because of my emotional outburst, but as she stands taller, schooling her features with utter disinterest, she commands under her breath, "Stay quiet," while sliding something into my palm.

"Aphrodite." The man doesn't smile with the approach, his stance pin-straight, like a soldier. He's so tall he casts a shadow over the three of us by merely standing still.

Without moving, his eyes find mine and then Adonis', lingering on him a second longer with a slight tick of his brow. "Pets? Really?"

Aphrodite folds her arms over her chest, her scowl alluring as always. "They are not of your concern, Ares."

He squints, lifting his hand in what appears to be a greeting, but Aphrodite knocks it away before we can think about grabbing it.

Seizing the opportunity, Ares grips her wrist and twists her into him. It would've been romantic if not for the disgust on Aphrodite's face when she spins around, her back to his chest.

There is nothing I can do to help. I'm no match for a God, especially not the God of War.

Adonis either doesn't know anything about the God or doesn't care as he steps closer. "Let her go."

I internally cringe, that second-hand embarrassment staining my cheeks on his behalf. He looks like a small boy ordering his father.

Unfazed, Ares nestles his chin in Aphrodite's neck. "Looks like your pup caught feelings."

Aphrodite's face softens into a look I can't decipher between pity and gratitude.

"Let her go," Adonis repeats, ignoring the plea in her eyes for him to stop.

"You need to tighten the leash." Ares doesn't take his attention from Adonis. "He is handsome, though. If you didn't have him collared, I'd take him for myself."

Others begin glancing in our direction. The last thing we need.

With an idea, I grab Adonis' hand, intertwining our fingers together like we're lovers, holding my body close to his and feel him both relax and stiffen at once. "Come, let's go see the rest of the gardens," I whisper in his ear, tugging his arm to follow.

With a promise to find us later, Aphrodite nods her approval, but not before giving me a warning squint that demands I behave.

Adonis' feet shuffle, reluctant to follow my lead, so I pull harder. Curious glances point in our direction as we make our way to the maze but quickly avert to a Goddess rushing past with a bleeding nose.

I pull us deeper into the maze, masking my rush with another elated giggle.

"Why did you do that? She was in trouble." Adonis' voice rises, unraveling his arm from mine.

"Everyone was looking at us. We needed to get away. Like you said, how are we going to find Kore if we don't look? You know as well as I do that she would grab a plate of food and head to the maze if she was here."

He glances back at the entrance and then deeper down the tall shrub walls in contemplation.

"I don't want to leave her with that man."

His resistance and favor for Aphrodite is beginning to ignite a rage inside of me that I didn't know myself capable of. We're here for Kore, that's all.

"Aphrodite can take care of herself. If anything, she'll probably manipulate Ares to leave her alone soon so she can find us."

"Fine," he says with a tone that insists it's anything but. His back muscles tighten, and his fists clench, but I don't want to push him any further, letting him lead the way down the green path.

I follow, but not before opening my palm to see Aphrodite handed me the small knife Sasha gifted me. My stomach knots.

The threat of this being a life-or-death situation is becoming more of a promise.

Chapter Thirty

KORE

Hermes leads us down the twisting hallways with such familiarity I'm certain he must have lived here at some time. As we pass rooms, he doesn't offer any description or tour like he had in the Underworld, instead his pace quickens with an urgency that leaves me stumbling and the rooms we pass a blur.

We're back in the main hall, passing pillars and gilded statues, when one of them comes to life, offering flutes of sparkling wine, the tray shaking in her hand.

I take one without needing any further encouragement, drinking it down and grabbing for a second one. A gesture the woman doesn't seem to mind and I'm sure it's because I'm taking weight off her struggling arm.

Rather than grabbing a glass, Dionysus reaches for the tray, insisting on helping the poor girl. She swivels out of his path and frowns.

"It's her duty to serve us." Hermes grabs two more glasses. "It's disrespectful to deprive her of doing her job."

"In that case." Dionysus grabs two of the flutes and thanks the woman with a wink. Still frowning, the woman turns on her heel and beckons us to follow, her hips swaying back and forth, mesmerizing Dionysus with hardly any effort at all.

Hermes' hand falls to the small of my back, the jolt nearly knocking the breath out of me. "Whenever you want to leave, tell me, and I'll fly us all out of here."

My nerves are a wreck, but his sapphires anchor me. *Everything will be fine.*

The muffled sound of a lyre and a soft, singing voice hits my ears first, and when the woman opens the double doors with a light push of her finger, the loud conversations flood me. There are too many talking at once, too many people in general, gathered in groups, eating, drinking, laughing, and dancing.

My chest tightens.

Elation, lust, wrath, pride, envy—every emotion hits me. My knees collapse and I'm on the ground, Hermes' and Dionysus' gripping my elbows before anyone notices, keeping me steady as my feet fail to. Neither of them needs to ask what happened. Dionysus felt it through our connection and offers the explanation to Hermes in a hushed whisper.

"You're okay, Little Bat," Hermes assures without offering any further comfort in front of such a crowd. It's Dionysus pushing his ability into me that has me secure on my feet again, the intoxication numbing away my empathic gift.

There must be hundreds of Gods and creatures I've never imagined possible gathered in this enormous garden. The gilded servers circle the perimeter offering trays with drinks I want to take back and food I want to gorge myself with.

Tall, neatly cut shrubs mark the giant maze I read about, mentally marking the location for later.

Flowers decorate every surface in neat clean rows, a specific flower belonging to their particular sections. I scrunch my nose at the neatness of it all. The one thing I truly admire is the ivy climbing the walls. At least they live freely.

It's nothing like my gardens back home—full of any flowers that find a home there—red carnations, purple hydrangeas, yellow daffodils, some I don't even know of but admire anyway. It strikes me that I'm not thinking about the one in the Mortal Veil, but the miracle I've grown in the Underworld. A home I need to forget.

Dionysus' arm drapes over my shoulder as Hermes leads us through a parting crowd.

The need to keep my head down is strong, my heart is pumping so fast I can feel it in my ears, but I force my head high, taking in as much as I can.

It's the blonde-haired boy playing the lyre that grabs my attention first, followed by the beautiful young Goddesses swaying their hips to the gentle melody of his instrument and the elegant voice of the dark-haired woman singing beside him. They must be the Muses and Graces I read and teased Dionysus about. Their beauty is something those words would never be able to capture.

When I finally tear my gaze back to the path, I can't ignore the turning heads and gaping mouths.

"What are they looking at?" I whisper to Dionysus.

"Us, love." He beams at the attention, lifting his chin to those we pass, offering them his wide boyish smile and a wink to swooning Goddesses.

I'm not as graceful. My insides wring, and my palms are sweaty.

I'm thankful to have the connection with him and that he lets me pull freely, feeling those flares of trepidation. "I'm way ahead of you." His eyes glisten and I know he's drunk on more than the attention.

We chuckle at our shared secret, now lighter and a little more calm with my head growing faintly dizzy. I'll have to stop soon, or I'll be a bumbling mess when it comes time to do what I need to.

Our mirth leaves the moment I see *him*.

The God is a giant, sitting on a large throne that towers over everything and everyone. He's dressed in all white, decorated with silver pins and jewelry that sparkle without any light having to touch it. His laugh is booming, and his eyes smile like Dionysus', while a man in a colorful outfit juggles different objects before the gathering crowd.

The God points and a streak of blinding lightning strikes the objects from the air, raining glass onto the poor man who ducks to cover his head.

Zeus.

A shrill comes from behind us.

Everyone turns to find Aphrodite as white as the little material barely covering her body, a shattered glass in her hands, and Ares attempting to help her. Immediately, my attention darts around, searching for Dora and Adonis. They must be here, too, but I don't spot them anywhere near the Goddess.

Zeus claps his hands together. "Wonderful!" His power is felt through that simple word. My own abilities recoil at it, not in fear, but like a snake readying to defend.

This is my father.

As we near, a woman approaches Hermes, saying something I can't hear before he steps to the side, allowing her to pass.

I don't have to wonder who this Goddess is. It's like staring in a mirror, except Demeter's eyes glisten brown as if she had been crying, whereas mine are violet flecked in gold and refuse such a reaction. Where my hair waves down my back, Demeter's sits above her shoulders in soft curls.

Dionysus has similar features, but Demeter is my twin, identical in nearly every way.

She looks nothing like you, Hades' voice filters through my thoughts yet again. If he were here, he would whisper facts about the Goddess, like he'd come to do in our *trainings*. A heat rushes to my cheeks at the memory, and I hate myself for thinking of him at a time like this, hate that his presence would put me at ease.

Come back, and I'll whisper anything you want in that ear. Bent over the desk, hanging from the tree, on the throne, on the dining table, wherever you want.

I resist the urge to smile too wide with Demeter staring at me. She would probably think I'm going mad, and I'm not entirely sure I'm not when I'm imagining Hades so vividly.

"I can't believe it." Demeter shifts like she wants to reach out, to hug me, to touch me, to make sure I'm real, but I throw my arms around her before she can, taking in her floral scent, her dense aura, and I can't help but wonder if I'm this uncomfortable to embrace, this stiff.

"I didn't think you were real." There's more meaning behind my words. I hadn't believed in the Gods, hadn't believed Demeter to be my mother, hadn't believed this moment would ever come.

When I pull away, Demeter copies the same greeting with Dionysus, who is less welcoming than I had been, offering quick pecks to both her cheeks.

"A toast!" Zeus' thundering voice brings everyone's attention to where we stand at the foot of his throne. I had been so consumed by the sight of Demeter, that I forgot about the God.

The gilded servers pass around new glasses, replacing my empty one with a deep red that smells like something rancid Hecate would mix together. Dionysus gives me the same questioning look when he smells his.

"To the return of my daughter, *Kore*, and my son, *Dionysus*." Zeus steps toward us, draping his heavy arm around our shoulders so hard that I almost drop my cup.

Dionysus looks natural standing here, like the long-lost son who returned home.

New guilt creeps up on me at the thought of Celius, what he would think if he saw me claiming to be someone else's daughter as if he wasn't my father my entire life.

A small piece of me can see it, the future I could have here. The loving mother, the dutiful father, and the handsome ladies-man brother.

It's a perfect life. One I had dreamt of long ago.

Come back, Hade's voice pleads with a gut-churning rage.

I can't, I shout back, feeling insane for entertaining my delusions.

My reason for coming here is more than a mere curiosity. Meeting Demeter had been one, and I refuse to leave until I succeed in the other two.

Quickly correcting myself, I become taller, and more confident, thinking of Hades' powerful grin and trying to master it. I watch Dionysus and attempt to mimic his natural happy-to-be-here presence.

A Goddess rushes past us, holding her nose, her wild hair reminding me of Hecate's, but I know who it is from the arrows down her back. Hermes turns and orders Dionysus and me to stay together before jogging after Artemis.

"The rest of my children, Apollo," Zeus motions to the lyre player, "Ares," to the warrior by Aphrodite, "Hephaestus is represented by his wife Aphrodite," Aphrodite's lips tighten. "Artemis and Hermes," Zeus waves to where Hermes chases Artemis inside, "and of course Hebe and Athena." He flicks his wrist to the strong woman beside his throne and a small girl beside her. "It's a wonderful thing to have family together again. And we have Ares and Hermes to thank for that. They'll be rewarded greatly for it."

A few frustrated sighs and low murmurs rippled through the sea of bodies. I've never felt more on display, their glowers faulting me for their failure at finding and returning me, for costing them the reward.

As Zeus tips his glass, the rest follow in unison, pushing past the horrid scent. Faces sour, mine included, at the bitter flavor. Dionysus already has our glasses refilled with my favorite wine to wash it down.

When everyone returns to their conversations, some whispering and sneering at us from a distance, Zeus disappears, and Demeter steps before me. "How did you end up in the Underworld?"

The question catches me off-guard. It's as if the Fates want me to be reminded of the Underworld and its king at every turn, refusing to let me move on.

"I fell." I brush an invisible hair from my dress at the awkward silence thickening between us. Maybe we're both unsure how to approach this, but I don't have time to play shy now. Demeter could easily be a way to get the information I need.

Before I can build the courage or find the right words, Demeter leans closer and lowers her voice, "Hades didn't harm you, did he?"

"Of course not." I scoff. "Why would you think that?"

Hades does have a reputation amongst the mortals, but surely these Gods must know him better. But when Demeter looks me over again, not like a mother would a fallen child, but a passerby during a lover's quarrel, my insides wither. I'll be sure to be aware of my facial reactions seeing how clear they are on her. "Is there something wrong with my dress?"

"No, sweetheart. It's... Well, that color isn't something we wear in the Heavens. It's too dark. It's more *his* color." I look where she motions to the crowd filled with much lighter-toned pastels, with an airiness to them as if the sun washed away the once vibrant colors.

"Don't worry." She continues her observations of me, noticing the scar along my shoulder. "We have an entire room set up with more *appropriate* attire. Enjoy the drinks, food, maybe dance?" She squeezes my arm and then disappears through the parting crowd.

"She's just as I remembered." Dionysus comes to my side. "It's like she wants us but doesn't know what to do with us."

"I suppose I don't know what to do with her either." My brother's presence alleviates some of the pressure, stopping me from picking at my cuticles. Maybe it's because we're soul tied, but I've never felt distant from him like I do with Zeus and Demeter and I'm grateful for it—to have a bond that is unquestioned.

It all comes to a halt when the dancers pull him away by his shirt. A few of them eye me too, but none of them dare when I set my scowl in place.

A tap on my shoulder has me spinning around, smelling the strong scent of the salty sea. By his appearance, it's clear that's exactly where he lives. His skin is golden with hair so blonde it nearly looks white from being caressed by the sun. "Care to dance?"

My head shakes before the words stumble out, "I don't dance."

"Everyone dances here." He guides my hand to his shoulder, gripping my waist and taking my other hand in his. Before I have a chance to pull away, we're already moving, or rather, I'm stepping on his feet.

"I'm Attis." He offers a charming smile that's too confident.

"Kore," the greeting comes automatically with my focus on our feet, trying to follow his fast pace. How had it been so easy with Hades, and now I can't figure out when to step back or forward? And now he's going left?

Everything is made worse when he lifts my chin to look at him.

"Rumor is you've been Hades' prisoner for weeks. How did you manage to catch his eye?"

"It must be my perfect beauty and pleasant charm." I refrain from rolling my eyes.

Attis' grin slips, finding no humor in my sarcasm. "You know he abducts women and keeps them as pets until they die, and even then, he gets to keep them longer because he can." His brow rises, dropping his glance to where my golden chain disappears between my cleavage. "Did he make you a pet?" He studies my neck as if there would be a collar, marking me as his. Little does he know that collar is flames and they wrap around my wrists.

344

My anger flares at the ignorance and even more at his arrogance, boiling over as his fingers tighten into my waist. A fury fills me that feels too aggressive for such a simple touch. I've experienced worse, so why does it feel like I want to burn this man where he stands?

He will burn for touching you.

Attis shrieks, taking his unwanted hold with him.

My jaw falls open.

Where my hands had just been, his top is singed, his flesh burned beneath. I start to apologize but the God doesn't give me a second before shooting me a glare and stalking off.

I'm acutely aware of the turning heads and the dancers that stop to stare, but I can't look away from my hands, baffled and confused at how I could have burned him. I don't have abilities with fire. I've tried and failed, haven't felt a flicker toward having such an ability.

I don't have time to think about this now. Before anyone else forces me to dance or stops me to talk, I make my way through the parting crowd, toward the hedges I mentally marked earlier.

Once inside, I remove the pages from my dress, showing me exactly which turns to take to avoid the dead-ends and misleading fountains and statues. My free hand glides along the passing bushes, feeling the roughness of their trimmed leaves that create the walls. Without the map it would be too easy to get lost for hours, possibly days.

On the last turn, a wide opening emerges at the end of the final walkway, revealing an enormous statue of three women, one holding her ears, another her eyes, and the last covering her mouth. The pool they stand at the center of ripples from the water trickling in.

It isn't the statue that has me nearly jumping up and down on my toes, but the asphodels along the shrubs.

I lie in bed, rubbing the butterfly on my wrist. I'm useless. Hades won't let me go to the Heavens, I'm not sure how to help the lost souls, and it feels like everyone has a secret. Hermes with his curse, Hecate with the Triple Goddess, Hades with just about everything, and Dionysus... well he's an open book.

My only skills include gardening, cooking, and selling. Selling isn't even my strong suit, considering I sell what people need. I could sell a fake personality, at times, when my mouth doesn't get the best of me. Here, I'm useless. I'm even horrible at chess.

"Now, now, Sweet Shadow." A dark mist fills my room. I leap from my bed, but a hand catches me before I reach the door. "You're anything but useless." Thanatos spins me back around, his wings stretched out, filling every corner with a darkness that once again calls to me.

"How did you get in here?" My heart skips. This isn't the kind of fear that sends my toes curling.

He eyes the vanity where books are marked and placed upside down to keep my place, right next to the pomegranate I planned to eat.

"I want to help you." He grabs the pomegranate and opens it with ease, handing me half of it. "This is from your garden?"

I nod.

"You haven't eaten anything from it yet." It isn't a question.

I shake my head, trying to decipher what he's looking for.

"That garden holds a special property in it. An oath made while eating what it's grown is more sacred than the River Styx." His eyes sharpen, holding his half of the pomegranate higher. "It's making a deal with the Underworld itself." He pauses, a tilted grin passing too quickly to take in. "Like I said, I want to help you."

"Why?"

"Because you're going to help me." He takes a bite of the fruit. "I see the fire and determination in your eyes, why Hades calls you a deviant. You are someone I cannot predict nor control, and I want to ensure that whatever happens, you succeed."

"Succeed at what exactly?" I look at the fruit in my hands, weary of what he's offering.

"Everything."

I rub the butterfly marking on my wrist. A cloud of dark mist appears a few feet away before Thanatos steps out of the dark shadows. His pale body looks sickly in the light as he looks around, confused not to be called to my room. "Kore." His face lights with a mix of awe and apprehension, his breath holding a weight as heavy as mine. "You did it."

"We have to move quickly." I hand him the last page that gave me the idea to harvest the healing flowers. "Make sure to keep the roots, or it won't work."

When I asked if Thanatos would take me here, he was nearly as angry as Hades for considering such an idea, claiming the Heavens is the last place I should be, that it's dangerous for someone like me, but of course, he didn't elaborate. After seeing Hades' scars, I can't entirely blame either of them for being concerned.

He isn't aware of every detail in my reasons for coming here, only this one, and it's imperative that I rush him out before I lose my nerve.

Our deal is clear. He'll help me succeed in every way so long as I agree to accept my fate. Fate is fate, accepting or rejecting it doesn't seem to be an option so agreeing was easy. After we ate the pomegranate, and before he left, he bonded the butterfly marking to a twin one he placed on his chest, where we can call upon the other with a simple touch.

We work quickly, digging up the flowers carefully to keep the roots.

What are you doing, Little Deviant? I push away Hades' haunting voice as I work.

"You should have told me."

"I couldn't. You would have told Hades, and you both would have stopped me."

He pauses to give me a look that says, *you obviously don't know me well enough to think that.* He would have stopped me, but he wouldn't have told Hades.

With a flick of his wrist, Thanatos conjures away the finished piles. "You did good." My heart fills. I wasn't entirely useless after all. With another flick of his wrist the empty shrubs are glamoured to appear full again. "When you come back—"

"I can't come back." I hang my head in shame, avoiding the voids I know I'll find swirling with fury.

From the corners of my eye, I see his shoulder tense, his head angling back eerily slow. "What did you say?"

"I'm sorry." The explanations sound ridiculous in my head, so I don't offer one. "The page I gave you explains everything you need to know. I marked all the books I used and wrote all my research and theories in a journal in the top drawer of my vanity."

"You're coming back with me." Thanatos stalks toward me. "We have a deal!"

I stammer back, stilling when I hear voices coming from the exit.

Hearing them too, Thanatos halts, pointing to his wrist with a promise that he'll find me soon before turning back to the waiting shadows, his head tilting at the fountain. "What a shame," he mutters, then vanishes.

The voices grow louder, and I refuse to find myself in another dancing dilemma.

I dive behind the fountain.

"Don't start a scene now." Zeus' voice holds just as much power while whispering.

"You sold her!" Demeter whispers back.

At the sound of it, I wish I would have just walked out instead of hid. This is part of my plan that will take time, and if they find me sneaking about, they'll likely grow suspicious of me.

"Can you wait until I place the silencing ward?" A moment later, Zeus' voice thunders back to its normal power. "I did what I had to do."

"You could have sold any other child, but you chose mine?!" Demeter yells with such anger, even I shudder and lower to the ground.

"That was who he wanted. We needed him out, and that was his price."

"*My* daughter?" I crawl forward a few inches, needing to hear them better. Peering around the edge, I can make out the back of Zeus' large frame and Demeter's green gown. "What is so special about her?"

The question stings. Unless Demeter has another daughter, they are talking about me.

"There is something," Zeus ponders. "Something about her eyes that I can't figure out. I set that reward to appease you, but it seems something more promising fell into my lap."

"I don't care. You don't get to sell my daughter to Hades without telling me."

"You were pregnant. She wasn't even born when I sold her. You barely held her before she disappeared. What does it matter? We got him to agree to never step foot in this veil. His influence is gone."

"You would never have sold one of Hera's children."

"She's my wife, of course I wouldn't." Zeus catches Demeter's arm before she can slap him, his laugh rattling the ground. "You didn't even ask why he wanted her."

"I don't care why he wanted her. He could make her his whore for all I care. Did you see her dress? She probably already is."

My heart plummets, my arms give out, and it takes all I have not to move. All hope for another chance at a mother is gone, but why would Demeter look for me at all? Why set the reward? I shake away my questions. This isn't why I'm here, I need to remember that.

"What is the issue then, Demeter?" Zeus grumbles. "The way I see it, it's a win for everyone. I got Hades out of here, you didn't have to be the mother we both know you didn't want to be, and Hades gets his whore."

The word stings every time they say it. They have no idea how accurate they are. Hearing Hades bought me, that I never stood a chance, never had a choice in anything, is such a splinter compared to the other blows.

"Consider yourself lucky Dionysus disappeared too, although I rather like him," Zeus adds with a glimmer of pride in his voice. "Cocky fucker, but—"

"You don't care that his whore is your daughter?"

"I can spin this any way I want. If anyone questions me—"

"*Off with their head and let Hades deal with the dead?*" Demeter lights up, all fury replaced with a chilling, repulsive delight. She laughs, rubbing her fingers up Zeus' arm. "She *is* beautiful."

"She is." Zeus rubs the side of her cheek, letting Demeter lean into it. The affection would have been romantic, envious even, if I hadn't witnessed their cruelty for myself. If Demeter didn't look exactly like me.

"Did it work?" She softens, nuzzling deeper into him.

I'm ready to look away to keep from spewing the bile rising to the back of my throat.

Zeus pulls away his embrace, turning and glancing straight toward me. No, not at me, above me.

"Hello again."

I suck in a breath as Ares pulls me from the ground by my hair. His smile is gruesome, and before I can say anything, he flips me around and yanks the back of my dress down. "Stop!"

Zeus tsks, louder than my fists striking Ares' arms that he catches and cages behind my back.

Demeter gasps. "I swear she's yours. I never— I swear it on the River Styx!"

I can't see them, but Zeus doesn't speak right away, seemingly unbothered by her outburst. "Yes, you will, and if what you say is true, then we have a problem."

I can't make sense of what they're saying, not as a blinding pain ripples through my ribs where Ares holds me tight against him, keeping me from moving an inch.

My hope of finishing what I started vanishes. My chance to leave left with the shadows.

Zeus steps into my line of sight with a sickening grin, and I see why others worship him. He's beautiful, with a look you want to trust while also fearing it. "Are you spying for him?"

"I'm not spying on anyone." I shake my head. "Or *for* anyone." I cry out, feeling my wrists ready to snap under Ares' grasp.

That burning rage courses through me again, and I hope my body will burst into flames, so he lets go.

"Looks like Hades had some fun." Demeter's snicker makes my blood boil even hotter, the scars on my back tingling from the night breeze, weighted under their scrutiny.

Zeus doesn't look impressed by her amusements. "You're not fully transitioned." It isn't a question. "Put her in the cell. We'll wait until she's transitioned to return her."

"No!" I struggle, doing anything I can to wiggle free.

Demeter grabs Zeus' arm, and for a second, I hope. "What about your deal with Hades?"

"My intention is to return her so he still can't step foot here."

"What about Dionysus and Hermes?"

"If they have my mark, they can do whatever they want. But she stays here until I say." His grin widens, and I know I made a mistake by not going with Thanatos. Every inch of my body wants to yank and pull away, to use my abilities to kill the God before me and vanish back to the Underworld, but I remain frozen, drained, and unable to call up any life around me.

"They usually break after a day or two."

Chapter Thirty-One

DORA

I keep my hold on Adonis' mouth tight, struggling myself not to go to Kore, but something isn't right.

We had been walking around the maze for what felt like hours without seeing anyone else. We heard Zeus' toast, trying to follow it back to the entrance, but found ourselves farther away, taking all the wrong turns, meeting dead end after dead end.

"Where are you taking me?" Kore struggles on the other side of the bush partition.

"Zeus, where *are* we taking her? You can't walk her through the crowd like this."

"Demeter," Zeus growls, frustrated. "If you keep questioning me, I'll lock you up with her. Do you understand me?"

The pounding in my chest can't be controlled, not as my body demands I leave, as my skin crawls, hands shake, and knees buckle.

Something about that low thundering voice gives me that same horror-struck feeling when we first entered the Heavens, but this time, I don't dare move.

"It's not uncommon for the guests of honor to celebrate a little too much." Ares' voice has Adonis fighting against my hold, our focus on the hedge parting us from our friend who groans with painful struggles.

"You fu—" Kore's voice is cut off by a blinding streak of lightning darting from the sky, striking on the other side. Its force, along with a deep cackle, has my skin shaking, bones vibrating, as if I, too, was struck.

The wait is worse than listening to the Gods berating Kore, hearing her dress rip, and the things they said. *Whore*, they called her, but I know Kore better than anyone. If she had truly been a prisoner or unwilling in any way to Hades, she would have disappeared into her mind and become a monotone shell. The sounds of her struggling suggests she's fully aware and willing to fight for herself.

When there are no snickers or faded footsteps, I let Adonis go, our chests rising and falling in rapid sync.

At his release, he rubs the collar around his neck, motioning for me to do the same. How could I forget? I can't rub it fast enough.

"What happened?" Aphrodite appears, looking us up and down before searching our surroundings. "Well?" She continues peering around the corners for any signs of danger, spinning back with such force, the braid atop her head unfolds down her shoulder.

Adonis speaks the words I'm too shaken to, telling a very intent Aphrodite everything we overheard. When he mentions Zeus didn't believe Kore was his, Aphrodite's chest visibly shakes.

"Did he see you?" Her wild eyes remain on mine as if the question were solely meant for me.

I answer with a shake of my head, still too nervous to speak for fear we will be found and thrown in the cells too—or worse.

It isn't Kore being taken, but my entire reality crumbling away. The Gods are nothing like I believed. They aren't caring, gentle, mortal-loving beings; they are cruel, every one of them.

"I don't have the energy to take you both back, but I need to get you both out of here *now*." She paces back and forth before stopping to take a long inhale. "All of our plans have changed, but I promise we'll get her out of those cells."

Her eyes shift to where the knife is tucked between my breasts. "If anything happens, I need you to find Thanatos. He's—"

"Death," I croak.

She squeezes my hand for the briefest second. "Thanatos or Hecate. Even..." Her throat bobs. "Even a Fury. I *promise* I'll come back for you."

At that, she and Adonis vanish without another word.

I would have been more surprised, more in awe, had Zeus' laughter echoing in the distance not sink me to the bench with a heavy dread. "It looks like our princess takes after her father, after all." The crowd laughs with him. "We won't be seeing her abilities today, but my son Dionysus will put on a show for you all when we return."

My knees bounce rapidly with every worry, every possible horrid scenario playing through my head, what they could be doing to Kore in those cells, what will happen if I have to find Thanatos or the Furies. A tremble rocks me as if we were in the midst of a freeze.

The Fates are cruel to bring me all the way here to fail.

"Alone in the gardens? Aphrodite's *charm* must have worn off?" That voice... I dare look down the row of never-ending shrubs, finding Pallas strolling toward me without any sense of urgency. "I told you I'd see you soon."

"What do you want?" I ask, hating how frightened I sound. As if this nymph needs any more reason to taunt me.

Pallas tucks a short piece of hair behind her pointed ear, making the sharpness of her cheekbones appear more sickly. "You're very pretty for a mortal. Yellow suits you." She tips a cup I'm confident doesn't hold water. "I can sense you're still pure, and Athena loves her *pure* priestesses."

I laugh. "Your senses must be off."

The nymph's gaze falls to the cup in her hand, and shrugs, her steps wavering. "Maybe, but there is something about you that I find myself attracted to. Would you consider becoming a priestess?"

"You mean slave?" I cross my arms. The Fates are truly cruel if they took me away from that life to throw me back into another one.

"The priestesses serve us, but they are not slaves. They join willingly and are free to leave as they wish. But why would they when they serve us?"

"You mean Athena?"

"'Thena, 'Thena, 'Thena." She mocks the name like a pouty toddler. I take the chance to glance up and down the walkway again, hoping someone will pass by to interrupt us. "Why would a mortal like yourself pray to the Gods for answers, offer to the Gods, and yet not be willing to serve us when we need you? It seems a bit unfair, does it not?"

"You speak as if you're a God, but you're just a water nymph, aren't you?" It comes out more mockingly than I intended, and Pallas' cocked jaw has me wishing I had just shut up from the start.

"You're a bit mouthy and mouthy things tend to be so because they're deflecting." Her eyes narrow, taking me in with a step closer. "What are you hiding?"

I look away, trying to act uninterested like I've seen Aphrodite attempt before, even as my ears perk at the familiar question—the one missing *doll*.

When I don't answer right away, the nymph paces into a slow, calculated walk, probably to keep herself from stumbling over. "What else do you have to live for? You have no husband unless that other pet was your husband, in which case he's Aphrodite's now. You have no children. With us, you'd travel the world. You can ask Medusa. She's a mortal like you."

The offered hand in the air begs for me to take it, to see the images that could tell me more about this curious nymph. An offer I can't resist and has me reaching for it on instinct, but when I lift my hand, Pallas retrieves hers, hissing with an intake of breath as if I'd hurt her.

"You are not one of us." We both openly stare at my long pink scar. "You swore on the River Styx and tried to break that oath? With who?" That narrowing glance returns.

Her clear distaste has me more on edge, wanting even more to see the nymph's past, to see what kind of danger I'm really in.

When I explain it was a test, Pallas' distaste turns hostile. "An oath on the River Styx is sacred. And yet you use it as a test?" She huffs furiously. "No mortal can swear on the river with consequences, not like that. What color does your blood run?"

She tosses the drink behind her back, the first sign that has me shooting up from the bench. When she reaches around her back, I turn to run but find myself face to face with the green wall, too thick to climb through.

Seven Gods.

I reach for the collar around my throat, praying Aphrodite has enough magic left in her to find me again, but before I touch it, my arm is yanked back. The smell of the sea takes over my senses as I cry out in agony, the blade too quick to stop.

Falling to the ground, I cradle my hand, tears pooling. When I look up, I see my black blood dripping from the knife and my shriveling reflection in Pallas' aqua eyes.

"Witchling." Amusement falls upon the nymph once again, clearing all previous disgust. "You could be something else, but at the end of the day, you're touched by evil."

Those words remind me of the knife tucked in my dress. My fingers fumble on the hilt before gripping it tightly, the blood making it harder to hold steady. "Leave me alone!"

The rustling of bushes and giggling has us both casting our attention toward the approaching couple.

A man in a red top, a color that's much too dark for this place, pulls a woman out of the shrubs. His attention lands on us, his eyes lowering to the blade I hold high in the air. "What's going on?"

"Nothing, young Prince." Pallas attempts to wave him away. "Just having fun with the little witch here."

"Come on, leave them alone." The woman pulls at his shirt, whining, "Let's go have more fun. I'm much better with my mouth than my sister is."

The man looks at me, taking in the blood dripping down my forearm, ignoring the pleading Muse next to him. "I happen to like witches. How's your mouth? You want to join our fun?" His smirk is charming, and in any other circumstances, I could have admired it more.

I'm about to answer no, but his squinting stare lets me know this is my way out. Before he can change his mind, I shout, "My mouth only gets me into trouble, but I do happen to love princes."

Pallas pulls at the collar around my neck, leaning into the side of my face with a whisper, "You'll come crawling to me eventually, witchling. And if you beg, I might just let you join us."

I'm certain that if this man hadn't helped, I would have left with more than the one cut.

Her lips brush my cheek before she's stumbling down the garden's path, where I watch until she disappears. I peek down at the fresh cut where all that remains is a smear of blood, no opening in sight, not even a scar.

That's... my core flutters. Witches can't heal themselves naturally, or so I've read.

A tug at my shoulders catches me off guard and I spin back with the blade still tight in my hand. I feel as it strikes something before seeing the man keel over, grabbing his ribs and hissing in pain.

"Oh, my Gods. I'm sorry! I didn't mean to."

"It's fine, love. It'll heal in a minute. It's my fault, really. I was a bit grabby with a woman holding a blade." He rights himself. "Are you alright or was I interrupting a special moment between you two?"

"Well, she didn't exactly get on her knees to pop a question, but she did practically tell me I'd have to get on mine and beg if I wanted to be with her."

"My kind of woman."

We both chuckle and his awkward stance has me grabbing his shirt and lifting to see where I stabbed him, finding his skin sealing the last of it before my very eyes.

The reprieve allows me to take in the black markings along his stout chest.

"You're a bit grabby, too. Again, my kind of woman." His throat bobs with another deep chuckle. "Dionysus." His hand waits for me.

I drop his shirt to take it, a blush rushing to my cheeks as he kisses my knuckles. "Dora, not Pandora, just Dora." My brows tighten when I feel that familiar rush, but no images appear.

His head tilts curiously before motioning for me to give him a moment. He helps the Muse, still clinging to his arm for dear life, to the bench, laying her down gently.

"She's sleeping." He smiles as if it's a joke. It's odd that the girl was so persistent and aware a moment ago and is snoring now. "You're Kore's friend?" My surprise must show because he clarifies, "I saw you in a witch's cauldron, and Kore told me all about you."

I want to ask more about the cauldron, about Kore, but something gnaws at me. When I touched Jason, I felt the calling to images that hadn't appeared either. "I'm sorry, can I?"

He lets me grab his arms freely without any restriction, looking down at me curiously while I focus. After checking both arms, my face falls. Still, no images appear. It could be a lingering effect of the gloves, but that doesn't feel right either.

"Very grabby." Dionysus grins. "I do have a lot of other appendages you can try doing whatever is making you focus so hard." My laugh leaps from my throat, a reaction that has his eyes smiling as wide as his grin.

"We have to go!" Aphrodite sprints toward us.

I seized his arm, praying he's the right one to say this to. "Zeus took Kore to the cells. She's not safe."

His charming smile drops.

As Aphrodite takes my hand into hers, the world around fades away, and the last thing I see is Dionysus running.

Chapter Thirty-Two

KORE

My head lulls from side to side. I try to breathe, but it's hard to draw in any air. Something causes my chest to tighten, and every movement feels as if someone has beaten my temples with hot rocks.

My muscles ache, my arms spasm every few seconds, and my mouth tastes of blood. There's something deeper too, something missing.

Through blurred vision, I see a man sitting in front of me, his head drooping to his chest, his arms—

A whimper slips past my lips.

No, no, no.

I try to run toward him, but my feet slip on something wet. My shoulders feel as if they're being ripped off my body.

Shackles pinch at my wrists, where they're chained above my head, connected to a hook in the ceiling.

"Kore?" Hermes' voice cracks, straightening himself and tugging at his chains.

"It's about time." As the woman sheds her white cloak to the floor, I realize it isn't dark cement, but blood—faded and fresh, black, dimmed gold, and crimson, dried, wet, and caked together. But that isn't what has me fighting against the chains, rattling them, pulling and yanking; every painful movement cutting deeper into my skin, blood dripping down my arms and onto my face. It's the thick brown whip twisting between Athena's hands like she's waking it up.

The *whoosh* to the ground makes me flinch, my heart pounding so loud in my ears that I can't hear Hermes begging me to stop fighting, to stop hurting myself.

The only thing that stops me is the tug at my chin, bringing me inches from Athena's strong jaw as she hisses, "If you tire yourself out now, it will draw this out longer."

It's like she's speaking another language because I don't know what she's talking about. I call to my magic, searching for any sign of life, but all I feel is depleted, like someone pulled it from my very bones and is holding it right at my fingertips.

"If you touch her, I'll skin you so slowly, you'll beg the Fates for Death."

Athena doesn't acknowledge Hermes' threats, so I'm not sure who she's talking to when she says, "Hades rubbed off on you."

"What do you want?" My arms tremble, trickling crimson.

I'm on my way.

Either my mind is trying to comfort me, or I'm nearing Death close enough to hear Hades coming to collect my soul.

"Athena!" Hermes shouts.

The sound of the whip smacks through the air.

I gasp for breath, waiting for the pain that never comes. Then another at the sight of Hermes' clenched jaw. It's so tight, his teeth might crack as fresh blood spills from his chest.

I plead for Athena to stop, to tell us what she wants, but the Goddess disappears where no amount of neck craning helps me see where she went. A second later, my arms rip from my body while I'm being pulled toward the ceiling. With my feet shackled to the chair, my body is taut, stretched to the limit without being torn in half.

This isn't how I'm going to die. I'm the seventh child, prophesied to kill Zeus, not be killed by him or the giant Goddess behind me. That is of no comfort now, though, not when there are things much worse than dying.

I tighten my muscles as much as the new position allows, anticipating the lashing. Whatever Athena is doing behind me has Hermes fighting against his restraints with no such luck, all they do is clink and clatter.

That jolt between us tightens and his panic floods mine.

I pull on my connection with Dionysus, and sure enough, it's still there.

A realization strikes me hard enough to shake my knees.

Are you real?

I don't have to wait for Hades' response, *Of course I'm real, Deviant.*

How? I start, but I know exactly how. Just as I know how I can feel that jolted tie with Hermes' and the soul-binding connection with Dionysus.

All clarity comes to a halt at the sight of Athena stepping between us once again. This time, she doesn't hold a whip, but a branding iron glowing and radiating a rusted heat.

"Consider yourselves lucky." Her pace slows, spinning on her heel before reaching Hermes, repeating the same torturing tease toward me. "The drinks tonight were laced with magic. Zeus' heirs were marked with this symbol on their back, and any other heirs of his that they come in contact with will bear the same marking." She pivots back. "A suggestion from Ares that earned him yet again another reward, and me doing their dirty work."

The Goddess rolls her neck with disdain.

"Neither of you have this marking. But seeing as how Zeus has already publicly claimed you and he doesn't like to be made a fool of, he's willing to continue the charade. You only need to bear his mark."

The iron shifts between me and Hermes, and as much as Athena had appeared disgusted by doing Ares and Zeus' dirty work a moment ago, the woman takes pleasure in the teasing. "Who's first?"

Her steps toward Hermes sends me thrashing against my chains, with less weight behind them as my muscles tire. My head is too faint from the amount of blood I've lost running down my wrists. My skin heats, sweating from the flames that blaze through my bones.

Hermes remains still, his features tight, not revealing any hint of fear or anticipation, but I can feel his heart thundering from across the room. It goes wild when Athena snickers with a turn of her heel and makes for me.

The monstrous woman doesn't tease this time. She yanks my dress clean off with one swipe, leaving only the golden chain around my neck.

When she attempts to grab at my hips, she pulls away as if burned by the touch. She tries again, this time for the necklace, but is left hissing away.

"I don't want or need to be Zeus'." As the words leave my lips, a deadly realization settles over me. If I'm not Zeus' then I can't be the one Hades has been looking for all these years.

"But this will be such a pretty addition to your current collection."

Athena disappears behind me.

I watch Hermes, anchoring myself deeper in his sapphires. *This is nothing. It'll be over soon,* a silent promise passes between us.

I've endured lashes before—I savor Hades' flames—this will be quick. *We will get out of this,* I promise right back.

My mouth flies open in a silent scream, the searing iron meeting the middle of my back. My body tightens to its limit, arching to flee where it burns my flesh, but the bitch won't let go.

Tears fall, sizzling down my cheeks.

When the iron finally leaves my skin, the wails free themselves, every bit of my weight hanging by my wrists when my feet fail to catch me.

A wave of heat ripples beneath my skin, focusing on that very spot, taking away the lingering burn.

I hadn't noticed the tip of Hermes' wings barely grazing my sternum, his body bowing to make the minimal contact.

I don't look away, letting him anchor himself right back into me as Athena comes behind him.

His jaw clenches. The sound of singeing and the smell of burning flesh penetrates the air again.

It's over.

I'll skin the mark off my back when we're out of here, but at least it's over.

The look on Hermes' face has the hair on the back of my neck rising. He doesn't look as relieved as I am.

"The shackles bar your magic, but when you transition, they'll turn gold." Athena points to Hermes' gilded shackles, then to where mine remain iron.

Woosh!

The crack of the whip snaps through the air.

My breath catches in my throat.

The burn is nothing like I remember, is nothing like the soft flames that Hades teases me with.

Sweat trickles down my temple, my body burns so hot I think Athena might have set me aflame, penetrating the slice on my back.

I swear I'm coming for you, just hold on a little longer for me. Can you do that?

Maybe this is me dying, and my soul is nearing the Underworld, where Hades is waiting for me.

You're not dying. The abruptness of Hades' voice leaves me wavering. I'm not Zeus' prophesized heir who will kill him one day. I want to meet them, but that being isn't me, which means that I could very well be dying.

"Why?" Hermes shouts. "You gave us the marks. Let us go! Let *her* go!"

Athena steps between us again, this time with a long-curved knife. "I don't question Zeus. He wants her to transition, and I'll make it happen. His only request was to leave a mark. As for you, he wants you to suffer and seeing her suffer seems to be doing the trick. Two birds."

"Can't even get his own hands dirty." Hermes spits at her feet.

"We both know the way he likes to get his hands dirty. Would you prefer it to be him?"

All color drains from his face.

"That's what I thought." The knife swings between Athena's hands as if she's trying to figure out which one she wants to wield it.

"It'll be over soon enough. When Hades finds out his whore is here, he'll come running. Zeus will take him or anyone he sends in his place." A loathing scowl stares back at me. "She's just a dangling carrot to capture a larger horse. And my bet is Hades will be here before the last guest leaves."

"You don't need to hurt her or have her transition to get him here. I'll bring him back myself."

My eyes snap to his, a motion Athena tracks.

"I don't think your friend liked that comment, Hermes." Athena cracks her neck from side to side. "I also don't think you're anything special, Kore, but Zeus' curiosity is piqued. Demeter's sworn on the River Styx that she never stepped out on him, which means someone

363

went through a lot of trouble to make sure you appeared as his heir. The question is who and why. An answer we might get once you fully transition."

The knife slides down my cheek, not hard enough to cut, but enough to elicit the fear Athena wants. "Don't worry, you'll go back to that desolated place once you transition. Or when Hades is captured."

I tunnel deep into my mind. *You can't come, please don't come.*

Hades doesn't hesitate. *There's no amount of begging you can do that will keep me from coming for you.*

Please Hades, I'm so sorry I ever left. I should have told you, but... If I'm dying, I'll see him soon enough to explain everything. *It's a trap for you.*

Do you think that changes anything?

My gut twists. This is my fault. *You can't*—I try, cut off before I can continue begging him to understand.

I'm not someone you need to stand up for Kore. I told you if it ever came to that, you needed to save yourself. Zeus loathes me. You need to curse me, do whatever it takes to show them how much you hate me. Swear on the river that you'll kill me yourself, and I'll be on my knees waiting with the knife that will do it.

You're not going to die. I'm not killing you and neither are they. Just swear you won't come. They said they'll release me in a few days anyway. I'll be fine. The lie is the hardest one I've told.

A dark chuckle leaves him, and I know there is no swaying him.

Oh, Litle Deviant, I'm burning that entire veil down if that's what it takes to bring you back.

I ignore the jolt calling for me.

Hades, I struggle to find a way for him to understand. *When you play chess*—

This is not a game.

That's exactly what this is! Protect the King, that's the goal. I'm a pawn, a low-level Goddess. I always have been.

Kore, I swear to Gaia...

Before he can finish, I throw up the wall to block my mind, thankful the shackles don't have any control over that. Using every bit of strength I have, I tug at the little glimmer I feel from Dionysus' connection and pull—deep.

I don't dare ask where he is, hoping he has the mark and made it back home.

As my head begins to swim from his abilities, I keep my focus on the wall I strengthen to keep Hades out of my head. I feel his presence lurking behind, punching, kicking, trying to tear it down, but I can't let him in.

He was the one urging me to stop when I was on top of Hermes, which means he can see what I see, feel what I feel. He's seen enough horrors the world has to offer—murders, rape, torture. He doesn't need to witness mine too.

If I could rub my wrist, I would call for Thanatos, but the shackles hold them too far apart. I'm stuck. My only option is to find a way to transition as fast as I can.

The sound of a blade crushing bone has my eyes snapping open. This time, Hermes grunts through his teeth, the knife sticking out of his shoulder. "I forgot to mention, if you don't fully transition with me, Zeus has a line of Gods ready to assist. A very eager one wants to repay you for a burn you gave him."

I keep my focus on Hermes, who gives me the same determined expression. We're both willing to do anything to get the other out of this place.

"Let's begin, shall we?"

Chapter Thirty-Three

HADES

There's no controlling the fidgeting in my knees as I bite at my nails. Habits I've long since rid myself of. If I didn't need a clear head, I would have been tempted to have Hecate find the Fairy Tonic or Gorgon Stimulant to numb me.

Every push, kick, or punch against the wall Kore built in her head failed to break it, but I can feel her behind it, her very presence antagonizing me to keep trying until I succeed. But with every call that goes unanswered, I grow more impatient, more restless, more fucking irate.

It was a day ago when I thought I had been in a dream, seeing and hearing her thoughts, the Furies cutting her. When I saw her crumbling in that throne room, I knew it wasn't a dream at all, no matter how deep of a sleep I was in.

I tasted the sleeping tonic on that tart but thought I imagined it. Stupidly I pushed away my instincts because she wanted me, all of me, and I wasn't going to deny her or myself, not after so long of depriving us both of it.

It was the lust that flowed through her, the glimpses of Hermes beneath her, that filled me with a rage I've never felt before.

The tonic was too potent to wake from alone, and it wasn't until a lost soul startled me awake, begging me to help Kore, who apparently ran off with a man the little girl described as Ares. That detail had my entire body burst with flames. The glimpses didn't show me that.

By the time I made it to the crossroads, it was too late. She had already crossed into the Heavens, one of the only places I can't step foot in, can't protect her from.

My hand flexes where the bones reformed from breaking them against the door that wouldn't let me through.

After destroying my study, I went to Kore's room.

Her apple scent was everywhere. The book of prophecies was open to the page I wanted her to read, *The Birth of Persephone*, the one prophecy tied to my own. I flipped through a few of the books she had marked, seeing she held interest in the asphodels, but a page was torn out. She marked pages on the death rivers, creatures with healing abilities, containment curses, and the Fates.

Her red slip was piled in the corner because, of course, she refuses to use the bin. Scissors, fabric, pins, all laid on the bed from a dress she'd torn apart and sewn back together.

That was when I felt her again, the ache in my rib followed by Kore's innermost thoughts. It was like I was sitting in the back of her mind, seeing distorted images and hearing fleeting thoughts.

I was forced to watch as the overconfident God took her to the dance floor. I could feel her repulsion for him, and I would have laughed if I wasn't livid at another God for daring to touch her.

When my power managed to filter through her and burn him, I ran to Hecate, trying to ignore Kore pulling Thanatos to her side. The little witch confirmed what I'd known for longer than I want to admit.

While the little deviant kept thinking it was her mind playing tricks on her, I had been attempting to break through more and more. The agony and searing pain that she was in when she finally realized I was talking to her broke me.

I wanted nothing more than to beg the Fates to spare her, to switch places, to storm the Heavens and burn anyone who crossed me until I threw her over my shoulder and brought her back home.

All I could do was funnel the healing flames to where the searing pain scorched her back.

By the time I was able to say the name a third time, the final time that would call upon the Triple Goddess—the one that would strip me of anything I cared for to make a deal to save her—Hecate hexed my mouth shut and banished me to my room to wait before I could make anything worse.

Since then, it's been hours of knocking on Kore's mind, hours since she pleaded for me to stay away with a brittle voice that she tried to stiffen.

My chest shatters knowing what room she's in, my hands trembling in the ball of fists that refuse to unfold.

I can't steady myself, stuck in this room, thinking of all the ways I'm going to inflict every bit of pain Kore endures onto Hermes and Dionysus, the former more for defying me and touching her, the latter is probably balls-deep in a Muse to even notice his sister missing.

The door opens, and no sooner am I on my feet toward it when Hecate steps through, shaking her head, and releasing the silencing hex.

"Fuck!" My fist meets the wall, already rebuilding the broken knuckle.

"I couldn't see her, but I could see the door. It is a trap. Zeus has guards all around the clearing."

That confirms the exact room Kore is being held in, and all hope that I had of being wrong vanishes.

The distress on Hecate's face makes it worse. There are three things that cause her to become unsettled: people touching her things, deals with the Triple Goddess, and Thanatos. None of which have ever had her dark eyes watering.

"He can't keep her there for long," she tries assuring me, failing as she clears the croak in her throat. "Not with your deal in place."

"I don't care how long he plans to keep her there." My anger is misplaced onto Hecate, but I can't stop myself from unleashing it on the nearest being, which just so happens to be her. "She's not staying one fucking night."

The door slams open, striking the wall so hard it bounces and is about to shut back before Dionysus pushes through, half-crazed. "They took them!" He lifts his shirt over his head and turns. "My back started burning. I didn't think anything of it until Zeus made me take my shirt off."

A lightning bolt surrounded by a double circle imprints the center of his spine, like a deep cut made with a knife.

Fuck. This is worse than I thought.

"Hermes?" I ask, already knowing the answer.

"Kore's friend Dora warned me that Kore was in trouble, so I followed Zeus after he made a big announcement that she was drunk and passed out. He pulled Hermes aside to take his shirt off, struck him with lightning, and then had Ares drag him inside." His chest is rising uncontrollably, unable to catch his breath. "He didn't have the mark."

Of course not.

I rake my finger through my hair, nearly ripping it out of my scalp.

"I tried." Hecate has her entire body under Dionysus' shoulder, keeping his trembling form from collapsing. "I tried to get them back, but he said he would only let them go if I came straight here to tell you he had them. He said he wouldn't hurt Kore."

"Because *HE* won't!" I growl so loud the room fills with my power, sweat pooling at their foreheads.

"That's not all."

I stop pacing.

"He... he knows things he shouldn't. He said if you didn't show, he'd tie her up using his lighting and do worse things than making her beg to come." He visibly shudders with disgust, pushing through to finish what he was ordered to say. "He's going to start with Hermes."

"Don't you finish another fucking word." My voice is clipped. "I'm going."

"No!" Hecate leaves Dionysus, letting him drop onto his knees to push me back onto the bed. "It's a trap! You idiot! Do you seriously not see what she tried to do? What she's *still* trying to do?"

"She thinks this is a game!"

"All wars are games!" Hecate's cheeks redden, her scar pale white. "We gave a willful, *deviant*, half-explained prophecies after telling her the one thing she never had was just beyond a door she couldn't open. We enticed her abilities out through you. Hades, I hate to admit this, but we created her exactly as you originally planned. She's going to do whatever it takes to ensure you're safe. She drugged us all because she went there to kill him. For *you*."

This wasn't what I wanted. Not anymore.

"Plans change." Everything was different the second I saw her in that stupid chair. The moment everything softened with her presence, like this veil came to life, sparking one in me with every scowl and quip. A newfound purpose filled me again, even if I didn't know what it was yet.

Hecate shifts her weight over my shoulders to keep me from throwing her off.

"She's not going to kill him." Dionysus has both of us twisting to see him bent over, whiter than he was a second ago. "She keeps pulling from me, but with how much, I'd be surprised if she was walking, let alone awake."

Good. I pray to Gaia she doesn't remember a single moment.

We still have to get to her without going through the clearing. "Where is Minthe?!" She would be able to swim through the veil, straight into one of their rivers. It would take her a while to find Kore, but—

"You sent her to the Mortal Veil," Hecate answers. Dionysus peels her off me at the perfect time because I was seconds from tossing her against the wall.

I curse myself for sending the nymph away now. I wanted her gone and it was a way to get what I wanted, *who* I wanted.

"Can you jump?" I ask Dionysus.

"Not with how much she's taken from me."

I could ring every God's damn neck at this moment.

Gods...

There is one *being* still connected to her.

I jump to my study without explaining myself, stalking to the one thing I managed not to throw across the room. Hel, I might have, but the table and its pieces are hexed to right itself.

The moving pieces on the map show Thanatos at his place, not too far away. Kore's piece, a tiny rose, is still in the Heavens right next to Hermes.

Throwing the table across the room won't move the two pieces I want to burn alive, won't change the fact that they are near Kore. Athena and Poseidon—the two Gods who would do anything for Zeus' praise.

The mares I left at the Heavens' door to bring Kore back if she came through are out front, and it's because of this that I won't murder Dionysus.

Thanatos holds as much trust for me as I hold for anyone, the ward around his home just as intricate as mine. Jumping isn't an option and running would take too long.

My fingers fumble with the straps to untie the stallions, figuring one will be faster than two carrying a carriage. Within seconds, its wings spread wide, and we're in the air, soaring to a being I never thought I would willingly seek for help.

It isn't long before the Furies circle me. "Go away before I rip your head off, Alecto!"

"Where are you off to, *King*." She sneers the last word but all I can think of is how Kore calls me that, how I hated being a king, but when she says it that's all I want to be.

My lips remain tight, focusing on where I need to go. Something else, something unfamiliar, has me shake the stubbornness away. "Zeus has Kore. I need Thanatos."

To any other creature the plea wouldn't have been obvious, but like sees like, and they know, they hear the underlying desperation.

Tisiphone darts ahead of us and Maegara shoots out to the left.

Alecto spins in the air above, wrapping her wings around herself, mocking my slow speed. "You know who she is?"

"I know enough, like how you cut her!"

"No, you don't." She twirls for show. "Did you know there were once four of us?" My head snaps in her direction. For as long as I've been alive, there have only been the three Furies that help me torture the wicked.

This isn't the time for a history lesson. I remain silent, thinking the ancient being will take the hint, but she continues anyway. With nowhere else to go, I'm forced to listen.

"Before the Titans there were us creatures, as they called us. Giants, Cyclops, Furies, and so on, many of us are in hiding or dead. Our sister was special, though. I believe your myths call her the Fertility Goddess. She became infatuated with one of these Titans in particular, and he with her. Myself and the other two kept our distance, not trusting these new Titans as they called themselves, but our sister wouldn't stop seeing him. One day, this Titan fell in love with someone else, and our sister was jealous, one of the essences she feeds off of. So, she changed herself entirely to look like one of them. We used to be able to sense her. Then, of course, the Gods and the wars came, and we were cast away. We haven't sensed her since. Until I cut Kore."

Thanatos' house is in the distance, but at the mention of Kore, I can't focus.

I don't know what to make of Alecto's story or why she felt the need to tell it now. Kore isn't as old as them, so she can't be this fourth Fury she speaks of.

"She's not our missing sister," Alecto adds, reading my unspoken question. "She is her daughter." A pause. "Kore is part Fury."

My chest sinks, understanding exactly why Alecto told me this now. I urge the horse faster. If Kore is the descendent of this fourth sister, and this sister is the mythical Fertility Goddess, then Kore is in more danger than I anticipated.

"What became of your sister?" I ask, nearing the ground.

"I believe you know her as Aphrodite."

Thanatos is standing in the middle of the sitting room, waiting for me to burst through. Tisiphone brushes past me, taking Alecto with her. As much as I want to punish Alecto for laying a finger on Kore, now isn't the time.

They can stay or leave; I'll do what I need to in front of all the veils.

"Tisiphone told me," Thanatos voice is as icy as his gaze.

I drop to my knees and tear the shirt over my head. My back burns as my skin rips open. Warm blood drips down my spine, pooling on the floor. My forehead sears as the skin tears and drips more heated ichor down my face.

I grind my teeth as my true form emerges.

My wings are sensitive against the air from centuries of being locked away, and I had forgotten how heavy the horns sit on my head.

"I need your help." I bow my head, lowering to touch the tips of Thanatos' feet.

He and I have had a forced understanding from the moment Kronos made me king in this veil. Death is one of the few who know my true form and understands why I must hide it.

This is as vulnerable as I can make myself, offering my pure form to Thanatos. A King before an equal. A God bowing before a Divinity.

He sneers, glaring at the horns on my head, but doesn't mutter a word about them. "If Zeus has Kore, it's going to be a trap to get to you."

"It is. But she's also with Athena and Poseidon."

"She's a strong girl. Besides, don't you need her fully transformed to use her?"

I remain bowed before him, even if I want to rip the horns off and gut my past self, and him for being so damn unfazed. From this angle, I can see something else lingering behind those white eyes. "You'd let her be tortured for a fucking prophecy?!"

"Wouldn't you? You mean to tell me that you wouldn't have sent her there if you knew she could kill Zeus after spending a few days of torture?"

"No!" I lift to his knees. The answer strikes me like the lightning my enemy wields. I would throw away all plans and plots to save her. "What do you want? You want this veil back? I'll do everything in my power to find a way to leave. You want the castle? It's yours."

"I want her." He knows the exact price I'll falter to pay. "Are you willing to give her up completely?"

My throat tightened.

No. I'll never give her up. I can't. She's *mine.* I don't care if she comes back never wanting to see me again, she's always going to be mine.

But she can't be mine if she doesn't come back, if they break her into nothing. And Athena and Poseidon *will* break her. It's why Zeus made sure to use them.

"She's not mine to give." The words are poison on my tongue.

"Actually," he glances at my horns, like he, too, wants to rip them off and gut me, "she is."

I wait for him to finish and can see the hesitation on his face, the bitter loathing as he explains, "I'm still very much connected to this veil and felt the agreement between you. You must have eaten from her garden and made a blood oath when she vowed to be yours."

That memory has my chest stutter.

"Come, I want to show you something." He waves his head for me to follow. "Keep your wings out."

I rise from the floor, stumbling from the unfamiliar added weight. "We don't have time." I groan when my wings hit the wall, forgetting to fold them in.

He leads us out back, to where the new grass grows wildly, and uprooted asphodels are piled in the corners.

"How did you get those?" I ask, astonished to see a flower that only grows in the Heavens.

"Kore. You've made her read so many damn books, they became surprisingly useful. Asphodels contain a certain healing property she believes will help the lost souls."

The one that woke me from that deep slumber mentioned Kore saying that she was going to help her, that she was going to the Heavens for a reason, but I pushed her off because I was too angry that Kore was gone at all.

That little deviant.

"Yes." I sigh. "I'd give her up if it meant saving her." I'll settle for watching her from the distance if I have to, for hearing her thoughts, watching her live from that pocket in her mind.

With everything we share, the mental bridge, the abilities, that pull… I had Hecate confirm my suspicion.

We're fated. I just didn't know if we're cursed or mated.

A lightness fills my body as the truth leaves my tongue. My wings stretch out feeling not only the relief of being free again but the tightening of the connection. A rope that could have been cut before now seals itself. The fire's song isn't the only one I hear and feel.

Thanatos grips my shoulder.

"Hades." My name is a warning as if he can also hear her agony. His hold is on the verge of breaking my bone. "I already started the plan. If you listen to me, we'll have her out of there within an hour."

I drop to my knees.

That other song that fills me is replaced with screams.

It feels as if all breath in my body empties into a dark void where my heart stops beating. Every thought ceases to exist. Everything around pales except the Divinity before me. The whites of his eyes glow a bright, golden light.

I shake my head as everything around me comes back to life once again, blinking to clear my vision. The eyes before me return to that off-putting white.

She's dying.

"You have five minutes."

Chapter Thirty-Four

APHRODITE

I make my way to the closet and begin stripping off the diamond bracelets.

"Why didn't we do that weeks ago?" Dora gawks with wide-eyed wonder as she clutches her chest.

As an explanation, I lift my wrists. "Zeus spelled these so even something as simple as jumping drains me. The Mortal Veil holds little magic, making me even more limited. What little I can do is restricted to the essence that is me. The part that he can't contain or control." The very thing that will keep Kore alive, or at least her soul and sanity intact.

Explaining the shackles that have held me back for centuries has me undressing faster, with an urgent need to rid myself of them once and for all.

"He's here," Adonis announces from the doorway, still pale from jumping.

Perfect timing.

I toss the cloak over my shoulders and make my way to the kitchen with the two mortals in tow.

Leaning against the counter, arms crossed, is Hephaestus, dressed in his soot and burn-riddled apron like he came straight from the fires he uses to forge his creations. The mask he wears covers half of his face, a smile carved into the metal to greet us.

River nymphs once caught a glimpse of him rinsing off in a river, and the rumors began, claiming he's gruesome, covered in leaky boils and hideous scars that never healed.

I know the truth. There are no leaky boils, but Zeus' hatred bestowed in the scarred flesh. Every inch of him is marred except for the part of his face not covered by that mask.

I like him best of all Zeus' children, but he's still one of the many flies caught in my web, as I am in his. That has always been our deal, use each other through body and schemes, so long as we never harm the other *unwillingly*.

"I haven't got all day." Hephaestus' voice is flat while he takes in the two mortals behind me with disinterest.

Without having to look at Dora, I know she's taking in his heterochromia and gilded shackles, remembering whatever vision allowed her to see him as Zeus' other prisoner.

"It's time." I can't stop fidgeting with my hands and twisting my own shackles.

His huff tells me he isn't the least bit surprised, which means he brought exactly what I need. "Are you *absolutely* sure?"

No, is what I want to say. Not one of my plans have gone accordingly, and I'm not entirely convinced the Fates aren't working against me to ensure I fail as retribution for tricking them, for making even them believe Kore was Zeus and Demeter's child.

My nod is slight but confident. There is no other way to save Kore.

Rubbing the tension building in my temples, I let out a sigh and tell him enough to understand why the time to free ourselves must be now. The squirrel behind me looks betrayed that I didn't really need her knowledge, or lack thereof, to remove the shackles. It would have served as a backup plan to the one already in place.

Hephaestus sucks in his bottom lip, the only acknowledgment that he's listening. "I'm not giving you mine, and with there being only the two unbinding serums, how do you plan to release—" He leans in with a snarl. "You can't be serious?"

The two behind me take a few steps back at his towering form, a form that would intimidate anyone who doesn't know him. His features both soften and harden, his jaw ticking. We are allies, nothing more, but he knows my history with Ares, the lying and manipulation, the suffering.

"I had no other choice. Ares agreed to bring her here and use his reward to unshackle me if I agreed to be his." I hold my confidence, so he doesn't see me wavering in my decision. It was the only way, but I can't lie and say I'm not afraid. Not much scares me but Ares does. "Besides, if I'm with him, it might be easier to find Eros."

Dora's head snaps to mine but I can't think about her odd reaction when Hephaestus tosses the box on the counter, his head shaking with disapproval. "You know the second she is free, Zeus will know it was us. You need to get your mortals settled, secure everything, and when you go to those cells you need to be quick. I have a source that says Zeus has the clearing surrounded, so if you plan on getting her out of there—"

"No," I shake my head. "We can't get her out of there. We just need her unshackled." Now that I'll be tied to Ares, it isn't safe for Kore anywhere near me. And Kore still has to make it to that clearing to become what was prophesized, for everyone's sake.

"You need to be *very* careful, 'Dite. You're making moves out of desperation."

Dora and Adonis watch us with building questions. Dora with wonder and Adonis with suspicion. Neither of them is leverage now, just mortals in the wrong veil, caught in the middle of a never-ending war.

My gaze falls to Dora as I think of Pandora, the one who told me the two paths Kore could take to her inevitable fate. It seems the Fates strengthened the one that led her to her father.

Kore and I both still have so much pain and suffering to endure, but I'm content knowing it's for the greater good—ending the wrong Thanatos and I made long ago *and* this stupid war, once and for all.

Lifting the vial from my pocket, I uncap it and drink, handing the last half to Dora. Tying her to me had been selfish and foolish, knowing the shackles bound me to Zeus, but at the time I couldn't resist. We needed the oath so we could trust each other enough to speak freely without lies or fear the other would leave.

When I told Dora this was where she was meant to be, it wasn't a lie. Pandora had also spoken of this girl's fate, and this is where our paths split for now.

"I need you to drink this and repeat after me." I say the phrase in the ancient language.

"Why?"

Good to see her naivete hasn't resurfaced. I hoped during our short time together, she would stop being so God-struck and learn to be suspicious and cautious.

"We need to unbind ourselves of the oaths we've made so when the time comes, you can run."

Dora looks as if I took away her dinner rather than offer her freedom.

"What's wrong? Scared you'll miss me, Squirrel?" I grin, not feeling any joy in it.

Adonis grabs my hand from the counter possessively, a quick motion that has me halting Hephaestus, who moves just as quick. The honor between these two men is admirable.

"We're not leaving you," Adonis says, refusing to let go.

Before I offer any reassurances that they would be better off and safe without me, Dora finishes the water from the River Styx and tosses the empty vial in the sink, repeating the ancient language.

A tether snaps between us, invisibly disintegrating, leaving us both rolling our necks from the lifted weight.

Hephaestus watches, his arms crossed, showing his growing impatience. His finger traces the shackles, eager to rid himself of the prison and get to his own hideout.

Thinking of him alone wherever he goes saddens me, but knowing him... "What about your little Grace? Is she going to miss your stalking?"

For the first time in the centuries that I've known him, Hephaestus' face is symmetrical to the smiling mask. "The moment you sent that old bag to get me, I made a stop before coming here." He kicks the brown bag next to his feet that instantly starts squirming.

My stomach dips reactively, knowing exactly what the poor Grace has coming to her. If she's lucky, she'll share his same tastes.

"See you around, wife." Hephaestus motions to the small box waiting on the counter, before gripping the bag and tossing it over his shoulder. "*Hopefully*," he calls back and leaves.

When Zeus forced us to marry, it had been a punishment for both of us. Kronos' pet and Zeus's hideous son, imprisoned within a marriage and bound by golden shackles. He had no idea how much a shared enemy could bring two people together.

CRUEL GODS

With Hephaestus gone, the tension in the air thickens. I demand they hold their tongues as we hurry to prepare everything. With time running out, we have to be quick, rounding every mortal to the safe house where I use every ounce of my magic to ensure it remains hidden and secure.

In detail, I explain to Dora and Adonis how to return and let themselves in, if yet another plan fails, and they find themselves needing a place to hide. Dora isn't happy when I tell her how to find the entrance to the Underworld or when I tell her that she needs to find the ancient witch, Hecate, the one being who can help her understand who she is.

Adonis isn't even phased when I tell him he'll be splitting from his friend, and something tells me it's because he doesn't plan to follow my instructions to go back to the Mortal Veil.

Thinking of Psych, I grin to myself, and the long list of tasks I gave her to complete. The old hag will probably die before finishing, and I'll have to find a way to pay a visit to Hades to bargain for the wretched mortal to end up in Tartarus.

Securing the box in my cloak, I take one last look around the prison I had made a home. The airy palace with the sea in the horizon. A place I'll never return to once I belong to Ares again.

Chapter Thirty-Five

KORE

Being able to hold my breath for long underwater doesn't help me, not with Poseidon holding me under with his frightening, enormous, hands wrapped around my throat. He waits until my body convulses, and my vision blackens to bring me back to the surface.

There is no relief when my sharp inhale is replaced with choking cries and screams as the whips start their strokes on their canvas—my back, arms, legs, stomach. There doesn't seem to be an inch they haven't touched.

I realized Hermes' curse the moment he lashed me with fallen tears. Forced obedience.

That's why he dropped me from the sky when I said to let me go when we first met, why he couldn't tell me anything, why he was so particular about his words, the constant mention of loopholes. But there were no loopholes for what they forced him to do here.

When they tried to force me to whip him back, I refused. They could maim me in every way, but they won't make me into a puppet. They won't take away my ability to say no.

That was when they brought the first God to have his fun. Every refusal to hurt Hermes since has been a new God allowed to do whatever they want, but I've pulled enough of Dionysus' ability that I barely understand what's happening.

The hardest part is not thinking of Hades. When my mind does drift toward him, I rebuild that wall and anchor myself deeper into Hermes.

His chest, arms, thighs, every bit of Hermes is covered in his cursed blood, just as I'm slick with mine. His wings droop where they're broken and bent at odd angles.

He still holds my gaze, anchoring himself right back. *It's almost over,* is the only thing we send down the link that jolts us a little every time.

The table they've been keeping me on is hard and stained with my blood and the room reeks of it, but I've been imagining it's the softest bed, surrounded by my favorite furs and cinnamon.

My head is so dizzy from Dionysus' ability that when I close my eyes, I can picture myself in the scaling amethyst tub instead of drowning in the salty one.

The doors clink open and close so many times I don't know who is in the room anymore.

"You have five minutes," Athena says, holding the exit open. "Let's go, Poseidon."

The Sea King tosses me back on my pedestaled table, ignoring my groans. "I want to keep watching. She's about to break."

I roll to the side that doesn't have broken ribs, or at least the side that doesn't have one protruding from my skin.

When I find Hermes, I let out a shaky breath. He's still here.

That relief is short-lived knowing there's another God here for me. This one must be different because my tormentors never leave, choosing to stay and berate me to transition quickly during every act.

After an uncomfortably long pause, Athena snarls, "No, she's not. Men always think women are weaker than they are. Trust me, she's got at least another hour left in her, and we need to check in with Zeus."

Poseidon groans and mumbles a string of curses. A moment later, the door clinks.

The promise of more torment with every passing second has me wiggling and praying to every God I know of to help me transition, to give me whatever aura they speak of, whatever final gifts I have yet to find. With so many different forms of torture, I'm not sure if I experienced the extreme cold or heat the final transition is marked by. I shiver and sweat on and off every day. My blood is almost all black without a hint of gold, but I must be close.

Bringer of Death

Someone cups my cheek, the soft touch teasing to be gentle, but I know better. Most have no imagination. They are too quick, too easily excited, and without much time, they rush.

I have time, though. I fantasize their screams that I'll elicit once I get out of here, promising myself to find every one who flipped me over. The ones who made me face them spin over cobalt spits, the ones who used weapons are used as pincushions, and the ones who dared attempt to harm Hermes are cut into pieces and fed to Cerberus.

"Kore." That voice sounds familiar, but my eyes burn from the salty tub to see anything but golden waves and dark cloaks.

Oh Gods, are they bringing in two now?

They grip my jaw, prying it open to pour something cold down my aching throat. It doesn't matter if this is poison or that it tastes of blood, I'm too thirsty to care about anything, drinking it greedily. They stop and immediately my wrists burn where the shackles dig into my skin.

I cry out, hating myself for letting them break me days ago. It feels longer, but with how much I've pulled from Dionysus, I can't keep track of anything.

At that thought, I pull deeper, feeling my brother's worry tugging me back. He's safe. If he had been taken, I would have felt it like I know he's felt every bit of what I've experienced. If I knew how, I would shut him out to keep him from this, but we never practiced control, choosing to relish in each other's gifts instead.

Soothing fingers stroke my wrists, and when I manage to crack my eyes, the shackles are gone.

"You're going to make it out of here. They won't break you." Violet eyes bear into me and for a moment I wonder how I can be looking at myself. "The vial I gave you at the sacrifice was ambrosia laced with my own blood to help release the cloaks and bindings I attached when creating you, and Hecate's when they hid you from Hera. I had to ensure you could protect yourself if you didn't come with me willingly. You're too headstrong for your own good, and as much as I want to apologize, I can't, Kore. I meant it when I said you were created for a bigger purpose. They can never take away what you truly are."

I try to ask how and why she, Aphrodite, is here, what she's talking about, but a man comes into view halting my attempt.

I'm positive I'm hallucinating again when Adonis' hand falls to my cheek, his mouth parted like he, too, wants to say something, but he's too busy searching over my broken body. "We can't leave her here."

His head snaps back to where Aphrodite is whispering something into Hermes' ear—where Athena ordered him to sit still without restraint as he watched everything being done to me, knowing he couldn't move or do anything to help.

They argue back and forth but their hushed anger is drowned out by my heartbeat pounding in my ears at the sight of Dora pushing Adonis away.

My tears fall freely as she pulls me into a hug, not realizing—and me not caring—that every wound stings at the contact.

She feels real. Her skin is soft, and she smells of lilacs. "I missed you so much," Dora says. "You have no idea."

I can't speak. The wave emotions are too harsh while I cry into her neck, gripping her shoulders like a lifeline.

As if the hallucinations couldn't get any crueler, Aphrodite breaks us apart. "You may have been bound to a mortal body for years, but you've always fed off emotion. Your very core could never be hidden." She grips my head, steadying it. "You're about to feel a lot of *desire* in this room, and we need you to latch onto it. You know that feeling you get in the pit of your core? That hunger and need crawling beneath your skin to give in and feed it?"

The balance.

"For you to survive the night, you need to give in. When you start to feel it, pull and keep pulling until that hunger satiates."

My tongue sticks to the roof of my mouth, keeping me from saying anything, but nodding in answer.

With the shackles gone maybe I can access my abilities.

Aphrodite doesn't need to cover my eyes, I know to close them to focus, but with the wine running through my veins, it's difficult to search for any emotions or life in the room.

"Remember, no one can take away what is deep in your blood."

That *feeling* appears.

Again, I don't need Aphrodite to explain anything about catching and pulling it in. Thanatos has helped me too many times for me not to forget the process.

Where red is pain, desire is purple, four mists stemming with it.

"That's it! Don't release it. Keep it for yourself. Use it!"

I pull the desire in, my head clearing by the second. My breathing evens out. Every cut in my body begins to close, the bones righting themselves back into place.

It's the pain in my upper back that has me clawing Aphrodite's hands from my face.

I fling back, arching off the table while my spine is ripped apart. The purple shadows fill me with desire beyond control, my grunts turning to moans as my skin not only hurts from the wounds but grows sensitive against the rough slab. The light air tickles, making me...

A hand wraps around my throat, but not enough to cut off my breath. "*Never* take too much. Satiate only."

Satiating was long ago, but at the warning, I release the shadows, and everyone in the room lets out a succinct, heavy breath.

I can't catch mine fast enough. Aphrodite's hand remains wrapped around my neck until she's sure I won't continue feeding off the desire or any other emotions I find.

It's what I find moving on both sides of me that takes my attention before I can contemplate doing just that.

Impossible. Black veiny wings spread out on either side of me, so long they droop to the disgusting floor. If my head wasn't so freshly cleared, I would have thought this was another hallucination.

I attempt to lift myself, but the weight of the wings pulls me back with such force that my head smacks against the table.

"You'll be fine," Aphrodite says, carefully pulling at my shoulders to help me sit. "You won't be fully healed, but it's a start. The vial melted your shackles and made it so you'll never be barred by any again."

Her eyes drop and narrow with sorrow. "With your family's history, you need to make sure you never take or give too much. The power you'll wield is infinite, but everything has a price. Even Divinities can go dark."

My mouth opens to speak, but my throat is too dry. *Divinity?*

"I'm sorry I can't tell you more, but we don't have time." Aphrodite takes my hand into hers. "Thanatos and Hermes know everything, and Hades knows more than he realizes. You're meant to be there. Please, don't ever come back here, not until the time is right."

"But," Dora starts, "we can't leave her like this!" She tugs at Aphrodite's shoulder, spinning her around and glaring with such fierceness I don't recognize her. The soft, naïve, fun Dora is replaced with someone who looks like they lost their lightness. The one a child loses when they grow up.

That familiar trust in Aphrodite shivers up my spine, commanding me to listen and do whatever it is that she says. If she wants me to stay put, then that is what I'll do.

I grab Dora, pulling her into another hug, this time taking in the love rushing from her, collecting it and sending it back where we're connected.

"I'm going to find you again," Dora promises.

Our hug tightens, our bodies saying the goodbye we can't.

A loud pounding rattles the door, followed by Athena's mocking call, "One more minute."

My heart races. How are they going to get out?

Seeing the fear written on my face, Aphrodite shakes her head. "Don't worry about us. She thinks it's one man in here with you."

"You'll be okay, Kore," Adonis says as if he's trying to convince himself, waiting by the door like he can't be anywhere near me, or so much as look at me.

It isn't the best goodbye, but better than our last and I don't blame him. I don't need to see myself in the mirror to imagine how horrific I must look.

"You've survived Pirithous, Metanira, and the sacrifice. You'll survive this too."

I frown at his parting words. *He knew about Pirithous?*

Aphrodite follows them out, but not before turning back one last time. "One day, you'll understand why I created you."

At the sound of the door closing, I shut my eyes and pull Dionysus' connection until the room is hazy. If I'm too alert, they'll know I'm healed, and I don't have the luxury of time to ponder on what happened,

386

the riddles within the exchange. Hermes apparently knows everything and can tell me later.

The door clanks.

"Oh Gods," Athena gasps, taking in the sight of my wings lying on the wet ground. "I guess it's your lucky day, princess. Poseidon's going to be upset he missed it."

If it weren't for Hermes, for what Athena would do to him if I failed, I would attempt to use my ability to hurt her. But I'm not entirely sure how to use it in a way that would help, not without the earth to pull from.

Athena strolls toward Hermes, wearing the white cloak soaked in our blood like a badge of honor. "Carry her." She smacks the back of his head.

His jaw tightens, gritting his teeth as he attempts to stand, wobbling toward me. His leg broke days ago, and whatever they're using on their weapons has made our healing slower, practically nonexistent.

"Squeeze your back and will them to shut." His voice is just as raspy from screaming as mine is.

"No," Athena orders. "Zeus will want to see them."

He lets out an irritated breath, his chest pumping against mine. He wants nothing more than to strike her down as much as I do.

"Put your legs around my waist and your arms around my neck."

He leads me gently to the edge, allowing me to straddle him and begin hoisting myself up, but it's harder than it looks. The weight of my wings pulls me back and it's Hermes' strength that's keeping my naked body sealed against his.

His fingers rub gently down my sore spine the entire walk. I have a feeling he's taking smaller steps to avoid wherever we're going, to soothe me a little longer before whatever comes next. I nuzzle deeper into his neck, stroking his scalp with my fingers.

It's almost over, he sends through the link.

Yes, but we're also on our way to see Zeus, according to Athena and no amount of freedom from that room can ease my fear. He should be proud of his daughter for her willingness to please him so thoroughly, leaving me marked as he had instructed, penetrating deeper than skin.

"Could you move any faster?!" Zeus' powerful voice sends a wave of terror, icing me over. Hermes tenses but doesn't stop the affectionate strokes down my back.

We're outside, the grand palace long behind us. The lush trees are the only things separating us from home. We're so close I can smell the white roses in the garden, the very ones I'm going to burn and regrow red.

Everything here is white and light. I *hate* white.

I almost smile.

They didn't notice the shackles were no longer barring my gifts, too focused on the new wings. I can feel the life around me, the trees we pass, the grass beneath us.

When we break the lining into the crossroad's rubbish-filled clearing, Zeus releases a relieved grunt as if he'd been holding his breath. I turn my head to see, but Hermes pushes me back into his neck.

"Get them up," Zeus orders.

Hermes' grip couldn't get any tighter and I instinctively grip him harder. I can't leave him again.

"Let her go."

At Athena's demand, his hold slips. I ready myself to stand, knowing he won't be able to resist the command, but the weight of the wings is too much. When his hands vanish, my knees buckle.

Hermes reaches out to catch me, but it's too late. It's the wings that hurt the most. The prickly grass makes them itch so bad I want to rip them off.

Before I right myself, a hand clutches my neck, wrapping damn-near all the way around, pulling me to my feet as I choke for breath. My feet dangle above the ground, toes barely grazing the grass as Zeus lifts me higher, bringing my face against his, his breath hot against my cheeks.

His kiss zaps my lips. "Did you have fun, princess?"

Blood drips down his forearm, but I know it isn't mine when I see a gash sliced down from his wrist to elbow.

"I'm going to keep all three of you as my personal pets, but I think you'll be my favorite." His smile deepens but I can hardly see it when my vision becomes spotty from the lack of oxygen. "It's why I didn't let them take you here." He cups between my legs, and when his finger curls, I kick off his chest, falling back onto the ground, more agonizing pain ripping right through me.

His howling thunders the sky. "Keep that fight, it only makes this more fun."

He tosses something to Athena, adjusting himself. "You'll find out just how much I enjoy this the second Hades steps through that door."

My arms shake as I lift to my knees. The door is right there, I could run to it, could try to make it through before—

I send the hopeful thoughts away. I would never make it in time and Hermes certainly wouldn't with his wings so horribly injured and his leg broken.

With the quiver in my lips and the twisting in my gut, I know Zeus is never sending us back.

"Get her up, Ares."

Rough hands pull at my shoulders, dragging me to my feet. It doesn't matter that I can't support myself because he spins me around and lifts me over his shoulder before I get a chance to see him.

"What are you doing?" I manage to ask the question I've been repeating in that room, but my voice is so scratchy I'm not even sure they heard me.

"I want to see you, princess," Zeus answers while Ares holds me up by the waist. Athena moves quickly, and I don't know what's happening before the spike hammers through my sensitive wings.

My shriek shakes the tree.

Excruciating is a word to describe a kiss compared to the pain that tears me apart.

The spikes don't stop. The bastards continue to add more, pinning me between two trees. There are so many of them that when Ares finally releases my waist, my body hangs by them without ripping.

Tears and snot run down my face as I continue to cry, forced to watch them do the same to Hermes across from me. The difference is that Hermes' wings are no longer attached to him, and they have to pin him by his arms.

"You know Gods don't have wings. I should have figured it out sooner, but even I can admit I was a little prideful to think my offspring possessed such interesting abilities." He's talking about Hermes. "And then there's *your* eyes." His attention shifts to me. "Not being mine makes sense, but you look exactly like Demeter. Except for those damn eyes. Do you know there is only one other being in existence with such a unique marking?"

"She wasn't there." Ares cuts in. "It's completely abandoned."

Zeus' chest puffs, his annoyance vanishing when he stands taller with an air of pride and confidence of someone who always gets what he wants. "I've had an epiphany since you arrived. One that I didn't think was real. Have you heard of a Fertility Goddess?"

My breath labors and my arms grow heavier at my sides. I shake my head tiredly.

I'm so tired that I lose track of Zeus until I spot him sitting on the bench between me and Hermes, his disgusting eyes raking up and down my bloody body with a lick of his lips. "It's a myth. One that I gave up searching for long ago. Until today, after Ares told me about your garden in the Underworld."

He adjusts himself again, and I swallow the bile rising, keeping my focus on Hermes rather than the monster between us.

Hermes' broken frame sags when a spike falls out.

His eyes speak for him, *I'm fine.*

I give a slight shake of my head, *No, you're not.*

The tightening of his jaw, *Stay quiet.*

My squint is my last response, last *promise*, an oath I don't need a river to swear on, *We'll get out of here.*

Zeus starts again, "This being, this myth, is a creator. With my blood mixed with theirs, we could create Zagreus, the curse-breaker prophesized to end this fucking war once and for all. He'll break the curses Kronos set in place. Us original Gods will be able to step into the Mortal Veil again. We wouldn't need mortals to survive. Kore, are you following?"

My head lulls to the side as I listen to his every word, his every breath.

"Not one for talking then? It's just as well. I'm merely wasting time anyway. It shouldn't be long now." His grin lifts even higher, growing more eager with every word I wish he'd stop saying.

I just want to go home.

390

Bringer of Death

"Do you know what happens when a God breaks an oath?" Zeus strokes the cut along his arm and continues, unaware of my regulating focus. "He's tortured. Physically, at first, but that's not even the fun part. Prometheus broke an oath long ago, and you know what happened to him? The stories will tell you he's chained on a mountain going mad, but that's how it started. See, he went numb from the torture, and then his mind went beyond hysterics, and he thought it was funny to feed himself to a bird."

The two Gods laugh with him. That's when I realize Ares has made his way next to Hermes and Athena is next to me, standing guard. "I want to see what Hades will do when he goes mad."

My heart drops.

"There she is," he says when my head snaps to him.

I want to thrash and pull and rip myself from these wings so I can tear him limb by limb. I would tie him up to a tree for months and never stop whipping him. I would find a way to heal him so I can break new skin again. But my body hangs uselessly. Lifting a finger takes too much effort.

The God before me snickers, striding toward me. "That's the look I want to see every morning with my cock shoved down that pretty little throat of yours, while Hades and Hermes watch from their cages."

It won't stop there though. He'll torture us all. It's in the way he touches himself with every sob that leaves me, every wince I make. He gets off on the brutality.

"I'm going to use their blood to fuck you until you birth Zagreus for me." His fingers grip my jaw, pulling my attention to him. "Using you will be so much fun, and you don't even know why."

I spit, spraying him with blood. I don't need to know why. With a gruesome smile, he licks the black heat clean off his lips. "And because you're such a needy little cunt who's practically begging for me, we can start now. Give Hades a show when he comes through."

He pulls me in, slamming his lips against mine. I bite him, making him laugh, his eyes filling with a hungry lust.

I'm not going to be bait.

If it means I'll never see Hades again, I'll stay here to ensure he remains safe there. The selfish part of me will die just so I'll end up back in the Underworld with him.

Home. A lightness overcomes me with the thought.

The tickling of a flame flickers deep in my bones as my veins sing with the life all around me. The very shadows that call to me now dance with the flames that fill me.

A dark laughter leaves my aching throat.

"You're mad." Zeus chuckles. "I fucking love it."

The grin that remains on my face startles him back a step. "I'm more than just a little mad. I'm going to find a way to kill you," I promise. "I'm going to watch Hades mutilate you before we feed you to Cerberus and play with your fucking bones."

The vulgarity is enlightening, but it isn't enough to balance that internal scale. He needs centuries of torture before that can happen.

Power I've never felt ripples through me.

Roots spring from the ground, wrapping around the arms of the three Gods. Zeus is pulled away, held in the sky by the roots I command. Athena shrills, being rooted to the ground, and Ares is tied to the tree next to Hermes.

Lightning strikes my shoulder, burning straight to my bones, faintly loosening my hold on my gift.

I do as Hades taught me and focus on the life beneath the ground, feeling them as if they're an extension of my own body.

I need every bit of power, crumbling the wall in my mind to tighten my hold on Zeus.

The second the wall drops, a dark cackle fills the sky. "Oooo, there is so much sin in the air here," Tisiphone shouts.

Megaera lands on Athena, gold spraying her black inky body as she slashes at the Goddess' chest before leaning over her and licking up the deep slices.

Thanatos appears before me, and never have I been so elated and relieved to see those white voids. "I'm sorry about this, Sweet Shadow."

Pain scorches through my wings as he pulls a spike from the tree, one after another. One falls free, pulling me down with it, but I'm still snagged on the other one, and it feels like someone is tearing my back apart all over again.

Lightning flashes and I brace myself against the tree when I feel Thanatos' support leave my hip. He falls to his knees and tries to stand when another bolt strikes his back, purple lightning streaking beneath his skin.

Shadows and mist roll along the grass, moving to surround Zeus, who lowers to the ground as my hold weakens.

"You're powerful!" Zeus rumbles, impressed.

Another lightning bolt strikes the tree I'm attached to, catching the branches on fire.

Thanatos rises from the ground just as Poseidon rams into him from the side.

I try to climb the tree to relieve the pressure off the one wing I'm hanging from, but my arms give out. Another groan escapes me, feeling it ripping from my back.

An army of Gods break the tree lining, their screams and war cries bursting through the clearing, but that's not what has me panicking.

I want to scream.

Blue flames fly across the sky, cutting off the Gods from the rest of us.

When I finally find him, I can't look away.

My heart jerks seeing Hades' body covered in cobalt flames, his eyes ablaze. His tattoos look as if they wield the fire right along with him. Wherever a God appears, flames dart for them. If anyone approaches him, he cuts through them with a long bident, using it as both sword and torch.

I watch as one God bursts into flames by a mere touch of Hades' arm. He doesn't stop at just fire, he stabs every God in his orbit, cutting each and every one down with every step.

"It's too bad you didn't collar her. No one knew she was yours," Zeus yells, sending lightning bolts his way. Hades dodges every one, deflecting them with the bident. "So, they all had a little taste."

Hades' eyes snap to mine. There is nothing friendly in them. If anything, seeing me makes the killings more brutal. The quick slices become ruthless, severing and searing off arms, heads, legs.

One God pierces his shoulder, a sight that has me cry out, but Hades doesn't even look affected. In one swift motion, he drags the sword out of him and cuts the God clean in half.

He doesn't give in to Zeus' remarks or taunts as he continues slicing his way, stepping through the line of cobalt he seared across the clearing to cut us off from the rest of the fighting.

I attempt to pull a stake but fail. My arms are too weak, the life around me fading.

Below me, shadows surround Poseidon, who's struggling beneath Thanatos fists and smothering mist.

Two Gods make it through the ring of fire, but Alecto is too quick for one, tackling him by his neck in her mouth like a dog catching a squirrel.

The other one darts straight for me.

Attis. The one I accidentally burned while dancing. The one who whispered in my ear about taking Hades' whore for himself, and how he couldn't wait to do the same to Hades when they catch him.

That pit in my core doesn't just stir, it becomes an inferno. And with the flames singing in my veins and the shadows swirling in my mind, I don't need to take in other's feelings to wield, I have enough pain and hatred to direct toward him.

The colors appear anyway. The entire clearing is full of suffering, agony, hatred, fear, and desire. But the man before me is different. My focus isn't on those emotions at all. I don't want to take away his feelings—I want to burn that golden light that throbs behind his eyes.

He doesn't deserve that light.

Now, that faint dark whisper that called to me when I first met Thanatos overcomes me, awakening something deep within me, latching onto that balance and tilting it until there isn't a scale left.

I *pull*.

And *pull*.

And *pull*.

And *pull*.

I pull, feeling and watching as that light dims until the God slows and drops to his knees.

It feels as if the entire world stops. There is no screaming or struggling. No fighting.

There is only that light.

That last glimmer.

The last spark.

Bringer of Death

I smother it and watch as shadows overcome him as if they have been waiting for the light to leave for eternity, have been starving for a chance to take over.

I smile as the last bit of light vanishes.

Thanatos pants on the ground next to Poseidon, his mouth hanging open. Athena stops struggling against the roots, as Megaera halts, licking her golden lips atop her. Tisiphone holds the whip she had been using on Ares. Alecto drops the God from her mouth. Hermes is on his knees as if he were mid-crawl toward me.

Every single eye is on me.

But mine falls to Zeus, attempting to find his light to smother too.

Hades doesn't stop, doesn't freeze for a second. He uses that pause to send flames throughout the clearing, and the screams begin again.

Zeus drops to the bench with his arms out wide where the roots are wrapped around them, his chest rising and falling in a rhythm that doesn't match his calm demeanor. His eyes widen when they met mine. It doesn't matter if it is panic or wonder, I want to pull them from his face, so he never gets a chance to look at me that way again.

But his light can't be penetrated like the other God's. I can see it, but I can't grasp it, can't pull it. It's like it's blocked by an invisible shield.

The three Furies are still looking at me in awe and then at each other, before bowing their heads and saying something in a language I don't understand, except for one word.

Persephone.

Zeus looks to the sky, sending lightning to strike the roots holding his arms.

I wince, feeling them wither and die.

Jumping down, he runs toward me with that sickening grin. I brace myself tighter on the tree, preparing for him to rip me off and jump me back to the cells.

He doesn't make it two steps before flames swallow him whole.

Hades.

He doesn't say anything as he steps before me, his hair a mess, his face coated with blood that isn't his, and those eyes blazing with a fire that could melt bones with a single look. A fire that could either light the world or burn it down, and right now, it's burning.

I focus where the blood runs down his chest from where the sword pierced him. He doesn't look at all phased as he works to pull my arms from the tree, wrapping them around his neck, and my ankles around his waist.

"Which one hung you up?" His jaw clenches, the only sign that he's in any pain. The tree shakes with the final spike he pulls from my wing.

"Ares," I whimper, "and Athena."

More Gods appear behind him, but before I can think to panic, they're all set aflame, Ares and Athena rolling on the ground amongst them.

There is a drop in my belly and the world disappears. The tree becomes the soft bedding. The grunts become fire crackling.

"Hermes!" I cry out.

A moment later, Thanatos appears with Hermes under his arm. "The Furies are taking the long way. I'm taking him to Hecate."

Hades doesn't let me go, not that he could if he wanted. My ankles and arms are sealed around him.

We're fine, Hermes sends through our link as his sapphires meet mine before being carried out of Hades room.

The room Hades carries me to smells warm and woodsy. I don't know where we're going, but it looks like we're outside. Glass surrounds us, revealing a night sky full of stars.

Night. Not day. There's no sun but the soft glow of the moon.

I sob.

I made it.

I'm home.

Something wet touches my wings and Hades grips the back of my head, pulling me in closer as that wetness rises to my thigh, my hips... I thrash against him.

"No! No!" I don't want to drown again. With my rising panic, my breath quickens. My pulse pounds against my skull. Every breath feels like I'm swallowing icepicks.

"Kore, I need to wash you."

When I open my eyes, focusing on our surroundings, I see we're in a massive bath cut into the floor at the edge of the mountain, the Underworld sparkling below. "I have you. I won't let you go," he

396

promises, squeezing his arms tighter around me to further emphasize his point.

The brutal warrior from the clearing is gone, but his face is stone with a sharp tick in his jaw. There is a softness behind those eyes that still hold that steel fire.

He summons soaps without going any farther into the pool, and I let him wash away the sticky blood, only stopping once to summon a glass of water. I want to drink the whole bath, but the little I'm able to get down burns too much for such a challenge.

I don't look at myself in the water's reflection or down at my body. Athena promised every cut would scar, and it isn't only my back this time.

My focus remains on the stars, hoping they will still be there if I blink.

"How long?" I ask through our connection, unable to speak.

"A few hours," he answers, knowing what I mean.

My head rests heavy on his shoulder. *"It felt like days."*

"It was for you." There's a harshness he's trying to keep under control but fails to clear away. As he sits us on the step, the water at our waists, I feel the pants he didn't bother taking off. "That room doesn't know time. A few hours here is days in there. A day here is weeks there."

"Five days," he confirms through the connection, answering the question I was too scared to ask.

We've been locked away for five days. Tortured for five days.

I tighten my arms around his neck, filling myself with his cinnamon scent.

"How did you make it there? What about the oath?" I don't know much about the oaths, but Zeus and Athena were certain he couldn't step foot in the Heavens with it in place, but also knew he would find a way to break through.

"Thanatos helped. I wasn't there long, so I'll heal. Don't worry about me, Deviant."

"Hades..." I jerk back, looking down at his chest again, to the cut that's webbing itself together. The sight makes me sick, and I begin wiping away the blood from his chest, his neck, his face.

His hands wrap around my wrists, stopping my manic movements to pull me in closer, as if he can't let any part of me go. *"For once, just fucking listen."*

We stay like this without talking while Hades continues to clean every inch of me long after the filth is gone. When he finally stops, I ask him to keep going, knowing I'll never feel clean enough.

"Gods are cruel," I quote, having heard it or read it some place I can't recall.

Hades hums against my neck. "But what does that make a Goddess?"

I tighten my arms without having to think, the plans already forming in my mind.

"Vengeful."

Acknowledgements

Thank you to everyone who has been a part of making this story come to life. When I first wrote Bringer of Death, I had no clue what I was doing. I only had a scene in my head with a growing story that spiraled (as everything does) to an entire series that I cannot wait to finish and share.

A huge appreciation goes to everyone who read the first edition that was originally written in third person. As I started my other series, Cruel Kingdoms, I tried my attempt at first person and fell in love with that format of storytelling and decided to move forward with the Cruel Gods being in first person as well. In making that decision, I chose to come back around and make that change to Bringer of Death. I am so happy I did! I love being in these characters head on a more intimate level.

As always, I will forever be grateful to Geena, Nadia, my mom, and my husband Nick for listening to me work through this story and so many others. Bristin, I can't forget you. You heard me editing chapter by chapter with the long lists of what's next, so you will always have my heart! AJ, here's the shoutout you asked for.

My true love goes out to my alpha readers, beta readers, ARC readers, and *all* my readers. None of my stories would ever be what they become without each and every one of you!